Kate Darby studied English Literature at Somerville College, Oxford, and Creative Writing at the University of East Anglia, where she received the David Higham Award. Her fiction has been read on BBC Radio, and she has published stories in magazines including *Slice*, *Mslexia* and the *London Magazine*, as well as winning prizes in several international fiction competitions. She teaches writing at City University, and co-runs the monthly live fiction event Liars' League. She lives in London.

THE WHORES' ASYLUM

Oxford, 1887. Even as Victoria celebrates the fiftieth year of her reign, a stone's throw from the calm cloisters and college spires lies Jericho, a maze of seedy streets and ill-lit taverns, haunted by drunkards, thieves and the lowest sort of brazen female as ever lifted her petticoats. When Stephen Chapman, a brilliant young medical student, is persuaded to volunteer at a shelter devoted to reforming the fallen women of Oxford, his closest friend Edward feels a strange sense of dread. But even Edward — who already knows the devastating effect of falling in love with the wrong woman — cannot foresee the macabre and violent events that will unfold around them, or stop Diana, the woman who seems destined to drive them apart.

KATY DARBY

THE WHORES' ASYLUM

Complete and Unabridged

CHARNWOOD
Leicester

First published in Great Britain in 2012 by
Fig Tree, an imprint of
Penguin Books
London

First Charnwood Edition
published 2013
by arrangement with
Penguin Books Ltd.
London

British Library CIP Data

Darby, Katy.
    The whores' asylum.
    1. Great Britain- -History- -Victoria, *1837 – 1901*- -
    Fiction. 2. Oxford (England)- -Fiction.
    3. Large type books.
    I. Title
    823.9'2–dc23

    ISBN 978–1–4448–1404–0

Published by
F. A. Thorpe (Publishing)
Anstey, Leicestershire
Set by Words & Graphics Ltd.
Anstey, Leicestershire
Printed and bound in Great Britain by
T. J. International Ltd., Padstow, Cornwall

This book is printed on acid-free paper

For Moira Darby, 1926–2011

If patriotism is the last refuge of the scoundrel,
love is a whore's asylum

George Delon (after Doctor Johnson)

Contents

Editor's Note

The following pages, in the following order, were recovered from the Fraser estate at Saclose Hall, Gloucestershire, in the early part of the year 1915, having been sealed and deposited with Dr Edward Fraser's solicitor, Cyril Tanner, to be opened only by his heir upon Dr Fraser's death — which sad event followed hard on that meeting, in the closing months of 1914.

The manuscript having passed into the hands of the current Editor, he begs, now that a yet blacker and bloodier shadow than that which falls across these pages has darkened Europe, to present to the public a story as extraordinary as it is cautionary, as appalling as it is, ultimately, uplifting, having at its heart the primacy of those two noblest of all emotions — Love, and Hope, and their final triumph over Death. The principals are no more, but the story lives on to instruct, affect, and warn all those whom it may touch.

If the reader should find infelicity, indelicacy or inaccuracy in the pages that follow, the Editor humbly entreats him to bear in mind that these words were wrested from the soul of a dying man whose reticence, kindness and modesty were a byword amongst his friends — friends who never, alas, guessed the terrible history of him and those he held dearest, nor the torment that haunted him, even to the end.

Despite Dr Fraser's evidently burdened state of mind when he composed the final parts of these, his last writings, we believe that the light of truth and sincere feeling shines from them, and any mistakes contained therein are entirely the Editor's own.

Rev. Jonathan Forrest, MA (Cantab),
D.Phil. (Oxon)
May 1917

Prologue

Letter to Captain Stephen Fraser,
Gloucestershire Regiment

Saclose Hall, Gloucestershire
9 DECEMBER 1914

My dearest boy,

When you read these words, and all those that
follow, I am afraid it must be because I am no
longer here to speak them to you; I shall have
fulfilled the predictions of my doctors and the
fears of my own heart, and will be beyond all
the cares of this world. I hope and trust that I
shall live to see you again, my son, in all the
vigour and valour of your youth — but if I have
learned one thing in my life, it is not to leave
anything to chance, nor save what must be said
until it is too late.

Perhaps I have too long ignored the shortness
of breath, the easy exhaustion, the pain that
constricts my chest and runs like lightning
through my limbs, for I did not wish to burden
your boyhood with the hypochondriac maun-
derings of premature old age, and so I sat and
cheered you at your cricket matches, and
stumped with you up hill and down dale in all
weathers; and though Dr Dunseath says I may

1

have shortened my life by many months in so doing, I believe rather the opposite — that the exercise of my failing physical faculties was the only thing that stood between me and invalidity. For how else to explain the fact that my illness has only really taken hold upon me since you have been away?

I miss you terribly, my boy — but you must not worry! I fully intend to hang on to life for a few weeks more, so that we may spend one last Christmas together, when you are back home on leave. For I am fortunate, as I discovered today, and shall have a little more time left to me, if I am careful — just long enough, perhaps, to set my affairs in order, which I now do, in these letters, memoirs and cuttings that I have preserved, and this final account of years and lives long gone to dust.

Six months ago I would not have had you know anything that might distress you; but you are a man now, and have seen blood, and killing, and death, at Marne, and at Ypres, more than I ever did or hope to; and you deserve to know the truth about myself, your mother, and your namesake, Stephen Chapman, the best and bravest friend I ever had.

The light is dying beyond the window. The snow heaped upon the hills glows ruby in the glance of the vanishing sun. There has been so much blood, and more still to come, they say; but it was ever thus.

I would write more; I would try to explain and excuse myself again — but these fading pages must perform that office for me, if explanation or excuse there can be for all that I once was, and did. But I am old and weary: my hand tires; my eyes mist and ache. These words and memories of so long ago have opened an ancient wound in my heart which only you can close again.

For the dead cannot shrive me now; your forgiveness, my dear boy, is all I crave. So come home safely, lift this burden of past errors and agonies from my old shoulders, and embrace once more your fond and fallible father,

Edward Fraser

BOOK ONE

The Memoir of
Edward Fraser

1

It is with a heavy heart that I take up my pen this day. Not two hours ago did I commit to the earth and commend to the Lord the body and spirit of my dearest friend in all the world, and one of the purest and most generous creatures I have known upon this Earth. It is in the interest of truth and the chastity of my own conscience that I set down these words, not to be seen by mortal eyes until the last of Stephen Chapman's family now living should go to their final reward. I would not have them know what I know; yet nor would I wish to enter my own grave with this dark secret upon my soul, and mine alone.

It is his loved ones, indeed, for whom I fear; for when this curse first descended upon my friend, I performed the same offices I might have expected of him had I myself been so afflicted; and thus managed to hide the true nature and cause of the poor fellow's illness from his unsuspecting family. Seven years have now passed since that day, and not a single hour has been free of the gnawing guilt of concealing what only I know — that awful thing for which, in a partial sense at least, I am responsible.

It is providential in the extreme that Chapman was a solitary bachelor, with few close colleagues (save that fatal one, the nearest of all), when the

7

sickness first came upon him. He had no spouse, no progeny, nor dear friends, excepting myself, to share in the horror of his affliction. That his surviving family saw their beloved boy, in his final, dreadful years, mentally debilitated to the extent that at the last he was quite beyond the reach of reason, unable to recognize his kin and calling down curses upon the heads of his friends, is awful enough; the tale of how he came by this terrible madness had to be concealed at all costs from those who were witness to its effects.

And yet, now that he has been taken at last, and as I do not know when God shall please to gather me up too, the tale must be told. My breast is too full of secrets, my heart too wrung with grief and exhaustion, my head spins nightly with horrible visions of his last days, with dreams of things said and left unsaid; I can no longer resist. The truth will out, or it shall kill me — as once, it killed him.

It was in early October of 1883, a few days before the commencement of the Michaelmas Term, that I journeyed down from Gloucestershire, a fresh graduate of the ancient Anglian seat of learning that is Cambridge University, to take up my place at the still more ancient (and only slightly less celebrated) University of Oxford. I had taken my Bachelor of Arts in Theology at the King's College with first-class honours, and intended to please both my father and myself by pursuing a Master's in Philosophy, and thence a doctorate in Divinity, at Worcester College, before devoting my life to one of two, as it seemed to me then, equally desirable paths.

At that early point in my life it was my avowed intention to explore the limits of my Christian faith and my own intellectual abilities, and depending on what I discovered regarding both, to end my days as either a servant of the Church or a purposeful wanderer in the lush groves of Academe. I was possessed of a vast curiosity and thirst for learning which, I was about to discover, I shared with my new room-mate (soon to be my first and best friend in the city), a medical student called Stephen Chapman. Chapman, a natural-born doctor if ever I met one, was pursuing his studies both in the scientific libraries of the University and, more practically, in the wards, lecture-theatres and dissection-rooms of the Radcliffe Infirmary, whose proximity had led him to fix upon Worcester as the most convenient college at which to reside for the duration of his training.

Both of us, grown accustomed to the bounty and regularity of dinner in Hall and the deference and convenience of University ser-vants, had elected to share a set of rooms with a fellow-student, rather than take private lodgings outside the college walls; thus it was that a random ballot allotted us a fine, modern set in the Garden Buildings, made still more delightful by the prospect from the sitting-room balcony of the glittering, wind-ruffled Worcester College lake. Having found ourselves thrown together by

9

hazard, we were well pleased with the arrangements, considering ourselves fortunate to have found one another. Indeed, we were both lucky and influential enough with the Bursar to secure the same set throughout our three subsequent years at the University, by which stage I was nearing the completion of my doctorate and Chapman — well, it shall be told in good time.

An intimate acquaintance, as required by my peculiar subject, with a number of ancient languages and their various alphabets, from Aramaic to Hebrew to Biblical Greek, has instilled in me a particularly keen faculty of memory; and I recall with perfect clarity the first time I laid eyes upon my poor late friend. Habitually an early riser, as those who aspire to the Church must be, or become, I had arrived in Oxford by the first train of the day and subsequently covered the short distance to Worcester by hansom cab, arriving at the college gates upon the stroke of seven.

I was admitted to the Lodge by a crabbed and elderly porter, who appeared to be three-quarters deaf and who treated my arrival with the irritation and contempt that this interruption to the perusal of his newspaper over a morning pipe no doubt merited. Nevertheless, he was prevailed upon to show me to my rooms; I was eager to settle in, due to a somewhat ungenerous desire to secure for myself whichever I considered to be the more commodious of the two bedrooms. I hoped to forestall my new room-mate by laying claim to my own quarters, and being thoroughly, comfortably installed before he had even enquired as to the distribution of accommodations.

In this quest, however, I was nearly frustrated, for scant minutes after the porter had grudgingly unlocked the oak-panelled outer door and vouchsafed me the key, I was startled by a peremptory knocking. I closed my portmanteau (my trunk, books and other effects were arriving separately by rail the next day), adjusted my cravat in the looking-glass of what was now my bedroom, and strode to answer it.

I opened the door upon a young man who seemed to have made great haste and effort in crossing the quad and ascending the stairs; he bore the signs of extreme exertion, panting heavily, his dark-blond, short-cropped hair disarranged.

'Oh I say, thanks, old man,' he said with relief as he beheld me in the doorway. 'The porter said he only had one key and I was beginning to think you must have gone out.' He smiled brilliantly and held out his hand to me in greeting.

'Stephen Chapman — how d'you do?'

He was a tallish, well-made fellow, inclining towards leanness, but with nothing of the pallor or languor associated with those such as I, who have no use for healthful exercise and instead stalk the vaults of shadowed, silent libraries for their sport. He wore a topcoat of summer tweed, cut rather dashingly, and trousers of brown flannel; and, taken all in all, bore the distinct air of being a young country squire surprised on his morning constitutional. His eyes were large and clear, set widely but not too far apart, and of a dark, aquatic shade of blue that seemed almost green in strong light; his handshake was firm and hearty, his whiskers short and fair, and his skin pinkish-pale and smooth as a boy's.

He appeared, when I first met him, far younger than his twenty-one summers, unlike myself, who, though only a year his senior, had already begun to develop the hesitant, stooping gait of a scholar and the incipient tonsure of a monk.

'I am very pleased to make your acquaintance, Mr Chapman,' I told him, grasping his outstretched hand. 'My name is Edward Fraser, and it appears that we are to share this set. Won't you come in?'

He did so eagerly, dragging behind him what proved to be the cause of his flushed features and heaving breast: a voluminous and weighty trunk of some dense black wood, which he was barely able to carry alone. I indicated his bedroom to him, and immediately volunteered to assist him in moving his belongings; although, as I mused out loud, it was scandalous that one of the porters had not offered to help him.

'Oh, he did,' Chapman assured me. 'The old chap, you mean? Brompton? He tried to take one end but when I saw the colour of his face I really feared that the strain would burst the poor fellow's heart.'

'Indeed?' I said, gasping as I lifted, for I was as unused to feats of strength as Brompton clearly was, although in those days I had youth and some health on my side. 'Were there no other servants about?'

'*The big lad dunt come on till nine,*' Chapman told me in a passable imitation of Brompton's phlegmy Oxfordshire drawl. Groaning, we lowered the behemoth to the creaking floorboards at the end of his bed. I straightened, not without some pain and a series of stuttering cracks emanating from my spine, and dusted my palms, relieved to have survived the ordeal intact.

'He would need to be a veritable Hercules to have assisted you with that,' I said. Chapman laughed.

'I know! I confess I indulge myself in far more books than any sane man would require — but in my defence, many are obscure works of pathology, rarely to be found in even the University's collection, and I must have them by me.'

'You are a medical man, then?' I asked, wondering when breakfast would be served in Hall, and whether I ought not to ring for some tea beforehand.

Chapman nodded, wiping his hands on his moss-brown trousers and glancing around the room, whose light, airy aspect and elegant proportions I was, perversely, beginning to envy.

'Hope to be, hope to be. Did my undergrad at Magdalen, but when I was assigned to the Radcliffe I decided to switch to Worcester for the rest of my time — not so far to walk, d'you see?'

'Of course,' I said, although at that juncture I had nearly as little idea of the topography of the city of Oxford as I did of the surface of the

Moon. 'And what is your particular area of interest?'

The hectic flush, which had drained slightly from his face since his initial exertions, surged once again to his boyish cheeks.

'Well, you know, medicine. As opposed to surgery, I mean. Medicine of the, er, the *corpus feminae, uteri, ovaria*, etc. Female reproductive medicine, in short.'

I could not prevent my eyebrows from rising. It was an interesting field of endeavour, and it was clear from his flustered speech that he hardly knew how to explain his specialism without a rather charming display of embarrassment and hesitation.

'And what's your field?' he asked swiftly, evidently desiring to change the subject of conversation as soon as possible.

'Divinity,' I told him, with the merest hint of internal amusement at his increased distress. 'I'm studying to be a clergyman.' His face ruddied further. 'Or an academic, I suppose.'

'Goodness,' stammered he, scarlet, unable to meet my eye, 'I'm awfully sorry. I didn't mean to offend — I mean, do you think it will be all right? I shan't — I can study in the library if — '

'Don't be absurd, my dear chap,' I told him, clapping him lightly on the shoulder. 'I am not so unworldly as to be unaware of the existence and purpose of women upon this Earth, and I admire those such as you who would work to bring more children into it. *Prodite et multiplicate*, as it says in Genesis. I promise you that I shall not object to your instruments and

14

chemicals, if you can tolerate my sermons and musty tomes.'

Chapman beamed broadly and stooped to open his trunk, the lid of which shot up in an explosion of dust and loose papers. He removed a stout small box, about the size to take an opera-hat, and pried up the top.

'That's most understanding of you, Fraser. A lot of fellows wouldn't take too kindly to sharing with a medic. We are notorious for our peculiar ways.'

The box popped open and he smiled as he carefully removed and divested of its black silk wrapping the object within, setting it in the centre of the green-leather-topped desk. It was a human skull, bleached and polished to a virginal whiteness and shining like a baby's tooth in the early-morning sun.

'This is Albert,' he said.

I made a slight bow towards the grim object.

'I shall ask the scout to send up tea for three, then?' I said.

Over the next several months, as Michaelmas became Hilary Term, and Hilary melted into warm Trinity, my acquaintance with Stephen Chapman deepened into a profound and affectionate friendship. Despite his eccentricities, my natural solitariness, and our differences in character and appearance, we were rarely out of one another's company; and though we were strangely matched, and must have seemed an odd pair as we strolled together along the banks of the Cherwell, deep in discussion, we became one another's boon companion, each the first to know of the other's triumphs and disappointments, sorrows and joys.

Our divergent areas of study might have argued a greater gulf between the two of us, both philosophically and morally, than proved to be the case; for we each found in the other an intriguing counterpart, a constantly renewed source of intellectual challenge, and a stern, enquiring lay critic of our own opinions and endeavours. I came to avoid my fellow theologians as far as possible, finding less stimulation in their companionship and the prospect of arguing, sometimes quite literally, the question of how many angels might dance upon the head of a pin, than in Chapman's languid yet incisive dissections of my own essays on the mysteries of the divine.

Here I must confess that my conversations with my friend were partly motivated by the fact that I had developed a powerful fascination, while an undergraduate at Cambridge, for the more *recherché* historical aspects of my subject, and the many faces which God has shown to the world since it was made. I found Chapman far more receptive than my academic colleagues to my ideas and discoveries concerning the strange and sometimes brutal worship of the cultures of the most ancient civilizations, and my appreciation of his excellent company was immeasurably deepened by the confidence which I knew I could repose in him.

Many was the evening when, vexed by a particularly obscure passage in the Talmud or puzzling aspect of Attic religious rites, I would expound to Chapman my theories upon these subjects (of which he knew no more than the average housefly), whetting the blade of my argument upon the sturdy stone of his scientific reasoning. In the absence of a competent supervisor (for Worcester's own Reverend Horsby was a dull, addled dotard more fitted to the contemplation of matters gastronomic than spiritual), I used my affable room-mate as sounding-board, proof-reader and audience, and he responded by doing me the same honour.

His tutors considered him a more than usually brilliant pupil, and had early in his studentship honoured him with what slightly prestigious and still more slightly remunerative offices were within their gift; thus he was frequently called upon to be second-demonstrator in the dissection-room, or laboratory assistant at some of the first-year chemical lectures. He continued tirelessly upon his own researches at the same time, making full use of the facilities afforded him by his indulgent professors, and would occasionally give a lecture or paper of his own to the undergraduate students in the faculty.

These talks were always well-attended, and often brought him favourably to the attention of the leading men in the School of Medicine; what was less well-known was that his first and most avid audience for each presentation of this kind was none other than myself. I, whose mind bent daily upon the imponderable complexities of the

17

divine, grew to conceive of no greater amusement and relaxation than to listen, enthralled and amazed, to Chapman's discourses upon the analgesic action of obscure poisons upon the nervous system, the wondrous deformities engendered in the womb upon a foetus the mother of which suffered from a certain disease, or the astonishing curative effects some chemical compounds had been proven to have upon ailments hitherto thought to be terminal.

In fine, Chapman and I were founts of knowledge and fascination each to each; and we drank from one another happily and deeply.

But do not think my own poor endeavours at devout scholarship had any great effect upon Chapman's moral character; it will not, perhaps, excite any untoward surprise that he partook heartily of all the vices commonly attributed to medical students at that time and place, the which are so often excused by the peculiar demands of their studies, and their obligation to work intimately and daily with the more gruesome aspects of mortality.

Chapman drank, both at table and in the more reputable public houses of the city; he was not immoderate in his consumption, but kept company (and, I am glad to say, also his temper and his head) with many who were — which sometimes occasioned in me fears for both his good character in the University and the ultimate condition of his soul. I also knew him to play at cards, sometimes for money, although never, I must make plain, in our rooms; nor did he ever boast of his gambling to me, out of deference to my own moral sensibilities. But many was the morning when I had risen with the sun to work on a little Hebrew translation or an essay on early Christian worship only to be greeted, as the toll of six rang clear over the quad, by the sound of Chapman returning from an all-night vigil at the card-table or in the rooms of a Magdalen acquaintance called Charles Kester, who hosted long evenings of port and poetry.

On these occasions I did not reprove my friend, for I well knew that his own robust conscience would do that work for me, once he had retired to bed and awoken again, heavy with the debaucheries of the evening, to attend his first lecture of the day. Instead I would await the smart knock upon the bedroom door, the hangdog salutation, and the sight of his innocent, smiling face, at once drawn with lack of sleep and hectic with wine and triumph, as he invited me to step out on to the balcony and smoke a cigar with him. At Cambridge I had led a particularly blameless existence, even for a theologian, and I confess that I had not taken up the habit of cigar-smoking until I came to Oxford; but slowly I grew to find the taste and odour of Chapman's Trichinopoly more pleasant than otherwise, and our companionable discussions upon the balcony, gazing over at the sparkling grey waters of the lake at dawn or dusk, came to be the feature of my days that I most looked forward to, representing as they did a calm and invigorating respite from my abstruse toils in the library.

I recall particularly one evening towards the end of our first year — during Eights Week, in fact, when almost every man in college was to be seen sporting the Worcester colours of salmon-and-black, in expectation of cheering our First and Second boats on to victory on the river — an evening, as I say, of early summer that was exceptionally mild and fine. I had been holed up in the Bodleian, chasing down certain rare commentaries, and Chapman had been hard at work in the dissecting-rooms all day, and, as was his custom, had disappeared to scrub the stink of the preservative fluids from his skin. We were both exhausted, and relieved to put the labours of our respective days behind us and to anticipate eagerly the Boat Club Dinner the next night, which was, by all accounts, a sumptuous and high-spirited affair in which the whole college — not just our admirable sportsmen — took part.

I was leaning on the rail of the balcony, contemplating the summer wind stirring gently the foliage of the great and venerable trees surrounding the lake, when my friend stepped out of the French windows to join me. Our balcony was narrow and somewhat precarious, but for our convenience, on these summer evenings, we would set out two chairs and a small side-table so that we could more easily take refreshment as we talked. Chapman had in his hand a bottle of the better college port, and two glasses; he set them upon the little table and took a seat, sighing with contentment and some weariness. He followed my gaze for a moment, then produced his cigar-case from his breast-pocket, opening and silently offering it to me. I took one and he lit mine, and then his own, with a long match. We smoked together in silence for close on five minutes before he uncorked the bottle and poured us each a modest glass of the ruby liquor.

'I hope,' I said, as the sun concealed itself coyly behind a towering oak, 'that you do not expect me to partake of port *before* dinner?'

I was a little in jest, but not entirely; I have never approved of excessive consumption of intoxicants and consider that the best way to eschew over-indulgence is to avoid temptation. Chapman chuckled and picked up his own glass.

'Come, Fraser,' he admonished, 'you are not quite a blue-ribboner yet, surely? What of Communion wine — would you decline that too?'

'I drink as much as is commensurate with my conscience and good sense,' I said, with a sidelong glance at my friend, 'unlike some.'

'You,' said Chapman, 'have a remarkably lop-sided view of stimulants, for an intelligent man.'

'How so?'

'Are you not the same fellow that I saw today at the Queen's Lane Coffee House, swallowing cup after cup of their foul brew, presumably in an attempt to keep yourself awake over some dry tome of Aramaic doctrinal law? If caffeine is not an unnatural stimulant, particularly to a cool brain such as yours, I confess I do not know what is.'

I smiled. 'Come, Chapman, you might be a medical man but I have not yet appointed you my personal physician. May I not drink coffee to my heart's content? It is a free country yet.'

'Indeed you may, but your heart might not be so contented as you imagine. You forget, I know your habits as well as I do my own; and I fancy that your febrile nervous-energy of a morning owes as much to black coffee as to your eagerness to begin another day in the theological stacks.'

I concede that he had me there; I had long relied upon the strong stimulant to see me through lengthy lectures and tedious days poring over crumbling manuscripts. I was amused and rather touched that my friend had taken notice of my little peccadillo, for all that it was hardly life-threatening.

I breathed blue smoke out into the golden evening, and watched it drift and hang in the still air, like a cloud of dust risen from a book which has lain long unopened. The smooth waters of the lake were gilded in the twilight; the low, harmonic toll of bells echoed from the direction of the chapel. It was an evening such as I should have liked to catch in a prism, to distil and separate each part, and play the rainbow of its perfection over the screen of my memory for all my days. But it was not to be. For that night marked a turning-point in the course of my friend's studies; an interest was kindled, and a decision made, that would ultimately alter our friendship beyond all recognition, and drag my unfortunate companion to the brink of despair, and beyond. But at that moment, all was sweet, serene and still in that hushed and lovely sunset scene.

'Very well, Doctor,' I said, 'what would you prescribe?'

He raised my full glass and placed it in my unresisting hand.

'The very best cure for an addiction to the invidious coffee-bean,' said he, 'is the occasional ingestion of the spirit of the grape. I speak, of course, as a chemist, a physiologist, and most importantly, a concerned friend.'

At last I laughed; I could not prevent myself.

'Very well; you have persuaded me. To your health, and my own.'

I sipped from the glass, but Chapman hardly seemed to notice the victory his eloquence had wrought; indeed, he was uncharacteristically quiet, smoking his cigar almost to its band before speaking again. I was seated upon his left-hand side, with a good view of his profile against the sunset before us; and even in the lowering evening light, I could quite clearly discern the marks of distress upon his strong features. His tawny brows were drawn together in concern or perplexity, and there was an enervated, unhappy tenseness to his normally easy and languid demeanour.

'What is the matter, Chapman?' I asked him eventually. 'You have hardly said two words together for ten minutes; I begin to suspect that the anatomy-class has deprived you of your tongue.'

He made a little grimace that was meant to

serve for a smile, and stared sightlessly into the bowl of his port-stained glass.

'You are not so far off, Fraser; indeed, I was thinking on today's progress and wondering what I ought to do.'

'My dear fellow,' I said, 'if you stand at the crux of two paths and wish to know which to choose, there is no better man to confide in than a philosopher of religion: we are forever telling people what to do. Some even contend that our advice can, on occasion, prove useful.'

Again my friend smiled; again he poured us each a measure of port into our crystal vessels. The last rays of the sun made the wine glint and glow in the glasses like blood.

'Are you then offering to return the professional favour, Fraser? I am your physician, and you are to be my confessor?'

'If you like.'

He sighed.

'Very well, then; I have a dilemma.'

'I had thought as much; you are poorer at concealing your inner concerns from me than you imagine.'

'*Touché.*'

He lit another cigar and offered me one; I declined.

'You know, then, that I have of late been pursuing a certain branch of medical chemistry; that I have been particularly interesting myself in those compounds which may have an effect on virulent diseases contagious through blood, intimate, ah, physical contact and . . . so forth?'

'I have heard you speak of it,' I admitted.

24

Indeed, as was our custom, I had been privy to the early drafts of a couple of his papers on the subject, and had found them most intriguing and enlightening.

'Well, Professor Marstone tells me that I have much potential in this area; that he would like to take me on as an assistant and that together we could make great strides in working towards a cure for many of the more ghastly and appalling complaints that afflict the unfortunates in our society.'

I hardly knew what to say, nor where the perceived problem could lie. I could see no discontinuity between this new opportunity and his own oft-stated desire to benefit himself and others by his work.

'Well! Congratulations, Chapman — I must say I can't see why this news should cast you down so — it seems a wonderful chance to help the wretched. Many a clergyman would be delighted to do as much good.'

I was hearty in my response, for I knew that, despite his occasional tendencies towards the more hedonistic follies of youth, my friend was a man of profoundly generous and improving principles, wishing only to relieve suffering and banish disease through his skill and studies. No man had less of a head for cheap glory than he — or so I had thought.

'Thank you, Fraser,' he said, 'but this is my conflict: Dr Williams, the obstetric surgeon, has also done me the honour of noticing my work, and has expressed interest in giving me individual tuition and a place by his side, and I am all torn up about which way to go.'

'What is at issue?' I wondered. 'Surely each has its own merits, but neither is an unsuitable path for one of your talents.'

He exhaled a soft stream of smoke. The coppery glow of dusk had by now subsumed itself in incipient darkness; the lake before us was lost to sight, the evening air was cooling, and the sky above our heads was a blue silk coverlet in which the evening stars were beginning to prick tiny, brilliant holes.

'My mother,' he said, 'always had an idea of me as a society doctor.'

'Indeed?'

Chapman rarely spoke of his family; I was aware that he had two elder brothers, and that his parents resided quietly in their country seat somewhere in Norfolk, venturing up to London warily during the Season.

'That is how she persuaded my father that I should study medicine, rather than go into the Church.'

'The Church?' I admit I was startled; Chapman was so evidently a scientist of the first rank that I could not conceive of his being engaged in any other field of study.

'Yes,' he said, a hint of amusement in his dry voice, 'it is traditional, is it not, for the third son?'

'I suppose so. But continue, please.'

'My mother had the notion that I would minister to all her country-gentry friends' fashionable ailments; that I would be some sort of black-bagged man-about-town, that one day I would cure the quinsy of the Queen and the colds in all the crowned heads of Europe.'

'Your mother is ambitious for you; what of it? I wish I could say as much.'

I had lost my mother — or rather, my father had — on my very first day of knowing her, for she had given her life in giving birth to me. This was one of the reasons I had always admired Chapman's dedication to a specialism that a more squeamish man might have shied away from as too bloody or indelicate to pursue.

My friend inclined his head.

'I have two choices before me, Fraser: obstetrics and pathological gynaecology. One option means that, although she will hardly be able to mention it over tea and dainties, my mother will know that I am in attendance at all the best confinements, and responsible for many a child of the nobility being brought safely into the world — for God knows the poor could not afford so elevated a midwife.'

'So you will deliver healthy babies — what could be wrong with that?'

'The other,' he said heavily, 'will give me the possibility of saving immeasurably more lives; it could relieve pain and banish ignorance in that part of society where suffering and lack of knowledge are ruinously endemic. It is exciting and challenging, immensely so; but, to my family, it will also appear both ignominious and obscure, and I am not sure my father will fund it, if he can even be made to understand what it entails. A researcher of venereal disease! My mother might not survive the shame.'

I shook my head. 'I concede that I am at a loss. What help can I give you, Chapman? Do you not know what you wish to do?'

'I do,' he admitted, 'and I am not sure I have the courage to do it.'

He turned his head towards me, looking me full in the face; and once again I was struck by the subtle shadows of discontent and confusion that had settled over his lineaments. He looked at once older and sadder than I had thought he could. Knowing what I did of his dedication to both his studies and his family, I could imagine the opposing duties that pulled at him, and winced inwardly.

'For what my words are worth,' I said, 'I am in a far less extreme, but similar position to you. I must soon choose between entering the Church and dedicating myself to the academic study — the dissection, perhaps — of what so many passionately believe. I do not wish to betray my obligations to myself or to my God — and, frankly, I often do not know myself what I should do.'

'So what is your advice?' he demanded eagerly.

'I might commend another man to prayer,' I said, 'but knowing how little that has availed you in the past, I will say this instead: examine your own heart, read what is written there, and follow its promptings. When your soul speaks stilly within you, attend to it; it speaks true.'

He favoured me with a long look in which was mingled a hard-won respect I had seen in his face but once or twice before, and a deeper aspect of gratitude and relief.

He nodded. 'Thank you,' he said. 'I shall listen, and try.'

I hoped then that my advice might lead him down the path truest to his natural inclination, and of the most benefit to the diseased and destitute creatures of the world. I know better now; and yet I do not think that, even had I been aware at that moment of the effect my words would have upon his decision, I should have been able to advise him any other way. Perhaps it would have made little difference in the end; who can say?

In any case, Chapman looked away at once, as though embarrassed to have said so much, and raised his glass to the departing sun. His old chaffing humour, which so rarely deserted him, and which made him such pleasant society to everyone he knew, was back upon him.

'Here's to the ladies, then,' he said. 'I shall undertake to save their bodies, if you will do the same for their souls.'

We grinned and touched glasses, and drank them off, and went down to dinner at High Table in excellent spirits, little realizing that both of us would live bitterly to regret this night.

The next three years were, by and large, most contented ones. Indeed, from my current vantage-point, they appear to me now as through a golden haze; the sort of honey-pale glow that hovers over scenes and places when perceived at a distance, but of which the actors in those scenes are, at the time, entirely unaware. I continued to trouble the librarians of the Bodleian and the Codrington with my presence (for I had eventually decided that I would be of more service to myself and mankind in general as an academic than a pastor). Chapman, for his part, expended his considerable energies on those worthy and admirable researches he conducted in partnership with his mentor, Professor Marstone.

Chapman had thought long and examined his conscience thoroughly, according to my advice, before choosing the discipline of pathology over that of surgery, and to my mind had made a most commendable and difficult decision. He was not without his setbacks and troubles — as which of us are? — and yet I must admit that it did my heart good to see how passionately and long he laboured in his chosen field, and how invigorated he was by both the theoretical challenges and the practical opportunities for good presented by the problems he and the Professor struggled to solve. He often confided to me that he felt sure he had chosen rightly; that they were destined to make astonishing advances in a sadly neglected and fascinating branch of medicine, and embarrassed me with frequent protestations of gratitude as to the soundness of my counsel. I, in my turn, offered up humble thanks to my Maker that I had been allowed to render my friend assistance and guidance in his hour of confusion, and that the outcome had proved to be so thoroughly beneficial to all concerned — except, perhaps, Chapman's poor ambitious mother.

In short, we were happy.

★ ★ ★

This happiness — or my portion of it, at least — was not, however, destined to last; and the cause of its slow erosion was, as it all too frequently proves to be between a pair of bosom friends, a woman. I do not mean anything at all crude by this assertion; the woman who came between us was certainly not contested by us as starving dogs may fight over a scrap of meat, and the situation which took so great a toll on both Chapman and myself was far more complex and sinister than a mere affair of jealous hearts. But I shall be plain, and tell all as it unfolded in that fatal fourth year of our friendship; this was now 1887.

It was in March of that year, in Sixth Week of Hilary Term to be precise, that Chapman returned to our rooms one Sunday at about eleven o'clock in the morning, in a state of high excitement and something approaching glee. Undesirous of idle visitors, I had sported our oak to discourage any who might approach, and was sitting at my desk, re-reading some of the minor Apocrypha in preparation for giving a paper later that week. However, as soon as I heard the swift patter of my companion's step upon the stair and the deafening bang of our outer door I surmised that he had something of great interest to impart.

My inner door was closed against intrusion, and he knew well enough that I did not like to be disturbed when writing lecture-notes, but I felt in need of a little respite and was, I admit, curious as to what could have exercised my friend to this high degree. I rose and opened it to discover him hesitating on the threshold, clearly in two minds over whether to interrupt my peaceful study. His face broke into a grin of delight, and he threw wide his arms as though to embrace me.

'You are not busy, then? I must confess that had you been engaged I do not know in whom I should have confided my excellent news, for I really feel as though I ought to tell someone, or burst!'

'My dear fellow,' I said drily, 'I am all afire to know what, so early on a Sunday morning, can have exhilarated you to this extent — for it is surely not the brilliant oratory of old Reverend Horsby?'

He laughed.

'Ah, but you do not know how close you have hit it!' he said. 'For it was as I was coming out of a sermon of Dr McCallum's at the University Church that the most extraordinary thing occurred.'

I raised my eyebrows, for it was certainly unusual for my friend to spend his Sunday mornings contemplating the inside of a church as opposed to that of his own eyelids; his attending a sermon was a curious development in its own right.

'Indeed?' I said. 'Then let us ring for coffee and some breakfast and you shall tell me all about it — for I do not doubt that both of us would be the better for some sausage and eggs.'

For my own part, I was not very hungry; but in truth, the past few months of intense work with Marstone had seen my friend labouring long into the night and frequently forgetting to take regular meals. He was growing thinner before my eyes and I considered it my duty to make him eat, not least so that that fire of enthusiasm which consumed him should have some fuel on which to feed.

He bridled and directed his glance out of the window, down at the floor; indeed, anywhere but at my face.

'Oh, you have something, but I shan't. Excitement has made me quite lose my appetite, I assure you.'

Chapman, despite his free, careless manner, was never much of a liar, and intimate acquaintance had made me an adept of his occasional dissimulations. I was perfectly aware that ever since his father had refused to fund his 'distasteful' medical studies, he had been cast down into a condition which, if not exactly penury, was, for a gentleman, perilously close to it. He had used up the small inheritance he had come into at twenty-one over the previous few years and, although he protested that he could easily manage on what little he made from assisting and odd teaching jobs, I knew he was behindhand in paying both his battels and (more crucially) his tailor.

Some six months ago I had dared to suggest that perhaps I could make him a small loan, but Chapman, both generous and proud almost to a fault, would brook no offers of assistance. Indeed, he was rather cold to me in his absolute refusal, and although we never quite quarrelled over the matter, I feared I had offended him gravely by even mentioning the subject, and it was a week or two before we were back on our old footing. In any case, I was concerned for him, and resolved to do good by stealth; so I ordered coffee for two and a large plate of eggs, bacon, toast, sausages and kippers which I knew I could never consume alone.

Once the scout had brought up the breakfast and retired, Chapman, who had been pacing agitatedly about the sitting-room, clearly desperate to deliver himself of his story, pulled out a chair and threw himself down opposite me. I poured two cups of strong black coffee and steepled my fingers, ready to hear it.

'Very well,' I said, 'now you may relate to me the thrilling events of this morning.'

'Well,' he said, 'you know I am not a regular church-going sort of man as a rule, and that I usually take Horsby's sermons in chapel as an opportunity to let my mind wander over problems at the laboratory — but a few days ago I was strolling down the High and saw a notice outside St Mary's on Radcliffe Square saying that Arthur McCallum was speaking this Sunday. The title of the sermon was 'Blood and Body; physical manifestations of the divine' and, as you know, I am interested in the reconciliation of the physical and the spiritual by religious thinkers, and particularly the attitude of the Church to my sort of work — saving your presence, of course.'

I nodded, toying with a fragment of bacon. 'Of course.'

'So, I decided I would vary my usual Sunday routine of utter indolence with a little expedition to hear the Reverend Dr McCallum on the subject. I rose, shaved, dressed in my Sabbath finery and set off, arriving at the church a little before nine o'clock — I say, are you going to eat that sausage?'

'No,' I said. 'Nor the bacon, nor the toast, nor especially the kippers, which have a sly and accusatory look. Won't you finish them for me? I hate to waste good food.'

He hesitated, a shadow of innocent suspicion in his eyes, for he could not bear charity, but then smiled and took up a fork.

'Very well, Fraser — I can't deny my encounter has made me more than usually famished. But to continue: the sermon, I'm pleased to say, broke many an unwritten law of devout oratory by being both interesting and intelligent; and as I emerged I was pondering deeply much of what the good Reverend had said. I wandered down the High with the vague idea of smoking a cigar and drinking a cup of coffee at your office' — by which he meant the Queen's Lane Coffee House — 'and thinking further on the matter, when I was waylaid in the most extraordinary fashion by a panting young woman.'

35

I could not conceal my astonishment at this revelation.

'What! At such an hour — and coming out of church, yet! I had understood such creatures did not manifest themselves until after dark, even in the centre of town!'

Chapman shook his head decidedly.

'No, no, you mistake my meaning — it was not some poor drab who accosted me, but a pretty and well-dressed lady of about five-and-twenty who bore all the signs of gentility; most well-spoken and apologetic for disturbing me, and most charmingly alarmed at her own forwardness.'

'I should think so too,' I muttered, pouring myself a fresh cup of coffee from the tall silver pot.

'Well, to cut to the quick of the thing, she introduced herself to me as Mrs Diana Pelham, a widow, and enquired earnestly whether I was indeed the Dr Chapman who, as she put it, 'has been making such extraordinary and brilliant advances in pathology as the research assistant of the esteemed Professor Marstone'.'

'An admirer of yours, then?'

'It seemed so. I refuted her accusation of brilliance, but admitted my identity, at which she exclaimed with delight, and proposed at once that we stroll a little way together so that she could put to me a professional proposition.'

'Very forward,' I remarked, somewhat acerbically. 'And yet you say she had the bearing of a gentlewoman?'

'Oh, assuredly; but there was a reason for her

36

unusual behaviour, you see — in our short acquaintance I have come to the conclusion that she is a quite fascinating and exceptional woman — but I will tell you what transpired, and you shall understand.'

I doubted it, and he may have seen my scepticism in my face, but I made no further remark, and he continued.

'It seems that Mrs Pelham is the daughter of a well-respected clergyman in Cambridgeshire, the beneficiary of a first-class education, and a lady imbued, as so many are, with the determination to do good in this world; but what is rarer, also with the talents to achieve her ambition. In short, a large bequest was made a year or so ago by a philanthropic nobleman — Charlie Kester's late uncle, in fact — to set up a shelter or refuge of sorts for those fallen women of Oxford who wish to give up their former life of sin and find for themselves some more worthy and useful role in society. The executors of Lord Kester's estate have been searching high and low for a suitable person to take charge of the day-to-day running of this charitable operation, and Mrs Pelham had but a few days before secured the position!'

'Most commendable,' I said. 'And your role is, perhaps, to deliver the inmates of their bastards so that they may the more easily redeem themselves?'

Chapman stared at me in open-mouthed surprise; the colour left his face and he appeared a little shocked by my strong words.

'Fraser,' he stammered eventually, 'that — that is unworthy of you.'

I threw my coffee-spoon down on the breakfast table in frustration.

'For Heaven's sake, Chapman, does it not occur to you that this Mrs Pelham and her home for indigent whores are quite unworthy of *you*? What on earth she thinks she is doing trying to involve you in any capacity in such an endeavour, benevolent and necessary though it undoubtedly is, I cannot conceive! Presumably she will next attempt to engage the Bishop of Oxford to christen their poor unwanted offspring!'

A hard, hurt look had come into Chapman's eyes; I suppose he had expected me to be as delighted and excited as he was by this bizarre occurrence; but, prophetically, I feared for my friend, and could see nothing in either the woman or her project which could do him any good.

'Now, Fraser,' he said, more gently than I deserved, 'you must leave off your sarcasm and your prejudices, for you have not let me complete my story, you know, and until you have the whole picture I think even one as sagacious as you may not fully judge it.'

I inclined my head by way of apology, and rested my chin on my hands, watching his bright, keen, thin face as he resumed speaking.

'It emerged that she had some slight acquaintance with my work through a sort of second-cousin of hers called Cornell, a medic at Hertford who had attended some of my lectures. She did not dare to approach the exalted Marstone, whom she wished very much to be a sponsor or figurehead of the shelter, and so determined to discuss the situation with me. It seems, in fact, that she had been puzzling over whether it would be better to present her case in person or by letter, when she saw me in church and made up her mind to take the opportunity to speak to me there and then.'

'And how did Mrs Pelham know you?' I enquired.

'By her cousin's description of me,' he said, smiling. 'Oh, and by the acid-stains on my cuff, or so she told me.'

'A veritable lady-detective,' I remarked. Chapman ignored the irony in my tone, and rushed on with his tale.

'She says that one of the most awful things that befalls the poor women in that station of life is the natural hazard of disease; that although for the most part they try to keep themselves clean, they cannot choose their clients, and that many a girl, be she never so young and fresh, is infected with a veritable cornucopia of complaints by the first old lecher she takes on.'

He stopped, suddenly and belatedly aware of the rather colourful picture he was painting for me.

'She did not put it quite like that, you know,' he added hastily.

'I am sure she did not.'

'But you see now, don't you,' Chapman said, appealing to me, 'where I come in?'

'I certainly see where she might wish you to,' I averred. 'You and Marstone are to treat these . . . doxies, presumably? Cure them of their foul illnesses so that they can retire to

39

embroider samplers, or whatever Mrs Pelham would have them do? Or, more likely, return to the streets until they should again require your services?'

Chapman shook his head. 'Not at all, Fraser — she proposes to run a sort of unfortunates' hospital, of which Marstone would be the titular head and I the consulting physician.'

My coffee had gone cold. I was half-amazed and half-afraid at his story, for I could see that he thought her idea a very fine one and could not guess at how it would certainly render him at best a laughing-stock, and at worst an untouchable among his peers, let alone society at large. Marstone for one would never sanction it, I was certain of that. From Chapman the serious researcher to Chapman the whore-doctor in one fell stroke! I had to stop this madness.

'Chapman, I must — '

'Fraser, you must let me finish!' he told me impatiently. 'She is going to set it all up nicely, shipshape and clean — she used to be a nurse, you know — and so not only could I do what was in my power to cure these poor creatures, but where cure is not yet possible, I may improve their health so far as I am able — perhaps with some of the new compounds Marstone and I have been working on — and study the progress or retreat of the disease!'

I digested this, turning it over in my mind, but made no reply.

'It is the most incredible opportunity, don't you see?' Chapman continued eagerly. 'We may be able not only to cure these women, but learn from them which remedies are effective and which are not against a huge number of illnesses!'

I felt a strong desire to step out upon the balcony to clear my head. This notion of Mrs Pelham's, and Chapman's alarming embrace of it, had set my brain spinning in myriad different directions. It presented so many problems — moral, social and not least ethical, given that the patients could not know the potential effects of newly discovered drugs any more than Chapman could — that I felt unable to grasp its vast folly all at once.

'And what of the ineffective compounds?' I asked. 'What if you kill them, or worse, restore them entirely? They will go straight back out to ply their trade again on the streets, probably believing themselves immune! Are you to cure these women of their diseases, which are no more nor less than the wages of sin, merely in order that they may return to being whores?'

Chapman shook his head violently.

'No, Fraser, you do not understand. They will not fall back into their former lives. Mrs Pelham says that those who wish to reform will be provided with suitable training — '

I could not help it; I burst out in bitter laughter. 'Those who *wish* to, indeed! Think, Chapman! What else can they do? What skills have they, or can they learn? What led to their downfall in the first place?'

He frowned. 'Fraser, I had not expected this of you: was not Christ forgiving of the Magdalene? Even you must know that only the most desperate and downtrodden creatures turn to street-walking as a profession: they do not choose to trade in their virtue — they *must!* There is no shelter for these women; no recourse, no asylum. They live on the streets or rent slum lodgings, and yes, many are unlettered and unskilled, but that is hardly through any fault of their own!'

'You will disgrace yourself by association,' I said quietly, through my teeth. 'You know what is whispered of those generous, moral gentlemen who stoop to raise fallen women! Their interest is never seen as pure nor their motives unblemished. Chapman, you will be tarred with the brush of whoremonger if you do this.'

He set his lips in a thin hard line and stared at me, his eyes luminous, stark blue as the morning sky laced with scurrying clouds.

'Let me tell you a story, Fraser — '

'I think you have told me enough.'

'Evidently I have not. This concerns a friend of a friend, a young man not unlike you or I: a little stupider, perhaps; a little more impulsive. But not somebody of whom society might in general say, 'This is a bad fellow.' '

'Indeed? And who is this paragon?'

'A cousin of Charlie Kester's; they call him Lucky, though I don't know his real name and I daresay it does not matter. A boy with plenty of money, a rather cruel sense of humour and a quick temper. It also concerns a girl, one of the drabs who plies outside the Ox's Head; a woman of the lowest sort, plunged in the direst poverty.'

I snorted with impatience. If he was setting

out to wring my heart with hard-luck tales, he would not succeed.

'When this young man encountered her she was weeping piteously; he asked her why, and she said she had been thrown out of her lodgings that morning because her rent was in arrears. She told him she had already sold everything she had of value and was in desperate straits.'

I could not restrain a cynical smirk. 'Oh, I do not doubt that is what she *told* him.'

Chapman shot me a hard look and continued. 'So, seeming to take pity on her, or a fancy to her — I am sure she cared not which — this young man offered to engage her to perform certain acts which he took great delight in depicting at length, as she stood and shivered in the rain, speaking to her from inside his coach, not deigning to descend. After he had named and detailed each perversion he — '

This was really too much for a Sabbath morning. 'I am not interested in further details, Chapman!'

'You will hear me out, Fraser; it is not what you think. After he had described each act he asked her for her price for it: in this manner he detained her, sodden and shuddering in a grim alleyway, for better than twenty minutes — and at the end of this obscene catalogue of vice, what do you think he said?'

'I have no idea.'

'He said: 'And how much to stand and listen to me speak this filth to you over and over; and how much to show your naked willingness to do anything for a mean shilling or two, for that is

43

what I have enjoyed most about our meeting? How much to sell yourself so cheap even a beggar could have you? Ah! Of course, I forgot: it costs nothing. Good-day.' And he drove off in his cosy carriage into the darkness, his manservant snickering at his side.'

A cruel and underhanded trick to play, to be sure, but I did not agree that just because their clients were worse, such women should be regarded by comparison as victims and saints, as Chapman seemed to think.

'And what moral am I expected to draw from this sordid tale?'

'Draw what you will from it: I will say only that Charlie's cousin relayed this incident to him in the character of a joke; and a mighty clever one, at that. And that is how these girls are treated; as less than human, as animals to be humiliated for sport, as worth no more than they charge, and sometimes less than that. No wonder, once they stumble, they sink so swiftly into vice! If that girl had had somewhere else to go, do you think she would have stood in the rain listening to such a man in hope of payment? If she had any other profession, or sanctuary, or chance at life, do you not believe she would grasp it with both hands?'

He spread his own palms wide, in an attitude of supplication. He was almost smiling in the conviction that even one so hard-hearted as I could not fault his persuasive logic. I knew that look; it was one of incipient triumph, and I would not give him that satisfaction. I turned away from him in frustration.

'Damn it, man! However tragic their plight, this is not your battle! Keep away from it, I say, and let Mrs Pelham exorcise her charitable impulses with some other dupe. If you must be a saviour, let you at least find persons worthy of saving!'

I was shaking with impotent anger at his obstinacy and obtuseness; I feared for the reputation, position and very health of my dear friend, an innocent of such high-minded gentleness that, were he to gaze into the pit of Hell itself, he would see no sinners, only suffering. Chapman watched my uncharacteristic outburst with anxiety and incomprehension in his wide eyes. I passed a hand over my face and found it cold and damp with sweat.

'Chapman,' I said, 'won't you give me one of your cigars? I think I must have a smoke in the fresh air.'

'Of course, old chap,' he said, slipping one from his case and passing it over. 'Are you unwell? You look pale as paper.' He sounded most concerned on my behalf; not, however, one-tenth as concerned as I was on his.

'Too much coffee, I expect,' I managed to say, and quit the room.

Outside, the morning was a glorious shout of spring; the brisk wind ruched up the sparkling waters of the lake, and the halloas of an impromptu game of cricket drifted faintly from the pitch on its far side. I smoked my cigar and thought about Chapman's words, and the mysterious Mrs Pelham's misguided project. Who was this unconscionable woman to proposition my friend — a respectable medical researcher with a mind and soul infinitely better and more valuable than those of a hundred diseased wretches! What sort of do-gooding fanatic must she be?

I recoiled from the portrait of her Chapman had painted, and yet there was something familiar about it — or perhaps about her name, an unusual one — that tugged a thread at the back of my brain . . . something I could not quite fix my memory upon, but which clanged loud as any bell the single word *danger*.

And yet, how could I explain to Chapman that ever since he had mentioned her — before, even, he had told me her outrageous idea — I had had a black foreboding about the lady who was seeking to involve him in her doomed experiment? There was no way. I could not tell him of my apprehension, he who dismissed intuition as a vestigial remnant of a past all enlightened beings had outgrown, as superannuated and useless as the appendix. He should have laughed in my face and refused to listen to me any further. I would have to try and argue him out of this appalling scheme. It would not be easy.

★ ★ ★

It was not easy: it was impossible, and it led almost to the dissolution of our friendship. Once Professor Marstone (much to my disgust) had given this preposterous endeavour his blessing, Chapman absolutely fixed upon taking the 'position', as he dignified it, at the refuge in

Jericho, which was to occupy him for two evenings a week. The reason we fell out, as I thought at the time irreparably, was that Chapman then had the abysmal idiocy to suggest that since Jericho itself was located tolerably near to the Radcliffe Infirmary, where much of his research with Professor Marstone was conducted, he should, for convenience's sake, move in to the area.

It must be understood that Chapman and I had long decided that when our studies were completed and our mutual time at Worcester was up, I should take up a junior lectureship which had been offered me by the Rector of Hertford College, and Chapman too would remain in Oxford to further his pathological investigations, attaching himself as a researcher to whichever college or institution would have him. But the main article of our pact was that when autumn came, we should continue to share diggings in whatever part of town we could best afford; for having found each other such congenial and interesting company for the last few years, we should have been loath indeed to lose the privilege of one another's close acquaintance.

We had spoken of taking a little place somewhere up the Woodstock or Banbury Road, as accommodation in North Oxford was known to be clean, respectable and cheap; but at no point until now had either of our minds bent towards the seedy, mazelike streets and ill-lit taverns of Jericho. The reputation of that quarter of the city had long done its Biblical namesake a shameful disservice, being notorious as the haunt of drunkards, thieves, beggars, pedlars and the lowest sort of brazen female as ever lifted her petticoats. Any eventual reader must pardon my forthright language upon this matter — but I mean to impress on him the thoroughly vile and abandoned nature of the area, and thereby explain my own vehement opposition to taking lodgings anywhere near it.

We argued long upon this point; he felt that I was unnecessarily prejudiced, I that he was suicidally foolish. We had left it far too late to make alternative living arrangements with other students, which meant that we were, effectively, yoked together if we wanted to live anywhere at all. Eventually Chapman, impulsive and determined as ever, packed his bags (excepting his enormous trunk, which he declared he would send for) and set off to walk around Jericho looking for lodgings on his own. Naturally enough, he was set upon by ruffians in Victor Street that very same evening, and limped back to the safety of the college walls much the worse for the encounter, having lost his travelling-bag, which, fortunately, had contained little of value.

Naturally, I commiserated with my poor bloodied friend, but inwardly I rejoiced, believing in my *naïveté* that this setback would surely reconcile him to living in some more decent, less dangerous part of town. Instead, it served only to strengthen his resolve; come Hell or high water, and whether it wanted him or not, Jericho would have him. For despite his chastening *fracas*, he had found a place to live — twice the size of our current accommodations at half the price, so he said — and was moving in the very next day.

Early on the morrow I was awoken by the crashes and groans of the porters removing his trunk; Chapman stood at the door, poor disembodied Albert (now his sole companion) in his box under one arm. Chapman's sad, strained face was stained with purple bruises; his cut lip swollen as he forced a smile, shook my hand and bade me farewell. It was one of the most pathetic sights I ever hope to see; and the only thing that rivalled it, as I discovered as soon as I had closed the door upon my dearest friend in all the world, was the hollow, dark and melancholy aspect of our rooms once he was gone.

★ ★ ★

I had resolved to take temporary accommodation in college while I decided what to do, and perhaps move over to Hertford when I took up my position there, if a room could be found at that late stage — but I did not reckon on the vagaries of my own will. Midnight the very same night found me standing under a broken gaslight, streaming with rain, shivering with cold, and banging fit to wake the dead upon the warped green door of a tumbledown workman's cottage in Canal Street. I was on the point of giving up and retiring to the nearest public house to enquire my way back to civilization, when the door shot open and I saw my friend's injured, astonished face peering out from a dim and peeling hallway.

His eyes lighted up to see me so unexpectedly, and he ushered me in, exclaiming at my folly at coming into Jericho at this hour, in the dark and the rain. He took my portmanteau and put it before the fireplace to dry, and fussed about me, hanging my overcoat on a chair, taking my hat and insisting that I imbibe some hot, spiced, mildly alcoholic concoction against colds which his mother swore by. The little kitchen was surprisingly cheerful and cosy, and Chapman seemed as at home in it as if he were back in the laboratory, mixing up alkalis in the test-tubes and washing out the retorts.

I sat and steamed silently; I had been a fool, no doubt, and fewer than twenty-four hours without Chapman's company had shown me exactly how much of one. Chapman handed me a smoking glass smelling strongly of brandy and enjoined me to drink it, which I did.

'No scouts to bring the coffee around here — I must shift for myself,' he told me cheerfully. I nodded my head and shivered; I could feel the rainwater in my boots pickling my toes. Chapman sat down opposite me and shook his head, his arms folded.

'Whatever possessed you to visit me at this ungodly hour, Fraser?' he asked. 'Was it some matter so urgent it could not wait until morning?' He clapped a palm to his forehead. 'Oh Lord, if it is my battels bill, tell the Bursar I shall have it for him by Tuesday — '

I cleared my throat. 'No such thing,' I said. 'Nothing so very urgent — only that I have not

50

come to visit: I have come to stay, if you will have me.'

He looked confused, then disbelieving, then finally grave. I had expected, and hoped for, his usual infectious delight at my news; but to my concern he seemed to have taken it quite the other way.

'Unless you feel that the rift is too — that you would not wish — ' I stammered. The truth was that his poor bleeding face had haunted me, until finally I could not bear it. I could not live a moment longer with the guilt of having abandoned my friend to his quixotic fate — or knowing that, friendless and innocent and unmistakably a gentleman and a scholar as he was, he would daily face the contempt and violence of the denizens of this low slum entirely alone.

Chapman shook his head.

'No, no,' he said, quietly. 'I quite understand why you thought me mad, and I know you spoke in what you felt was my own interest. I was just thinking how exceedingly lucky I am to have so good a friend as you, who would not only risk his skin in coming once to Jericho, but every day from thereon by living in the place.'

I hastened to assure him that anyone would have done the same; that it was nothing.

'At least,' I said, 'the next time the Victor Street vagabonds come after you, there will be two of us to contend with.'

At last that unquenchable spark of humour flared up in his face, and he chuckled. For my part, my heart throbbed with a relief so intense it almost nauseated me; and as I raised my glass to my lips I could not prevent it knocking gently against my chattering teeth, nor my hands from trembling.

Despite my misgivings as to the sordid and dangerous character of our new neighbourhood, our first few months in Jericho were fraught with few inconveniences greater than the incessant leak in the ceiling of Chapman's bedroom, and no worse threat to our well-being than the mice who scratched ceaselessly behind the kitchen skirting, and bore away any little crumb of food we were foolish enough to leave out. Chapman worked industriously at his various places of employment (including the shelter) from dawn until dusk, and I performed my duties at Hertford with application and no little pleasure — for there is a strain of showmanship in my blood on the distaff side, and teaching and lecturing have always come naturally to me.

Although, as a consequence of our commitments elsewhere, we rarely saw much of one another during the working week, we treasured every Sunday as a day of companionable leisure, sacred to discourse and the discussion of our respective weeks. I would regale my friend with the latest High Table gossip, and Chapman, for his part, would tell me of his recent advances and setbacks in the laboratory. However, in deference to my sensibilities, he never spoke of his labours at Mrs Pelham's establishment, for he well knew that this aspect of his career still made me uneasy; and so we rubbed along pretty well.

As autumn wore on, I was pleased to discover that Chapman had not been mistaken about the economic benefits of living in Jericho, and as the weeks passed in a busy blur of action, I grew to appreciate the advantages of the area. Not only was the rent on our little cottage a most reasonable, almost nominal sum, but our purse was made to stretch still further by the low prices of the shops and cafés (one could not call them restaurants) in the area — for indeed, such cheap goods and refreshments were all the poor could afford. Our accommodating landlady, Mrs Genevieve Shimmin, known to the more informal lodgers in her other properties as Ginny, 'did' for us for a small consideration, and all in all we made our little home as snug and cosy as any occupied by a pair of student bachelors might be.

We occasionally ventured out of an evening to the sole vaguely reputable tavern in Jericho; a squat modern brick public house with a swinging red sign called the Harcourt Arms, where there was a fire in every room and the brawls were merely sporadic. This relative peace and serenity were due in large part to the strict rule of the landlord, a former merchant-seaman called Randolph Quire who measured six feet in height and almost as much in circumference, and who became quite friendly towards us once he discovered we were fellow-residents of the area, and working men, of a sort.

'I had took you for young men on the town at

first,' he confided in me one evening, 'and didn't want no trouble, for there is only one reason fellows from the University ever come around these parts, and it ain't the fine flavour of the beer.'

I smiled and thanked him for giving us the benefit of the doubt; but I returned to the snug with a heavy heart, for the living reminders of Mrs Pelham's 'project' were all around us constantly — in the streets and outside the gin-shops and lower types of inn, if not (thanks to Quire) in the Harcourt itself. I suppose I feared that their shamelessness and vice might imprint themselves somehow on my innocent friend Chapman. In this I was proved right, after a fashion — but in such a bizarre and roundabout way, that I coldly comfort myself I could not possibly have predicted from whence the danger would come.

★ ★ ★

We had been in our little house on Canal Street for about four months, and had made it quite cheerful and comfortable (most especially for the mice), even in the dark and chill of what was now winter, when one day Chapman came back from the laboratory with a spring in his step and a shimmer of mischief in his eye.

'What is it?' I asked immediately he entered — for he could no more hide his moods from me than a dog could speak. In reply, he threw two gilt-edged cards down upon the kitchen table.

'What do you think? Professor Marstone has recalled rather belatedly that he has an important lecture to deliver at the Royal Free Hospital in London, and therefore cannot possibly use his tickets to the Medics' Ball tomorrow evening!'

I examined the cards; they were indeed thick white tickets, heavy and stiff as canvas, permitting entry to the Ball in question.

'And he has kindly donated these to his impoverished assistant!' I cried with satisfaction — for in truth, I knew how dearly Chapman loved the glamour and romance of such occasions, and how sorely he missed the revels he had forgone through his ill-paid dedication to the craft of healing.

'You have it in one,' he told me. 'He knows something of our situation, of course, and absolutely *insisted* I take them — would not let me leave the lab until he had wrung from me a solemn oath to attend!'

'He is the most generous of men,' I said heartily.

'Oh, assuredly! And so while Professor and Mrs Marstone are sleeping soundly in their beds at the Great Western Hotel, you and I will be swanning about in white tie, toasting the beauty of the ladies at the Ball!' He grinned and executed a little bow.

'You and I?' I repeated in confusion, for I was quite unused to enjoyments of this type, and had naturally assumed that he would wish to take a female companion — almost certainly the redoubtable Mrs Pelham.

Chapman threw open a cupboard and grabbed a tin of dry biscuits, crunching through two at once with all the avidity and decorum of a famished wolf.

'Sorry,' he said, 'I have had nothing to eat all day — we were performing a particularly delicate series of titrations and I couldn't leave the bench for fear of them going wrong.'

I forgave him with a nod, and brought the teapot over to the kitchen table.

'I had thought of asking Mrs Pelham,' he confessed, once I had poured him a steaming cup, 'but I was afraid she would not consider it quite proper to attend an event of that type with — well, a professional colleague, I suppose. None the less, I should probably have chanced it, but for the happy coincidence that she mentioned only this evening that she is going in any case!'

'Oh,' I said, my anticipation of the night's amusement dampening slightly.

I rallied, however, reasoning that this must mean she was being courted by some other foolish fellow, and that my friend's heart was in no danger from that quarter — for Chapman, when he spoke of her, was always full of the highest praise, and to hear him talk I could not forbear to think that he held her in unusually high regard among her sex.

'She has a beau, then?' I observed casually — and was somewhat nonplussed when Chapman shook his head.

'No indeed,' he told me, 'she is far too dedicated to her work (as am I, you know) for things of that nature — old Kester's sot of a son used to hang about the shelter, professing admiration of her endeavours as well as her person, but she drove him off — for he once had an ill reputation with the girls hereabouts, at least if his cousin Charlie is to be believed. No, that medic relation of hers from Hertford is bringing her — he is qualified now! Fine chap, name of Cornell.'

'I see.' I fancied I knew the name, from a few mentions of the fellow at High Table, but rather to my disappointment could recall no ill having been spoken of him.

'Well, he has no sweetheart, and knows Mrs Pelham to be interested in medical matters — and, you know, she is awfully pretty, quite the ornament to any chap's arm, so she is going with him. Although she confided to me that she is quite at her wits' end as to what she owns that will be fine enough to wear!'

He laughed fondly at this evidence of feminine perplexity. Her habitual widow's weeds would not, I imagined, suffice; but perhaps she had not funds enough to discard her sombre black for half-mourning. I must have frowned as I thought of the woman, for Chapman caught my concern.

'Why, tell me, what is it?' he said cajolingly. 'I declare, you look quite Biblically stern!'

I shook my head and smiled, and said that I had been wondering whether it was quite appropriate for me to attend such a frivolous and no doubt somewhat free-and-easy occasion.

Chapman scoffed away my fears.

'Nonsense, old chap! Why, you are beginning to resemble one of my graver cadavers! You are not in a vicarage yet — and nor, I warrant, will you ever be — you are too clever for that. And besides, it is quite within the remit of a junior

57

lecturer to indulge in the odd night of fun and frolics. It'll do you a power of good. Perhaps you'll even meet a young lady!'

Unmoved by the extremely remote prospect of a romantic encounter, I nevertheless agreed, with little further persuasion, to accompany him — but I felt cold and sick at heart. For I could not ignore the daunting likelihood of being introduced at some point to the woman with whom Chapman spent so many of his evenings; of whose praise he was unendingly full; who had captured his imagination and admiration and, I half-suspected, also his heart — in short, the mysterious Mrs Pelham.

I had hoped our paths would never have to cross — that she would remain, as it were, a theoretical female, just as we know those friends who have gone overseas to exist, though we do not see them from one year's-end to the next. But it was not to be. I excused myself and ascended the stairs to seek out my old white tie and tail-coat. I felt as though I were dressing for someone's funeral.

Oh, what shall I say of the stars, the sparkling frost, the thousand glittering candles and glancing crystals of the chandeliers! What can I tell you of the glimmering silks and rich velvets, the Polar white of the gentlemen's starched shirt-fronts and the glowing gold of the ladies' curls, that my reader may not, with far greater alacrity and vividness, conjure up from all the balls he has seen or known! Ah! They shone, those youths and maidens — they shone as the lake at Worcester shines briefly at sunset — as one great, gilded mass of soft fire.

As may be surmised, I was favourably impressed by the glamour and elegance of the occasion, having led a very quiet life at both Cambridge and Oxford, despising the regular College and Commem Balls as idle, wasteful fripperies, and rather looking down on those who would turn their minds from their studies and bend them purely on pleasure in such a fashion. But as I beheld the quiet beauty of the cloisters (for the venue was my friend's *alma mater*, Magdalen) transformed into a candlelit garden of light and laughter, my heart could not but thrill within me at the exquisite loveliness of the sight.

Admittedly, I was less enthusiastic when it came to dancing, and was certainly more inclined to lean casually against the ballroom wall with a glass of punch than to join in the foxtrot; but I took pleasure in watching Chapman enjoy himself with his old cronies from Magdalen and his newer ones from the Radcliffe. Everywhere I turned I encountered sumptuous food, handsome women, and plentiful drink. Chapman seemed in his element — and so, after a glass or two of Champagne, felt I. I even began tentatively to hope that the evening might pass without the dubious pleasure of Mrs Pelham's company — but, alas, that good fortune was denied me.

Chapman had been dancing with a comely and energetic young lady of bright eyes and high colour, when at the end of their gavotte, he was hailed by a tall red-whiskered fellow with the air of a rugby player about him, whom I thought I recognized. This man was holding by the elbow a lady of perhaps twenty-five or -six years with glossy black curls, shiny as a stallion's flank, an almost anaemically pale complexion, a small, delicate figure and fine dark eyes. She was smiling widely, and her teeth gleamed a brilliant white in the candle-light against the flushed rose of her lips.

I knew that lovely, fatal face instantly, and the blood drained from my own.

They made their way across the room, where Chapman disengaged himself courteously from his dancing-partner, and greeted them both with evident delight. He turned to introduce me.

'Fraser,' he said, 'may I present my good friends, Mrs Diana Pelham and her cousin, Dr Neil Cornell? Mrs Pelham, Dr Cornell — my best and oldest friend, Dr Edward Fraser.'

We shook hands and nodded cordially to one another, I succeeding in avoiding the gaze of Mrs Pelham, and tried to make a joke to cover my horrified confusion.

'I am not one of your Hippocratic fellowship, you understand, Dr Cornell — a doctor of Divinity merely!'

Cornell laughed good-naturedly, but at the mention of my subject, Mrs Pelham's dark eyes inadvertently and instantly sought mine; I was staring hard at her, unable to drag my gaze away, and our glances intersected — or rather, collided, for we both started involuntarily, and our mutual awkwardness was obvious even to Chapman. I was the first to recover myself. After all, I suppose I had always known, somewhere in the dark recesses of my memories of long ago, whom she must be.

'Mrs Pelham,' I said, 'surely I have had the honour of meeting you before?'

Her colour rose further and she shook her head decidedly, her black curls tossing.

'I should think not, Dr Fraser,' she stammered ' — that is, I do not believe so.'

Her dark eyes pleaded silently with mine; and the memories tumbled unbidden before my mind's eye, sharp and clear as stars on a frosty night. A shaft of dusty sunlight . . . the bitter taste of China tea . . . a discarded shoe, emerald-green, and over it all, the stifling heady smell of oil paints. I studied her pale face closely in the light of the multitudinous candles, and I knew I was right.

'But I am certain of it, madam!' I insisted. 'Some years hence, to be sure, but we have encountered one another on several occasions prior to this. In Cambridge, was it not? At the School of Art . . . and elsewhere. We had a mutual friend, I think? A painter.'

I was smiling with every appearance of happiness and surprise at having serendipitously rediscovered an old friend; but Mrs Pelham looked faintly aghast, as though I had made some unexpected and quite unforgivable *faux-pas*.

'No . . . no, sir, I really cannot recall having made your acquaintance before now,' she said faintly. That voice again! It assured me in my identification. However soft, however low, I remembered it only too well, drifting from behind Valenti's easel, dropping like a petal from a first-floor window in the still summer afternoons of yesteryear.

Cornell was clearly uncomfortable at her insistent denial.

'Well, I don't know — that great-aunt of yours lives in Cambridgeshire, doesn't she, Di — might have seen this chap in church, don't you think?' He barked a laugh like a parade-ground command. 'Maybe you — ha! — you collared him like poor old Chapman here?'

She glanced at him and fire flashed, ever so briefly, in her black eyes. He dropped his gaze hastily; for all his bulk and bluster, Cornell was patently a little afraid of his lovely cousin.

'Perhaps you just don't remember, my dear?' he suggested timidly.

She nodded, looking away from me, feigning weariness of this tiresome theological boor who was so ill-mannered as to pretend to know her. Chapman broke the awkward spell by begging the honour of a dance; she agreed with relief, and I swiftly suggested to Cornell that we hunt up a waiter with a tray of Champagne. He agreed heartily, and promised to meet his cousin in half an hour at the eastern end of the cloisters, where there was a refreshment-table. She bade me a cool farewell, her eyes never once resting on my face.

I bowed shallowly over her extended hand, and planted my lips on the air an inch above the white silk of her glove.

'Good evening, Mrs Pelham,' I said, although it was not the name by which I had once known her.

★ ★ ★

Chapman was uproarious and more than a little intoxicated when he finally returned home at past three o'clock the next morning; I, on the contrary, was cold, sober, and quite incensed. At the beginning of the evening, Chapman and I had made an agreement that, should we somehow become separated in the crowd or lose one another for more than an hour, we would both immediately repair to the front quad, by the Porter's Lodge, where there stood a little stall providing coffee, chocolate, and hot-toddies, and rendezvous there.

When, after returning with Cornell, I could not discover my friend or his dancing-partner anywhere in the ballroom, I was at first puzzled, then angry; then afraid. For the next twenty minutes, Cornell and I were forced to wander about the place, searching for them, all the while making stilted small-talk (of which I have precious little at the best of times) until he could find his cousin. Pleading exhaustion, I declined to join them, but begged Cornell that he would send Chapman over to me at once if my friend appeared.

I can only conclude that he did not, as I waited for a full half-hour on a cold hard bench outside the chapel, and met with nothing but curious glances. Finally I bethought myself of our pact, and hurried to the stall by the Porter's Lodge — but he was not there either. I asked after him; the vendor had seen no-one matching his description — or rather, had seen everyone, for he was an old, near-sighted fellow and all of us identically dressed young men must have looked and sounded entirely alike to his unsophisticated discrimination. I thanked him, and purchased a hot-chocolate to recompense him for his trouble.

Fortunately I had a case of cigars with me, and whiled away the time smoking, admiring the beautiful old college buildings, and composing a forceful and elegant denouncement of my friend's appalling manners, to be delivered to him as soon as he showed his face. But still he did not arrive. I bought a hot-toddy, strong with rum; then another, then a third; by this time it was nigh on two o'clock in the morning, and the revels about me showed no sign of dying down.

I stood up abruptly, furiously, and demanded of a rather frightened porter that he call me a cab; I would not stay in this place a moment longer. As I waited outside the gates, I realized how very cold I was; the rum had momentarily warmed me, but it had worn off, and the sere chill of the night seeped into my bones. It had been snowing, softly and prettily, at intervals throughout the evening; and, glancing down, I saw that the shoulders of my tailcoat were lightly rimed with flakes. I had sat so long waiting for Chapman that I had allowed the snow to settle on me, for all the world as though I had been one of the statues outside the chapel, or a gargoyle adorning the guttering.

The pit of my stomach burned with anger and humiliation; the cab drew up and I threw myself into it, a black and dangerous mood slowly developing over my soul on the twisting, bouncing journey back, as silver nitrate blooms on a photographic plate.

★   ★   ★

I paid off the cabman and let myself in to our lodgings, which were, as they always became when both of us had been absent more than a few hours, black, chill and rather damp. I lighted a candle, made a small fire in the kitchen grate, and sat up angrily to wait upon my friend's return. I was almost done in when I heard a

65

muffled thump on the front door — a noise that spoke more of a body slumping drunkenly against it, than of a knock demanding entry.

There was a metallic scratching of keys, then a black silhouette flung the door wide and swayed in through the short passage to the kitchen. Chapman did not seem especially surprised to see me already at home and waiting up for him — he merely threw himself into a rickety chair, focused that dazzling smile of his somewhere over my shoulder, and asked whether we didn't have any more Champagne in the house.

I glared at him icily. 'We never had any at all, you bloody fool.'

'Oh,' he said airily, 'never mind. Tea will do.'

I could contain my indignation no longer.

'Where on earth have you been all this time, Chapman? Do you know what hour it is?'

He swung a lazy hand.

'Twelve? One?'

'Nigh-on four in the morning, Chapman! How came you home? Have you been robbed? For Heaven's sake, man, you know Jericho at this hour — you are damned lucky to be alive!'

He smiled and winked at me, most impertinently.

'I have a guardian angel, Fraser.'

'You certainly must have, to wander these streets alone!'

'Her name' — he paused to write it on the air with a weaving forefinger — 'is Diana.'

My skin turned cold. I leaned forward in my chair; Chapman's beatific features were illumined only fitfully by the flickering flames in the grate.

'What have you done, Chapman? Where did you vanish with her? If there is any dishonour at all in this, you must tell me.'

He grinned foolishly.

'My dear fellow, there's not a particle of it! I am sorry, of course, that you and I lost each other, but I have passed the *most* delightful evening and I trust you have too. Perhaps you found your own guardian angel, did you?' He smirked conspiratorially at me.

'I have no need of one, thank you,' I told him stiffly.

He steepled his hands in mock prayer.

'Ah yes, the Lord will provide.'

'Don't you laugh up your sleeve at me, Chapman,' I said in a hard, quiet voice. I put out my hand and shook his shoulder; he shrugged me off.

'Fraser, Fraser! I cannot blame you for being jealous, Heaven knows, but I should have thought you'd be happy for me! Is not love the greatest joy to which Man can aspire?'

'I cannot speak of what I do not know, Chapman, but I will say this: if you are talking of love — if, as I am forced to conclude, you fancy yourself in love with Mrs Pelham, there is nothing but sorrow and shame in it for you.'

He arched an eyebrow and fumbled in his case for a cigar.

'Oh really? And how, innocent of love as you are, would you be able to tell that from meeting her once, for thirty seconds?'

I hung my head. Ever since seeing her again a few hours past, I had hoped it would not come to this. My tale did no-one any credit, but especially not Mrs Pelham, and it hurt me to have to recount the whole sorry story, even for the sake of one so dear to me, and so worthy of my protection, as my friend.

'I can swear to it, Chapman, because I have met her many times before. Oh, she may deny it — but I knew her once, long ago, back in Cambridge, and I consider it my bounden duty to inform you of exactly who, and what, she really is.'

BOOK TWO

The Tragedy of Antonio Valenti

Now I break from the record of my Oxford days, and must instead turn back the leaves of the years to a time that seems as remote from the present as are the striving Heavens from the Earth — to a time of my own youth, and innocency, and my first encounter with the madness of men that may be wreaked, whether knowingly or not, by the mystery that is Woman.

When I first went up to King's as an undergraduate in the year 1880, I was a shy and timid creature, even more so than when I stepped off the train at Oxford some three years later: a mere sapling of a boy with an immense love of learning, but with hardly a tongue in my head, nor a friend in the world — at least, not in the world of Cambridge.

My father, a King's man himself, who had rowed to a Blue with the current Provost, had packed me off from the North Wayneflete railway-station with enough money (so he claimed) to last me until Christmas, and a trunk almost entirely full of books from our patchy library, as well as my elder brother's old academic and formal wear, altered to suit my more modest dimensions. 'Waste not, want not' was Father's creed; and even as the carriage was pulling away from the platform he continued to warn me sternly against the dangers of profligacy and debauchery, concepts I was far more likely to encounter between the pages of a dictionary than in any practical endeavour of mine.

I was accommodated on a staircase with a number of boisterous, sports-playing fellows whose society attracted me not in the least; but after a few weeks I was happy to make the acquaintance, while admiring the Constables in the Fitzwilliam's picture-gallery, of a young man whose interests and temperament seemed wonderfully to match my own.

He was a handsome, swarthy, fine-figured fellow called Antonio Valenti — from which you may surmise, as did I, that he was of Italian ancestry. His mother was English, however; and he spoke the language as his native tongue, having been educated at Harrow School. As we chatted, it soon emerged that Valenti (a great admirer of Turner) was himself an artist — and by artist, I do not mean the sort of milksop watercolourist or dilettante weekend-sketcher one finds amongst 'accomplished' young ladies and effete undergraduates.

No, Valenti was as fiery and passionate in his painting as his Mediterranean heritage might suggest; he was utterly committed to the pursuit of his art, and had a surprisingly deep and eclectic knowledge of many other subjects via the history of his own.

We walked together to a nearby tea-room, and over our cups we discovered a mutual interest in classical mythology and ancient religion — particularly the more obscure and mysterious rituals imported by the Athenians from Thrace and Phrygia, a thousand and more years before Christ. In short, by the time we parted I found myself thoroughly pleased with his company, and hoping to enjoy more of it very soon, for I had promised to lend him an unusual volume I had picked up in Hatchards of Piccadilly, on the subject of the sacrificial rites of Bacis. I walked back to college in an excellent mood, slipping through the great black gate just before curfew, and thought no more of it, save to muse upon what a fortunate fellow I was to have found such an agreeable new friend.

Valenti and I continued in our acquaintance some months, meeting regularly to attend exhibitions of paintings and sculpture, and the occasional lecture on pre-Christian culture to which he accompanied me as my guest. Although a little older than me, he was not a student at the University, but rather at Ruskin's recently founded School of Art, where he was the most brilliant and promising pupil of the renowned Macaré. He had a sort of garret-studio in the poorer part of town, which none the less boasted a fine view over the city spires, whence we would sometimes retire when the day's labours were over, to talk further on religion and painting.

Perhaps this all sounds puppyish and whimsical, but it was a most rewarding friendship for both of us. He would often grant me the intimate privilege of viewing his work, both the finished canvases and those in progress, and seemed to place a flattering degree of importance on my opinion of them. There were only a few paintings he refused to show me; these, he told me with a rather Luciferian smile, were quite unsuitable for my English eyes, and my clerical sensibilities.

He described them, rather coyly, as 'studies of the human form, in an ancient classical style' — well, any man of the world may crack that code as easily as did I! He meant that they were nudes got up as nymphs and naiads and goddesses and so forth. I felt certain that, having beheld the majesty of Canova's *Three Graces*, I could cope well enough with the sight of a housemaid in a disarranged toga — but I did not care to press the point (nor indeed to appear prurient), so I respected his wishes.

As summer blossomed over Cambridge, Valenti began work on a collection of pieces for a small exhibition, and at about the same time, I took to the library to study for the first part of my Tripos examinations. So, one way and another, I had not seen him for perhaps six weeks when, on the afternoon of my penultimate paper, I found myself, quite by chance, wandering back to college via a route that passed Valenti's lodgings.

I decided to surprise him with a visit, intending to invite him to celebrate with me the end of my examinations on the morrow. I knew him to be at home, for I could hear his rich baritone soaring from the open window; he liked to have music whilst he worked, and since he possessed no instrument, habitually provided his own accompaniment. His rendition of '*Aura, che intorno spiri*' greeted me as I ascended the stairs, hot and panting; and although I knocked several times, he cannot have heard me, for his voice was tremendously powerful, and I could barely hear myself.

Finally, I tried the stiff old handle of the door. It opened with unaccustomed alacrity beneath my fingers; Valenti had evidently oiled it since last I visited. I pitched forward and half-fell into the studio, bewildered and embarrassed beyond anything when I realized the nature of the situation I had literally stumbled into.

Before me stood Valenti in a paint-smeared smock, his palette in one hand, his paintbrush in the other, and his mouth a perfect 'O' of surprise. Behind him was an easel on which rested a half-finished portrait of a young goddess rising from a lake or sea; and behind that, only partially obscured by the canvas, was the model herself, frantically clutching a volume of white gauze somewhat reminiscent of a bride's veil to preserve her modesty.

Naturally, I at once averted my eyes and staggered blindly from the room, slamming the door behind me and throwing myself against the wall of the staircase. Be assured that I was as red as any Turner sunset, and twice as warm! But before I could regain my shaken composure, Valenti strode out on to the landing, laughing like a man who had just heard the greatest jest of his life.

He flung his arm about my shoulder and guided me by main force into the studio, despite my protests. I kept my eyes tight shut until I was assured by both the young lady and my friend

75

that she was now decently attired, and when I finally opened them I fixed my gaze firmly on the floor, as I stammered heartfelt apologies for the unpardonable invasion of my friend's rooms, and my shocking trespass on his model's privacy.

They were both laughing gaily by the time I had finished, and with hindsight, I am not a bit surprised. Now I see what a pitiful, whining wretch I must have seemed to them both — a half-grown virgin schoolboy who had unwittingly intruded upon an adults' game.

Still chuckling, Valenti poured a small glass of some strong Italian liqueur, and made me drink it. It burned my throat, but it brought me back to my senses, and more or less to my usual self. Valenti and the girl both stood watching me and smiling.

'Now,' said Valenti, 'will you not permit me to introduce you to my very charming model and friend, whom you must call Venus, as I do? Venus, this is Edward Fraser, the theological acquaintance I have mentioned.'

She smiled vaguely, perhaps recognizing my name, and made a little curtsey. She was now demurely clad in a long green velvet robe with an embroidered placket, after the fashion of the women of the Pre-Raphaelite movement. She had dark, shining curls which tumbled in pretty disarray about her pale face, small pearly teeth, and a pair of the brightest, blackest eyes I had seen on any woman in my life — although, as I say, my acquaintance with the sex was at that time rather limited. I inclined my head gravely, and Valenti clapped his hands together in amused satisfaction.

'Well, I'm glad you two have become formally acquainted,' he said, turning to the girl. 'I think, Venus, this ends our session; I trust I shall see you again next Wednesday, at the same time?'

She smiled her assent; he approached her, put a few coins into one delicate hand, then seized the other and bent over it in an excess of gallantry. This seemed to charm her, for she giggled; a high, sweet, melodious sound.

When she had gone he turned to me with an apologetic shrug.

'I did warn you,' he said, 'that some of my paintings were not at all suitable for a clergyman-in-training.'

'Well, yes,' said I indignantly, 'but I never asked to see them; and I must say that I never expected to walk in upon the subject of one here in your own house!'

Valenti frowned in bafflement.

'And where else did you imagine I would paint the studies?'

I confess I had not the faintest idea where modern artists commonly kept their unclothed young ladies; I had merely naïvely imagined that it would not be in their living-rooms. Naturally, I had seen some still-lifes and so forth in progress when I had visited previously, but I had trusted that this was as far as modesty permitted him to venture, at least *chez lui*.

'I . . . I do not know — I suppose I presumed at the School of Art?'

Valenti laughed delightedly.

'I wish they were as free-thinking and liberal as you, Fraser! No, no, the School would not at all approve of the work I do in my little studio here; as it is, when these go on display — *if*, I should say, they are allowed to go on display — I shall be obliged to lie that I used rather more imagination than I may honestly claim to possess.'

'Oh,' I said, unsure whether this was better or worse.

Valenti strode rapidly across the room and rescued his bottle of liqueur and another glass. He filled and raised it to me in salute.

'In any case, my friend, it is a pleasure to see you; I have missed our little talks. Where did you disappear to?'

I explained about my examinations and he commiserated, but while he was describing his own difficulties in finding the right models for his Thracian series of paintings, his eyes suddenly narrowed and he smiled that half-wicked Italian grin.

'Do you know,' he said, 'I think I shall change Venus's name?'

'You mean to say it is not her real name?' I asked, startled.

He gazed at me pityingly.

'Of *course* it is not her real name, you ninny. I don't want to know their real names any more than they want me to. I call them after the first figure they sit as, and that way I always remember perfectly what they look like and who they are. At the moment I have a bounteous Juno, a ghostly Persephone, and a rather winsome Echo on my books, as well as the lovely Venus, of course. Except that when you made your *commedia dell'arte* entrance just now, you gave me an idea; I shall paint her as Diana, and so she shall be called. I am dissatisfied with the Venus in any case; it is lazy and derivative.'

79

'Why Diana?' I asked curiously. I had discerned nothing of the fierce huntress in the model's languid, slender beauty.

'And you a classical scholar! Have you forgotten the story of Actaeon already?' asked Valenti, raising his eyebrows.

I called the legend to mind, and laughed.

'He surprised Diana while she was naked, bathing in a forest pool,' I said. 'Ah! Of course! Very clever.'

'I rather like the idea,' mused Valenti. 'And I think she will, too. She's an awfully good sport, you know. Quite unlike the scheming little prudes I am accustomed to dealing with.' He turned to me and knocked my glass with his own.

'To Diana!' he said.

'To Diana!' I echoed.

'Let us hope she does not cause you to be torn apart by dogs, as did her original!' added Valenti cheerfully. And he grinned at me, and we drank his fierce liqueur down.

I did not see Diana, as Valenti now insisted I call her, for some weeks after that day; my visits to Valenti's studio continued frequent, but after my initial, mortifying experience, I made certain to warn him in advance when he could expect me. During my time there I met and spoke to some of his other friends and models — every one of whom, I hasten to add, was always fully clothed and taking tea in the most civilized manner in the world when I entered the room.

Whichever painting Valenti was working on would always be propped upon the easel in the corner — sometimes, if the subject were suitable, displayed uncovered for me to admire; more often with its face turned to the wall. This piqued my curiosity, but only a little; and I looked forward to the day when I might view the finished pieces upon a gallery wall, for I wished my talented friend every success.

Valenti frequently spoke of his models, both in their presence and out of it; it seemed to make little difference to him. I suppose long hours regarding them as visual objects merely had led to his considering them almost as part of the furniture, even when they were sitting next to him; in any case, they did not seem to mind, and some, indeed, laughed and were flattered when he spoke chaffingly of their backgrounds and habits. It was in the course of one such conversation that I was surprised to discover Diana had less humble origins than I had supposed.

'It is a most curious story,' said Valenti to me, as he poured more tea from a pot he had painted himself in the Grecian style, with darting satyrs and fleeing fauns. 'Diana, née Venus, is quite the jewel of my collection now; but when I first saw her I really thought she was just a little serving-girl like the rest. The lower classes always produce the most exquisite females, of course; they grow in the slums like roses on a dungheap.

'I saw her walking around one day in the Fitzwilliam (the very gallery-room in which you and I met, in fact), dressed cheaply but fashionably, as these poor girls do who put on the airs of a gutter grandee to pretend they are better than they are. Her thrice-mended shoes told me she had no money, but what fascinated me was the way she was looking at the paintings — really *looking*, you know, as you or I might; as though she knew something about them and could understand what they had to say.

'Most of the other museum-visitors go there for entirely unartistic reasons, as you know; to gossip and parade themselves, if surrounded by their own sex; to spoon and make eyes at one another, if in mixed company. Certainly none of them have the least interest in the works before them. But Diana displayed two unusual attributes: she was unaccompanied, and she was evidently there for the pictures.

'After observing her discreetly for a quarter of an hour or so, during which time she was so completely absorbed that she did not discern my scrutiny, I respectfully approached her and asked her her opinion of the collection (we happened to be in the sculpture room).

'Her reply at once intrigued and puzzled me. You, I fancy, have not really heard Diana speak — and for the very good reason that her accent betrays her surprising history. Not only was she eloquent and knowledgeable, but her voice was not the drab Cambridgeshire drawl I had expected; in fact, she was quite tolerably well-spoken and had clearly received a much more extensive education than many well-to-do young ladies these days enjoy. And yet her threadbare clothes and pallor spoke of a poverty more shabby than genteel. I could not fathom the paradox.

'I asked her frankly how she came to know so much about art. She told me, as frankly, that her father had been an artist, of a good family which had disowned him when he embraced the Bohemian life and married his model, Diana's mother, a beautiful dancer from Paris. Her mother died when Diana was but a child, and her father raised her himself, educating her at home, and making what little money he could by teaching art to the scions of his former peers, and selling his own work for whatever he could get.

'The physical strain of ceaseless labour and want was too much, however, for his weak constitution, and he, too, died when Diana was barely fifteen, leaving her both friendless and penniless. From that day she'd had to make her own way in the world; and after a wearisome stint as a governess, then as a drawing-mistress at a school for young ladies, she had found employment more suited to her, as companion to a retiring and infirm spinster of advanced years, living just outside Fen Ditton.

' 'It is not so bad,' she told me with a pretty little sigh, 'but oh! it is a dismal house; the shutters are always drawn, for the light hurts Miss Bellingham's eyes. From October to May you cannot see outside, and it is always cold as the grave.'

'Her employer granted her a half-day every Wednesday, however, which she would use to travel into the town and enjoy such entertainments as were within her modest budget; she told me that she spent most of her free time either at the public library or the picture-gallery, or, in summer, at the Botanic Garden.

'Normally it's rather an awkward situation asking someone to be your model, you know — so many girls, especially the more stupid and vain ones, imagine at once that you mean to ravish them, and begin twittering nonsensically about the police before one can explain. But, knowing that I was speaking to the daughter of a painter, and one, moreover, with an excellent knowledge and understanding of art, I had no hesitation in putting my proposition to her, being well aware that she needed the money and would take my offer of employment in the pure and artistic spirit in which it was meant.

'To my delight she accepted at once, and struck a rather shrewd bargain with me — she may look innocent, Fraser, but she is quite the negotiator! She would sit for me every Wednesday, on her half-day — her employer, fortunately, understood that young ladies sometimes need more dazzling amusements than macramé and Bible-reading, and she was not expected back until eight that evening, so we would always have six good hours together.'

'What a romantic tale!' I exclaimed, when he broke off to pour more tea. 'It is quite as good as anything by the Brothers Grimm — indeed, it reminds me of *Cinderella!*'

Valenti grinned. 'She certainly stands in need of a Prince Charming to rescue her,' he said, 'for she is daily terrified that her employer will discover her secret second career. She insists I paint her in such a way that her face is never seen; and yet she will not give up modelling for me — I pay her too well!'

I was somewhat unnerved by Valenti's evident relish in having the poor girl at the mercy, as it were, of both his generosity and his discretion — but his next words disturbed me still further. He leaned forward and lowered his voice as though, miles away in Fen Ditton, the subject of his conversation might catch his whispered words.

'I don't mind telling you, Fraser,' he said, 'that I would do a lot for that little girl; an awful lot — and when my work begins to sell, perhaps I shall be in a position to offer her more than a few measly shillings for an afternoon a week. I should like to spend my life with her, you know, and I do believe she returns my affection — at least, she has given me certain signs that she might. I must just hope that some insinuating schoolmaster does not beat me to the punch!'

I did not ask what these 'signs of affection' were; frankly, I did not wish to know. Instead, I nodded; but my private reaction to this revelation was one of acute discomfort and foreboding. Valenti was handsome, personable, and of excellent stock, for all that his people were not rich; he certainly did not need to set his sights so low as a poor part-time model without money, friends or family. Many a young English gentlewoman with a hefty dowry would gladly have taken him; and in Italy I fancy he should have had his pick of the loveliest heiresses in the land.

But, as has time and time again been proven, men are, alas! stubborn as mules when it comes to women; and often all that is required to convince a fellow he is in love with a girl is to tell him flat out that he cannot have her.

I walked home from Valenti's studio in a pensive mood. His frank admission of his love for Diana had, I own, surprised me, for he had always struck me as a devil-may-care sort of fellow; charming indeed, but himself immune to feminine charm. I supposed (for at that time I could not judge, never having heard her speak two words together) that she must be an extraordinary sort of girl to have won his passionate and capricious heart; and yet I was still uneasy. Her punctiliousness in the matter of payment, which amused Valenti as might a child's avidity for shiny pennies, sat ill with me; she had a somewhat unbecoming interest, in my view, in the business aspect of their artistic arrangement.

The only time I voiced this opinion to Valenti, however, he shrugged it off, telling me that I, who had never known poverty or want, could not possibly understand those who had to live 'upon a knife-edge'; that she was only trying to protect and provide for herself, a vulnerable woman, alone and friendless, in a hostile, unforgiving world.

I was somewhat insulted by his implication that I was unworldly (perhaps because I felt the truth of it in my bones), and revolted by his sentimental attitude — for though he romanticized her as a friendless orphan, she had friend enough in him; and moreover it was evident to me that she was no child, and certainly no fool. I could not refrain, in my secret heart, from associating the hard-headed practicality of her attitude to money with that of those women who trafficked in an altogether different market, though one not so far removed as I should have liked. Let her keep accounts when she had her own household to manage, said I to myself, and not before! Avarice in a man is unattractive; in a woman, however lovely, it is unnatural, and dangerous to any man weak enough to indulge it.

These were my thoughts; but out of deference to Valenti's affection for the girl, I did not confide them to him. Who knows what tragedy might have been averted had I done so? But I kept my counsel. It was not, after all, my business. What knew I of women, or of the world? Foolishly, I ignored my instinctive distrust of Diana. My silence, as so often, was to cost me, and those I cared for, dear.

★　★　★

I had still greater cause for unrest a few months later, at the beginning of the Michaelmas Term, when I was asked to dine at High Table for the first time in my short academic career. Only a handful of the three hundred undergraduates were asked each week, and I was very sensible of the honour done me by the Fellows of the

College, and the gratitude I owed my tutor. The other two students who were also thus distinguished that night were a geographer whose name I forget, and a young Classicist with whom I shared some classes, by the name of Henry Hereward.

I am sure you can guess what transpired when Henry and I and our Latin tutor discussed the love sonnets of Petrarch and our own future ambitions in swift succession. The wine flowed, as did the conversation, and by the time the port came round Hereward had divulged that he was 'violently in love' with 'the most perfect creature': a girl whose outward charm was matched only by her sweet soul and delightful temperament; who rivalled Athena in wisdom, Helen in beauty, and Penelope in faithfulness.

I admit that not for one second did I connect this paragon of feminine virtue with the mysterious, taciturn Diana — not, at least, until Hereward, by this stage somewhat the worse for wine, mentioned visiting her at the house she shared with 'some elderly female relation' in the village of Fen Ditton. Astonished, apprehensive, yet hoping against hope that his beloved was not who I suspected, I pressed him for a physical description.

He chuckled and clapped me on the shoulder.

'Oh! I can do better than that, old chap,' he said, and reached into the long pocket of his coat, producing a new-looking leather-cased photograph of an attractive young lady with exquisitely pale skin, laughing black eyes, dark, shining curls and a direct, intelligent gaze which seemed to outstare even the eye of the camera.

'Had it made a month or two ago,' he said. 'I wanted something to show my father. A peach, ain't she? Poor as a church mouse but I've enough for both of us — and of a good old family, too. I ask you, Fraser, who wouldn't be proud to marry such a creature?'

There could be no doubt; she had pearls at her ears and throat (gifts, doubtless, from Hereward, whose ancient Catholic family still owned much of Northamptonshire) and was wearing a black bombazine dress, far grander than anything I had ever seen her in — but it was unmistakably Diana. I managed to stifle my strong reaction, and returned the photograph to Hereward with a murmured compliment.

I steered the conversation towards her family history, and was more than a little shocked when he repeated the same story she had told Valenti — with a number of small but striking differences. In this version of her autobiography, her father was a clergyman cast off by his people after converting to Catholicism to marry her mother, the youngest and loveliest daughter of an illustrious family. Again, he had died when his daughter was only fifteen, and she had been raised in a charitable school of the Church of England; but (said Hereward) she longed to return to the faith of her father, her childhood and her true soul. No doubt she had surmised that any union with him would be at the price of her reversion to Catholicism, and so she had presented herself to him as a ready and willing subject.

I left High Table that night with a heart both hardened and heavy. As I walked back around the Great Court to my staircase, and the high chill eyrie of my study-bedroom, I was sunk in thought. My mind was awhirl; I did not know whether Diana was the daughter of a painter or a priest, whether she was sincere in her affections towards my poor friend Valenti or the moon-struck Hereward, or both, or neither! — but I knew beyond doubt that she was a liar, and an adventuress; absolutely the most dangerous kind of female.

Hereward, I was certain, would be aghast to learn of her modelling, not to mention the fantasies she had spun him about her background; and Valenti deserved to know that his sweetheart was setting her cap at a man who, though vastly his inferior in looks and talent, had twice his influence and five times his meagre wealth. It was clear to me what sort of woman she was; it remained only to persuade both her swains to discard her at once, and for ever. I did not know how I would achieve this, and had no certainty, even, that I could; but I made up my mind there and then to do my utmost to save both my friends from the clutches of this scheming minx.

In this resolve, as you will have surmised, I utterly failed; and in such an abject fashion that it pains me to recall it even now. With hindsight, it is obvious that I did everything wrong; not one particle of credit devolves to me from the whole sordid affair. For I lost two friends on that fateful night, and I do not think I shall see either again until Judgement Day is upon us. One of her suitors was killed outright, and the other forced to flee the country, his health broken and heart scored.

And this is how it all happened.

★   ★   ★

At first Valenti would not believe me. He laughed me out of countenance; he even had the temerity to suggest that I — I! — was envious of the 'profound and sincere' affection that existed between himself and Diana. He challenged me on every aspect of my tale until I began to doubt the evidence of my own eyes, let alone my own veracity. He insisted that Hereward's fiancée must be another girl with some slight resemblance to Diana. He wondered aloud how many dark-haired young women with elderly guardians might reside in Fen Ditton; in short, the strength of his cynicism would have been enough to chasten me into silence, had I not had the strongest reason and resolve to make him accept the truth of my words. He bundled me out of his studio rather roughly, though he smiled still at what he called my 'solicitous folly' — and would not admit me again for a week.

Fortunately (or so I thought at the time) what finally prompted me to stop vacillating and persuade my friend of his beloved's betrayal was this: in the intervening days, when Valenti had sent me to Coventry, it came to my ears that Diana had accepted Hereward's proposal of marriage. There was to be an informal engagement-party that very night at the Café Flore, to which Hereward's friends and acquaintances, myself among them, were invited. I immediately called upon Valenti to inform him of this development.

'It is the simplest thing in the world,' said I to him, not without some coldness, 'for you to prove me mistaken — come with me as my guest to this happy occasion, and you shall be granted the pleasure of meeting the lady herself, and her noble fiancé.'

Valenti glared at me. He had been painting when I entered and, though he had flung down his brushes and abandoned his canvas, still wore his charcoal-stained smock, so great was his turmoil and anger at what I had told him. He ran a paint-blackened hand through his hair and glanced irresolutely between myself and the half-completed work on the easel.

'Is it not enough that you must interrupt my work with these fairy-tales of yours, but you must also drag me half-way across town to disprove your idle fantasies?' he demanded angrily.

'This is no brain-fever,' I assured him, 'or if it is, it infects your reason, not my own. The regard in which you hold Diana is entirely misplaced; and I could not forgive myself if I did not try my utmost to disabuse you of your mistaken love for this creature.'

My hard words seemed to decide him. He tore off his smock and began changing into his well-worn evening-clothes. I had already dressed for the occasion, determined to go and confront

Hereward myself, whether or not Valenti agreed to accompany me. I moved over to his pencil sketches and portfolios, and began sorting through them. He stopped his frantic dressing and stared at me in open astonishment.

'Good Lord, Fraser, have you run mad? This is no time for art criticism!'

I remained calm, turning over each sketch and study, searching for what I needed.

'You forget, Valenti,' said I, 'that yours is not the only heart imperilled by this affair. I mean also to show Hereward what a viper he has clasped to his bosom.'

'Enough!' he cried, striding across the room and snatching the drawings. 'I'll hear no further maligning of my darling's character until your accusations are proved to be founded on fact — or rather, as I hope and trust, entirely unfounded. What, pray, are you searching for?'

'Why, for your portraits of Diana. You say that she will not let her face be seen in the finished paintings, but I am sure you have done many a preliminary sketch for the nude studies. Hereward is quite as romantically obstinate as you, and he will never believe ill of her unless we present him with proof of her secret career as your model.'

It was clear that, though reluctantly, Valenti saw the truth of my argument. Angrily, he pushed me away and reached for a worn black leather portfolio, sorting through it with swift expertise, his hunched torso, bent over the table, blocking my view of the folder's contents.

He was murmuring as he leafed through, and I

fancied I caught the names of goddesses from the ancient and pagan pantheons of Egypt and Thrace; Isis, Bast, Cotytto — names which filled me with foreboding, for I surmised that Diana was represented as each of these dark deities in those sketches he would not allow me to see. Finally, he selected a large canvas, apparently finished but unmounted, stared at it a moment, then rolled it into a tight scroll before I could catch more than a glimpse.

'The sketches are no good,' he said grimly. 'This is the best. It is a study of the figure more than the face; but if what you say is true, it should be enough.'

It occurred to me that Diana's own reaction upon seeing Valenti would likely do more to convince Hereward of her guilt than any number of paintings; but evidence was needed, and evidence, damning and irrefutable, we had. Outside, in the black, rain-hammered street, we hailed a hansom and ordered the driver to take us to the Café Flore with as much haste as his sleepy horse could muster.

Valenti, dishevelled, brooding and suspicious, sat beside me, staring straight ahead, saying not a word for the duration of the journey. As we drew up before the Café's grand entrance, the horse steaming, he turned to me with fire and fear warring in his eyes.

'You know that I come here not because I believe *you*, Fraser, but because I believe in her. If Diana is not this Hereward's girl, I shall turn straight around and leave, and you will oblige me by never calling upon me again.'

I bowed my head in acknowledgement; and, together, we went in.

★ ★ ★

The restaurant was in merry uproar when we entered, and for some minutes Valenti and I lost one another as we fought through the revelling throng. Hereward was a popular fellow, and had, as so many rich young men at University do, a wide and somewhat wild acquaintance.

At last I caught a flash of his face, laughing from a raised dais on which stood a large round dining-table with twenty chairs and as many bottles of Champagne, with which his closest friends were toasting the health of his lovely fiancée.

This dais or rostrum overlooked the entire dance-floor, and although the company occupying it seemed a little more sedate, as befitted gentlemen when a lady was in their midst, I still discerned snatches of chaffing conversation and bursts of laughter which spoke eloquently of what the Bard, in *Macbeth*, describes as 'the general joy of the whole table'.

I own that my courage nearly failed me at this moment; for it suddenly struck me that what I was about to do would almost certainly destroy the happiness of two people, if not three. I thought, for a second, as I detected the elusive glow of felicity in Hereward's keen eyes, that perhaps it was not too late to turn back; to reconsider. And then I turned, and saw Valenti.

He was stood, still as Death himself, in the

midst of whirling activity: the laughing dancers moved around him as though he were a statue; the laughing drinkers saluted one another with brimming glasses over his head.

He was a pitiful sight. His hair had been brushed every which way by the wet wind of the street outside, his shirt-front lacked a stud, his unlinked cuffs flapped free, and his trembling hands were still dirtied by oil paint, despite his rushed attempt back at the studio to make himself presentable. Compared to the immaculate and dashing Hereward, he seemed a poor second choice indeed. My heart ached in my breast as I followed the direction of his gaze up to the slight, still figure on the rostrum.

Diana had her back to us, and had not yet seen Valenti, but it was unmistakably her; just as it had been in Hereward's photograph, just as it was in Valenti's painting, which he still squeezed, rolled and drooping, in one hand.

Valenti seemed for a few moments to have lost his power of speech, but then he gave a hoarse cry, which sounded a little like 'Diana!', startling the fellows around him for a brief second. Perhaps she did not hear him; she did not turn.

Upon the dais, the boisterous company poured Champagne and joked, oblivious. My breath laboured in my lungs; I could no more speak than move. My whole being was concentrated on the back of that lovely dark head, the line of that slender pale neck.

Remembering himself, Valenti cleared his throat, called her again; this time by her own name — or at least, the one by which Hereward knew her.

'Anna!' he cried.

There was no hush, no cessation in the noise and movement all around us; but I knew that this time she heard him. Her whole body stiffened and her head twitched around, sharp as an animal's that senses the approach of a predator in the silence of a moonless night.

I think that Hereward must have heard too, or seen her sudden, frightened reaction; for he leaned over the table with concern in his whole demeanour, pressing his large hand over her own, small and gloved and motionless upon the crisp white linen.

Valenti called her again, and Hereward rose and peered over the baluster, something of anger, almost of fear, in his stance. Perhaps he had always suspected, always known? He stretched a smile from tense lips and looked about for the speaker.

'Hallo down there!' he cried. 'Are there more for our party?'

His eyes lighted upon my face, and relief broke like sunrise over his anxious features. Diana remained sitting with her back to us, unmoving, like a creature at bay and despairing of deliverance, hoping to escape notice by remaining quite still.

'Fraser!' said Hereward, gesturing me forward. 'My dear chap, what a delightful surprise! So good of you to come. I had not expected to see such a retiring fellow as yourself at our celebration; but come up, join us, and welcome!'

I glanced at Valenti, whose normally swarthy face was dead white in the brilliant gleam of the chandeliers.

'I hope you do not object, Hereward,' I said, 'but I have brought a friend. A friend of both of yours, I think, who has come to . . . pay his respects.'

I indicated Valenti. Hereward's eyes narrowed as he took in my companion's somewhat disreputable appearance; but he nodded curtly, and together, struggling through the slow-yielding masses of the venue's raucous clientèle, we ascended the shallow steps.

As we approached the table an uneasy silence fell; it was abundantly clear from Valenti's expression that he did not share the exultant mood of the gathering. Nobody was quite sure what to make of us, least of all Hereward, who seemed both alarmed and puzzled by my friend's haggard looks and ominous silence.

At last a bold, preening Irish fellow called Jameson broke the unnatural moment with a high, peacock laugh.

'Come now, Fraser, introduce us to this 'mutual' friend! — whom, I daresay, I have never seen before in my life!'

I turned to Valenti; he seemed still devoid of speech. Diana looked straight ahead, past him and myself, to some other thing that only she could see; perhaps her future, perhaps her traduced past. I shall never know what she felt at that moment, but I cannot say I truly believe that it was remorse — unless, of course, at the discovery of her deception.

Valenti, white as the very table-cloth, approached the edge of the circle and bowed deeply, first to the astonished Hereward and then to Diana, who yet refused to turn her head or meet his eye. He moved a silver wine-bucket aside, then spread his canvas scroll on the tabletop, for all the world like a Turkey-rug seller displaying his wares.

'An engagement gift,' he said in tones so soft as to be barely audible, and yet so redolent of the banked fires of a terrible passion that each of the assembled company could discern every word.

'A gift,' repeated Valenti, 'for the happy couple. For the bride and groom.'

The image that met Hereward's eyes was one I had never seen before, except in part and unfinished: it was Valenti's final painting of his model in the attitude of her divine namesake, painted at my unwitting instigation, in a style that alluded at once to classical portraiture and to the more romantic work of the Pre-Raphaelites.

Every dark hair upon the goddess's head was individually rendered; every tautened muscle strained through the ivory-pale skin until it threatened to break the surface of the canvas itself. Her head was turned away from the viewer, startled by the dirty, graceless creature in the background, which had come crashing through the undergrowth to interrupt the naked deity's solitary ablutions.

Of the face, nothing could be seen but a quarter-profile; the long dark lashes of the eyes were just visible past the sweet curve of her cheek, and the distinctive, curiously sharp angle of the raised jaw revealed a blue vein in her swanlike neck that seemed almost to flutter with a racing pulse.

One slender hand clutched at her bosom; the other was flung out in astonishment, raising a spray of droplets from the limpid pool in which she bathed. Just beneath the bend of her wrist, the swell of Diana's breast was visible; a tiny, dark mole stood in sharp relief against the alabaster skin. Valenti had caught her exactly; a wild thing surprised, a beautiful, feral creature poised at the moment of flight.

Hereward gasped; his eyes were wide and amazed as his gaze travelled down from the averted face to the braced and tensed body, which seemed, in Valenti's rendition, to be more divine than human, and still, somehow, more animal than divine.

His brows knitted together as he beheld the naked torso, and he stared as if the painting might draw him into itself, fixated upon a single spot; the sole flaw, indeed, in the goddess's perfect, barely mortal beauty — the black dot just below the curve of her breast. In that moment I saw that he had recognized his beloved; and that he had not needed to see her face to do so.

I had suspected she was wanton, but not, I confess, that she would have debased herself so far to acquire a husband, even one so desirable as Hereward. I do not say that she had yielded up that treasure prized by all maidens and men, and sacred to the holy bond of matrimony — but it was plain that she had allowed her fiancé to glimpse at least some part of the beauty of which he believed himself both guardian and sole possessor.

A harlot's shop-window, a seductress's promise; it made no difference. Hereward was as horrified by the copy as he must have been delighted by the original. He cleared his throat harshly, and when he spoke, it was with difficulty.

'This,' he said, and he gestured at the painting before him as though it were something bloody a cat had left in the scullery, 'dishonours both of us, sir, as much as it does the subject of your brush. What do you mean by presenting me with it?'

Valenti regarded him coolly, triumph written in every line of his face.

'Only to show you the truth of your bride-to-be; what she is, and what she does, and what she will do — for money, you understand.' His fine lip curled. 'I see now that there was no love in what she did for me, what she revealed to me; that there never was. That she has been dazzled by your family and fortune, I might forgive her; that you have been dazzled by her beauty and brilliance, I cannot but forgive you — but I must know whether you will forgive your betrothed her . . . youthful indiscretions. I should not like either of you to enter such a holy state without full knowledge, each of the other.'

There was a sneer in Valenti's voice, and on his handsome face, as his gaze flickered between the two; Hereward flushed and furious, Diana statue-still and marble-white. No one around the table moved; it was as if the breath had left every body, and the motionless tableau stretched out, absurdly, until Hereward broke it with a peal of dreadful, low laughter.

'I suppose I must thank you, sir,' he said, 'for showing me what an exquisite creature I was to marry. If only she were inwardly as lovely as is her outward form, I'd swear I had been engaged to Mary the Virgin, not the Magdalene.'

Still he did not look at Diana; still he held Valenti's gaze with his own dark and burning eyes.

'My dear,' he said softly to her, 'I think you may go. This is not a fit place for a woman of your . . . artistic sensibilities. And as for your gift, sir' — here he grabbed a steak-knife lying at his right hand, awaiting the arrival of the meal — '*this* is what I think of it!'

Before Valenti or any one about the table could prevent him, Hereward darted in like a striking cobra, and sliced a great gash through the canvas, slashing across the naked form of Diana, and ripping the painting nearly in half. There was a dreadful ragged, dragging sound as the blade gouged into the table beneath. Valenti gave a wordless cry and leaped forward to protect his work, throwing his arm over the ruined canvas just as Hereward plunged the knife down again.

There was a shocked gasp from the gathered company; and then a vast and terrible hush.

Blood dripped on to the painting from Valenti's left forearm; the tablecloth was flooded with red where the flesh and tendons of his arm had been laid open by Hereward's blade, almost to the bone.

I recalled with dreadful clarity Valenti standing before me, earlier that evening, in the midst of painting, hesitating; the brush held delicately between the long fingers of his left hand.

'No!' I cried, interposing myself between Hereward and the crumpling Valenti. The knife dropped, gory and forgotten, from Hereward's shaking hand. I wrestled Valenti upright and began to bind his bleeding, injured arm with a linen napkin; he seemed hardly to realize what I was doing, but kept his eyes upon his rival, staring at Hereward's face as if to commit it to memory, despite the cruel fact that he would not be able to paint it; not now, nor ever again.

'O God! You will pay for this,' he whispered to Hereward, his voice tight with agony.

'A doctor!' I called, desperately. 'Someone! Fetch a surgeon!'

Valenti twisted in my grasp. Despite the blood running freely from his wound he was still far stronger than I; it was like trying to restrain a dying beast.

'What need have I of a surgeon?' he said, his voice dead and black. 'There is nothing to be done. Blood for blood, Fraser.'

He raised his tousled head and spoke again to Hereward.

'You,' he grated, 'you have ruined my finest work. You have destroyed my future. I challenge you, sir. A duel. Pistols, tomorrow at dawn, upon Midsummer Common. O, do not fear' — and here he laughed, awfully — 'though perhaps I'll never paint again, I can shoot straight enough with my right hand. Blood for blood. And if you will not face me tomorrow, by God I will hunt you down until you do.'

He dropped his head in the general direction of the company; a grotesque parody of courtesy.

'Good-night, gentlemen,' he said. And then he took a long look, a look of such sadness and reproach and pitiful hatred such as I hope never to be subject to, at the downcast face of his erstwhile sweetheart.

'Good-night,' he said, 'my love.'

Then, with a brutal effort, he wrenched himself from my grip and staggered down the stairs, a mad grin upon his white face, a red trail at his heels.

Silence followed Valenti as he limped slowly from that dreadful scene: silence and disbelief, and two pitiful creatures whom now, I felt certain, even darkness would not sully itself to touch. One was Diana; and the other, myself.

Valenti did not sleep that night.

I know this, for I spent each torturous minute of that long vigil with him, from the second he staggered out of the Café Flore until he strode on to the misty field at six the next morning. Do not think I was idle during that time, however; far from it. First, I knocked up an acquaintance — a student doctor, like my future friend Chapman, though not half so skilled as he

— explained the urgency of the situation, and begged him to repair Valenti's dreadful injury as best he could.

Throughout all this, Valenti moved like a man in a dream or a swoon. It frightened me to see how little notice this avid observer, this artist who had always been so alive to the world about him, now took of his surroundings. Even when the young surgeon was sewing together the bleeding edges of my friend's wound, his shaking hands stitching flesh to flesh and sinew to sinew, hardly a sound passed Valenti's lips; he sat limp as a rag-doll and compliant as a dog, uttering nothing but the occasional sigh, as though briefly troubled by some sad, fleeting recollection.

Once the arm had been dressed, I escorted Valenti back to his studio (for it was now well past the hour of my college curfew), lit the fire and brewed a pint of strong coffee, braced with a dash of the almondine Italian liqueur he favoured, called *amaretto*. He had followed me meekly through the city's midnight streets; and if the driving rain or the bitter cold troubled him, he did not show it. He might have been made of stone for all he seemed to feel the chill. I sat him before the hearth and placed a hot cup of coffee in his hand; he did not taste it, but let it cool in his unmoving fingers.

I spoke to him more desperately than I have ever spoken to anyone in my life; with even more urgency than when I told this very tale to Chapman before a guttering Jericho fireside.

I spoke to him of his family, and his honour; his talent, and his career; of his duty as an artist and as a man; of his obligations to his friends, his calling, and himself. I could, with as much effect, have talked of the price of tobacco or the weather in China; he was deaf to my entreaties. In vain I tried to persuade him to rescind his challenge; fruitlessly, I told him that Hereward was well-known as a crack shot (this was only something of an exaggeration), and that the painting could be mended or restored — the girl won back, even, if he so wished. Nothing moved him. He was beyond my reach.

Even now, I cannot truly say which of that evening's grotesque events most grieved my friend. Whether it was the damage inflicted by Hereward upon Valenti's finest work, the appalling wound to his arm and his prospects as a painter, or the terrible blow dealt to his proud heart by Diana's betrayal, I suppose I shall never know. Each taken singly would have caused him profound pain and grief; together, they felled him.

The hours passed, and still Valenti gave no sign of heeding me; but I persisted. I invoked God, I appealed to his common sense, I even threatened to inform the constabulary of the deadly appointment he and Hereward had made — all to no avail. At last, as my voice failed in my throat and sleep threatened to overtake me, he turned his head towards me and found my eyes with his own.

It was as though a statue had moved. The sinews in his neck cracked; he raised himself slowly from his chair, with the doomed, ancient weariness of Atlas shouldering the heavens, and shuffled over to the table whereupon lay the scattered sketches of Diana, abandoned at our earlier hasty exit. He turned them over meditatively, using his good right hand; gazing at each with such frowning intensity that it seemed he would absorb the image entirely, leaving nothing but a clean white sheet.

'I did not think she could do such a thing, you know, Fraser,' he said, at last. I flinched, startled to be addressed. After so many hours of useless entreaty, I had no idea what to say. But he did not desire an answer, it seemed; perhaps, hardly aware of my presence, he was simply thinking aloud as, when painting, he was wont to do. He went on, his voice light, almost casual.

'I thought I knew her.' He smiled fondly down at some image I could not see. 'Every inch of her. Ha! I thought — do you know, I really believed that she loved me? What a fool!'

I shook my head and cleared my throat; but my words were exhausted.

'Do you remember that ring she used to wear on her little finger?'

I could not say I did; but it mattered little, for he continued, his head bowed, his voice hollow and soft.

'I gave it her; it was my mother's. Of course, we could not be engaged until I had enough money to keep us both, but it was a pledge, a token of my intentions. Of our love — or so I thought.'

His left fist clenched involuntarily, and only partially: the fingers flexed, twitched and trembled, and a fleeting expression of agony

107

crossed his features; I do not know whether with the pain of his wound or the recollection of the grievous damage. I have had the misfortune of seeing other such injuries since; they cripple and paralyse, and there is nothing to be done about them. Once the strings have been cut, there is no repairing them, and the instrument to which they belonged must be laid aside or else smashed.

'She stopped wearing the ring some months ago,' he said evenly. 'She said she was afraid her employer would find out she had a sweetheart. I suppose that was when she met Hereward. What use had she for a poor little garnet-and-gold trinket when he could stud her with diamonds and drape her with pearls?'

Valenti laughed and stared through the window before him at the nacreous grey of the pre-dawn sky.

'I tried to give her all she deserved, of course; but painted jewels could never be enough for a woman like her.'

I do not know what he saw, out there in the twilight, but he shook himself briskly, as though suddenly cold, and glanced back down at the portfolio with a tiny, final nod of his head.

'Well, enough of this. I've looked my fill at that girl; as, I think, has Hereward. It only remains for honour to be satisfied. How ridiculous if one of us should die over this, when neither of us wants the wench now! I hope it shan't come to that. Still, the gods love a farce.'

He turned to me with a broad, bright, mocking smile; and for a second I saw what he and Hereward had in common; a sort of restless daring, and a willingness to see the consequences of their actions, whether brave or foolish or both, through, right to the end. It is the spirit that built the Empire; I have seen it in other men, often enough to recognize it, seldom enough for it to be remarkable. All those others are lost, or dead.

I understood in that moment that if Diana had indeed loved either man, she had probably loved both. Not that her true affections made a jot of difference, for both Hereward and Valenti were men who did not share; nor did they forgive.

Valenti shrugged on his coat, draping the left shoulder like a cape over his wounded arm.

'Come,' he said; and I rose, and followed him out of the door.

★ ★ ★

Duelling, thank Heaven, was no more legal nor much more common then than it is now, in what we laughingly call our enlightened age; but Cambridge was ever a bastion of outmoded tradition, and it was certainly not unheard-of for drunken fellows to call one another out over some matter of cards, honour, or women from time to time. Of course, neither the University nor the city condoned such wanton violence, and so any contests which took place, whether with sword or pistol, were unofficial and, perforce, conducted in secret.

But so pernicious and all-pervading is gossip, that writhing, insinuating thing that penetrates each college dining-room, sports-meeting and drinking-den, that by that grey dawn it was common knowledge in every corner of the ancient University that there was to be a duel out upon Midsummer Common; and it was to be to the death.

Hereward, perhaps, had put this fatal rumour about to make himself look more dashing and fearsome; after all, there is no boast so rash and vaunting as that of a cuckold. Every man around that table had got a good look at Valenti's painting, at the naked figure of the woman Hereward had worshipped, and he must have felt the shame of that far more keenly than Diana ever could. Or so, I imagine, he thought.

So Henry Hereward was fighting, that damp, mist-breathing morning, for his own honour as a man; just as Valenti was taking his revenge for Hereward's attack on him as both man and artist. And the woman over whom (it was whispered on all the college staircases, around every court) they fought? She was nowhere to be seen. With hindsight, her circumspection was understandable. After all, in trying, too success-fully, to snare one then the other, she had been cast off by both — and even if both lived, she knew well enough that neither would welcome her back.

And yet I could not forgive her absence. Assuming she had some small measure of feeling for either of the men she professed to love, however much it might hurt and appal her to contemplate seeing him die, she had failed in one of Woman's most sacred duties — that shared by both Marys as they watched Christ die on the cross — of supporting, of bearing witness, of bringing however meagre a moiety of succour.

The Common was as a still pool in that pale and ghostly dawn, and crossing it was like wading underwater through a clear, green lake. The tall grasses bent as we passed; the dew clung to us, glittering in the nascent sun like broken glass. In the distance, we spied figures; far more than we had thought. There should have been only three; Hereward, his second, and some neutral arbiter to oversee the propriety of the match and ensure that both duellists behaved honourably.

But there were more: far more than three. It seemed to my astonished eyes that half Cambridge was out on the Common that morning, wrapped in gowns and overcoats and mufflers, shivering with cold or anticipation, waiting for one of the men before them to die. My disgust at this prurient audience turned me sick at my stomach; I begged Valenti to let me scour them from the field. I promised to shame these idle spectators into allowing Hereward and himself the dignity of a privately settled score, but he merely shook his head and smiled.

'Let them watch,' said he. 'It is no more brutal than cock-fighting, and a good deal more voluntary. Perhaps they will learn something from it.'

'Such as what?' I said incredulously.

'Such as not to fight a damned duel,' came Valenti's grim reply.

The arbiter was Frederick March, a graduate

student at King's who was known slightly to both Hereward and myself; he was a fencer, and had duelled with sabres while travelling in Prussia, or so rumour had it — in any case, he bore an impressive scar along one side of his chin, and walked with a slight limp.

Naturally, I was seconding for Valenti; the irritating Irish fellow, Jameson, was Hereward's second, and looking very nervous about it. Hereward, flushed and frowning, seemed to have taken rather more drink than necessary to stiffen his resolve; I could smell brandy on him, and his eyes were bloodshot, though his step and stance were steady. It occurs to me, looking back through the mottled glass of many years and miseries of my own, that their fiery red appearance on that raw morning may have been due to an excess of weeping the night before: I suppose I shall never know.

Hereward handed a polished wooden gun-case to March, who removed the pistols, examined and loaded each with a single bullet, then returned the firearms to their case and presented it to Valenti. Valenti barely looked down, picking up the nearest and weighing it judiciously in his right hand, his left arm hanging uselessly at his side.

The pistols were fine-looking things, sturdy antiques; their steel barrels were polished to a dark silvery sheen and the wooden stocks oiled and smoothed to fit snugly into one's hand. I wondered whether a few hours ago they had been macabre fireplace ornaments for Hereward's study — and whether they would return thence once this bloody business was done, as still more piquant conversation-pieces. The thought made me rather light-headed — at once nauseous, and possessed of a peculiar urge to laugh.

Hereward hefted the other pistol and March set down the box. The damp grass steamed and the dew shimmered in the sunrise; there was a murmur from the distant, half-invisible crowd as the duellists turned their backs on one another and March raised a red silk handkerchief in his right hand and began to count aloud the paces. I walked alongside Valenti, measuring the steps with him as I might have paced out the length of a grave-plot.

'Ten!' cried March. Valenti swivelled to face Hereward, small and far away, ethereal now in the mist rising from the green earth, Jameson at his side. It occurred to me to wonder what, if both shots were fatal, we two should do. I had been praying all night; silently, I prayed again.

The handkerchief trembled in March's hand. In the sweet, freshening breeze I fancied I heard the murmur of bees; but it was only the blood buzzing in my head. When he let go the scrap of silk, when the silk touched the ground, then both parties could fire at will.

'Fraser,' said Valenti calmly, 'if I live through this, as I hope to, do not for God's sake let me take her back.'

He turned his head, and in his dark eyes there was a pleading, abject look I had not seen before.

'I shall die first,' I swore.

Valenti smiled slightly and turned back to face his enemy. 'Good,' he said conversationally. 'She is most persuasive, you know,' he added, 'and I love her so very much.'

'Seconds retreat!' called March, and Jameson and I stepped back a few paces from our respective friends; safely out of the firing line, or so we hoped.

March's thin fingers clenched and released; the red silk square fluttered swiftly to the ground like a winged bird. I closed my eyes.

A gunshot rang out.

I waited for the second report, but it did not come. Or had both shots been fired so close together that they had sounded like a single gun?

I opened my eyes. Valenti stood before me, a look of bewilderment on his face. His right arm still held the pistol before him and he was lowering it slowly, staring keenly at the other end of the field. I turned to look. Hereward was down, lying on his back in the grass as though pushed over, a burst of blood blooming on his white shirt-front, high on one side of his chest, somewhere between shoulder and heart. He was not yet dead; he was trying to struggle up on his elbows, but his arms kept failing him. Jameson circled him like a dog, exclaiming and darting back and forth, half-maddened with shock.

'I must have knocked out his arm,' said Valenti wonderingly. 'He never got a shot in.'

'Did he even try to shoot?' I mused aloud.

'Yes, oh yes,' he said distractedly. 'Another tenth of a second and he would have got me; but he hadn't a chance to pull the trigger.'

He began jogging towards Hereward and Jameson; the first stretched full-length, the other bent over him in an attitude of despair. I stumbled alongside; they grew nearer, clearer in the pale thin fog.

'He'll need a doctor,' muttered Valenti. 'Why did I not think to ask your surgeon friend? Damn it!'

He turned his head as he ran and shouted to the cowering, silent onlookers.

'Are none of you medics? Look lively, in God's

name! This man needs help!'

A great noise banged against the yellow sky. Valenti, who had been running full-tilt, staggered and rolled in the wet grass, flopping like a drunk down a stair. Hereward lowered his good arm and dropped his pistol on the ground. Jameson knelt next to him, his hands over his ears, in an agony of terror. Hereward pushed himself up, half-sitting, his hand pressed against the wound in his chest. His bleeding had slowed considerably. He was evidently not nearly as badly injured as we had first thought; perhaps he would survive after all. A couple of men from the crowd had peeled off and were running towards him, shouting about bandages and pressure. I felt grimly certain he would not succumb.

As the commotion and fuss about Hereward swelled, I dropped to my knees beside Valenti. He lay on his breast in the grass, drenched red now with his heart's blood, his head twisted awkwardly to one side. Hereward's shot had got him through the throat; had torn open his jugular. His eyes were fixed and wide, staring past me along the plane of the Common, towards the scarlet blaze of the rising sun.

My hand was shaking as I stretched my fingers to touch his bloody, lifeless face, still warm, bathed in morning light; but there was nothing I could do for him except close his empty eyes.

The notion of a man's honour is one with which, I admit, I have always wrestled. It is a peculiarly evasive conceit, which shines as brightly, yet can mislead men as surely, as a will-o'-the-wisp dancing over marshes. Many thousands have died for it, and some, especially in these latter days, profess to care nothing for it. It has historically been most prized by the aristocracy; and yet, like the divine spark of life itself, honour is democratic and universal, and each of us, be he never so mean, is born with his own proper portion of it.

Honour shares further qualities with the soul, in that it is at once nebulous and sensible, indefinable and yet essential — and once lost, it takes with it some irreplaceable part of what it is to be a man. And once lost, it cannot be regained at any price.

★　★　★

Henry Hereward, as he was half-dragged and half-carried by a quivering Jameson from the bloody field, was a man who had forfeited his honour. He had come to the Common to defend that part of a man's credit and reputation which resides in a woman's virtue; but his own brutal cowardice had stripped him of that far greater portion which is found in one's own moral character. What he had done — what all of us present on that sad and echoing field had seen — was murder, plain and simple.

Perhaps when he saw Valenti running towards him across the grass, he had panicked, thinking my friend meant to finish him off with a final shot; no doubt that was what he told himself.

Hereward probably consoled himself (still, perhaps, does) with the excuse that a similarly wounded man, a half-drunk man, a man not thinking straight, would have done the same as he; and yet we had all seen March load the pistols, and knew there was no second bullet in Valenti's gun.

Perhaps he had feared Valenti's superior physical strength and passionate fury, so amply on display the previous night at the engagement-party — and yet he must have heard my friend's pleas for help for his fallen opponent. No. He knew it, and I knew it; we all knew it: Hereward had behaved in the most disgraceful, despicable and ungentlemanly fashion. He had violated the laws of God and Man, and deserved more than almost any other person I have met in my years since to be punished for his crime.

And yet, as Valenti's life bled out on to the sparkling grass, none moved to apprehend his murderer. Every spectator, mist-veiled, ghostly, was still and silent as the grave itself. As Hereward staggered upright in Jameson's trembling arms, lurching away cravenly from the scene, the mark of Cain was upon him — but it was as if all who watched him go had been paralysed, or struck blind.

Even March's visage was pinched and stark white, but for the livid curve of his scar, as he watched Hereward's shameful progress from the field of honour. I had not seen an expression of disgust so pure and absolute since the night before, on Hereward's own face, as he had glanced from Valenti's painting to his dishonoured bride-to-be.

I have no defence for my own behaviour in those moments; none of us there had. I examined my conscience and found it stained; I had been tried in the fire, and found myself sorely wanting. To be human is to be quixotic and fallible, consumed and beset always by terror and doubt. The dark side of our capacity to aspire to holiness and virtue is that we must always feel upon us the gravitational drag of weakness and sin, and sometimes discover ourselves unequal to resisting its force.

For our collective failure to act was not due solely to the shock and horror of seeing a man die: it was fear. Fear for ourselves, shallow and shameful. Fear of the black thing that had cast its shadow over the sun, that had come so close we had felt the breath of its passing. I knelt beside the body of my friend and watched his killer stumble away, and I did not stir: I could not. It was as if I were made of something infinitely lifeless and heavy; of clay, or stone.

Sometimes, if we have the great fortune in life to be both wise and good, we are exalted and transported to a realm more beautiful than imagination. I have felt this extraordinary sensation perhaps twice or thrice in all my years; Valenti, too, used to speak of something similar which descended upon him in the fever of creation, or just after he had completed some work at the extreme limit of his capabilities.

He described it thus: it was, he once said, as if he had been fast asleep, and was suddenly startled into wakefulness by the lightest of touches; 'the brush', as he put it, 'of feathers;

perhaps the hem of an angel's robe — and I felt that if only I could reach out and grasp it — draw it to me . . . ah! What could I then not know, or be!' Of course, he could not touch that ineffable dream. None of us can: not in life, anyway.

I looked up through blurred eyes and saw that almost every witness of that dreadful scene — spectators, Jameson and all — was gone. There were but three lonely figures remaining on that field as the morning sun began in earnest to burn off the mist, which had until then served as both our blindfold and our cover. These were poor Valenti, myself and March, the arbiter, his silken kerchief crushed tightly in his hand as he stooped over the place where Hereward had lain.

March was quivering with anger as he snatched at the pistol Hereward had let fall. He grabbed the thing up, and tossed it with loathing into its polished, ornamental box, which now seemed like a little sarcophagus, tainted with the deadliness of the instrument it held.

He approached where I knelt, dumb and drained, guarding Valenti's sprawled body. He limped slowly up to us, his mouth a thin, grim line, stopping a few yards short of Valenti's outflung right arm. The second pistol now lay at March's feet, wet and gleaming. March picked it up and contemplated it.

'If I thought I could get away with it — ' said he, and stopped, turning the empty barrel of the pistol carefully downwards, to point at the scarred earth, his fingers whitening around the grip.

'If I thought I could get away with it,' he repeated in a softer voice, 'if I thought we should all escape punishment but for Hereward, I'd give him to the beadles ten times over.'

He grimaced, twisting his scar up in an ugly jagged line, and shook his head.

And at last I knew what it was that every vanished student on that field had been afraid of — had disappeared so swiftly in order to escape. It was nothing so grand as death, of course; we were young men, and the things youth fears are far more ominous than extinction. We feared our parents. We feared our tutors. We feared for our University places, and our degrees; our scholarships and our reputations and all the other petty things that made up and gave meaning to our timid, sorry little lives.

March, in wishing aloud that Hereward should not escape punishment, had as good as admitted that he would. It was not, of course, certain that even had we reported the whole affair to the proper authorities, he would have stood trial — for the rich often find it convenient to ignore or rise above those aspects of the law not amenable to themselves.

And had we given Hereward up, there was no doubt that everyone involved, but particularly Jameson, myself and March, would have been immediately rusticated, if not sent down; for the University took a very dim view of violence among the student body. To conspire in the staging of an illegal duel was bad enough, but to have permitted a man to die as a result was, as Valenti might have put it with that ironical smile of his, the very height of indiscretion.

March proffered the pistol to me and I shrank back instinctively; I have always been morbidly afraid of handling firearms. I shook my head and he strode forward and thrust it at me again.

'Take it, you fool!' he said. 'Don't you see we must pretend that this was an accident?'

'A — an accident? How?' I stammered.

March leaned closer and spoke softly and slowly, as if to calm a child.

'Valenti went out for an early-morning stroll, taking pot-shots at the wildlife. It was foggy; he was tired. He tripped in a rabbit-hole and his gun went off . . . '

I continued to stare uncomprehendingly; the idea of anyone shooting rabbits with a duelling pistol was so ridiculous that I felt an idiot smile creep across my face. I must have seemed a grinning dolt indeed; for March's blue eyes narrowed impatiently as he knelt beside the shell of Valenti, wincing as the weight shifted to his bad leg. He placed the butt of the pistol in Valenti's hand and gently bent my friend's fingers about it.

'You were crossing the Common to see the First Eight on the river,' he continued quietly, 'as was I. We were going to watch the training together.' His hands were nimble and precise as he arranged Valenti in a more natural, less agonized attitude. I watched his long fingers as they moved, and saw there was a cross-hatch of silver scars on them, too.

'We stumbled across him,' said March evenly, 'and, naturally, we shouted for help.'

'Naturally . . . ' I echoed, still not really comprehending his purpose. Surely we could not explain away a corpse in so incredible a fashion, unchallenged? Surely Valenti's murder could not be suffered to go unavenged?

'You stayed with him while I went to fetch help,' said March. He rose, the pistol-case containing the other gun in his arms, and backed away from me, eastwards to where the rays of the ascending sun played on the small, deep stream known as Marysbrook which ran through the meadow, a rushing, swelling tributary of the great Cam.

March limped swiftly towards it and flung the other pistol far upstream, where it sank into the tumbling waters with a silent, bursting splash. He filled the gleaming mahogany box with stones from the stream's steep bank, and when it was full, locked it, and sank it at a sharp bend in the brook's course, just below a weeping-willow tree. Then he stood again and started back towards me, an expectant, demanding expression upon his white face. I had not the least idea what I ought to do.

'Help!' he yelled suddenly, angrily. 'Help! There's a man hurt here! Help!'

Catching on at last, I added my dazed, feeble cries to his own. Eventually some of the First and Second Eights, who had been heading out to the Cam to practise for the forthcoming regatta, heard our cries and came to our aid. They were not to know that it had always been too late. They helped us carry Valenti's sad, cold remains back to King's, where a sleepy college doctor found a suitable place to lay him out until the city morgue opened.

I suppose I did not truly realize and accept that my friend was gone until the moment when the doctor, having decently arranged Valenti's poor damaged arm and torn throat so that they did not show too horribly, drew the sheet up and over his still face. I almost spoke sharply, to stop the man; I almost reached out to stay his hand — but then I remembered that Valenti was dead, after all; and I did nothing.

★ ★ ★

I had told myself, and everyone had assured me, that there was nothing further I could do for Valenti; but I was wrong. After a brief, exhausting interview with both the University police and the Cambridge constabulary, March and I were permitted to return to our college rooms on condition that we did not stir beyond the gates without explicit permission. Numbly, I ascended the stairs to my cheerless chamber and fell — almost swooned, so stunned and fatigued was I — upon the narrow bed, dropping dead asleep at once.

I woke with a gasping start at around eleven that evening. For a few brief, suspended seconds, I hardly knew where I was, nor could I have said what had passed in the previous twenty-four hours. For some reason I could not fathom, I felt afraid as I looked about my familiar, mean little bedroom; unsettled, as though some dreadful thing hovered above me. Then, as my brain shook off the cobweb of sleep, the memory of the last day's events settled over me like a shroud.

I buried my head in my hands, pressing my fingers hard into my eyes to push away the images that burned behind the lids. Alcohol was forbidden in the rooms, so I was forced to calm myself by drinking two or three glasses of water from the pitcher at my bedside. Upon the night-stand lay my Bible; I picked it up blindly and opened it in the middle of Ezekiel, on a passage so strangely fitting that I almost began to believe in Bibliomancy:

> Then I said unto her that was old in adulteries, will they now commit whoredoms with her, and she with them?

And I realized that there was one final service I could render Valenti, and that I must do it tonight.

★   ★   ★

I dressed swiftly, in my oldest and darkest clothes (and it may be imagined, given my prudent habits and sober dress, that these were tolerably old and dark), left my candle burning near the window to preserve the illusion of occupancy, and crept quietly and carefully down the stair. I knew that the porters had been instructed not to let me past the gatehouse; but the courts were muffled in darkness and silence, as though a heavy black snow had fallen.

I knew, too, that the news of Valenti's death

and Hereward's disgrace had spread through the college like wild-fire — my fellow-students had regarded me strangely even as I had stumbled back to my staircase that morning, acknowledging nobody. I was not surprised that most had chosen to stay indoors rather than roam the lonely grounds on such a sad and ill-starred night as this. I was not the only person about; but I was one of very few, none of whose faces I could descry as I passed them, no more than they could discern mine beneath the hat pulled down over my brow.

The great gatehouse of the college, however, was lit up merrily as a Christmas-tree; I should not be able to pass through it without being discovered. But as long as there have been college walls to keep undergraduates in, there have been young men willing to climb them to get out; and at nineteen, sound in body, light and lean-framed, I was as agile as I would ever be. I passed through to the Back Lawn, where the walls were lower and easier to climb, and swiftly scrambled over, dropping with a smacking thud into the quiet street on the other side.

It was a chill, cloud-shadowed night; only the occasional star peeped from a heaven that seemed filled with grey smoke, and although my eyes had adjusted to the darkness, I could hardly see two yards before me. But even had I been blindfolded, I should have known the way to Valenti's studio, for I had walked it so often in sun, rain, wind and snow; morning, evening and midnight too.

I knew where his key was kept (for he was

somewhat absent-minded and did not trust himself to carry it about his person around town) — and I knew that I needed to hurry, for his parents lived close to Cambridge, and would surely come down to claim their son's body by the next morning. Sad birds, as they say, have the swiftest wings.

As I ascended the stairs to Valenti's rooms, the hair at the back of my neck prickled; and although I was here with the best possible intentions, to perform one final office for my friend, a shiver of cold apprehension passed over my aching body. I stood without the portal, fumbled for the key in its old place, and found it; turned the key in the lock, and flung wide the heavy door. It made no sound; the hinges were still well-oiled, as they had been ever since my unannounced entrance of so long ago.

The room was silent, greyly shadowed in the weak light of the sickle-moon, and quite empty. Or was it? I darted forward instinctively, a soft cry escaping my lips, as I espied a pale, still figure at the edge of my vision — and then I saw it was only an old dressmaker's dummy with a wig-stand atop its shoulders. Valenti sometimes used this object instead of a live model, when sketching background figures — nymphs, dryads and so on. It wore a long pale-blue gown and had a rough turban wrapped about its blank head. I wanted to laugh at my own foolishness, but in that waiting stillness, found myself strangely afraid to.

I was assailed by the uncanny sensation of being watched. Was that candle-smoke I could smell? A long, tattered muslin curtain stirred in a draught from the window. But the windows were closed; I remembered pulling them to when we left for Midsummer Common that morning, twenty-odd hours and, it seemed, a lifetime ago.

I advanced gingerly, prepared to grapple with any intruder concealed behind the drapes — and then recalled the broken pane at the top of the casement, high up and impossible to repair. I retreated to the threshold and softly closed the door to the stairs, lest anyone had followed me. I groped over the table for the candle-stub and matches Valenti habitually kept there, found both, and lit the wick.

Instantly the room gained an aspect at once more cheerful and more chaotic. The barely controlled disorder of the studio seemed even greater than usual now that Valenti, the master of this realm, was gone. I had not realized we had left it so untidy; but my memories of that dreadful night when we had sat up together after the confrontation with Hereward and Diana were somewhat blurred, and shot through with distorted images that seemed to come more from a dream or hallucination than from my own experience.

I glanced about to see whether anything in particular seemed out of place, seeking the source of my unease. All appeared more or less as it should. The dummy model stood in the far corner; the wine-coloured chaise-longue and India coffee-table dominated the rear of the room, and Valenti's easel and sketching-table stood forlornly by the window, where the best light fell in the morning. Everywhere lay scattered paintbrushes, scraps of paper, broken stalks of charcoal, loose leaves from sketch-pads and note-books, paint-tubes, and the swags of brightly coloured cloth which Valenti used for backgrounds. The surfaces and floorboards were abundant with silk vegetation, which grew wild about the place, draped over the backs of chairs and stuck in empty paint-jars. Valenti had preferred imitation flowers for his still-lifes — they were only twice as expensive as the real thing, he said, and lasted very much longer.

In short, the whole room wore the air it always did of being something between a garden and a green-room; a child's dressing-up box tipped into a florist's shop. Strewn with discarded costumes, rich fabrics and ersatz greenery, ripe with colour and potential, it waited for him, as a stage awaits the actors of a play; as an orchestra awaits its conductor, lost and purposeless without that which gives it life.

Perhaps the presence I had sensed was exactly the opposite; something was gone which should have been there.

With an effort, I roused myself from my reverie and lifted the candle: I had come here for a reason, and much remained to be done. I moved towards the table on which were strewn the portfolios where Valenti kept his preliminary sketches. A number of the folders lay untied and open from the night before, when he had raided them for those studies of Diana he had cryptically censored as 'no good'.

There were many of these large leather

binders, old and worn but otherwise unmarked, all apparently the same; and flicking through them, the pictures seemed to be in no sort of order. A still-life would precede a landscape, followed by a hasty profile or a sketched nude. It seemed I would have to examine every last piece of paper to find what I sought. I placed the candle at my right hand, and sat down to my task.

Valenti had always been as prodigious and prolific in his art as he was in all else. His aesthetic tastes were eclectic, and he had a wide and varied set of friends, of whom I was but one — and, it seemed, he rejoiced in sketching every thing and every one he saw, and some things he could not possibly have seen, unless in a laudanum-dream.

I discovered portraits of tinkers, athletes, scholars, serving-girls and cabmen, mixed in with studies of flowers and sunsets, fruit-bowls and fairies, dragons and human skulls — but I did not find what I was looking for until I reached the third portfolio, which was filled with sketches for his goddess-paintings.

There was Juno, the heavy red-headed model (by profession a kitchen-maid), whose bountiful flesh overflowed her unfastening toga; here, a slip of a girl, barely out of school, portrayed coy Echo or weeping Niobe. I cast these aside impatiently; they were daring but not indecent, and besides, he had shown me the final paintings of which these were mere preparatory shadows. They were not what I had come for. Where was Diana?

Valenti had been so peculiarly protective of the pictures he had made of her that I had eventually surmised he was hiding something — and if he concealed them from me, I could not imagine his wanting his parents or professors at the School of Art to see them. It was my last duty to protect him from the low and unseemly imputations that some would surely put upon his more intimate sketches, should they come to light.

I found the folder I wanted at last, shoved down between the table-leg and the window-frame, half-concealed by the billowing curtain. It gave me a pang to think that even as he was rushing to confront his rival in love, he had thought to spare my feelings, and Diana's modesty (if she could be said to possess such a thing). Overcome with grief and pity, my vision abruptly blurred. I pressed my eyes until the burning stopped, lighted another candle, and opened the portfolio.

The first few sheets were innocuous enough: Diana wrapped in gauze and silk, posed in various attitudes, one of which — head turned, back arched in startlement — I recognized from the painting Hereward had destroyed. Valenti had evidently settled upon that position, and there were two or three more detailed versions past which I progressed, seeking what I knew I must eventually find. The next series was the failed Venus, which he had abandoned early on for the portrayal of Diana and Actaeon. They were out of sequence, then; or perhaps as I went on I was going back in time to earlier sketches

— excavating the past.

I was not prepared for what I saw when I finally reached the drawings tucked at the very back of the book. I was even less a man of the world then than I am now, and my only exposure to the female form had been through art — Valenti's own, and that displayed in the South Kensington Museum and the Fitzwilliam — and the occasional mystified glance at some of my surgeon-acquaintance's anatomical textbooks.

The first was of Diana as a goddess, but one which I did not immediately recognize. I was familiar with the religious iconography of a number of different mythologies, both classical and modern, but I was shocked by this depiction of a strange deity. She was shown as an abandoned and licentious creature, sprawled askew upon the steps of what seemed to be, from the pencilled inscriptions, a Babylonian temple. I leaned closer, trying to read the faint symbols upon the lintel by the feeble light of my flickering candle.

At that moment, some soft sound startled me; my attention had been so completely claimed by what lay before me that all around had seemed to fade into darkness. I was suddenly recalled to my surroundings, however, by the return of the unnerving feeling that I was being observed. The hairs at my nape stirred as though someone had breathed gently upon them. I turned abruptly in my chair and half-rose, holding the candle aloft. Its tall yellow flame throbbed and guttered in the breeze from the broken pane.

'Who's there?' I said tentatively, and my voice

was dead and echoless in the low, tenebrous room. Unsteadily, nervously, I surveyed the studio. My sight was mazed by the wavering shadows, and I could not be sure that no-one lay concealed somewhere in the frozen tumult of furniture and props. Not a creature stirred; but still I felt that invisible gaze upon me, stronger than ever. Despite my belief in things spiritual and ineffable, I was never one of those credulous fellows who put stock in tales of ghosts and suchlike supernatural nonsense — but alone in that dark, empty room, I confess I was shaken.

It occurred to me for an instant that perhaps the bonds between Heaven and Earth had not yet quite dissolved, and that my friend's departed soul was still somehow connected to this place, where he had spent so much of his time and passion. I whispered his name once, twice: silence was my only reply. I noticed nothing out of place or disarranged; so, after one last look around, I turned my back upon the studio, and sat down again to examine the sketch of the Babylonian figure.

As in the painting of Diana bathing, the form was fully displayed, but the face was barely visible; thrown back this time in extreme agony, or perhaps pleasure, the tendons of the supple white neck taut as wires. A litter of golden coins surrounded the figure, as though she had been pelted with them, and treasure spilled from every fold and orifice of her body, so that she seemed either to be suffocating on the largesse, or else it was erupting from her person, as she vomited, wept and bled gold. This was the apotheosis of whoredom; some ancient, cruel divinity long predating the Bible, a goddess with many forms and many names. Ishtar, Astarte, Inanna . . . Valenti could have meant her to represent any one of them, or all three.

I turned the picture over, holding it by its edges, not wishing to touch the foul thing. The other, irrelevant sketches I swept off the table in a single motion. I searched on. Some of the characters portrayed I knew of; some I did not; some I could barely bring myself to look at. They piled at my left hand.

In one, the Thracian goddess of birth and death, Cotytto or Cybele, was pictured in the midst of an orgiastic rite, her priests castrating themselves in imitation of her son and lover Attis. After this came angels and demons from the Old Testament and the Cabala. In another sequence, Diana appeared as the Woman Clothed with the Sun described in the Revelation of St John, hideous in the pangs of birth, the moon trampled beneath her feet, a starry coronet twisted upon her head in a blasphemous parody of Christ's thorny crown.

Beneath these lay Naamah, the Pleasing One, from the Ancient Hebrew texts — the angel of prostitution, tormentor of children and mother of demons, and bride of Samael. Valenti seemed to have no particular source of inspiration, save that all his subjects were infernal or divine: in not one of these terrible pictures did Diana portray a human. I recalled his peculiar interest in my own field of study; the conversations we had enjoyed concerning mythology and religion, and shuddered with sudden understanding.

There were more; very many more than I care to remember. It occurred to me with dawning disgust that this carnival of depravity was what Valenti must have meant by the 'signs of affection' Diana had shown him.

I rose abruptly from the table and surveyed the waste of paper before me, the drifts of writhing, abandoned figures; the tangle of limbs and confusion of half-averted faces. I gathered sheaves of the obscene drawings and stuffed them willy-nilly into the last and largest portfolio. Every scrap of paper, every draft and study of a dubious or licentious type, every unwholesome subject was swept into the folder's leather maw. I left only that which could be looked upon without shame or revulsion; the more tasteful goddess-drawings, the still-lifes and landscapes, the portraits and profiles. I struggled to tie the portfolio, now bloated with paper; when at last I had secured it, I heaved the thing under one arm and took up the guttering candle.

I approached the door with soft and hesitant footsteps, not wishing to trip over any of the discarded objects littering the floor; afraid of breaking the hushed silence. At the threshold I took a final, wary look around before I snuffed out the candle-flame, closed the door, and locked it firmly behind me.

★ ★ ★

It had rained while I tarried upstairs, sorting through Valenti's work, although such had been my absorption that I had not heard it fall. The clouds had dissipated, and the cobbles shone slick and black beneath a sky full of sharp stars. I waited some minutes, until I was sure that the roads nearabouts were clear of other night-wanderers, then stepped out on to the street, hugging the portfolio to my chest, and set off back the way I had come.

As I hurried from that silent place, I cast one final glance behind me, looking my last at the studio. My shock at what I saw was so great as nearly to cause me to drop my precious burden; and it certainly explained the unsettling feeling of being observed which had overcome me as I sat at the sketch-table.

For, although I knew I had extinguished the candle, the window of Valenti's studio was lighted once more. Gazing, transfixed, I caught the looming flicker of a pale face, framed by dark curls, at the pane. I turned as cold as if I had seen a ghost, and shrank into the shadows; but she had not marked me. Indeed, she seemed to be frantically searching the room: a single candle-flame flickered and darted about the studio, casting strange, swinging shadows on her determined figure.

I stood still, as though in a trance, and watched until her silhouette disappeared from view and the flame went out. Then I came to myself, and strode swiftly away down the blackest and obscurest alleys leading back to King's, twisting and feinting lest she should attempt to follow me. I had thought Diana fled; but she must have got word of Valenti's death and returned in the middle of the night to claim something of his — or hers — that she could not permit anyone else to find.

I comforted myself that if it was her own lewd portraits she sought, she would have no satisfaction. The nudes in the blameless classical style, along with the elves and chimeras, flowers and tradesmen and skulls, and the various sketches and studies of an innocent nature — in short, all that was decent and respectable — I had suffered to stay. The remainder, that cornucopia of blasphemies, was clutched grimly to my breast; and I swore to myself, as I moved silently along the black alleys of the town, that neither she nor anyone else should have them, at any price.

★   ★   ★

Back in my cold college room I lit the oil-lamp and threw my awkward burden upon the bed, where it lolled, black and bulging. I unpicked the hasty knot, and the folder sprang open, sketches sliding out on to the rough blanket. I had no desire to see any of them again, but could not avoid the horrible images. I shuddered to think what Valenti's parents and peers should have thought of my poor dead friend had I not fortuitously intervened to keep this filth from their sight.

I tipped every last piece of paper from the portfolio, shaking it to ensure that no scrap remained. As I went to close it, however, I saw a thin, worn white corner protruding from a pocket in the front cover. I tugged at it, bringing it out slowly into the light.

It was a much smaller drawing than the rest, done in pencil and, apparently, in some haste. It slipped from my shaking fingers and landed on the floor askew; seen upside-down, it seemed to be a portrait of a youth reading a book that looked familiar to my weary eyes. The face was partly obscured by waves of thick, darkish hair, and the head half-turned away — I had remarked that Valenti preferred profiles and odd angles. When I knelt to pick it up, I was so astonished that for a moment I did not consciously recognize the familiar face which gazed out from the page, eyes downcast, looking past and through me.

It was my own.

I sat down rapidly on the bed, crushing the rest of the portfolio's contents beneath me. It was a peculiar giddy shock to realize that the drawing in my hand was of myself, transmuted via the artist's skill to something other, something stranger and finer, than any mere likeness. In my confusion I could not think when or how he had made this sketch; but then I saw the title of the book I held in my pencilled hands, and began to remember.

Valenti sketched all the time, incessantly when alone, and frequently in company — it was a nervous habit, almost; an impulse he could not control, an activity which at once energized and soothed him. He could not keep the pencil from his fingers nor thence from the paper; and even when we were engaged in our late-night conversations about everything and nothing in particular, he would often be doodling or scribbling as we spoke, lying back on the moth-eaten chaise-longue smoking his pipe, with the drawing-board propped up on his knees.

I would sometimes look up from my reading, in the midst of a companionable silence, to find that he had downed his paintbrushes and taken up charcoal and sketch-pad, and was furiously drawing away. Perhaps I was obtuse, or perhaps I have a smaller portion of the vanity that attends us all; but I never once dreamed that he might be sketching me.

I focused my gaze again on the picture in my hand. Without narcissism, and without, indeed, boasting excessively, I own that I was much more handsome in those days than I am now, and before my hair began to recede, which was unusually early (in my twentieth year), I wore it rather long. It was lustrous and thick, and of a peculiar dark auburn colour; people had used to remark upon it.

It was the strangest thing in the world to see my own image upon that piece of paper, for I had never been drawn before; my only portraitist hence had been my shaving-mirror, and so I was hardly able to tell whether this was a true rendition of how I appeared to others. It was like me enough in feature, I suppose; but there also lingered about it a certain quality of innocence, of freshness, that I had never been sensible of having — or at least, I had called these attributes by their proper names of *naïveté* and callowness.

But in that little, hasty sketch, I saw something

of my friend's regard for me; or perhaps I should say, for the man I was, or could have been. When I looked at it, I viewed myself anew through my dead companion's eyes, and through that forgiving filter I seemed less weak and full of sin than I knew myself to be.

I slipped the drawing carefully between the tissue-thin pages of my Bible, taking great pains not to smudge nor stain it. I closed the empty black folder and stowed it safely beneath my narrow iron-framed bed. The picture of myself, I kept; for even in the extremity of my weariness and distress, I knew I could not bear to part with this memento, be it never so small, of my most beloved, most talented friend.

Every other slip of paper, every scrap and sketch and image, I gathered into my arms, placed in a great heap before the weak, struggling fire in the grate, and, slowly and methodically, burned.

BOOK THREE

The History of
Henry Hereward

The birds were fluting softly in the tree that overhung our kitchen window in the small house on Canal Street. The watery light of dawn streamed in through the grimy glass; bright patches illuminated the black-and-white chess-board of our ash-dusted floor. My mouth was dry as sand, desiccated by speech as it had never been by years of silence. My eyes were sore with wakefulness and my eyelids heavy, but my spirit felt inexpressibly light, freed of a long-carried burden.

I had told Chapman a truncated version of the preceding narrative, omitting no detail, however tawdry or personally painful, which I felt would assist in persuading him that the woman he now professed to love was one and the same as Diana; and was fatal.

Chapman was hunched over, his tawny head hanging listlessly between his shoulders, so that I was not at first sure whether he slept or woke; but when I had finished my sorry tale, and the stillness that followed it had settled upon the room like dust after an explosion, or sunlight after a storm, he bestirred himself and raised his head, looking directly at me.

'Is that all?' he asked; and his voice was low and his face hard.

My confusion at his response must, I suppose, have amused him; for a faint, parched smile twisted his dry lips.

'*All?* Why — why, yes, that is all,' I stammered. 'Is it not enough? Do you wish to hear more?'

'Certainly not,' he said coolly. 'Why should I?'

I did not know; I myself had no desire to speak further on the matter.

'Perhaps you require more proof of — I do not know *what* I must prove to you, Chapman! Is the word of a gentleman, of your nearest friend, not enough?'

He stood, his tendons cracking and joints clicking. My own muscles ached dreadfully with tension and tiredness. I felt as if I had not slept in weeks; recounting my miserable tale had also been partly reliving it, for I had never told another soul the full account of what had transpired all those years ago. I had certainly never admitted my rôle in the destruction of Valenti's drawings. I had felt no guilt at the time, and still do not; but the look Chapman gave me seemed to say that there was something in my actions of which I should have been ashamed. I could not understand it.

'I think,' he said, 'you have *proved* enough.' He pushed a hand through his lank hair, still damp from the night's snow. 'And I also think that I am very tired, and should like to go to bed.'

I started from my chair and made to take his arm, but something in his face warned me to drop my hand before I touched him.

'I am sorry for it, Chapman, sorrier than I can say — but there it is,' I said stiffly — for in truth, I could hardly bring myself to mourn a love so misdirected, so ill-conceived and so doomed to be stillborn. 'She is utterly unworthy of you, and at last you know it. And though I have not seen her face from that day to this, I know as sure as there is a God above us that poor Valenti's Diana and your own Mrs Pelham are the same woman.'

He still said nothing; but a slight, cold smile lifted his lips. Undaunted, I continued.

'It's an unpleasant thing, certainly, but I had rather be the bearer of unwelcome news than stand idly by and watch her destroy you as she once destroyed another of my dearest friends — '

My voice caught in my throat, and I was obliged to stop speaking. It was as though someone had their fingers about my neck, and was throttling me. I had not reckoned with the depth of the silence I had broken, nor the raw strength of the memories unearthed. I had mistakenly imagined that after so long, their power would have diminished, as a corpse rots in the grave, or a liquid, left long enough in an open vessel, evaporates, leaving only a few dry crystals behind. I was wrong. My recollection of the events I had narrated was as vivid and fresh as if they had occurred only yesterday. I had buried my secrets and sealed them with silence, and was dismayed and astonished to find that they were still horribly alive, with all their original power to agonize me.

Chapman gazed at me steadily: I could no more read what was behind his eyes than I could decipher hieroglyphics.

'I do not know what more I can say — ' I continued in desperation.

'Then say nothing,' he told me curtly, and with that, he turned on his heel and left the kitchen. I heard his heavy tread on the stairs, and thought of going to bed myself. I remembered lying in my cot at King's after burning Valenti's drawings, weary beyond words and yet sleepless. I had turned to the Bible, as I always did, for comfort; but that night it had not soothed me. Yet, at last slumber found me as the mid-morning sun slanted in through my high, narrow window; and then I had slept like the dead.

It seemed I could do nothing further tonight.

I retired to my room, knelt by my bed, and said prayers for my own soul and for Valenti's, as well as that of Chapman and of the woman whom I could not refrain from thinking of as Diana. Then I undressed and climbed between the cold sheets, drawing the blanket up to my chin. I took up my Bible from the night-stand, in between my pocket-watch and my carafe of water, and opened it. It was a sturdy, handsome tome, ponderous and large enough to eschew the tiny print that is the hallmark of the pocket-Bible.

I turned to the place where I knew I should find most comfort, feeding my soul on what had finally afforded me enough peace to sleep on that dreadful, waking night back in Cambridge, six and more years ago. A slip of paper of drawing-thickness marked the spot. It was the pencil-portrait of myself Valenti had sketched, which I had trimmed and carefully preserved in the safest spot I could think of, between the pages of my bedside Scripture, marking the place of David and Jonathan, and guarded on either side by the books of Samuel and Ruth.

I had meant to read on; to comfort myself with Solomon's wisdom, but I did not. Instead, I stared at the picture before me until it seemed that I was looking through, rather than at it — until I began to imagine Valenti's face on that page instead of my own, and then Chapman's; until at last Bible and picture both fell from my heedless hands, and I saw nothing but the scarlet darkness behind my eyes, and my own tumbling dreams.

★　★　★

When I awoke, dazed and stupid, and with my head aching fearfully, in the late afternoon, there was no sign of Chapman anywhere about the house. I had slept long, and for some minutes upon waking, was quite disorientated as to the hour. The walls seemed to echo with Chapman's absence, as once Valenti's studio had resounded to his. I do not mind admitting that it made me a little afraid.

Fortunately it was a Sunday, and since I habitually worshipped at a different church each week, partly to examine the architecture and partly in hopes of stumbling across an inspiring speaker who would encourage me to tarry, I knew I should not be missed anywhere. I shaved and repaired as best I could the damage that emotional strain and excess of alcohol had done to my appearance; I dressed sombrely, as befitted the Sabbath, and stepped out of doors.

Outside, the sun burned low in the sky; the slender branches of the sapling in the garden shone in the late-afternoon light and swayed in the soft breeze, but I cared nothing for them. My heart was overcast, as with a grey thunderhead; my very soul felt grimed and black. I could not bear to spend another night sitting up alone, in the vain hope that Chapman might return. I thought of tramping the alleys for an hour or two to burn off my restless energy, but it came on to rain as I wandered, the dull drear sound of it splashing upon the dirty Jericho streets.

I concluded at last that I would repair to the Harcourt Arms, ask of Randolph Quire whether he had seen anything of Chapman, drink a glass of beer, and consider my wretched situation in as calm and rational a fashion as I could.

The landlord had seen nothing. Rather to his surprise, for Quire knew my abstemious habits, I consumed two pints of ale, hardly noticing what I did. Eventually, when the hands of the clock lacked a quarter of nine and I was the only remaining customer, having sat in morose and miserable silence for the better part of three hours, I bade good-night to Quire, turned my collar up against the ceaseless drizzle, and walked the short distance home.

Chapman was there, hunched in the kitchen chair in his stockinged feet, his back to me, and his shoes, clumped with pale Oxford mud, drying before the fire. He heard me enter; he could not have been unaware of my presence — but he did not greet me.

'I . . . I had thought you had gone,' I said.

He half-turned, smiling without warmth.

'Gone where? Where have I to go?'

'I thought — perhaps — you had quit the place for ever?' I admitted.

He laughed shortly.

'Oh! Do not doubt that I would have if I could, but I cannot. I cannot afford to stay anywhere else. Now if I were a whore' — here he chuckled again, bitterly, as at a private joke — 'why, I should know well enough where to find asylum; but I am nothing but a poor medic, and so must return to my proper bed or else sleep in the gutter.'

'I must say I'm glad of it, Chapman,' I said, adding hastily, 'that you are here, I mean.'

He turned his face back to the flames. 'Well, I am not. We are yoked together, Fraser. It is vastly inconvenient and discomfiting, but there it is. No-one regrets the circumstance more than I.'

Oh, that chill, measured tone of his! I remember it still, and its effect upon me. I felt as though he had stuck me through the chest with a sliver of ice. At that moment I was very glad he could not perceive my stricken face, for I, who had learned so early and so well to hide what I felt behind a mask of indifference, should have shown my naked heart to him. The moment trembled and died; the misty rawness passed from my eyes, and I was calm again.

'You had been out so long,' I said evenly. 'I could not think where you might be.'

'I have been walking.'

'All day? Where?'

'Along by the canal. Through Portmeadow.'

'In this rain!'

'Yes,' he said tightly.

I started forward; stopped myself.

'But Chapman, you have no galoshes . . . why, you have nearly ruined your shoes with mud — '

He swung around, his face livid with disgust.

'For God's sake, Fraser! Don't fuss about me like an old woman!'

I was startled and a little afraid at his outburst.

'I — I am sorry.'

'Anyone would think you cared a damn for my well-being,' he continued, snarling, 'but of course you and I both know what a ridiculous notion *that* would be — you who care only for yourself, and your own puritanical prudery, and the wretched phantoms of your inflamed imagination.'

I recoiled as though he had struck me. His harsh words stung me like a whip — and yet, I suppose, they were no worse than those he had listened to last night concerning Diana.

It was abundantly clear that I, with my well-meaning and ill-considered confession, had achieved what all the drudgery and privations, poverty and natural hardships of a young doctor's life could not; I had made him suspicious, ill-seeming, morose. I had killed, perhaps for ever, that part of his spirit which laughed and rejoiced; was trusting and blithe and carefree. Perhaps I had poisoned the well of love itself.

Against all my more exalted instincts, I hoped so. A man in love is as blind and unthinking as a bull in rut, or a wild creature in pain; he is all animal feeling, and nothing of human reason. I know that now, of course; I did not, despite

Valenti's example of long ago looming so vividly before my mind's eye, fully comprehend it then.

Passion is a beast, like a lion or a wolf — and I was surely no lion-tamer. I withdrew to my own chamber, where I lay, fully dressed, upon my cold bed. I did not hear him ascend the stairs; I did not see nor speak to him at all the next day, nor the day after that. Chapman had cast me aside, into the pit of despair, and I could not begin to think how to climb out.

★　★　★

So it went for the next several weeks. Never can two men who shared the same domestic space, and who were not within the confines of a monastery, have had so little intercourse with one another. I shut myself up in the Bodleian and in my teaching-room at Hertford; Chapman took refuge in the Radcliffe and at Mrs Pelham's Victor Street establishment, where now he worked almost every night. When I caught my rare glimpses of him, he looked haggard, and visibly thinner. But I said nothing, for I knew too well that any words I uttered would be taken as malicious.

If I had not happened to be crossing the Hertford front quad one morning, on my way to give a tutorial on Attic worship to two uninterested and indolent students called Willsburgh and Edis, it is quite possible that I should never have overheard the following snatch of conversation until it was too late for me to act.

On the way to my tutorial-room, I found

myself trailing a tall, thickset, ruddy fellow I belatedly recognized as Cornell, the cousin of Mrs Pelham whose acquaintance I had briefly made at the medical ball at Magdalen. He was striding along determinedly, his long gown flapping in the fresh breeze, when he was hailed from across the quad by an undergraduate.

'Cornell!' the other student called jovially. 'It seems congratulations are in order!'

'What do you mean?' Cornell replied impatiently. The undergrad set down his books on a nearby bench and bounded around the quad towards him.

'Why,' he panted, 'I hear that pretty cousin of yours is to be married to the surgeon chap you admire so much — Chaplain, is it?'

'Chapman,' said Cornell. 'Yes, indeed. A capital fellow, brilliant brain — a pity he has not a little more money — then he might have been all she could wish. But not too bad a match, after all.' He grinned broadly. 'Thanks, old man! I shall pass on your compliments at the engagement-party.'

Cornell took his leave of the young man and strode away, his head in the air and his eyes on the distance. In my eagerness to avoid recognition, I lost my footing on the uneven flags of the quadrangle and stumbled against the wall, pale brick-dust dirtying my gown. I need not have panicked, for he overtook me without a glance, as though, indeed, I were not there; and for a second, as my head span and I leaned against the cold stones, I felt my own insubstantiality.

At that moment, 'engagement-party' seemed

to me the two most dreadful words in the English language, recalling as they did the tragic events in Cambridge of yesteryear. I could not tell if I was more shocked and upset that Chapman had proposed to Diana despite my advice, or that he had not bothered to tell me the news, which he must have known would affect me very deeply. Perhaps he planned a midnight flit for his honeymoon, leaving me alone in Canal Street, the lonely master of our empty, tumble-down castle?

Somehow, I made it up the stairs to my study; somehow, I sat through my two students' wretchedly ill-written and under-researched essays on the cults of Ancient Greece. I angled my chair towards the window and stared out, watching the wind play with the tossing branches of a birch outside, as they droned interminably on. Then I gave them both a beta minus and dismissed them.

It was not at all easy to find out what had become of Henry Hereward in the intervening years. After word of his disgraceful cowardice on the field of honour had got out — as it inevitably had to, with such a scandalous open secret and so many witnesses to attest to the sordid story — his former associates began to shun him, and the doors of those he had counted as intimate friends closed upon him, and quite rightly too. He would have been sent down, had the University or City authorities been able to prove a scrap of what had happened; but they could not. No-one who was there that fateful morning would have dreamed of speaking to them about it. It was considered, ironically, to be a matter of honour and discretion.

But with his shame bruited abroad and discussed at every card-party and salon to which he was no longer invited, Hereward's life at Cambridge soon enough became hardly worth living. It was in the middle of the subsequent term that he discovered a pressing need to take an extended tour of the Continent for his health (for the injury Valenti had given him, though not fatal, remained severe), and after that nothing more was heard of him. I don't suppose I was alone in thinking it good riddance indeed.

I had not imagined I should ever again care to seek him out; but now I needed him; or rather, to convince Chapman of the truth of my tale, I needed the painting of Diana which I believed Hereward still possessed.

I wrote to some acquaintances from my under-graduate days, and also to King's; but my former friends' addresses were some years out of date, and the Domestic Bursar of the college was the only one of my correspondents to make any reply. His brief letter stated that nothing had been heard of Hereward in several years; that his last-known address was a *palazzo* in Venice; and that he still owed the buttery eighteen shillings and three pence, which the Bursar would be grateful (should I ever catch up with the young gentleman) if I were respectfully to bring to his attention.

I sent off a missive to Venice and received a passionate reply, scrawled in a slovenly feminine hand and, apparently, in some haste and anger, telling me that he was gone out of Venice these six months past 'and not caring a Jot for who, or What, he leaves behind him'. It gave an address in Bloomsbury to which he had had his things sent on after his departure from the floating city.

The next Saturday morning, then, I stood upon the platform of Oxford railway-station, wearing my best suit, hat and travelling-cloak, a Gladstone bag in one hand and a newspaper rolled tightly in the other. I bought a third-class ticket and stared at the paper all the way up to Paddington Station, incapable of absorbing a word. I was acutely aware that in my breast-pocket was all the money I had saved throughout my time at both Universities, scrimped from my father's somewhat stinting allowance — and that I might well be parting with a large portion of it very soon.

At Paddington, I eschewed the underground railway, which would have taken me to King's Cross, ten minutes from Bloomsbury, and instead determined to walk the whole distance. It was a fine, crisp day; and besides, I believed the exercise and the air, thick though it was with unfamiliar smells and sounds, would do me some good.

I was quite unfamiliar with that part of London, and had only a penny-map bought at the station by which to guide myself; but fortunately I have always had a country boy's naturally excellent sense of direction, and I found that as I strode

155

along Marylebone Road towards Euston, I was rather enjoying my intrepid excursion.

I had of course visited this great city, the engine of the civilized world, on prior occasions: once, when I was fourteen, for the funeral of a distant uncle or cousin (I forget which), and several times since, for the purposes of academic research, to various bookshops, as well as University College and the Reading Room of the British Library on Great Russell Street. Despite this, however, I had never actually trodden the thoroughfares of the metropolis for more than a few minutes at a time; I had merely jumped into a hansom cab and been driven from one echoing, cheerless interior to the next; from church to station, from dusty archive to lofty lecture-hall.

The address given in the letter from Venice was of a house off Lamb's Conduit Street — a charming *cul-de-sac* just by Holborn, closed to traffic at one end, and lined with small tea-rooms, various clothing and food emporia, and a surprising number of book-sellers. It was perhaps half past noon by this time — a decent hour, or so I reasoned, to call upon anyone — so, having fortified myself with strong coffee and some toast at one of the delightful cafés, I walked up and down, searching for Emerald Street.

I found it at last upon the eastern side of the road, little more than a narrow passage populated by a few tall, gangly buildings in decided need of repair, their overhanging upper storeys shadowing the doorways. Number Three was distinguished by a tiny, neglected front garden, separated from the street by black iron railings scabbed with rust. I straightened my cravat, knocked the last of the London soot from my coat, and banged firmly upon the door.

I stood there so long I began to believe that the servant had not heard me, and had raised my hand to knock again, when the door burst open abruptly and I found myself being regarded with bleary disdain by a portly, ruddy-faced gentleman of perhaps thirty-five or forty with ill-trimmed side-whiskers. He was clad in a dirty silk dressing-gown, worn over what appeared to be the evening-clothes of the previous night — or possibly of several nights ago.

'The master's not home,' he drawled ironically, in a faint Irish brogue. 'I shall tell him you — ' He stepped forward, examining me more closely, a whiff of stale whisky causing me to recoil. His face was uncannily familiar, and although I could not at that moment quite place it, I felt sure I had seen this fat, dissolute creature somewhere before.

'Harry!' he shouted abruptly, still staring at me. 'It is not Rosen's man! He doesn't look like *anyone's* man,' he added, contemptuously.

He wiped his thick mouth with his sleeve, his eyes narrowing.

'Damned if I don't know you, though . . . Harry! Come and have a look!'

I did not relish being observed as though I were a zoo-exhibit, and treated with about as much courtesy. I determined to assert myself.

'My name, sir, is Edward Fraser,' I said icily. 'I wonder whether Mr Henry Hereward might be at home?'

'He might,' said a voice from the shadowed hallway. A second man stepped forward, shading his eyes from the bright midday sunlight. He cut the most extraordinary figure; he, too, wore soiled evening-clothes, his white tie loose over his breast, his shirt-studs missing and the shirt itself open at the throat, disclosing a dirty neck, a sunken chest of springy dark hair, and a yellow rime of wear around the inside of his collar which matched the tidemarks on his trailing cuffs. He held a smeared crystal goblet half-full of red wine; his thin, hollow-cheeked face was marred by a large, unkempt moustache, and, incongruously, the whole ensemble was crowned by a yellow, drooping Panama hat.

'Christ,' he said. 'It's *you*. What in God's name do you want?'

'A few minutes of conversation,' I said. 'That is — I merely wish to ascertain whether you have something I would like to — to purchase from you.'

My gaze darted between the two; I was not sure which was the more repulsive and sinister figure. 'I have money,' I added, superfluously — for they both looked as though they needed it, and I was sure that, even on so brief an acquaintance, had they not sniffed some potential financial advantage in conversing with me, our acquaintance would have been still shorter.

'I should damn well hope so,' said Hereward, and laughed; a hacking, barking cough, like the rasp of an angry dog. 'Well,' continued he, hoarsely, 'in that case we ought to let him in. We can't let a chap with money loiter on the step all day, can we, Jameson? Mr Rosen might see him, and then there would be an end to his wealth and felicity.'

Jameson — for it was he, and with shock, I now recognized him — sniggered, and stood aside to let me enter. Hereward's helpmeet and lackey had changed greatly since last I had seen him upon Midsummer Common, and not for the better. The years had not forgiven him his vices; indeed, he seemed to have swelled with them, like some noxious mushroom. Not without trepidation, I squeezed past his soft bulk into the black, musty-smelling hallway, clutching my bag to my chest like a maiden aunt at a country market.

Hereward stood perfectly still, only his goblet trembling a little in his fist, a queer, mocking smile upon his cracked lips. Then Jameson closed the door behind me with a creaking thud, and I was plunged into near-darkness.

★ ★ ★

As my eyes adjusted to the gloom, details emerged slowly about me, like fish swimming to the surface of a murky pond. Half-burned candles were stuck haphazardly into wall-brackets, drowned in their own wax. Tarnished candelabra balanced on the occasional-tables littering the hallway like hurdles in an obstacle-race. The house itself was not ancient, but the interior had evidently not been touched since the place was built; not even to the extent of laying on gaslight.

The hall, once, perhaps, wide and gracious, was narrowed by the clutter heaped up against the peeling walls; discarded newspapers and correspondence (among which were prominent several red-inked tradesmen's bills) consorted with empty wine-bottles, some of which I upset as I tried, half-blindly, to follow where my hosts led. I sensed their amusement as I stumbled behind them, unsure of where to step, and in constant peril of losing my footing among the rubbish strewing the floor.

A set of double-doors was flung open, and though it was a tolerably warm day for February, the fire in what must once have been a fine library blazed so fiercely that candles were superfluous, for the tall yellow flames lighted the whole shuttered room. Hereward plucked a cheroot from a mantel-shelf box and lit it at the fire; the stinking smoke in that thick, close air offended me, but I suppressed my cough.

'Well,' said Jameson archly, 'this *is* a surprise.'

'I am sorry to call upon you unannounced,' I said, addressing Hereward. 'I wrote enquiring as to whether I might come by, of course — but as I did not receive a reply I am not certain my letter found you.'

Hereward smiled, and his white, regular teeth, perhaps the only part of him untarnished by time and debauchery, shone in the firelight.

'Oh, I expect it found us,' he said carelessly, 'but I doubt whether we have found *it*.'

I recalled the wine-stained invoices and letters lying upon the tables and floor in the corridor. No doubt my polite, hesitant plea languished there still, alongside more urgent but equally ignored correspondence.

'Harry doesn't like the post,' observed Jameson. 'He says it's only ever bills and bad news.'

160

'Jamie's right,' Hereward said, still smiling. The end of his cigar burned orange and he exhaled slow, blue smoke with his words. 'Well, Fraser, which are you, bill or ill-tidings? I can hardly believe you braved the journey to town just to buy something from me. For as you can see, I have nothing of value left — excepting, of course, my virtue.'

This quip prompted a high-pitched chortle from Jameson. Hereward joined in, but his laughter deteriorated into a fit of harsh, bubbling coughs, as though his lungs were full of poison. He clutched a stained handkerchief to his mouth; then noticed me watching him and turned away, as if ashamed. I glanced at Jameson, who stared levelly at me, seemingly unmoved by his friend's plight. I placed my bag on the unswept carpet. I had not been invited to sit, so I remained standing.

'I have a proposition,' I began — and did not quite know how to continue. I had agonized for hours over the phrasing of my letter to Hereward so as to sound neither importunate nor insolent — but now all my eloquence left me, so unnerved was I by the bizarre pair before me, and the peculiar, offhand nature of my reception.

'Oh for God's sake just sit, Fraser,' said Hereward impatiently. 'You look like a travelling-salesman. If you stand upon ceremony you'll stay there till you drop.'

Gratefully, I did as I was bid, lowering myself cautiously on to a worn chaise-longue. Hereward threw himself on the sofa opposite me, the burning cheroot drooping between his lips.

Jameson came around behind Hereward's couch with a bottle and refilled his friend's glass silently. I was not offered any refreshment.

'Well, Fraser, what d'you want?' said Hereward. His tone was abrupt, his head cocked idly to one side in the attitude of a curious animal. Jameson leaned his crossed arms on the back of the sofa and observed me as if expecting me to do or say something amusing. The combined scrutiny of the two was distinctly unsettling.

'It's about a painting,' I replied, bluntly. Hereward raised an eyebrow, but there was no light of recognition in his face.

'A painting?' echoed Jameson. He frowned quizzically at Hereward. 'We sold them all, didn't we, Harry?'

'All the ones we could,' Hereward agreed, thoughtfully. I believed I saw comprehension dawning upon his features; it was not pleasant, for I surmised that the more he knew I valued Valenti's canvas, the more delight he would take in driving as hard a bargain as he dared for it. Still, he had what I wanted, at least — for how many other unsaleable works of art could he own? Of course, he could not have auctioned Valenti's painting, not with that ugly tear through it. It was probably rolled up in an attic somewhere. I hoped it had not deteriorated too much in the mean time. I prayed that Diana would still be recognizable.

'I think you know the work to which I refer,' I said. 'I'll give you a good price for it, though I am, as you may conjecture, not a rich man.'

Hereward nodded.

'This is to do with that Italian fellow, isn't it?' he said. He tipped his head back towards his fat friend, keeping his eyes on me. 'The painter, Jamie — do you remember?'

Jameson stared hard at me with a curious expression of surprise mingled with recognition, a look almost (I shuddered to think it) of fellow-feeling.

'Indeed?' he said. 'I remember him. A talented

163

fellow. Handsome, too.'

'Handsome enough for Anna, anyway,' said Hereward, with a thin half-smile. 'I found him less attractive after he put a bullet in me.'

'And you in him!' I rejoined. Hereward and Jameson exchanged a significant glance.

'He was a luckier man than I, Fraser,' said Hereward. His bout of coughing had left his voice ragged; still, he drew hard on his cheroot, and the tip glowed against the dark hollows of his face.

'How can you say that?' I demanded hotly. I was struggling to remain collected and calm, but the strangeness of my surroundings and the peculiar experience of encountering Hereward and Jameson again as haggard grotesques, caricatures of the young men I had known a handful of years ago, had shaken me more than I could have anticipated. Hereward's face hardened and he leaned forward into the firelight.

'What use is a man who is not whole?' he asked bitterly. 'What good's an athlete missing half a lung? Or a soldier with a bullet lodged in his breast? I'll tell you — none at all! I envy your friend. I should have been better off dead.'

His face was so close that I could taste his breath on the air between us — tobacco-sour, wine-sweet. His eyes, once clear and wide, had sunk deep into their orbits and stared blackly from beneath his knotted brows, like those of a murderer or martyr. Perhaps the trip to the Continent really had been for his health. Perhaps he was less a debaucher than an invalid? Pity welled in my breast: I wondered whether I had not horribly misjudged him.

'A soldier?' I said, bewildered.

'My father wanted me to take a commission,' he said. 'Perhaps, then, what happened on Midsummer Common might have been forgotten — after all, the Army values sharp shooters.'

He looked, then, as though he wanted to laugh, but could not — or did not dare. A black cast had settled over Hereward's features; it would not take much, I surmised, to rouse him to anger or plunge him into a profound melancholy.

'Leave it, Harry,' murmured Jameson.

Hereward twitched with irritation.

'Why don't you get us more port?' he said. 'Let's discuss this like civilized men.'

Jameson vanished through the double-doors, leaving Hereward and I alone together. It was not a situation I relished. Hereward leaned back and addressed himself dreamily to the tenebrous, smoke-haunted ceiling.

'I think I know what you want,' he said. 'But I must admit that I really cannot conceive why — or rather' — and here he fixed his penetrating dark eyes on mine again — 'why you would have it *now.*'

'My reasons for desiring to possess that painting can be of no possible consequence to you,' I said stiffly. 'I imagine the question uppermost in your own mind is how much I can be persuaded to give you for it.'

'That,' he said, smiling, 'is why I am so curious.'

At this point Jameson returned, bumping in

with a tray upon which stood a bottle of inferior port and a couple of indifferently clean glasses.

'Ah,' said Hereward, 'now we can get down to business.'

Jameson refilled Hereward's glass and poured two more, for myself and him. He then heaved his ungainly body on to the chaise-longue beside me; I felt it sink beneath his weight. Hereward watched him with fond indulgence in which there was, none the less, a hint of scorn.

'Well, Fraser, now we know what you are after, perhaps we can waste a little time on pleasantries?' he said.

This was the last thing I wanted to do; but what choice had I?

'I do not wish to detain you unnecessarily, of course,' Hereward continued smoothly, 'but, frankly, Jamie and I receive few visitors nowadays — and really *none* from the happy Cambridge years. A friend comes up from Oxford occasionally to try his luck at the card-tables, but he's poor entertainment, for he usually loses; God knows why they call him Lucky. You, however, are, I am certain, full of interesting revelations. So, you see, it would be a crying shame to bid you farewell before we have reacquainted ourselves properly.'

I ignored this invitation to gossip, suspecting that the less I revealed to Hereward, the wiser I should be.

'You are a difficult man to find,' I said. 'I heard you were in Venice, but a Miss Welles informed me otherwise.'

Hereward raised an eyebrow. 'That slut!' he said. 'Still there, is she? Living off my hard-won credit, no doubt.'

Jameson laughed, slapping his meaty thigh.

'She's a wily little thing, Harry,' he said. 'She'll marry you yet!'

Hereward shot him a look full of bile; then turned to me.

'Not as wily as some we have known,' he said, 'eh, Fraser?'

I shrugged. 'I cannot say.'

He stared at me, his expression calculating and quizzical.

'Were you — forgive me — you were surely not in love with the girl *yourself*?'

It was such an extraordinary suggestion that I was surprised into laughter.

'Hardly!' I exclaimed.

Hereward seemed amused by my reply.

'No,' he said thoughtfully. 'I had not really imagined so. Not after all she put poor Valenti through. Then it is a sentimental souvenir, perhaps?'

I said nothing.

'But such a painful one,' he mused aloud. 'Why should anyone wish to gaze upon the image of his dead friend's mistress? What comfort could it afford? What is there to be gained?'

His head snapped towards Jameson beside me.

'Jamie,' he said, 'your thoughts?'

Jameson pondered deeply, savouring the conundrum.

'I believe there are three possibilities,' he said at last. 'One: clearing Valenti's memory — though

167

it's rather late for that, of course. Two,' he continued, bending his smug, insinuating gaze upon me, 'blackmail. Anna has reared her lovely head again, perhaps married, perhaps rich — and Fraser here has found himself in trouble somehow and wishes to extract what he can from her using the painting as leverage.'

My face reddened, and it was not entirely due to the heat of the blazing fire.

'I think we can discount that,' said Hereward drily, 'given Fraser's unblemished character and disappointing lack of guile.'

'Perhaps,' said Jameson, 'but he blushes so prettily! Besides, we must not dismiss any possibility, however remote. Thirdly,' he went on, examining me minutely, as though calculating my whole moral self, 'persuasion. Or should I say, *dissuasion*? Perchance she is playing her old tricks on someone else, someone close to poor Reverend Fraser — ah! I have it! She has another dupe in her clutches, and this is the last, desperate measure to get him out!'

Hereward smiled in indolent delight. 'Oh Jamie,' he said lazily, 'what the Limehouse dens have gained, the world of academia has lost. He's hit it, has he not, Fraser? And now, I think, I am in a *far* better position to name my price. Wouldn't you agree?'

I was mortified that my motive had been so easily and swiftly penetrated; but I did not give him the satisfaction of an answer. I gritted my teeth and dropped my gaze to the threadbare carpet, wondering how long I should be obliged to tolerate this queer game of theirs; this sinister farce.

'If his new friend's tangled up with Anna, I'm sure he'd like to know the full story,' said Jameson. I disliked his tone: there was amusement of an idle, petty kind in his voice, the anticipation, no doubt, of some sordid tale.

Hereward lit another of his foul cigarillos and settled himself back on the sofa.

'I suppose you recall the unpleasantness on the Common as well as anyone?' he said.

'How could I forget?' I asked grimly.

'Indeed. I expect you think I behaved disgustingly, and I daresay I did. But' — and here he turned his painful gaze on me — 'do not you forget that I was in fear of my life. Still am — '

He paused, as though he would say more; then continued in a more philosophical vein.

'If you corner an animal,' said Hereward, 'there's no telling what it may do to save itself. Wounded beasts are wild. And, despite the trappings of civilization — which, as you see, Jamie and I are doing our best to throw off — that is all Man is: a dying animal. Some more so than others.'

He drank off his glass. Jameson silently refilled it.

'After the . . . altercation, I went at once to a doctor I knew,' said Hereward. 'A man I'd used before, for less serious but rather more delicate situations. He was more medic than surgeon, but he had expertise enough to confirm what I already knew — that Valenti's bullet had pierced my lung — and to tell me what I was not then aware of, namely that it had also grazed my heart, and was lodged so close to that organ that it could not be removed without — well' — here he grinned, wolfishly — 'killing me, to put it bluntly. Rather poetic, don't you think?'

Jameson stared across the room at his friend, his eyes dark and wide, listening as raptly as a child to a beloved story.

'I hope I do not bore you, Fraser,' Hereward said solicitously. 'Jamie knows the whole thing, of course, but we needn't bother about him. It is quite his favourite fireside tale.

'In any case, I was made to understand that I must lead a very quiet life from that day: no strenuous exercise or late nights, a calm and regular routine — in short, everything that made life worth living was summarily denied to me lest any moment might be my last.' He touched his breast gently. 'The bullet is still in there, you know. Sometimes I can feel it. The slightest exertion, the mildest of excitements . . . ' He snapped his fingers and laughed lightly.

'Well, you may imagine my dismay upon receiving this news. Worse, Anna was still around, beside herself with grief at losing her adored Italian, but desperate to win me back, now her lover was no more. Naturally, I did not apprise her of my delicate condition, and so she still believed me a fair prospect.

'She kept suggesting — insisting, in fact, with a most unfeminine zeal — that we marry quietly elsewhere. She was out of her wits almost, you understand, else she would have known how impossible it was that I should ever wish to see her face again. She even tried to blackmail me

— but we'll come to that. In any case, I tolerated her, because I believed — wrongly, as it transpired — that she might still be useful.

'Valenti had given her a key to his studio; and in my desire to mitigate the stain of dishonour upon my character — I still cared for such trifles then — I decided that I would blacken his name in the University, and thus lighten, by contrast, my own.'

'You would have desecrated his memory!' I cried, aghast. 'Have you no shame?'

'None,' said Jameson approvingly.

Hereward smiled at me without mirth.

'Calm yourself, Fraser,' he said. 'Don't you know you cannot libel the dead? Besides, I should only have exposed to the world what he had been painting in secret, surely what he would have wanted. Anna maintained that he had always been an untameable spirit, aesthetically. He was not without talent, of course, and morally he was a . . . free-thinker — rather like myself. I sometimes wonder whether, had it not been for our unhappy shared interest, we might not have been friends.'

'Never,' I muttered savagely.

'Well,' said Hereward, with a pleasant show of teeth, 'we shall never know, shall we? In any case, that very night I sent Anna to collect his more rococo sketches for a little exhibition, to be mounted at my own expense, naturally. I promised I would destroy all paintings of her and use only the work involving the other models, for she had told me that there were plenty more pictures of an erotic nature hidden in his studio.

171

She would have agreed to anything. Imagine! She still thought I'd have her after what she'd done, the silly slut!'

He dissolved into wheezing laughter; Jameson started up nervously from the chaise-longue, but the fit subsided and, to my distaste, Hereward continued.

'However, she returned practically empty-handed. She claimed someone had been there before her and ransacked the place — but naturally, as she had sworn to me that only she and Valenti had keys, I did not believe her. I became quite angry, didn't I, Jamie?'

Jameson nodded his assent.

'I'm rather surprised the exertion didn't do for me there and then, actually — especially so soon after the duel, with my wounds still half-open and bleeding.' He touched his breast again, reflectively, stroking the old injury like a pet. 'In any case, I made rather a mess of her, and incidentally solved the blackmail problem too.'

Though I feared its answer, the question sprang unbidden to my lips.

'What do you mean?' I whispered.

'Oh, only that she was carrying something she claimed was mine, that I did not want, and by which means she hoped to force me into marriage. Suffice it to say that when Jamie escorted her out, she had nothing left to bargain with.'

I sank my head in my hands. The sickness I had felt the second I entered this horrible place washed over me again like a polluted sea. I thought I understood his implication, and began to believe that no matter what her crimes, even Diana could not have deserved such ill-treatment at this devil's hands.

'I did love her once, you know, Fraser,' said Hereward, in a soft, wistful tone, 'and I wish all had not turned out as it did; but I told you I was mad. I was a wounded beast that night: it's a wonder I did not kill her. Jamie intervened when she began to bleed, didn't you, Jamie? He always was soft-hearted.'

Jameson looked away. He seemed to have shrunk into himself, his bulk now more pitiful than imposing.

'I regretted my impulsiveness the next morning, and determined to give her some money, for I was rather afraid she would go to the police, despite the humiliation. She took the cash readily enough — rather a lot, I might add — but she didn't hold her tongue.' He grimaced bitterly.

'Oh, I stuck it out at Cambridge for a bit, for form's sake, but — well, word gets around. Not only a killer, but a coward. She'd confessed to her friends, or one of her other beaux, perhaps. I could have ridden out Valenti's death, given my side of the story, but to raise my hand to a woman — even such a woman — was unforgivable!

'And so we went abroad. I had to be careful of my health, now, and so Jameson came with me as my companion. He was happy enough to quit England, too, weren't you, Jamie? Some little indiscretions, financial and otherwise, were catching up with him. We spent a very pleasant

173

few years on the Continent, enjoying the gracious society of the English abroad wherever we went. Venice, Paris, Brussels, Vienna — all opened their arms wide to us.

'The wonderful thing about expatriate British society is that they're so starved of civilized company they will practically bite the hands off a pair of eligible gentlemen who can dance well and talk nonsense with their lumpen and thick-witted daughters. That is, until rumours surface of a certain incident in Cambridge . . . ah, well. We saw a lot of very pretty towns on our travels, and a deal of pretty girls too — didn't we, Jamie? — though none of them for more than a season, for obvious reasons.

'Anyway, we lived as well as we could out there until Europe became a little too hot to hold us. Fortunately, Jamie's uncle had come into this place — left him by some elderly and rather untidy relative, as you can see — and wanted a tenant to occupy the house and prevent thieves from ransacking it while he was up at his country seat. We have made it as comfortable as we can.

'Alas, we are short of funds — but we manage, and I fancy it will be several months before our reputation catches up with us. Until then, when anyone enquires, I am an Afghan veteran with a bullet next his heart, or sometimes a consumptive poet seeking my Muse. Plenty of time to borrow a few guineas and break a few hearts. And even when we are exposed, who shall say it will not stand us in good stead and make us the toast of the town? This is London, after all!'

He raised his glass in a grim toast, and drank

it off. I did not touch mine: I had no taste for it. Hereward tipped his head on one side and studied my face with interest.

'I do believe he's heard enough,' he said mildly. 'Be a good fellow and fetch the daub, would you, Jamie?'

Jameson lumbered to his feet and left. I sat motionless and ramrod-straight on the chaise-longue, staring into the fire in order to avoid Hereward's gaze. On the periphery of my vision, however, I noticed him stroking his moustache contemplatively and staring at me.

'You must value the happiness of this friend of yours very much,' he said eventually, 'to tolerate all this for him. What is his name?'

'Chapman,' I said, dully.

He nodded silently.

I turned my head and looked at him full-on. Black after-images of the flames danced over his sunken features. 'Was all that true?' I asked.

He inclined his head. 'Every word, I'm afraid.'

'Why do you tell me this? You cannot be less than abhorrent to yourself. Can you not see you are a monster?'

'Yes,' he said, his eyes lost in darkness, 'I know it.'

'Then why?'

'That woman,' he said slowly and seriously, 'is bad luck. More than that; she's a curse. One man has died because of her. The other — well, look at me! I do not say she does it deliberately, but everything she touches turns to misery and horror. There exist people like that, you know; they are not inherently evil, but evil attends them

175

— follows closer than a shadow. That is why I told you. Why else would I malign and incriminate myself? If your friend Chapman is in love with her, trust me; if you do not end the attachment, and end it soon, he is doomed. I have done . . . things I had not thought myself capable of. I have lost everything: my health, my wealth, my prospects. My family believes me to be dead, and I would not wish them to know otherwise.'

He seemed about to say something else, but at that moment Jameson returned with the painting and sundry drawings, vanishing again immediately to allow us to conduct the negotiations. I unrolled it and glanced at it long enough to ascertain its authenticity and condition. I sorted through the pencil-sketches as well; I could hardly bear to look at them, but I had to be sure. They would cost me a pretty penny, but there it was. The devil would have his due.

'Very well,' I said shortly. 'How much?'

I did not care to haggle or bargain. All I wanted was to leave that squalid place as soon as possible. Hereward was gazing at one of the pencil-portraits of Diana which lay across the table between us. Her hair was down about her shoulders and she stared out from the page as though at something approaching her from out of darkness. Hereward shuddered and shook his head.

'Don't give anything to me,' he said. 'I don't want money for these. You are lifting a curse from me.' He raised his dark head and his eyes pierced me to the soul. I shivered to look in

176

them. 'I truly believe that, Fraser. I thank you for it. Just take them away.'

'Then to whom — ?'

He waved a languid hand, speaking in gasps, his scantness of breath returning.

'Jamie will show you out,' he said hoarsely. 'Give the money to Jamie. I have been living off him for a long time. I don't wish to be a . . . He is a good friend to me. Pay him what you think is right. Whatever your friend's safety is worth.'

I nodded, taken aback by this excess of sincerity on Hereward's part. He was exhausted and quite white. Looking at him, thin and sunken upon the couch, I wondered if I might not be the last to hear that secret tale from his lips.

'Fraser!' he called abruptly, as I made to exit.

'Hereward?'

'Good luck, old man. If you are as loyal a friend to Chapman as you were to Valenti; as Jamie is to me . . . ' He smiled, as at some private joke, closing his eyes. 'He probably doesn't deserve you.'

'Good-bye, Hereward,' I said, awkwardly.

'Farewell, Fraser.'

In the vestibule, Jameson was nowhere to be seen. I found an old envelope, folded half the money I had brought inside it, and left it on a table, having written Jameson's name upon it. I had some qualms, but Hereward's insistence on remunerating his friend rather than himself had moved me strangely. Besides, I had never taken anything from anyone without paying for it fairly, and I was not about to begin now.

Then I took one last, appalled look around at the ramshackle scene, stepped gratefully through the front door, and pulled it shut behind me.

★ ★ ★

The sun was low and louring in the sky by the time I reached Paddington Station, returning with the swift aid of a hansom cab. I thanked Heaven for the driver, one of those dour, silent men who do only what is required of them, and not one iota more. I had no inclination towards idle chatter, haunted as I was by the furtive sensation of being a criminal escaping from the scene of a successful robbery with his ill-gotten loot.

The sketches were carefully stowed between the covers of an ecclesiastical journal in my Gladstone, but the rolled canvas was too large to be secreted in my bag without crushing and possibly damaging it further. I clutched it at my side as casually as I could, yet every minute I carried it, I felt utterly conspicuous, as though everyone about me must know what I held and what it meant, and might at any moment demand it from me. I have never broken any law of this country, and am always extremely comforted to see a policeman, but I was suddenly made aware of what it must be to be a wanted man, and quail with shame and terror at the tread of heavy Metropolitan boots or the shriek of an official whistle.

At Paddington, I paid off the cabman and, hurrying to the nearby parcel office just before it closed its doors, bought a long cardboard tube in which to conceal my treasure. Once the thing was safely disguised, I felt a great weight fall from me; I strode straighter and taller, swinging the long thin cylinder like a cane or a baton. Building plans, or a map, perhaps, could be carried thus, I decided, and so I tried to maintain the air of a gentleman-cartographer back from Stanford's in Covent Garden. Ironically, innocence being my default state, I had never been obliged to counterfeit it before, and was rather afraid I was not especially skilled at the masquerade.

I was certainly somewhat pink, and perspiring freely, when I exchanged my third-class return for a first-class single ticket at the station office; and, by the time I had walked briskly down to the extreme end of the platform in hopes of finding a compartment to myself in which to examine my purchase thoroughly, quite out of breath. But my luck held; after peering in at successive carriage windows, startling some of the sitting tenants, I discovered a first-class compartment empty of passengers, and swung myself into it.

Once inside, I closed the heavy door to the platform — would that I could have bolted it! — raised and secured the window, and pulled the blinds down. I removed the journal (the *Christian Register*, I believe it was) and stowed my Gladstone on one of the luggage racks. When I had done all this I sat, straight as a sapling and taut as a drawn bow, and waited for the journey to commence; only then could I be assured of remaining for a time undisturbed.

With a screech of wheels and whistles, and a heavy sigh of steam, the train drew slowly away from the bustling station. I raised the corner of the blind and watched the magnificent edifice of Paddington recede, attended by a feeling I knew perfectly well to be both ridiculous and superstitious; that only once we were speeding through the open fields outside London could I consider myself truly unobserved. The tube was held rigidly upright at my side; the *Register* placed square in my lap, my ticket face-up, awaiting inspection. Once the guard had examined my ticket, I was free to do the same — if with rather more trepidation than deference — with the sketches and painting for which I had paid so dearly, and upon which depended so very much.

As the locomotive hurtled headlong through the encroaching countryside, towards the city where Chapman and Diana both moved, entirely unaware of my desperate plan to tear them asunder, I made my inspection.

First, I checked the corridor, lest any perambulating stranger should accidentally burst in on me; it was empty. Then, swiftly and with trembling, fumbling fingers, I popped open the lid of the tube and drew out the canvas. It made a soft, hushing sound, as if beseeching stealth, as I withdrew it, and I was almost afraid of what I would see portrayed on that oblong of cloth when I unrolled it — for the light in Hereward's den had been treacherous indeed, and the central figure, though unmistakably Diana, had seemed to leap and twist with the guttering flames in the grate.

I must have examined that painting to within an inch of its tattered life; I do not know how long I pored over it, only that I have never inspected any work of art so thoroughly as I did that one, all alone in the ill-lit first-class compartment of an Oxford-bound train, with no gallery-guide to aid me and no other image to distract. At last I rolled it up again into a tight cylinder, and thrust it back in its cardboard tube. It was enough; it should be, anyhow. And yet doubt nagged at me, aching in the back of my head like a rotten tooth.

Anyone who had seen Diana, the turn of her head, the fall of her hair, even the lax, lilting attitude of her wrist at rest, could not fail to identify her from that most admirable portrait — but the conclusive proof, the full-face, was lacking. I knew that Chapman would comprehend instantly whose image he was presented with; but knowing and admitting are, as any defendant at the Old Bailey will attest, two quite separate things. I did not wish to give him the flimsiest pretext to disbelieve me — for in my fevered brain, his rejection of myself was so intimately bound up with his embrace and acceptance of her, that the two seemed almost one.

Had she been a man threatening my friend's integrity and happiness, I should have known well enough how to persuade Chapman to my view; but against the subtlety and evasiveness of a woman, what weapon will prevail, what armour is proof? And yet . . . the *face*! Where was the face Chapman would demand as evidence? Where were those large dark eyes, lasciviously wide, gazing out at something that both frightened and excited her — at —

I turned suddenly and cast around for the *Christian Register*, snatching it up and riffling its pages; I could picture exactly that expression, on exactly that lovely face, and I had seen it not two hours ago, on a yellowing scrap of drawing-paper in Hereward and Jameson's unsavoury lair, by the dirty-red glare of a fire. It was in here somewhere, a full-face picture, innocent enough in itself, but proof of the connection — enough to establish that this was that same model who had posed for the painting of the goddess I held.

I found her at last. There she was, tipping drunkenly off the train-seat, charcoal and cream but still eminently recognizable — and recognizable, moreover, in a study that was unmistakably a preliminary sketch for the final canvas that rolled about the floor in its cardboard container. The same position of the body — cut off at the waist, indeed, and immodestly covered with a rag of what Valenti had used to call irreverently 'goddess-gauze' — that identical pose — it could not, would not be denied! There was even an unfinished, tiny figure of Actaeon in the background. It could not have been more perfect.

The only difference between the pencil-drawing and the final image was that whereas in the painting her face was arched away from the viewer, in the sketch she stared out at him — at me — full-on. Perhaps Valenti had meant to imply that the observer himself had surprised her at her ablutions; that the viewer's own lustful gaze would see him torn to pieces by vicious hounds — I did not know. All that mattered was that the woman in the picture was the same — that she was, incontrovertibly, that very raven-tressed, ivory-skinned gamine who contained within her the seeds not only of Actaeon's destruction, but that of the artist who painted her, the aristocrat who loved her — and, I most fervently and impiously hoped, herself.

I slipped the precious sketch back between the pages of the *Register*; I snatched up the cardboard tube that held the painting, tapping it impatiently against my thigh. The train made a sigh and a long screeching moan, as of infinite weariness and pain, and came to rest at Oxford Station. The journey had passed swiftly; but time disports itself in strange ways when one stands upon the very threshold of past and future.

'Come, my dear,' I said softly — and anyone passing would have thought me a little crazed, sitting alone in the compartment, with nothing but a long map-case, a Gladstone bag and an ecclesiastical tome to address — 'and let me introduce you to your fiancé.'

★ ★ ★

I do not know whether it was better or worse, as it eventually fell out — I had imagined such a confrontation, such a scene of passion and reconciliation, of apology and forgiveness, that I suppose anything else should have disappointed me. But the long and short of it was that when I returned home, Chapman was not there.

I refused to be baulked in my righteous revenge. I knew that wherever he was, he must return home to sleep, and though it was early yet, I was fatigued by the exertions of the day. Let him not hear it from my own lips, then — let Valenti's painting, and his damning pencil-portrait, speak for me. In truth, I cared not whether I was present to witness my moment of triumph, for I knew it must fall on one side or the other, and that Chapman must throw in his lot with me, or with her only — for never the twain should meet.

I entered his room, still and cold and dark as the tomb. The fateful painting I laid upon his bed, with the little full-face pencil-sketch lying against it. To the rough paper I appended a note of but five words, which would tell Chapman all he needed to know:

BECAUSE YOU WOULD NOT BELIEVE

Sleep and myself have never been easy bedfellows. I am one of those unhappy men whose slumber is as light as a cat's, and as difficult as that creature to coax when it does not wish to approach. Add to this an inability, however exhausted I am, to slip back into the cool waters of sleep when once I have been haled out, and an insomniac tendency that meant many a night at University found mine the only light burning long after the chimes of midnight had sounded, and you may begin to imagine how nervous and wretched I was after two full weeks without sight or word of Chapman.

The morning after I had left the pictures and note upon his bed, all three — and he — were gone. The first night that he did not come home, I comforted myself that he had been caught up in some emergency at the laboratory or the shelter, and braced myself for our meeting on the morrow. But when he did not return the next day, nor the day after, my disappointment at being cheated of the confrontation I had rehearsed a dozen times in my head gave way to a growing fear for my friend's safety. I pushed it away, reminding myself that he had shown no similar concern for me; had abandoned me, indeed, without the courtesy of a word or note of farewell. Anxiety and anger warred in me for mastery; pridefully, vengefully, I hardened my heart against the former, and gave myself over to the latter.

But still I could not rest.

I stared sightlessly at Greek texts in the Theological Library until the night-attendant roused me from my torpor. I could not sleep; so I haunted the streets about our Canal Street abode, peering into the thick-bellied window-panes of the public houses, staring out the alley shadows until they vanished, or proved to be nothing more than a heap of rags or, occasionally, one of those ruffians whose grim work is performed by low gaslight, or better still, no light at all. The sooty kitchen echoed its emptiness; the cold ashes of the grate rebuked me with my neglect. I returned home only to try to snatch a few hours' oblivion in the chill dark of my bedroom: yet, without Chapman's presence, the house had become as repugnant to me as a tomb.

Appointing myself my own confessor, I spent hours bowed and contrite, in church and out, praying, cajoling, bargaining; it eased neither my conscience nor my anxiety. Dazed with watchfulness, with waiting, I went to bed at noon, shattered in mind and body. I bound my eyes and stuffed my ears, proof against the loudest knock or footfall — and yet all this meant was that my nightmarish visions had freer rein to caper across the black screen of my closed lids.

I saw Chapman and Diana, eloped; abroad, perhaps; Diana laughing triumphantly as they burned the pictures I had given him. Diana jostled on the street, or (O febrile fancy!) in some low, benighted tavern; Chapman defending her honour in that thoughtless, passionate way of his, and ending shot, stabbed, beaten beyond recognition, his life ebbing as she bent over him, her dark curls loose, her lips parted, her head half-turned away . . .

Oh! What did I not imagine as I twisted on my comfortless bed? All manner of awful things — and every last one dissolving into Chapman's deathly white face, and the accusing stare in his sightless blue eyes. I concluded that sleep, if it ever came, would bring only dreams still more dreadful. My fervid visions would not let me rest. Without him, I was less than half myself — I

186

was delirious, deranged, distracted; for, try as I might, I could not drive his face from my mind. I cursed him for a traitor, and a fool: had he but listened to me at the first, had he trusted a friend's word over a woman's wiles (I assured myself) there would have been no rift; it should not have come to this. What would I not say to him, when I saw him again! How sternly I should scold him for his lack of faith in me, and yet how readily would I forgive him, if only he returned!

I sat up in bed and unwound the cloths from my aching head; I pulled the cotton-wool from my ears. Pitchy darkness assailed my sight, and silence surrounded me. I was suddenly terribly afraid. I stumbled blindly, hastily into my clothes and left the house, walking so far and fast that I hardly knew where I was, questing the streets for a glimpse of light, however tawdry; of life, however low. And so I continued, night after sleepless night, seeking without finding, searching without admitting to myself that I did so; a wanderer, lost among the lost.

★ ★ ★

They grew to know me, the night-people of Jericho. It was strange to discover, during my first encounter with one of the gentlemen of the shadows (those protectors, proprietors and persecutors of the street-walking girls) that I, once so timid, so halting, so apprehensive of physical harm, was now so gripped by my visionary misery that I felt nothing but a mild sense of disappointment when a man who stepped out of the darkness of a side-street and shook his dirty fist at me proved not to be Chapman. He offered to relieve me of my purse or my life; but my wild laughter must have frightened him, and after staring for a shocked moment, he backed away: a coward, of course, unwilling to engage with such a reckless stranger to fear.

Indeed, by the end of the first week of my tortured vigil, my appearance must have been alarming enough; hollow-cheeked and fiery-eyed, I had gone to give a tutorial and my students had visibly quailed before me, as before some demon inadvertently summoned. It took a fainting-fit in the Senior Common Room, whence I had stumbled to revive myself with strong coffee before my afternoon lecture, and a stern interview with the Principal, to make me understand that discretion, in this instance, was the better part of valour. It was made plain to me that if I wished to regain my fitness to teach, or indeed retain my position, I must not return to Hertford until my 'illness', my 'nervous-exhaustion' (what a green-sick girl that made me feel!) had passed. I ought to have been grateful for the college's concern; instead, it set me adrift, a bark on the storm-churned seas of the night.

How I yearned to be indifferent to Chapman's fate, as he was to mine! How I wished I could sleep sound in my bed, not knowing where he laid his own head, nor caring to know! But how abjectly I failed. I had tried to excise him from my heart — but it felt as if my heart itself had been cut out. I must know what had become of him; I must help him, if I could. Only let him not be gone from me for ever! I prayed for his return, swearing on my soul that all would be forgotten, as with the prodigal son, if he would only come back alive and well. There was no answer, save the relentless ragged beat of the blood in my head. Enough of this! I rose from my aching knees; I strode from the church, I let the door thunder behind me. There was no succour here.

I combed the streets by dusk and dawn. I sought out every friend and acquaintance of Chapman's whose name I could remember. I asked at each haunt he had ever frequented. I even, at last, bent my steps towards Mrs Pelham's benighted asylum, intending to swallow what pride remained to me and beg of her his whereabouts — only to be told brusquely by the raddled blonde Cockney who answered my knock that the lady was away, and should be gone some weeks. No more information was vouchsafed me, and the only answer I received to further petitioning was the door closing in my face.

My wanderings took me further and further afield, as I tried, vainly, to tire myself out in hopes of snatching a wretched rag of slumber when I returned home footsore, wet, and despairing. Always I imagined that the figure ahead of me might be him; over and over the sight of a blond head, the sound of a ringing masculine voice, or the glimpse of a lean silhouette against the halo of a gas-lamp deceived my poor heart into fibrillations of agonized hope. Surely that was — ? Could it be — ? At last, it must — !

It never was.

I must have covered more of Oxford, its suburbs and outlying villages in those days and nights than I had in the several years of my prior residence in the city, criss-crossing the map like a maddened spider, the paths I took curving and returning, hatching and gridding the town until I truly believe I had searched every square inch of the cursed place. I could barely see, I could hardly walk, and who knows whether I missed Chapman a dozen times as I stumbled heedlessly beneath the glowering moon — but I did not know what else to do.

I could not tell which I dreaded most — that he was dead, or that he was still alive, hating me, evading me; fearing me, even. The tears of the rain mocked me; the hard, icy wind chided water from my eyes, and my own fatigue compelled me to weep, soundlessly, whether I would or no. It was merely a physical reaction to exhaustion, I knew; but when the whores and their masters saw me returning to our cold abode dawn after dawn, my face shining wetly in the numinous grey light, they looked at me with strange apprehension, and moved away.

If madness has a border, I was preparing to cross it; if it has an edge, I was its whetstone. Even in my profoundest misery and vastest despair, however, I was more fortunate than I realized; for had I known then what I eventually learned, I should have fallen to my knees and thanked God that however wretched I was, I was not Chapman.

Chapman had been lost to me for some weeks, and I was half out of my senses with despair. Having quartered every street and square of the city over the past fortnight and more, I had taken to walking home from my excursions along the towpath beside the Oxford Canal. This smooth body of water runs to the west of the town proper, by the railway-station, alongside the walls of Worcester and Jericho, under myriad pretty bridges and past dozens of gaily painted narrow-boats and barges, and finally north through Portmeadow to Summertown and beyond.

This I did, not because of the cheerfulness of the prospect, or the opportunity it afforded me for quiet contemplation (for Lord knows, that was the last thing with which I wished to encumber my debilitated brain) but because of a vague memory — I sometimes believed it was something I had imagined to comfort myself, to give my restless wanderings a definite end and purpose — that Chapman had taken to walking there when he was troubled and angry. I had a vivid image of him standing, drenched and defiant, on the chessboard tiles of the kitchen, having made his way back home beside the canal, the mud crusting his worn boots, as it now did mine every eventide. Alive or dead, on land or in water, I continued to hope that it was there I should find him.

I cannot say with absolute certainty whether it was dawn or dusk when I came across the two river-men. I was trudging wearily along the squelching path, the mud sucking with listless appetite at my aching feet. The sun was a raw wound across the sky, swabbed by dirty rags of cloud, shafts of light stabbing through the treecanopy and into my swimming eyes like shards of broken glass. The rains of late had been heavy, and the normally sluggish waters of the canal were in spate, fairly racing along beside me; a lock somewhere having evidently been opened to prevent them bursting its banks.

I heard their voices before I saw them, but thought little of it; these river-men have their own set of vocal signals, cries and whistles by which they communicate when manoeuvring their craft along the canal. But as I gained the little bridge which arched over the water at about the half-way point back to Canal Street, I saw two stocky boatmen waving urgently at me; whether to beckon me toward them or shoo me away, I could not tell.

Mazed and tired as I was (it was the only state I knew now, and was like treading through some grey, comfortless dream where everything presented itself to me flat and flimsy as a paper silhouette) I approached the men to enquire what I could do for them.

'May I help you, my good fellows?'

'You'll be 'elping us if you stay away from the canal, sir,' said one of them, the elder of the two, rather abruptly. He wore a greasy brown felt hat and greying side-whiskers, and had an air of pompous authority.

'Indeed?' I was rather piqued by his brusqueness, and could not imagine what offence I had committed by walking privately and quietly along the towpath.

'Aye, sir. We've been asked to keep folks clear if we can. The water's 'igh and some poor soul was found in it not three hours ago.'

'Good Lord,' I said, stepping back from the edge of the swift-flowing waters. 'I trust they were not drowned?'

The younger man, a sturdy, ruddy fellow, not much more than an overgrown boy, shrugged and shook his blond, close-cropped head.

'It's to be hoped not, sir, but I saw the body myself when Mr Edwards drug him out — like a drowned vole he was, and I don't hold out great hope for him.'

It seemed improper to ask the question on my mind — whether the cause had been the hazardous footing hereabouts, violent assault, or even self-murder — so I softened my voice, turning to the elder man (presumably Edwards).

'An accident, I suppose? The going must be treacherous in this heavy weather.'

Edwards snorted. 'That's what the boss says; that's why we're out 'ere warning walkers off the path. I brung 'im in,' he added, with grim modesty, 'and I seen a lot of bodies — young girls what try to do themselves in after their gentlemen go off them, beggars and suchlike what have a rum too many and tumble in the drink. But this one I couldn't say 'ow it 'appened, for all Mrs S. swore 'e must've missed his footing in the mud.'

'Mrs S.?' I echoed.

The younger man chipped in. 'Mrs Shimmin, her that runs the 'hotel' in Jericho.' He exchanged a sly glance with his companion. 'Perhaps you know it, sir?'

I suppressed my indignation at this piece of impertinence and answered carefully. 'I have heard tell of the place, but Mrs Shimmin also happens to be my landlady. Was she acquainted with the fellow?'

'Seemed to be,' said Edwards, 'but she wouldn't say 'ow. Me and Alexander carried him as far as Ginny's, for you know 'er door never closes, and it didn't seem right to put a gent in the women's shelter, however dead 'e was. We was just going to send word to the Radcliffe Infirmary for them to come and get him when Mrs S. catches sight of the fellow's face and goes white and red at the same time.'

'Indeed?' I could not imagine the scene: I had never seen that impassive woman turn a hair at anything, no matter how extreme the circumstance.

'Aye, sir,' Alexander confirmed eagerly. 'Looked like she'd seen a ghost, she did. And then she all but pushed us out the parlour and said not to bother the hospital, she'd take charge of him herself.'

I frowned in surprise. 'She would not allow him to be taken to the Infirmary? Why ever not?'

This was quite at odds with what little I knew of the woman, for though she could be both hard and firm in her dealings with tenants, a stout, kind heart beat beneath her stern exterior. She would surely not have denied a poor half-dead soul his best chance at life, unless some harm might come to him there, or some strong reason prevented his admittance, unless —

O God, could it be? That it had come to this!

'She wouldn't tell us why, sir,' Edwards was saying. 'Just said she'd look after 'im, and to see usselves out. If I didn't know better I'd say she was a little touched up 'ere.' And he tapped his sweat-stained hat.

'Perhaps,' Alexander suggested, with ponderous wit, 'she'd been on the gin.'

'Is he still there?' I asked, and in my urgency, my voice broke absurdly, so that both men stared at me with alarm and trepidation. 'Is he? Tell me!' I insisted.

'Aye, sir, if'e's not yet in the morgue,' said Edwards, with a startled glance at Alexander. 'We laid 'im out on the sofa in the parlour and I doubt 'e's stirred from there.'

'Thank you,' I gasped, and, dispensing with the formality of a good-bye, turned from the two astonished men and fairly ran from them up the slippery, mud-churned towpath, sliding and stumbling on the sodden ground, the breath in my breast short and burning, my limbs aching, my eyes astream with sudden, wind-borne tears.

'Careful how you go, sir!' I heard them shout as I reached the next bridge, already panting and breathless, and then the avenue of dark green into which I plunged severed me from their shrinking figures, and I too was lost to their sight.

Ginny opened the door to my frantic knocks, after what felt to me like a lifetime of pounding. She was dressed with her habitual plain neatness, and exuded an air of calm that was almost aggressive in its stoic complacency.

'Thought you might turn up,' she said shortly. 'He's in there.' And she twitched her head towards the room to her left. I pushed past her, staggering down the hall. She closed the door behind me and followed me at a leisurely pace.

'I sent word to your house, but nobody was in,' she told me. 'I didn't know what they'd make of it at the Infirmary, so I told the river-fellows to leave him here. I knew he'd be all right with some brandy inside him and a bit of rest. Hush now, he's sleeping.'

With an extraordinary effort, I stopped myself from bursting into the parlour, and eased the handle down with exaggerated gentleness, opening the door as quietly as my shaking hands and heaving chest allowed.

'Here,' said Mrs Shimmin, 'you can wipe those muddy boots and all. That's a new rug.'

Mad with impatience, I pulled my boots off and cast them aside. Perhaps the thud of them dropping on to the parquet woke him; or perhaps he had been lying quietly conscious for some hours, but when I entered the room Chapman was supine on the day-bed, gazing towards the door. His face was grey and drawn, and his hair plastered like pale, soft weeds to his head, but his blue irises burned feverishly in their bloodshot orbs, seeming almost to be the only part of him still living and capable of expression.

'He's still in his wet things,' Ginny remarked disapprovingly. 'He'd not let me take them off, though I told him he'd catch his death and stain my sofa into the bargain.'

'Mrs Shimmin is right,' said Chapman in a hoarse, soft rasp. 'I have been most discourteous. I sincerely apologize for the inconvenience, Mrs Shimmin. I insist that you send the cleaning bill to me.'

She shook her head in brisk dissent. Was there a hint of abashment in her mien? 'There'll be no need for that, Doctor, I'm sure,' she said. 'Just you lie still and rest now.'

He smiled faintly at this, as if remembering only distantly what smiles were for and when it was appropriate to use them, and turned his livid gaze upon me. But his eyes were blank and expressionless, like those of a statue or carved mask.

'I have imposed long enough on your hospitality, thank you. And if Dr Fraser would be so kind as to assist me, I am sure we can make our way home together. Do not' — and here he raised a white hand, steady and commanding, to forestall any attempt to sway him from his purpose — '*please* do not dream of doing anything further for me, Mrs Shimmin. You have already been far too kind.'

He made another poor attempt at a grin, teeth flashing like an animal's between drawn, white lips. 'Physician, heal thyself — is that not what

197

they say? I'm well enough, just a little shaken up. Fraser will escort me.'

Thus prompted, I moved uncertainly to his side; he slung an arm around me, and I took his frail weight on my shoulders. He was lighter even than he appeared, and had never been a hefty fellow: had it not been for the wiry strength of his grip I should almost have imagined myself bearing up a boy, not a full-grown man. His skin was chill and moist, as though he had but lately been hauled from the waters, or were in the throes of some fever. As we made our way awkwardly past our hostess, like the limping losers in some absurd three-legged race, he grasped at her hand and held it tightly; too tightly, perhaps, for the shadow of a wince crossed her normally impassive features.

'Thank you,' he said in an undertone, 'for not letting them deliver me to the Radcliffe. You may have thought me insensible, but I heard what you said. It would not have done for me to fetch up there: a hospital is the worst of places for gossip — it spreads like a disease, and — well. Questions would have been asked. Speculations made. I am most grateful.'

She quirked her lips in a thin smile and nodded firmly, once.

'It was nothing,' she said, holding his gaze for a long moment, and opened the door.

★　★　★

He would not lie down; that is what I remember most clearly of that dreadful night. He refused absolutely to take to his bed, and I could barely prevail upon him even to sit. To my considerable exasperation (for I knew well enough from my own restless condition that sleep would avail my friend more than anything else), I was forced to half-carry, half-drag him into the kitchen, and heave him into our only armchair, his damp garments dripping unheeded on to the floor. He tried to struggle to his feet, but I pushed him down firmly and, kitten-weak as he was, he could not resist. I did not make a habit of taking strong drink, but there is no better medicine in some situations, particularly with a man at the extreme edge of his physical endurance, who has suffered an icy-cold drenching to boot. I shot a glance at Chapman, whose wet head lolled helplessly against the back of the chair, and reached into our topmost cupboard for the half-bottle of brandy I knew he kept there.

I poured a generous tot into a mug and pressed it to his lips; he felt for it blindly, like a child, and fitted his numbed hands around it as though it held some warmth greater than the false fire of alcohol. I watched as he tipped it back and took a gulp; darted forward as he began to cough and choke, the strong liquor scorching his throat. He brushed me away with feeble impatience.

'I am well enough; I have swallowed a little river-water, that's all.'

'Is there anything else I can get you? Will you have coffee, or — '

I hardly knew what else I could offer him. Our stocks had been sadly depleted since he had left;

I'd had no appetite for what food remained and had allowed it to spoil in the pantry, to Mrs Shimmin's vocal disgust. I saw no point in buying more; or perhaps I had meant to, and forgot. I realized that I could not recall the last time I had eaten.

He shook his head fiercely.

'No,' he said. 'No. This is good. This will do.'

'But your head — a bandage, a compress?'

He had sustained a large and ugly bruise to the rear of his skull; it was purple and soft as overripe fruit, and crusted with blackish blood. I did not know whether he had been the victim of some violent robbery, or had met with his injury by accident, and was unwilling to overtax his strength by asking.

He smiled vaguely, staring at the floor.

'It's not so bad. Just a bump.'

'Stephen — '

He raised his blue eyes to mine, and at once I felt terribly cold, as though sunk in the canal myself, the waters closing over my struggling head.

'As a physician, I assure you,' he said in a low voice, thick, even so, even then, with something like amusement, 'there is nothing more you can do.'

'But Chapman — ' I stammered, 'my dear fellow, I — '

He shuddered so violently that the mug almost jerked from his tight grasp; as he thawed, the chill of the kitchen was settling upon him. I leaped to my feet.

'What a fool I am! Of course; a fire, I shall

build us a fire. You must be — wait, I shall have it going in a moment — let me just — '

Chapman watched me through half-closed eyes, sipping slowly on the brandy as I dashed about the kitchen, trying to gather enough coal and kindling to pile in the grate and warm us both through. The matches spilled from my trembling fingers; but he sat patient and silent, staring at me with a strange, dreamlike expression upon his exhausted face. When the fire at last sputtered into a frail blaze, and I sank to the floor in relief, he put his mug down and scraped his armchair a little closer to the flames. I had draped a blanket, torn from my bed, about his shoulders, and he huddled into it, the rough grey wool dark against his white face.

We sat in silence for a long time, the light of the fire playing mesmerically over our faces, the damp wood crackling and hissing in the silence. I did not know what he was thinking of, what he had seen in that strange and fearsome no-man's-land between life and death, nor what had driven him to venture in so far as to be almost lost to it; and I was afraid to guess. And yet, appallingly, he smiled. It was, however, a smile utterly bereft of warmth; a joyless rictus such as I had seen upon the faces of the whoremasters and denizens of the night when some new depravity or brutality caught their attention, or piqued their base and jaded palates. It was an expression hardly human: I shivered to see it cross the face of my friend.

Suddenly, he shook his head and coughed, retching; he reached for the brandy and I passed it to him. He poured himself a rough measure, the glass neck of the bottle jittering on the mug's clay lip, but did not drink. At last he spoke. His voice was a dry, harsh croak, nigh-on inaudible against the chatter of the flames. It had in it a tone of the deepest despair, a thing I had never hoped to know in him. I bowed my head and did not look at his face; I dreaded what I might find in it.

'What must you think of me, Fraser?' he said softly, ruminatively.

I knew not how to answer; indeed, I hardly knew what I thought, or whether I thought at all. Grief and gratitude were so closely commingled in my heart that I could not tell one from the other.

'I think — I know that you are my friend. That whatever you — that your reasons are . . . '

The words faltered and died in my mouth. I looked across at him helplessly. He watched me curiously, that unnerving smile still haunting his features.

'Did you not, then, receive my letter?'

My heart leaped, a vicious joy blazing in it. So he had not abandoned me without a word, after all! He had attempted to make some explanation or effect some reconciliation at least . . . How selfishly glad I was!

'Letter? No, indeed. I scoured every post, believe me.'

He smiled hollowly. 'I dropped it off for you at Hertford. I did not wish you to have it . . . too soon.'

'I have been somewhat ill recently,' I confessed

— though omitting to explain the reason for my late indisposition. 'I have not been at the college for a fortnight.'

'Ah well. How very like *Romeo and Juliet*! One must never trust to letters — they go too easily astray. So it did not find you — but you found me, in the end.'

'Thank God!' I exclaimed.

He glanced sharply at me. 'That remains to be seen. But you must be wondering, then, whether I have been a victim of some towpath footpad, or of my own evil impulse? I know you, Fraser.'

The question had certainly crossed my mind, but I had quashed it firmly.

'Can you say which?' I remembered the wound at the back of his skull. 'Can you recall?'

He nodded, then winced suddenly at the movement, pain flashing across his face like a twist of lightning.

'Oh, I know, all right. But I am not sure you shall want to, for all that you are my confessor.'

Again he shuddered, as if caught in a sharp blast of wind, though the fire now blazed brightly and the kitchen was growing snug and warm. I jumped up, desperate for movement, for action; something to break the silence that threatened to form again between us like night frost.

'Don't speak,' I said. 'Save your strength — you are shocked, you are chilled to the bone.'

I dashed up to my bedroom; but there were no more blankets to warm him. The river-men, however, had dredged up his coat along with his wretched half-drowned self and left it with Mrs Shimmin; and I had wrung it out as best I could and hung it upon the hat-rack to dry. It was better than nothing; it would do. I grabbed it up and came back into the kitchen, closing the door behind me to keep the heat in. The room smelt of river-mud and spilled brandy; I noticed the bottle was a little emptier than before. I laid the black coat over Chapman's knees. He stared down at it as if he had never seen it before.

'Where did you get this?'

'It was nearby you, in the river. You must have fallen in with it on.'

Fallen; I fervently hoped it was so. An unfortunate accident; dangerous, nearly fatal, but an accident none the less. Chapman fumbled the coat open; it had lost its last button and presented a sorry sight. He seemed puzzled.

'Where are they?' he muttered.

I did not ask what, but stood silently, watching him search and turn the damp garment over slowly, dazedly, in his mud-streaked hands. He thrust one hand deeply into the left pocket; too deeply, indeed, for he got his arm in almost up to the elbow. He pulled it out, found the pocket-flap upon the right, and performed the same manoeuvre. A queer, rattling, choking laugh bubbled up in him, like tar in a pit. It rocked him slowly from side to side, as sobs rack a keening woman.

'What, Chapman,' I whispered, very much unsettled, 'what is it?'

His eyes swam with awful mirth; he wiped them on the bedraggled coat, burying his face in it momentarily, then looked up with that lost and despairing smile I had remarked before.

'I didn't want there to be any blood,' he said emptily. 'No blood, no fuss. Drowning was all I could think of. I was always rather afraid of water — do you remember? Never rowed. Never swam. But there are more terrible things than drowning. I thought it would be a clean end. So I loaded my pockets with stones, every one I could find — '

'My dear fellow, no . . . '

'Yes,' he said. 'I walked into the river. A doctor knows how to die. I remember the fire in my lungs. The freezing cold, the blackness . . . The stones should have weighed me down.' He banged his fist in sudden, agonized fury against the chair-arm. 'They should have kept me down!'

I leaned heavily against the wall, my skull throbbing; I saw again that misty field, pebbles in a gun-case — a noiseless splash, and the river closing over it. Cold was rising again in me like dark water. Chapman shook his head, wrenching at the thin material of the coat as if to tear it apart.

'The lining gave way,' he said, a light, regretful wonderment in his voice, 'and so here am I, a poor sodden would-be suicide with pockets full of holes.'

He bent over the coat, clawed its folds into his two fists, and began laughing again, eerily, silently. His breath was jagged and shallow, as though he were struggling for air. I stood back, helpless and aghast.

At last he let the coat slip unheeded from his lap and reached blindly for the mug of brandy.

He swallowed a little and gazed into the fire, the grin that played about his features fading like a ghost at cock-crow.

'Christ,' he said softly, 'what must you think?'

'I will not judge you,' I said, surprised at the conviction in my own voice. 'Lord knows nobody is worse qualified to do so than I. But you *must* tell me what befell you, Chapman.'

'What I did,' he muttered. The orange flames danced in his shining eyes.

'If you wish; whatever you wish. Whatever will unburden you.'

He closed his eyes and leaned back in the chair. The empty mug swung lazily from his drooping hand. He turned his head away in a gesture of immense and profound tiredness.

'I cannot tell it over. It is all in the letter. Alas! I had planned for it to reach you too late, but not so late as this. My poor friend, what agonies you must have suffered! I never meant to cause such pain.' He blinked at the fire. 'I suppose we never do.'

He sighed — almost a sob — and sank his damp head in his hands, speaking through his fingers.

'Leave me, old man. I'll do well enough alone, now. Don't worry; I shan't attempt to cheat Fate again. I know when I am beaten.'

'But what — '

He turned from me, staring into the snickering flames.

'Leave me, Fraser,' he muttered. 'If you must know, read the note. I can say no more. It is all in the letter.'

206

BOOK FOUR

The Testament of Stephen Chapman

My dear Fraser,

As soon as you read these words, I suspect that you may well guess at once what I have done — what I am, as soon as the ink on these pages is dry, about to do.

Do not start up from your chair, Edward! It is already too late. The events of the past weeks are over and done, and my destiny sealed — for good or ill, who can tell? Nevertheless, I entreat you, do not clutch at your brow, or run off harum-scarum to raise the alarm, or indeed do anything but hold this letter in your hands and read it through, carefully, to the very last word. This final boon I crave of you.

What I have done — will do — cannot be undone by God or Man. All you or I can hope for, my friend, is that you are able at last to understand why I do it. I do not presume to imagine that you might eventually forgive my actions, for my sins are far from venial and this last most mortal of all; but perhaps, in time, you shall.

I hardly know how to begin to explain the state of mind in which I now find myself, nor indeed that misery which has wrenched at my soul these weeks past, when you, if I know you, will have been seeking me vainly in all the wrong places. Dear as you are to me, old fellow, I believe sometimes there is a splinter of ice somewhere in your heart which puts you at one remove — whether below or above, I cannot say — from the rest of the impulsive human race. Hence I fear that much of what I shall tell you will seem as wild and incomprehensible to your phlegmatic soul as the starkest ravings of a lunatic.

Love is a disease; no doubt of it, and one which has proved mortal to many men down the ages — but life too is a disease, taken in the long view. Merely by existing we hasten our own inevitable end. I have always thought it a curious irony that in loving we are truly awakened to life; and yet by waking, by living, we take our first step towards death. The only certain immortality consists in never having truly lived; that, perhaps, is why I was always queerly certain that you should outlast me. The unpierced heart may as well never have beaten at all.

But I am babbling — forgive me. I am so terribly tired. When I glimpse my own face in the glass I am shocked that it is not already sunken and corpse-pale, even translucent, as ghosts are said to be when summoned in séances. It will take more than a table-rapper and some floating muslin to raise me soon! And yet my own body's abiding strength and insolent health continues to affront me. I should be slipping away, staining a white silk handkerchief ruby with delicate coughs, like Violetta in the opera, or little John Keats on his deathbed. But no!

This body is a traitor. It aches to live, Fraser: it has tasted love, albeit tempered with despair; the heart within it has twisted and burned, almost to bloody ashes, and yet the warm fall of dawn light across my hand as I write these words is wondrous to me. I constantly forget my dark purpose in the sheer sensual delight of breathing the sweetness of air, or the astonishing beauty of a spectral sunrise. I am seduced from my destined path a thousand times an hour by tiny and exquisite joys which I never before noted; but I shall follow it none the less. It's true that they cling fastest to this world who are closest to leaving it; so it seems with me. As a doctor, I have always found this phenomenon fascinating; as a philosopher and theologian, no doubt you would disapprove this want of self-control, this lack of resignation to one's fate.

There I go again, ascribing sentiments to you which, for all I know, are quite against your natural temper. I know you are not such a cold fish as you seem, Fraser; but what I do not know is whether you have, deep at your core, enough heart's-fire truly to understand what I am about to divulge. I must trust to your affection for me; I must trust to your discretion. I must put my faith in a hundred things beyond my control; and I must make you once more, as long ago you promised to be, my confessor.

But enough of what I must do; the first and most urgent of my obligations is to tell you why, by the time you read these words, I shall already be dead.

You did your work better than you knew, Fraser. When you told me of Diana's history, I was not as unmoved as I pretended. Oh, all that I said was true enough — my feelings for the lady were and remain unchanged; indeed, the crucible of recent events has strengthened them beyond what I believed possible, and that is why I am taking the only way left open to me to assure her future health and happiness. I really was furious that you had stooped to such a low trick in your attempt to drive a wedge between us, but the damnable thing is that in the end, it was the strength of my love for her that undid me. I was betrayed by my own heart, you might say.

I have Othello's flaw, Fraser, the green-eyed monster that stalks all lovers. Sooner or later each of us feels the breath of this shadow-creature, jealousy, upon our neck; hears its insinuating whisper in our ear, and at last we must heed it, whether we will or no. Sense does not come into it, I am afraid; it is all sensibility. Even you, my friend, must agree that logic and love are rarely on nodding terms.

What was I jealous of, you may wonder. Of what? Why, of everything! Of the men she has known, of the men who wish to know her; of the tradesmen and cousins, of her casual acquaintance, of the whores, even, those poor wretches on whom she lavishes her time and care, unthanked. Of the pillow cradling her head, of the sunlight on her face, of the air she breathes — of everything of her that is not mine. This, you would tell me, is madness, and you would be right, for love is a disease of the mind as well as the body. 'The lunatic, the lover, and the poet / Are of imagination all compact' — never a truer sentiment was expressed!

A lunatic was what I was — what I still am, though now I have yet greater reason to despair. The tragedy of the mad is often that they do not recognize their own madness, but in this respect at least, I was sufficiently self-aware to realize that the exquisite agony of my jealousy was far from rational. I decided to treat my symptoms as I would those of any other disease: I attempted to manage my affliction.

When I first began to fall in love with Diana, I knew that if she suspected the extraordinary force of my emotions, my love-sickness, it would frighten her. She has been betrayed by men before, you see — indeed, you know it better than I. Men who vowed always to love her, never to hurt her. Your friend Hereward was exceptionally convincing in that regard, I believe. I came to understand that she feared violent love as much as passionate hatred. And she was right to. It's the most dangerous thing on Earth, Fraser. It debilitates, it deranges: it destroys.

I love her as she is, do not mistake me; but that painting you left showed me all she could have been. It showed me what had been stolen from her: what she once was, and what she might have become, had life treated her more gently. Whatever else your friend Valenti was, he was certainly talented. That damned painting lives and breathes! And there she sat upon my bed, a flower pressed beneath glass, unspoiled, unchanging, and quite unreachable.

I couldn't bear to look at it, Fraser; it was like seeing that saddest of spectres, the lost ghost of happiness. I determined at once — at last — to confront the original.

I left the house immediately and found her in her study at the shelter. I knocked loudly and peremptorily on the closed door. This detail fired my blood; I knew she kept the door to her room ever open, so as to observe the girls' comings and goings, as well as to provide easy access and counsel to those who desired a private conference. I beat back my indignation as I waited for her to answer my knock. Perhaps she was hearing the sad history of a new arrival — still, I would make her see me. My business would not wait.

After a few moments she opened the door, slipping into the hall and closing it quickly behind her — but not quickly enough to conceal the fact that no woman occupied the chair before the fire. Instead, I saw a pair of long, languorous male legs, crossed at the ankle in a lounging attitude. My heart clenched in my chest; I guessed without being told to whom those elegant limbs belonged, and that suspicion fuelled my disgust and fury.

Diana regarded my pale face and trembling hands with alarm as she leaned her back against the closed portal; God knows what emergency she must have thought I heralded.

'What are you thinking, Stephen — do you know what hour it is? The girls are asleep!'

'Not everyone is, I see. You have a visitor?'

'Yes, I do. A . . . friend of the shelter.'

'But no friend of yours, I trust?'

She noted the change in my demeanour and, with the quick, false intuition of women, found only one thing to which she could readily attribute it.

'Stephen,' she said in low, forbidding tones, 'have you been drinking?'

'No,' I told her. 'I am not drunk. A damned fool is what I am.'

She looked shocked; frightened, even.

'What is wrong, Stephen? What have you done?'

This was too much.

'What have *I* done? I!' It was all I could do not to laugh; agony battled hysteria in my over-full breast. 'What have *you* done, Diana? To whom have you lied? What deceit will you attempt next? That is what I would know!'

Her face was wax-white.

'What can you mean, my love?'

I drew back as she came towards me, her arms outstretched in an attitude of pleading. I could hardly bear the look of innocent sorrow upon her sweet face.

'Tell me first who is in your study, Diana.'

She dropped her eyes. 'I have already done so.'

'His name!'

She raised her gaze to mine, defiantly. 'It is

Lord Kester, and I do not see why that should anger you so.'

So I was right. Lucius Kester, son of the man whose bequest had funded the shelter — scion of a disgraced dynasty, and every jot as wayward and debauched as his father had been before his deathbed conversion to piety and good works. He had made a habit of imposing his company upon Diana when the shelter was first established, pretending a charitable interest in her labours, attempting to worm his sly way into her affections by a hypocritical semblance of concern for the girls newly in her charge. The man hadn't a generous fibre in his whole dissolute being, and I didn't trust him further than I could throw him — and had told Diana as much on many occasions. His visits had been a bone of contention between us while they lasted, but I had not encountered him for some time, and was not aware that his interest had been rekindled. Certainly I had never before found her receiving him at such an extraordinary hour of the night.

The blood roared in my head. What possible reason could there be for her behaviour, but that she was melting before his amorous advances, pressed ardently in my absence? I apprehended what I had before secretly dreaded: that he and his money and his counterfeit sympathy would win her away from me, just as Hereward had seduced her from her poor true lover, Valenti. History was repeating itself before my eyes.

'Why is that man here?'

She lowered her eyes. 'It — it is a matter of business, concerning the finances of the asylum. I was obliged to receive him.'

I snorted with fierce, bitter laughter.

'A matter of business? At this hour? Please do not think me as callow as I have been in the past, Diana. What is his true purpose here? Tell me!'

She quailed at the low fury in my voice, and would not meet my gaze.

'It is urgent,' she muttered. 'It could not wait. I swear to you, there is nothing of what you think in it. Please go, Stephen! I must conclude our conference. It is important, and — confidential.'

'Surely we have no secrets from one another?' I said, sour sarcasm leaking into my tone.

'No, my dear, of course not! Only . . . it is a sensitive matter. I promise, this is the last time. I will tell you all, just as soon as I may. Only please believe me — and I beg you' — here her voice dropped to a panicked whisper it stung my heart to hear — 'please leave us.'

'Us', yet!

'Believe you? How can you ask such a thing, after the lies you have spun — not just to me, but to the other men who loved you, to everyone you have known!'

Her dark eyes flashed and her hand flew to her mouth.

'What other men? There are no other men! O Stephen, this is madness! I implore you, trust me!'

Trust! Ah! That was the word that broke me. The brazen hypocrisy of it. *I*, trust *her*? I felt like weeping, but I breathed deeply and mastered myself, looking hard at her to detect the faintest flicker of remorse when I showed her what I knew. Slowly, I drew the rolled canvas from inside my topcoat, and watched her face pale and eyes widen with guilty apprehension. I shook it out and held it before her, wordlessly; she turned her gaze away, as though it pierced her to look upon it — as well it might!

'Fraser has told me everything,' I said.

There was a moment of silence when her lips moved to form words, and could not, and her slender form swayed in shock; and yet she recovered, and held herself upright once more, and stared at me straight, with a strange, calm resolution.

'What has he told you?' she asked softly, hopelessly, as a prisoner in the dock might ask to hear the charge brought against him.

'That you were the mistress of a painter, and of a libertine,' I said. 'How one died, and the other lives. That you are a curse to all who love you — a whited sepulchre, full of corruption; a beautiful tomb, hungry for the souls of men . . . And I did not believe him! I defended you, fool that I was, because I love you — fool, *fool* that I am!'

'No!' she cried. But I could see in her face that it was true; all true.

'Do not lie to me, Diana,' I pleaded. 'I beseech you, do not lie.'

218

'No! I never . . . You don't understand!' she said.

'You are a widow, of course?' I sneered.

'Yes — why, yes! My husband died young, of a fever . . . '

'Ah yes,' I said. 'Your 'husband', Henry Hereward?'

'I never told you his name,' she whispered, paling.

'Nor your own, it seems, for Fraser says you did not go by Pelham when first he knew you. It is as well that I know. It is better that we part this way, with truth, if not honour, on both sides. Very well. I shall leave you with your latest victim. Good luck to him, and good-night to you.'

I turned to leave, blind with hot tears, but she darted past me quick as thought, pressing herself against the front door, and would not let me pass.

'Let me at least tell you my part of the story,' she begged, and the tears flew from her pale cheeks like dew from brushed leaves. I despised her at that moment, loving and abhorring her with equal fervour. I could not believe another word she said. And still that man, her hateful interlocutor, lounged within, awaiting the conclusion of their 'conference'.

I cast the accursed painting at her feet and pushed her aside roughly, not caring, in my impetuous rage, whether I hurt her. I wrenched open the door, and turned to face her broken figure in the low light of the hall. The innocent, painted gaze of her past self mocked me from the floor. Diana's dark head was bowed over the canvas, her tears spotting the cracked image, as she tried to gather it up, or perhaps rend it, I knew not which.

'I'll hear no more lies,' I assured her in a voice thick with fury, and then I turned my back upon her, and walked away blindly into the driving rain.

I expected no welcome at home, Fraser, for I knew then how deeply I had wronged you with my mistrust. I was crazed, and muddled, and wet through, and knew of only one place that would welcome me in that condition — so I went straight to the Harcourt.

I knew what I needed, and I went and got it. I'm up on the required dosage of that medicine in my own case, and that's more than any tee-totaller (saving your conscience) can claim. Quire kept them coming, but when he locked up, I was still as sober as a theologian. I could not return to our lodgings; I did not know where I should find shelter in weather so foul. So I postponed the decision, determining instead to carry on drinking. I do not seek your blessing for this, Fraser, nor your forgiveness; I merely tell you things just as they fell out.

I think you know the Ox's Head — not as a patron, naturally, but by reputation at least? It is a filthy inn, where whores congregate just beyond the circle of light cast by the single, low-burning gas-lamp on that perilous street. It is the sort of low tavern one imagines thriving in plaguey London before the fire cleansed the slums; a place whose very walls exude squalor and dim, drink-dappled despair. When I first stumbled across it, I confess I was astonished that such a place was suffered to exist, even in the darkest corner of Jericho, for every sort of vice is flaunted and any sordid pleasure openly available for a miserable pittance. Many of Diana's girls once plied there, and some, I regret to say, occasionally lapse so far as to return on slow nights or when drink, poverty or solitary despair overmasters them. The Ox's Head is where the most raddled and disease-racked prostitutes, the most hopeless opium-addicts and inebriates, and the most violent, degraded criminals go to drink, for it turns none away and, moreover, does not close so long as the cloak of night protect its clientèle from whatever they fear most; whether illumination, discovery or sobriety. Naturally, then, it was there that I bent my steps. Where better to lose oneself? Where better, reasoned I, to forget?

I entered, jostling through the crowd in a manner that showed I was in no humour to be approached or trifled with, and got a bottle and glass from the bar: I meant to get as drunk as possible and did not intend waiting upon any-one's pleasure to do so. I took the rough brandy and my tumbler to the darkest corner of that dark place, to brood and seethe, after the indulgent, self-immolating fashion of frus-trated lovers.

I sat drinking, sick with anger and grief, and by now assailed by guilty remorse, both at refusing to hear Diana and at disbelieving you. I tortured myself liberally with the thought of Diana and Valenti together, of Diana and Hereward, of — God forbid!

— Diana and Kester; of the men who had plucked her as one might pluck a beautiful flower and, as casually, trampled her beneath their feet. I longed to save the girl in the picture from a future that was already past; an idiotic, romantic, entirely useless notion. As you may have gathered, I was by this hour somewhat intoxicated. I had reached the sentimental stage of drunkenness, dwelt there a little while, brandied tears poised trembling in my eyes, then descended into self-pitying fury.

It was Sukey Dollond who did it. I should likely have stayed huddled in my shadowy corner, swigging and brooding, until dawn, had she not spied me across the room. That girl has eyes sharp as a cat's, I swear (a damned useful thing in her profession), for she instantly recognized me.

Sukey is a Southwark girl originally, London born and bred, recently escaped from the violent drudgery of servicing sailors to a softer life in Oxford. She was one of the 'regulars' who used Diana's shelter as something between a clinic and a flophouse. Alas, what Diana had meant to be a half-way station for such women as genuinely wanted to exchange their dreadful trade for another more virtuous and useful, has rapidly become a sort of common-room for street-walkers to meet and gossip. I may admit that Diana long ago gave up hope of rehabilitating any but the most promising cases, and resigned herself to the fact that (as you once warned me) many of the whores of Jericho are admirably suited to their profession, and have neither patience nor skill to succeed in any other.

In any case, blowsy little Sukey, all of twenty-one, was one of the latter class; lazy, uneducated, and uninterested in self-betterment save in the practical sense of doing less work for more pay — but with a cheap, gaudy sort of wit and Cockney quickness that made her a popular novelty among the students, just as they might be amused by a mischievous monkey or a talking dog. She had given many a medical student his first lesson in human anatomy, as she never wearied of boasting, and regularly threatened to do the same to the Good Doctor, as she styled me. It was her crude way of flirting, I suppose, which she used with all men alike, whether potential customers for her wares or not.

Indeed, she averred that every man was always in the market for what she offered; some just did not know or could not admit it. When I protested, she made one concession. 'Except the queers,' she said, 'that's a whole different marketplace, let alone stall.' Even you must have encountered the type, I imagine — buxom, brassy, obvious; heavy-handed and light-fingered. They are ten-a-penny, but Sukey was brighter than most; and her exceptionally sharp ears and eyes would, in the age of Queen

Elizabeth, have made of her a wonderful agent of espionage.

Spotting me in my corner of the room, she crossed to greet me, never mind that I was obviously desirous of nothing more than solitary oblivion, and nothing less than company. I sank back into the shadows, clutching my bottle jealously to me — but she had seen that too, and proceeded shamelessly to attempt to cajole me into giving her a tot.

'Fancy seeing you in here, Doctor!' she said, winking at me in that sly, suggestive way she had. 'Doing a bit of chemical research?'

'The deleterious effect of alcohol on the working classes,' I mumbled, trying to edge further into the darkness. I had no wish to encourage her attentions, so neither stood nor offered her my chair. Undeterred, she sat on the corner of my table.

'None of that nonsense . . . Sukey knows what you need, don't she? A nice girl for a little bit of fun? Stop you mooning over that bluestocking sweetheart of yours. What's she done to you now? I thought congratulations was in order?'

She leaned over to look into my averted face, swaying alarmingly.

'You shouldn't be out of bed, Sukey,' I said. She had been laid up with a venereal disease I had seen before in the girls who came down from London or had clients there; a highly unpleasant tropical ailment carried by the sailors from the Dutch Indies, and spread around whilst on shore leave. It began with high fever and a blotchy, violent rash, followed by a few days of sweating and vomiting, but usually went into remission on or about the third day, only to return, redoubled, a week later in the second, more sinister phase of the illness. When I had ministered to her two days previously, she had been shaking and writhing like one possessed; but the remission period was evidently upon her, and so she had discharged herself, walking the streets to make up for lost earnings.

225

She stared at me with amusement.

'It's Saturday night, Doctor! A girl's got to work. Believe me, I'll be back between the sheets soon as I find a bloke willing to join me.'

She winked and nudged me with her elbow. I raised my eyebrows, but made no reply to this crude jest.

'Well, dear, if you're not after a chat, for Christ's sake give me a drink at least!'

She grabbed my empty glass and held it out. She'd already taken plenty, it was clear, but her thirst was not slaked.

'Come on, love,' she wheedled, soft and sloppy, 'pour a girl a glass.'

I was extremely reluctant to do so, as you may imagine, for I have seen these girls in their cups before, and it is a dreadful and degrading spectacle — but she had the air, by now, of a belligerent beggar who has determined upon extracting money from a prospect and will not quit until he succeeds. I reasoned that if I obliged she would be mollified and cease bothering me. So, foolishly, believing myself wise, I poured her a generous measure. Her grey eyes lit up avidly with the surprise of greed unexpectedly satisfied, and she drank half of it off in a gulp.

'That's better,' she said, wiping her chapped lips. 'Now, what did you want to talk about?'

'Curse it, Sukey, I've nothing to discuss with you! If you insist on soliciting — against my express orders, I might add — haven't you better men to sit with on a Saturday night?'

She laughed and her tangled yellow ringlets tumbled forward.

'Plenty more agreeable,' she said, with a knowing smirk, 'but none better,' and she looked up blearily through her sandy eyelashes and winked again. 'Down the hatch, Doctor,' she murmured. 'Join me, won't you?'

I shook my head. 'That stuff is no good for you — worse than usual, in your weakened state. You are not well, Sukey. Don't you remember, I said that even if you felt better, you must stay in the sick-room and rest!'

The heady stench of brandy gusted into my face as she laughed again.

'Don't you worry about me, dear! It's you I'm concerned about. What'll us girls do if you die of melancholy? What'll Our Lady do?' (For that was the girls' impudent nickname for Diana, which they called her by when she was out of earshot or her back was turned.) Her sneering tone angered me, and I forgot myself.

'This has nothing to do with Mrs Pelham, and I'll thank you to speak of her with respect!'

My petulance did not move her; Sukey had seen far worse displays of anger from her clients, as the cuts and bruises she frequently sported could attest.

'Nothing to do with her, eh?' she drawled, smiling. 'And nothing to do with Lord Lucky's being back in town, either, I'll wager? Come up again from the country, with a purse full of money and a heart full of 'charitable intent', and don't we know it!' She leaned closer and

added, *sotto voce*, 'Never mind what his britches is full of — you don't need to be a
seamstress to tell. Didn't take *him* long to
come prowling round his favourite place again.'

I tried to appear sanguine and careless, but
her words unsettled me greatly. So the visit I
had interrupted was not the first of late — O
God, even in her absence, Diana deceived me
still!

'Making eyes at your fee-ancy, ain't he?'
Sukey continued, relishing my discomfiture.
'Coming over all Gladstone, wanting to rescue
us street-girls with one hand and topple our
virtuous Lady with the other. He don't fool
me, though he's pulling the wool over *her* eyes
all right — you'd think he was a frigging
deacon, all the high and mighty moral noises
he was making tonight! Fair turned my stomach, it did. He used to be fun, and generous
with it. A bit too free with his fists, but a girl
can't have everything.'

This piece of gossip confirmed my worst
suspicions. The man the girls called Lord
Lucky was the same Lucius Kester Diana
had been entertaining earlier, a minor viscount with more expensive and contemptible
vices than he had thousands in the bank
— of which there were not a few. The early
death of his father (though some said, not
early enough) — the very same who had
willed half his fortune to establish the refuge
in Victor Street — meant he had come into
his title and inheritance by eighteen, an age
at which young men, especially those in

whom dissipation is tantamount to an heredi-
tary disease, need most closely to be
watched. His guardian, an elder cousin called
Charles, who was an erstwhile acquaintance
of mine, was, alas, even further gone in
debauchery than Lucius himself, and had
allowed his ward the run of his fortune, so
long as he was invited to share in its pleasures.

A few months ago Kester had made rather a
nuisance of himself about the shelter, hypocriti-
cally professing an interest in Diana's
rehabilitation work, but keeping one eye on the
rescued girls — especially the youngest and
most vulnerable — with a view, as it subsequently transpired, to luring them in to cater
for his decadent circle at the John Wilmot
Club. The Club, named in dubious honour of
the legendary debauchee and rake John Wilmot,
the second Earl of Rochester, was notorious for
its sinister orgies, and had been the scene of
some of Kester's most whispered-about indiscretions.

This had not, apparently, come to the ears of
Diana; for I was morally certain that she would
not have permitted him to set foot over her
threshold had she heard the black rumours
concerning him. I had spoken to her a number
of times on the subject of Kester and his
unsavoury reputation, but hypocrites make
excellent dissemblers, and she properly (and
infuriatingly) refused to believe ill of the man
until presented with definite proof. She insisted
that his interest was sincere, and that he was

generously condescending to involve himself in the project to which much of his father's money had been dedicated. Hence I was helpless to persuade Diana of the danger he represented to any woman, let alone one such as she, who combined beauty with charity, and intelligence with an optimistic, almost naïve, innocence.

I had been relatively absent from the shelter these past few weeks, working on a series of experiments at the Radcliffe with Professor Marstone, so had not witnessed Kester's recent visits. But now, as I realized what could and might well happen this very night in Diana's study with that man — who was perhaps drunk, possibly invigorated by cocaine or some other noxious stimulant — I became seriously concerned for her safety, both physical and moral.

Idiot! What had I been doing, sinking into sottish self-pity while she was sitting alone and defenceless against that rake's improper advances? I would go to her. I must!

As you may have gleaned from the lurid and contradictory impulses besetting me, I was by now far drunker than I believed myself to be, and when I rose to leave I staggered and swayed, clutching the table for support. Sukey pushed me back down on the bench, and helped me to another few fingers of brandy, swigging her share directly from the bottle.

'Oh dearie me,' she said solicitously, 'you are in a bad way. So it *is* that what's got you riled up. I don't blame you, but there's no harm in him these days, I'm sure! He was most respectful when I saw him tonight — just as quiet and pious as a Bible-lamb!' She grinned. 'His Lordship likes to visit after dark, see, so as to do good by stealth. Matter of fact, they was still *conferring* when I sneaked out — that was about ten o'clock, I suppose. She must have been very interested in what he was saying, for she didn't notice me leave, though I wasn't too quiet about it.'

Since ten! A conclave of two hours could be nothing but seduction — or conspiracy, against what or whom I could not fathom, but my jealous blood, laced with bad liquor, was beginning to race. I leaped to my feet, but Sukey darted out a grubby broad hand, quick as a hawk and as strong, it transpired, as steel, to restrain me.

'No — stay,' she said, decisively. 'I remember now, he said he had a party to get to later on . . . somewhere beginning with W, Wilcote, I think, a friend called John. He begged Our Lady to accompany him — he said it was to be most elegant and refined — but she could not be persuaded, though he described it beautiful, like he'd seen Heaven shining in a dream and remembered a piece of it.'

'Wilcote?' I knew of no such town. 'Are you certain that was the place? Wolvercote, don't you mean?'

She tossed her head impatiently.

'No, no, it was Wilcote, or Woolmot, something like that. What's it matter? He'll be long gone by now, and Our Lady saying her prayers.

So you and me can have another drink, can't we?'

She sighed smugly at her conclusion, and reached again for the bottle, but I stayed her hand.

'Was it Wilmot, Sukey — John Wilmot — can you remember? Tell me!'

A smile of recognition dawned, and her eyes brightened like those of a backward child who has unexpectedly stumbled across a correct answer.

'Wilmot — why yes, that was it! One of Lucky's friends, I suppose. I thought it was that sort of name.'

'John Wilmot is no friend of his — or anyone's,' I muttered.

So he had a rendezvous at the Wilmot Club, and had had the damned temerity to invite Diana along, as though it were a garden-party or a tea-dance, knowing full well she would refuse, but laughing up his sleeve at her the whole time! It was insupportable.

I rummaged in my pocket and spread all my money upon the table; I happened to be carrying more than usual about my person, and Sukey's grey eyes sparkled at the sight of it.

'Lor',' she said, 'you *are* on a spree! What's all that for, now?'

I gathered the coins into a sliding, shining pile and pushed it towards her.

'It's for you, Sukey,' I said, 'on condition that you return at once to the shelter, and rest — not just tonight, but tomorrow too. This should cover your losses.'

She squinted suspiciously across at me. 'How d'you know what I make of an evening?'

I shrugged. 'I wouldn't presume to guess, but I know you have not been well — lost your bloom a little, perhaps — and moreover you're exhausted from your illness. Take the money, Sukey, and go back to Victor Street.'

Her eyes narrowed and hardened.

'What you saying? Don't think I'm up to it? Too old and wrung out, am I?'

Exasperation made me reckless: I should not have said what I did, but I wanted to impress on her the gravity of her situation and the hopelessness of plying her trade further that night.

'For God's sake, Sukey, nobody wants a sick whore!'

'And nobody,' she said softly, viciously, 'gives a whore, specially a sick one, money for nothing in this world, though I can't answer for the next. What d'you *really* want from me, Doctor?'

'For you to take greater care of yourself!'

She laughed scornfully. 'Don't give me that! You're all the same, dancing around what you're really after, pretending to be moral, hating yourselves and scared of us. Come on now. What you paying me for?'

'Believe me, Sukey, I have no ulterior motive — '

' — whatever the bleeding hell one of them is — '

' — my concern is only for your well-being — '

'Well, if you don't want me to go with a

233

feller in here and earn myself a bit of honest cash, who *do* you want me to go with? Because I don't take no charity!'

I made no reply. Her voice softened and warmed, her eyes searching my own.

'If it was you, Doctor, I wouldn't take money. I wouldn't tell Our Lady; I wouldn't say nothing to a soul. We all got something we want, ain't we? Even you?' She dropped her eyes in something grotesquely like modesty. 'Even me.'

I shook my head. I could say nothing without hurting her; enraging her, even. But it was as if I had faded like a ghost: she stared through me, supplying her own answer.

'Not good enough for you, I suppose. Don't you think I know that? Never stopped anyone before, though they curse themselves after, God knows. Men. Christ! Was there ever a stupider animal? When it's guarded like the Crown frigging Jewels you'll kill yourselves to get at it, and when it's offered you on a platter you'd rather eat poison. No wonder Our Lady's got so many admirers. Me, on the other hand . . . well, maybe you're right. Too worn-out, too sickly, that's me. I ain't even good enough for Lord Lucky no more, never mind that I know what *he* likes, and there's not many come back for more of that. But fresh blood's what he's after.'

'What do you mean?'

She glanced fleetingly at me, recalling my presence.

'When I left tonight I went out the back way,

and who should I see but Mary Ann skulking around opposite; shrank back into the shadows, like she was waiting for a particular gent and didn't want nobody else bothering her. Well, I give her a wave and she near jumped out of her skin. I asked about her appointment and she said his Lordship said to wait for him: he was going to a party and promised her a crown after if only she'd come along. Well, I've been to a few of Lord Lucky's gatherings — not the fancy-dress ones, mind, I steer clear of that lot — and I told her she'd be expected to earn her money, but that a crown was a damn good price, what with her being only fifteen with no tits to speak of, and not even a virgin.'

'So she stayed? He took her?'

'More than once, I should think,' said Sukey archly, and started toying with the mess of coins before her, stacking the farthings and pennies into unsteady piles and pushing them over again with the tips of her ragged nails.

Mary Ann was a girl who had appeared a few weeks before. An orphan, she had been beaten, abused and whored out by her stepfather since the age of twelve to supply him with drinking-money. She was a thin, mousy creature who looked much younger than her years (it was doubtless this which had piqued Kester's interest) and her backwardness and simplicity were such that they amounted almost to a mental defect. It made me shudder to think that Mary Ann might be in Kester's hands, and those of his fellow Club members.

I'd known a few of these rakish types in passing, through Magdalen friends, and I had laughed along with everyone, half-disbelieving and half-scandalized at the tales they told over port and cigars of the Club's degenerate and sordid activities. But since I had come to work at the shelter, since I had understood the degradation these girls withstood daily, I had felt ashamed that I hadn't had courage at the time to take the boasting culprits outside and knock them down. I could not let a girl — nay, a child — so fragile in health and understanding as Mary Ann, suffer such men's depraved attentions.

'Don't worry, Doctor,' said Sukey, reading my expression, 'after what she's already gone through, she'll survive.' A smile ghosted her lips. 'That's what we do.'

Her face in the half-dark was like that of an ancient goddess or carven mask from the Orient; impassive, sensual and crude. Though none knew better than I that she was neither strong nor hard as she seemed; that she deserved protection as much as any woman, however low fallen, looking at that cruel loose mouth on her, I could hardly make myself believe it. But Sukey was not in danger from any man tonight (in fact, rather the reverse) whereas Mary Ann — and, perhaps, still, Diana — most certainly were. Through the sottish miasma of my thoughts, an idea swirled; at the time, it seemed a wonderfully clever solution.

Sukey was evidently determined not to retire

this evening, and was convinced that the money I offered required some favour in return. Mary Ann would by now already have gone with Kester, and I was tolerably certain I knew where.

'Very well, Sukey,' I said, 'if you insist upon working tonight, here's your chance, and an easy job too. There's that much again for you if you go at once to the rooms above the Tolling Bell in Pembroke Street, and take Mary Ann out of there. That's where the Wilmot Club convenes; they have kept a suite there for years, and they dare not use any part of college property these days, for fear of being caught and sent down.'

Her eyes glittered with interest.

'You know plenty about this Wilmot bloke, for an upstanding doctor,' she said. 'Could it be you wasn't quite so full of moral scruples once upon a time?'

'Never mind how I know,' I said, 'just go there, and get Mary Ann away. Do anything you have to.'

She slanted an eyebrow. 'Anything?'

'Yes, Sukey. Say . . . I don't know, say that she is ill — the pox, or the clap, or whatever will frighten them. Say she's half-gone with it already — you know how simple she is — they'll believe easily enough that she is soft in the head.'

'And what if they cut up rough? You know as well as I that rich boys don't like having their toys took off of 'em, not when they've paid in advance.'

'But didn't Kester promise her the money after?'

'If she's lucky, and a bruise or two to remember him by.'

'Then she is not bought and paid for!'

She chuckled grimly. 'Makes no difference. Quality's used to getting everything on tick.'

A devil entered my soul.

That is the only way I can describe it, Fraser, and in a fashion that you, above all people, will understand. I am not a paragon among men; I have gambled and drunk, cursed and caroused; I have given in to my lust and greed and — oh, many temptations that may beset a youth. Any venial sin you care to name, I have probably committed, if no more than the average fellow of my age and station. But I have never broken my Hippocratic oath and I had hoped never to do so, either by omission or commission, until that demon, born of drink and fury, whispered to me precisely how I should exact my revenge upon Kester.

Primum non nocere: this is the guiding principle of the oath, and of all the doctors that ever lived, from Hippocrates on. Do not seek to infect where you can cure; do not break where you can mend; never hurt where you can heal. First and last, *do no harm*.

'First,' I told Sukey, 'you must tell him you are a gift.'

Her brow creased. 'What?'

'A gift from an anonymous admirer. Get Mary Ann away, and if they kick up a fuss — only if they complain, mind — offer yourself

238

instead. A real grown woman instead of a skinny, addled girl, sent to do whatever he bids. He's used you before, you say — well, why not again, especially when he can have you for free? Toffs are no less avaricious than common men; if they see a shilling in the street they will pick it up, and if they are offered something *gratis*, they will take it, and no questions asked.'

Sukey thoughtfully sipped the last lick of brandy in her glass.

'I never reckoned you'd be so full of ideas, Doctor,' she said drily. 'Proper little libertine, ain't you?'

'I only wish to help Mary Ann,' I told her stiffly. 'And since you scorn my charity, and insist on working for what was freely given, I am enlisting your assistance.'

'Oh, don't get me wrong,' she said, 'I don't mind Lord Lucky, and I'll gladly swap places with Mary Ann, for I'm accustomed to his ways and she ain't. I'm just surprised at you, I suppose.'

'Well, you should not be,' I said brusquely. 'No matter what superior airs you may think I affect, as you so astutely observed, us men are all the same at bottom, and I am as much a man as anyone else.'

'Oh,' she said with a darkling grin, 'very much more so, I should think.'

She stood and made a brisk toilet, brushing the worst of the ash and grime from her dress and wiping smutches from her skin with a licked finger. She pinched her cheeks, bit her lips and shook her curls, and now with the brandy-flush in her face, and the candle-light shining in her grey eyes, she was quite unrecognizable as the pallid drab who had accosted me earlier. She looked like the mother of all Magdalenes, as though there was nothing she could nor would not do — for there was something magnificent in her then, Fraser, something elementally powerful and fierce; and I was almost afraid of what I had done.

Then she tossed her head, and walked away swiftly and steadily, out into the foul night and on to the Tolling Bell.

I thought of the disease swarming in her body, relishing the irony that Kester, who had ruined so many, should be ruined so in his turn — for the pathogen stays in the blood like malaria, and once infected, there is no true cure. Oh, awful though it sounds, I confess I was thoroughly pleased with my night's work, Fraser — for I flattered myself that I had, by proxy, both punished my rival, and prevented the violation of an innocent.

And I was left alone with no company save an empty bottle, a ravaged heart, and the vengeful devil who had made his home in my soul.

I woke the next morning beset by more than one devil, I assure you, Fraser; a whole circle of hell seemed to have emptied its demons into my skull. My head banged and throbbed like a cracked bell; my stomach twisted like an eel, and my mouth felt dry and sere as a clean-picked desert bone.

There was, however, far worse to come. As I struggled upright, cowering from the harsh blast of sunlight that dazzled my shrinking eyes, it dawned upon me that I was not in my own bed, nor even in our home on Canal Street, but lying in a room I had never seen before in my life.

As you may imagine, myriad explanations of how I had awoken in a strange bed, in a strange house, raced through my bewildered mind, each more awful than the last. I lay, fully dressed, upon but not between the unclean sheets of a sagging bed. The bedroom might equally have belonged to a Jericho working-girl, an undiscriminating boarding-house, or indeed an honest drudge whose struggle to keep up appearances was proving all too unequal. The bedstead was narrow and of iron; the mattress at once thin and lumpy. The curtains bedecking the cracked and grimy window-panes were cheap frayed cotton, their gaudy floral print faded by the sun. The blanket and sheets were coarse and worn. The wallpaper had peeled off in patches near the ceiling and bubbled up elsewhere; due, no doubt, to the damp that also explained the chamber's pervasive, musty odour.

Before venturing outside the room, I ascertained with relief that I was still in possession of my valuables — my pocket-watch, cigar-case, and so forth — before twisting the doorknob and stepping out of my dilapidated sanctuary into the house itself.

Thankfully, there was no-one on the landing,

and every other door was closed. I had no desire to intrude on or startle any of the house's sleeping inhabitants (my watch informed me that it was but a quarter of seven o'clock in the morning), so I slowly and softly descended the stairs.

My suspicion that I had not strayed far from Jericho grew stronger as I tiptoed down the squealing treads, for the abode itself was built on the same pattern as our own little cottage; on the first floor a large bedroom at the front, with two smaller behind it, and on the ground, a narrow hallway with the parlour off it and the kitchen at its end, at the heart of the house.

As I squatted upon the bottom stair and attempted, my clumsy hands shaking, to lace my boots (for I had come down in naked feet, for quietness' sake), the door to the kitchen eased open and a square unkempt head poked around it.

'Ah,' it said ironically. 'You're up, I see?'

The door opened fully and I beheld Ginny Shimmin, our landlady and also proprietress of an informal sort of hotel on Wellington Street which provided temporary accommodation — usually measurable by the hour — to the street-girls of Jericho and their clients when the weather was too cold, or the customer too dainty, to conduct the transaction *al fresco*.

Ginny's house, like the Ox's Head, was open for business around the clock, and she was said never to sleep — partly so as to free up a bed for amorous guests, but mainly to be on the alert for new arrivals. Her ear was unnaturally quick to discern the footsteps of those who would sneak off without paying the bill — and, more sinisterly, the cries of girls who had inadvertently brought back a 'bad 'un'. The girls at the shelter whispered that when she was not inspecting her other slum properties, she was always to be found in her back kitchen, seated in a massive black rocking-chair, staring into the fire with eyes half-slit like a watchful dog's; never moving, ever vigilant.

I commenced a stammering, dry-mouthed apology, but she waved me into silence.

'Don't you worry, love,' she said in her warm Oxfordshire burr, 'it wasn't half as busy yesternight as Saturdays usually are — the unseasonable weather, I suppose — so I didn't lose anything by taking you in. Couldn't have lived with me conscience if you'd been robbed and murdered anyway, not in me own street. Got lost on the way home, did you, dear?'

I rose, my boots half-laced, and tried to thank her, rummaging in my trouser-pockets for money to cover the expense of my stay (enough for four or five normal periods of residency, I guessed) — but was dismayed to find them quite empty.

'I do not know what to say, nor how to thank you,' I muttered. 'I was sure I had a dozen shillings on me yesterday — I cannot have spent so much in a single evening . . . I confess I don't know where it has gone, and I have nothing with which to recompense you for your hospitality.'

She grinned. 'You did the exact same thing

last night, Doctor — tried to pay me out of your pocket, but I said then and I'll say now, fluff and buttons ain't no use to me. Besides, you're a good tenant, and you're kind to the girls around here — and if you do right by them you do right by me, so I don't mind returning the favour.'

And with this she closed the door firmly, leaving me standing penniless, perplexed and extremely dishevelled, in the hallway. I finished tying my boots and headed for the door, but as I opened it on to a painfully sunlit, glistening street, Ginny's grey, tousled head reappeared.

'If you're wondering where your money went to, you could ask Sukey Dollond.'

'Sukey?' I echoed. The name provoked a series of dim, jumbled recollections; a dark-blonde curl twisted around chapped fingers, a flash of grey eyes, the sour savour of bad brandy.

'You was muttering about her as you come in last night. Sukey this, Sukey that, don't get into trouble . . . I ain't saying she took it, mind; but she might know where it went.' One eyelid fluttered briefly in a wink. 'If you catch my meaning.'

'I am most indebted to you, Mrs Shimmin,' I said with as much dignity as I could muster, bowed, and left the house wondering what on earth I had done — and why — the night before.

I tell you Fraser, had the physical torments of my hang-over been the most painful experiences to be visited upon me that day, I should have been fortunate indeed. But by the time I had repaired to the early-opening coffee-house on Little Clarendon Street, where you and I used to meet of a morning — do you remember? — I had, to my regret and mortification, managed to piece together the previous night's events in rather too great detail.

Some things remained obscure to me, of course, such as exactly how much money I had pressed upon Sukey (for she had counted it, not I), and the precise nature of the instructions I had given her — but the gist of my behaviour and intentions I recalled only too well.

I remembered the jealousy and despair that had brought me to the Ox's Head; I remembered Sukey's tipsy wheedling and clumsy advances, and above all, her unsettling news that Lord Kester had Mary Ann in his power. And finally, I remembered what I had paid her to do; and was beyond reckoning aghast at myself.

Finishing my coffee with a grimace, I started back towards Victor Street and the shelter. It was by now eight o'clock on Sunday morning, and I knew Diana would be preparing herself for another long, thankless day spent attempting to improve, however infinitesimally, the lot of the unfortunates under her roof and her care. I shrank to recollect the baseless suspicions I had entertained regarding her indulgence of Kester; how terribly unworthy of her I was, especially after my behaviour of last night! My step faltered; but I resolved not to compound my errors of the evening before with a failure of courage the morning after, and kept upon my way. I was filled with remorse at having refused to hear her side of your story — for does not the proverb tell us that *tout comprendre, c'est tout pardonner?* Since I had known Diana, she had been the very model of womanly modesty, industry and forbearance: did that count for nothing? What right had I to judge her without allowing her to speak in her own defence?

My principal motive in venturing there (apart, of course, from apologizing to Diana for my appalling behaviour) was to ascertain whether Mary Ann had yet returned — for, having nowhere else to go, she must perforce have made her way back to her proper bed in Victor Street, or else passed the remaining hours of darkness on the dangerous streets. If Mary Ann was safe — and, perhaps as vitally, if she could tell me anything of what had occurred at the Wilmot Club last night — I might be able to undo or ameliorate some of the damage I had already caused.

If Mary Ann was not there, and neither was Sukey . . . Well, I dreaded to think what that might mean, and forced the idea from my mind until such time as (God forbid!) I should be confronted with its stark and ominous reality.

My feet dragged as I approached the shelter; despite my attempt to look rationally upon the situation, and give the events as I recalled them the most optimistic interpretation, I quailed to think what I had done. The black logic of my overwrought brain told me that I had as good as ravished Sukey myself by sending her to Kester — what mitigation was it if I had thereby rescued the vulnerable Mary Ann from a dreadful ordeal?

The fact remained that I had placed Sukey directly in the path of a man whom I knew to be violent and vicious, and (less troubling, but still reprehensible) I had also given her money for sexual services. No matter that Sukey had not attended to me personally; no matter that in so doing she had saved a child from abuse — I was still a cur, and a pander. And to Kester, of all people! On sober reflection, I could hardly apprehend the horrible depths to which I had, however briefly, sunk.

My poor head ached with the implications of my drunken act of revenge. I hoped fervently that both girls were safe under Diana's roof, rolling their insolent eyes in exasperation at her piety, groaning as she roused them from their too-brief slumbers — but somehow, I suspected that my visit to the shelter would bring no relief from my mounting anxiety.

In this, however, as in so many things recently, I was wrong — for as I mounted the scrubbed stone steps and rang the bell, I glimpsed a pale, blank face gazing at me moonishly from a first-floor window. Could it be — Mary Ann? Diana quartered the younger girls in the upstairs dormitory, for she considered them more impressionable, and more vulnerable, and that was the room in which she herself slept, the better to keep an eye on them.

You may imagine my astonishment and relief, Fraser, when the door opened to reveal Sukey, standing with eyebrows raised and hands on hips, for all the world like a stern matron preparing to berate a late-returning son.

'Oh, it's *you*,' she said, unsmiling.

'Sukey!' I cried. 'How delightful to see you! You must forgive my words of last night — I confess that drink had the better of me, and I most humbly apologize.'

'Never mind all that,' she snapped, moving aside to let me pass. 'You'd better come in.'

I entered the cool darkness of the atrium, where, to my surprise, I discovered a gang of girls huddled in the hallway, milling in confusion like so many flustered chickens.

'Why, what is all this?' I wondered aloud. 'Should you not all be at breakfast? Where is Mrs Pelham? I must speak with her.'

Sukey closed the door and crossed her arms, reproach and accusation in her look.

'That's the thing, Doctor,' she said. 'We don't know. Our Lady's missing.'

I will not describe here the days and nights of confusion that followed, for they were as fruitless as they were frustrating. The local police-force was singularly uninterested in Diana's disappearance, their entire efforts apparently devoted to investigating a daring and lucrative series of burglaries at Christ Church. The mysterious vanishment of a respectable, charitable lady evidently came a poor second to discovering the avaricious felon. A certain Sergeant

Beaton, who openly disapproved of Diana's work, seeming to regard her as no better than the girls in her charge, even suggested that she had 'taken herself on a little holiday', something that 'these flighty sorts' were wont to do; I was advised 'not to fret about it, sir, for these girls usually turn up sooner or later'. I came extremely close to punching him on the nose and thanking him not to refer to Diana in such disrespectful terms. Instead, I held my peace and, concluding that the proper authorities could or would not help me, resolved to conduct my own enquiries.

I asked after her on the streets and in the homes of her acquaintance. Her cousin Cornell had no idea whither she might have gone; nor did any of the girls in the refuge, few of whom could even swear to when or where they had seen her last. Reluctantly, I attempted to secure an audience with Lord Kester, whose malicious hand I thought I descried in her sudden disappearance — but I was told by the porter at Magdalen that my Lord was at best an irregular visitor to the college, and, his lodgings being beyond its walls, he could throw no light on the matter. His landlady listened suspiciously to the story I poured out on her doorstep (for she did not do me the honour of inviting me in), laughed shortly, and said that he came and went as he pleased, and that sometimes she did not see him for weeks on end. Even my attempted bribe, paltry as it was, cut no ice; she sneered at the coins in my hand, and shut the door smartly in my face. I received much the same reception at the Tolling Bell, the land-lord of which steadfastly refused to utter a word regarding the whereabouts of any of the Wilmot Club members; his mouth, too, no doubt, silenced by silver.

I was in despair. All I could do was throw myself into my own, and now Diana's, work — for the girls still needed shelter, food and medical care, and I knew that my selfless dar-ling would desire above all things that the routine of the house she had worked so hard to establish should not be broken, even in her absence — even in the event of her —

But I am getting ahead of myself. Let me say only that the next few days were torture to me; that I barely slept, and that every waking second was consumed by thinking of her, wor-rying about her, and searching ceaselessly for her. I must add that Sukey, extraordinarily enough, proved invaluable during this terrible time. I have often noticed that it is under the greatest duress, in the most trying and distress-ing situations, that the true quality of a person's character is revealed — some buckle under a burden laid suddenly upon them, while others summon new strength from the very adversity that besets them. Sukey was one of the latter type, and I thanked God for it.

Once she realized Diana was gone, and that no-one could say for how long, or whether she might ever return, she grasped at once the absolute necessity of carrying on as normal for everybody's sake. Without her I should have crumbled, Fraser; that is a dead certainty. She took over the domestic arrangements, becoming a veritable mother-hen to her wayward sisters; counting them in and out again, as eagle-eyed as a young Ginny Shimmin, cooking their meals and organizing all the thousand other little things Diana had once taken upon herself, from the laundry to the daily grocery-shopping.

From the day of Diana's absence, not a drop of liquor passed Sukey's lips; nor was she ever abroad for longer than it took to fetch in the washing or pay off a tradesman. Her transformation was quite remarkable; and though she retained her customary irony and levity, this was now directed towards raising the girls' spirits, and had far more of generosity in it than weary malice. She was quite adamant that 'Our Lady' would return, and devoted herself to ensuring that she would have nothing to complain about when this inevitably came to pass; not the cleanliness of the halls, nor the industry of the inmates. Despite the sickness sleeping in her blood, she was utterly indefatigable, consistently cheerful, and apparently tireless. She took many a care from my shoulders and on to her own, and when I felt ready to drop with grief and weariness, would always offer a wry remark or a helping hand. Oh! I wish you could have seen it, Fraser, you whose faith in the redeemability of humanity has not always, I know, been unshakable — it would have gladdened your heart and restored your hope. Sukey was my rock: I could not have borne those days without her.

It was the Friday afternoon of that week — nigh on five days since Diana's disappearance, after I believed I had exhausted every possible line of enquiry, and had begun to repose more faith in prayer for her return than in my ability to bring it about, that I made my first real discovery. The shelter was almost empty of residents, and Sukey was at the Covered Market. I determined to use this temporary lull to discover from Mary Ann exactly what had passed on Saturday night, hoping to unearth some fresh clue to Kester's whereabouts.

Sukey's account of events after she left the Ox's Head had been precise, brief, and unilluminating; according to her, she had shown up at the Tolling Bell as instructed, entered the party, and discovered Kester gone. The rest of the fellows were lounging about the room in attitudes of mazed and exhausted satiety, the air was heavy with opium-fumes, and she had found Mary Ann curled half-naked on a chaise-longue, stupefied with laudanum. Seeing that nobody present was in any condition to object, she had half-dragged, half-carried the waif downstairs, flagged down a cabby, and returned to the refuge with her charge at around four in the morning. She could not say whether anyone had been in Diana's study at that time; only that the door was closed, and Diana was not in her bed.

I had, of course, already quizzed Mary Ann as to whether she had seen or heard anything of Diana on that evening, but she had merely

252

mutely shaken her head, and, given her debilitated state, I had pressed her no further. Still, the notion of Kester being at the root of the mystery stole over me until it was an *idée fixe* — for in my desperation, I grasped at any straw of hope as avidly as a drowning man. What had been the meaning of his visits — and her toleration of them? And where was he now? I must find some clue, for I could not bear hopeless inaction, and my brain was tearing itself to pieces, picking over the scanty facts again and again with an obsessive restlessness dangerously near to monomania.

It was about two in the afternoon when I went upstairs bearing a glass of hot milk, the beverage Mary Ann customarily took at this time, and rapped gently on the dormitory door.

'Come in,' she said, with her usual timorousness, as though it were a bailiff and not a friend who knocked without. I pushed the door open: Mary Ann lay in her cot, curled foetally, her gaunt frame lost in the thick woollen nightgown with which the ever-watchful Sukey had provided her against the February chill.

I set the milk on the table beside her bed; she sat up, regarding it without much interest, and her eyes refocused on the street below the window, where a couple of carters were standing by their impatiently tossing horses, passing the time of day. I had noted that Mary Ann could sit or lie for hours like this, gazing blankly out of the casement at whatever passed in the street, whether a full-blown fist-fight or the gentle swirl of fallen leaves in the running gutter. On these occasions she seemed to have fallen into some kind of reverie or trance, for she was hard to rouse, and her whole soul came into her brown, darting eyes as she avidly watched the life going on beyond the pane. The poor girl was unlettered and had very little conversation; I suppose that she had learned under the sway of her cruel stepfather to find her entertainment where she could.

'You ought to drink it, Mary Ann,' I said. 'It will help you rebuild your strength.' For she had developed a slight fever after her Saturday-night ordeal, and was not quite recovered yet.

She shrugged, never tearing her gaze from the inaudible but animated conversation across the street.

I offered the glass to her, and she took it with a sigh, like a beleaguered child. I lowered myself on to the bed opposite.

'Mary Ann,' I said seriously. 'I wish to speak to you about what happened on Saturday before Sukey arrived. It may not be pleasant — but you must tell me everything you can remember of that evening.'

She buried her face in her glass and gulped, perhaps hoping a sudden willingness to drink would mollify me. I continued undeterred.

'Sukey says that a certain gentleman offered you a large sum to accompany him to a party on Pembroke Street. Now, is that true?'

She gave a tiny but definite nod.

'Good girl. Of course I understand your regret at giving in to temptation, especially when you were doing so well in your classes and had taken such an interest in Bible-study; but I am not here to judge, Mary Ann, only to see if perhaps you know something — anything, my dear — which might help me find Mrs Pelham.'

She stared at me a moment, uncertainly, perhaps wondering whether she could trust me with her tale; then conquered her doubts, looked me square in the eye, and began to speak.

'It was the gentleman they calls Lord Lucky, Sukey and the other girls,' she said hesitantly. I nodded in encouragement.

'He said he wanted a companion for a party, and was prepared to pay me an awful lot of money to go with him — but when I got there . . . Lord! It was like no party *I* ever been to.'

'Go on, Mary Ann,' I said, smiling.

'Oh! It was awful — a fearful lot of men, all dressed nice like his Lordship, all with voices like your own, Doctor — saving your presence — quality, I mean.'

'Did you recognize any of them?'

I reasoned that if she could describe any of the men there gathered, at least I might identify the culprits. And though I knew well enough that no judge in the land would take the word of a whore over that of an Old Etonian, a description would give me an idea of who had information, and the leverage to squeeze it out of them.

'None, except his Lordship, and that only by his high, hoarse voice.'

'Describe their faces, girl,' I demanded, exasperated at her slowness. 'Were they fair or dark?

255

Bearded or clean-shaven, stout or lean?'

She stared at me with trembling lip.

'That's the worst of it, sir! I cannot say, for they all wore masks.'

'*Masks?*'

Of course. Grotesque, impressive and, for the members of the Club, who would naturally wish to conceal their identities, a practical necessity.

'Horrible ugly things they was, though well-made and costly, you could tell — foxes and wolves, and skulls, and jesters, like they wear at the St Giles Fair.'

'What of the other girls, then? Were any present when you entered, or were you all alone?'

I suspected that Kester and his comrades had rounded up a brace of doxies, probably the starving street-girls who plied around the Plain and its three tines of Cowley, Iffley and St Clements — for in this, as in everything to do with the Wilmot Club and its libertine namesake, licentious variety and gluttonous excess were the rule.

'Oh no, sir. There was some girls there already, about my age, a-crying and fussing when I come in.'

'You were not afraid, though?'

She shook her head avidly.

'Oh no, Doctor, I was — terrible afraid! I didn't know what they'd seen or done before I come, and so I was most scared for myself, though I tried not to show it.'

She leaned forward confidentially, her brown eyes wide.

'Sukey says men can smell it on you like dogs can — fear, you know — and if they sense you're scared of a whipping, why they'll take it upon themselves to give you one, if only for sport.'

My blood quickened, and questions tumbled from my lips. 'When did Sukey arrive? At what hour? What had passed?'

Mary Ann creased her pale brow. 'Two or three in the morning, I suppose — and it was the queerest thing too, for it seemed she had been sent.'

'Indeed? By whom?'

She looked away, sheepishly.

'Well, sir, I know it may sound bold to say so, me being what I am, but — why — by Providence, I almost thought.'

'Mary Ann,' I said, ' 'not a sparrow falls but that He knows it' . . . '

'I know that's what they say, sir. Miss Diana most earnestly begs me to believe it, and I try, but it is not often I can.'

'Tell me what happened,' I said softly.

'Well, Sukey was most determined that I come out of there — I'm sure I don't know what had got into her, but she would not hear no for an answer.'

'Indeed? And how did they take it?'

'Awful hard, Doctor — they said they'd got me and by God they'd keep me and no poxy slut would stand in their way. She took up the poxy part of what they said and said I had all manner of disease, that I wasn't fit to lie with a beggar or a Bedlamite, and she'd been sent to replace me by a friend who wished to remain anon . . . a noni . . . '

'Anonymous?' I supplied.

She grinned at me with relief.

'Yes, Doctor, that's the very word. What's it mean?'

'Never mind. What did you do?'

'Well, I didn't fancy losing the crown I'd been promised, but every minute I stayed in that company I grew more frightened.'

'Why was that, Mary Ann?' I asked gently.

'Lord Lucky,' she said, giving me a swift, hunted look. 'He left around two; said he was going on a 'special errand'. Promised he'd come back with — with a great surprise, a treat, he said, though not for the girls, that's certain. The look in his eyes when he said that — well, sir, it turned me cold. There's something . . . not right about him. Something a little mad.'

I thought of his high-strung strangeness, his shrill, bursting laugh, his avid quickness and restless eyes. I'd met him but once or twice at Charlie's parties, years ago; but even then I had distrusted him implicitly. He had always struck me as a queer, unnatural sort of young man.

'Say what you mean, Mary Ann. I promise you, I shall not betray your confidence.'

'Something,' she said in a little voice, scarcely more than a breath, 'something murderous.'

It will come as no surprise to you to learn, Fraser, that this exchange ended my tête-à-tête with Mary Ann, for the poor creature was white and trembling, having quite exhausted her feeble strength in recounting the events of the night in question. It seemed that the remaining gentlemen, doubtless weakened in their resolve by the excesses of the evening, had given in to Sukey's insistence, albeit with a very bad grace, and had let them both go. Intriguing and sinister though it was, however, Mary Ann's account profited me little in my search for Diana.

It seemed that Mary Ann's reservations regarding the Providence that notes the fall of a sparrow were more justified than I cared to admit. Certainly, though God may be watching every living creature as and when they drop or disappear, He often proves to be the sole witness. As Sergeant Beaton had implied (lumping Diana in with the run of whores in a manner that made my fists itch), one Jezebel more or less on the streets excites little notice or concern among the general run of humanity, except perhaps for her sisters in the trade, who will squabble over her 'patch'. As far as most people are concerned, women of the night come and go as they please; and when the night takes one — well, it was always destined to close over her head in the end, so why not sooner rather than later? Unless there is some sensational or grotesque circumstance attached to her death or disappearance, no-one laments her absence nor prays for her return. Every day, in every city of what we are pleased to call the civilized world, these feebly flickering souls are snuffed out with as little ceremony as you or I might snuff a candle-flame; and the darkness in which their compatriots move grows a little deeper.

I tramped the streets of Oxford the whole of the next week without unearthing the smallest hint of Diana's whereabouts. Every evening, after discharging my duties at the Radcliffe or the shelter, I hastened the dilapidation of my already sorry boots patrolling Jericho and the alleys around Pembroke and Christ Church. I even ventured as far as the Plain some nights, to speak with the girls who plied there and discover whether Diana had come amongst them. When she could not rest, I knew she often kept vigil in the night-time streets, handing out cards and speaking to the girls, urging them to come to her for succour. Some knew her, indeed; but despite all my imprecations, could not say where she had gone, or by whom she had last been seen.

My last resort was to return to the lodging-house in Wellington Street run by that unsleeping Argus, Ginny Shimmin, whose kind hospitality I had so lately abused. Once I had thought of it, I cursed myself roundly for not having tried her before; for if any one person could speak with authority of the goings-on in Jericho, it was assuredly she. Mrs Shimmin knew all the girls and their regular clients by sight, and sat at the centre of an enormously efficient network of rumour and gossip. She might tell me in an instant whether Diana had been seen over the last fortnight.

It was about seven on a Friday evening when I knocked upon that unassuming black door, and waited, intemperately tapping my feet, for the heavy bolt to slide back, vouchsafing me entry. I could hear Mrs Shimmin's heavy, measured tread in the hallway as she approached; this time I had brought enough money not only to pay for my impromptu sojourn of a fortnight before, but also handsomely to recompense her for whatever new information she might have. Sometimes, Fraser, when attempting to coax secrets out of such women, my silver tongue proves unequal to the task, you know, and a handful of silver speaks more persuasively.

In either case, I was prepared; and as the door inched open I readied my most entirely charming smile to greet the proprietress. The expression on her square, severe face was one of extreme umbrage; annoyed, no doubt, to be roused so early in the evening by one whose intemperate lust could not wait — but when she saw me her scowl softened and she pulled the door wider to admit me, daintily stifling a yawn. As I had suspected, she slept by day in order to watch all night.

Waving aside my apologies for disturbing her, she showed me through into the kitchen. A kettle chuntered over the hearth, and having poured us both a strong dark cup of tea, she settled back into her rocking-chair, and squinted at me astutely, eyes glimmering in the flicker of the fire.

'Well, young Doctor,' she said at last, 'I take

261

it you ain't here for a social visit; or did you want to re-engage that room you had the other evening?'

I laughed sycophantically at this cynical piece of wit.

'I have come to settle my account,' I told her, pressing a couple of coins into her extended hand — more than covering what I owed, for, as you know, I coveted her help.

She counted the money in her palm with a single sharp glance, and stowed it away in her apron-pocket, smiling her approval.

'Well, and with interest, too! I shall retire to my little cottage beside the sea before I know it, at this rate.'

'I must confess, Mrs Shimmin,' I told her, 'that this is by way of a down-payment; for I wish to pick your marvellous brains, if I may.'

She raised a sparse grey eyebrow. 'Ask away, my dear, if you think there's anything in this old head which might be of use to such a learned gent.'

'It concerns Mrs Pelham,' I told her.

'Our Lady, is it?' Her lips twitched. 'Yes, Sergeant Beaton said she'd done a moonlight flit or somesuch. Got too much for her, I expect: all them good works will take it out of a body. Tell me, did you ask Sukey if she'd seen her?'

I sighed. 'Mrs Shimmin, I've asked everyone, you must know that. Nothing escapes your notice — which is why I have come to ask *you*.'

Hearing the gravity of my tone, Mrs Shimmin set aside her cup of tea and leaned forward in her chair, clasping her large, coarse hands before her.

'Do you really think she's gone, then? And not of her own accord?'

'I am afraid I am convinced of it. She vanished the Saturday before last and has not been seen since. I wondered whether, perhaps, you might have heard any news of her?'

Her thin, bloodless lips set themselves in a downward-curving line.

'The night you come in drunk was the last night anyone saw her, then?'

I bowed my head.

'The same.'

She nodded grimly. 'And who was the last person to speak with her?'

I smiled ruefully. 'From all of the enquiries I have made, it appears to have been me.'

'Well, you at least are in the clear, for you come in alone; and I can vouch that you didn't stir until the next morning, for I know everything that passes in this house.'

'I do not doubt it,' I assured her. 'But what I wish to know is whether you have heard anything of her since that night — for I can find no trace of her, and I am extremely anxious for her safety.'

'Are you now? She'd be honoured, I'm sure, to be the cause of such concern. She's usually the one what cares for lost women.'

I remembered my confrontation with Diana; my rude insistence on knowing the purpose of Kester's visit; my sneering innuendos and venomous parting shot.

'Naturally, I care for her very deeply. She is a valued colleague, and . . . '

'And the rest,' grinned Mrs Shimmin. It seemed that word of our engagement had found its way, like every other piece of news in the area, to Ginny's sharp ears.

'The last time we spoke we had . . . a disagreement,' I admitted. 'I was in a rage when I left — over nothing, really, or so it seems now. We did not part on good terms.'

Mrs Shimmin's face darkened and grew sour as she received the import of my words, and the blood flew to my cheeks as I felt her chastening gaze upon me.

'I hoped at first that she had gone somewhere for a few days to think and recover her composure — that I had temporarily driven her away — but now I believe the situation is far more serious, whatever Sergeant Beaton says.'

Mrs Shimmin nodded, her usual air of ironic good humour quite gone.

'Who was she last in company with? Apart from yourself, of course?'

I cleared my throat; glanced down at the cracked kitchen tiles, and then out at the grimy window. The man's name had grown so hateful to me by this time that it near choked me to pronounce it, almost as if I were subject to the old superstition that when one speaks of the devil, he is sure to appear.

'Lucius Kester,' I said.

Mrs Shimmin shook her head in grim dismay and abruptly rose from her rocking-chair, sweeping past me to stoke the fire.

'Lord Lucky, eh?' she muttered, stabbing the glowing coals with the poker.

I nodded.

'Sukey said he was sniffing around again; I'd hoped the rumour was false.' She paused, as if recalling something, and her shoulders slumped. 'Course, she always was one of his favourites. Prided herself she could handle him. Silly girl.'

'I have been enquiring after him, too,' I said eagerly. 'It seems that he went from his audience with Mrs Pelham straight to a private gathering of the John Wilmot Club. Others were present, but Kester was the only one Mary Ann could name. But he left before Sukey arrived, and neither girl can tell me any more than that.'

'Mary Ann?' Her face cleared. 'Ah, the little Atkins girl. So his taste has turned to halfwits, now?' Her jaw tightened and she sighed. 'That family's blood is bad. His cousin Charlie's a wrong 'un as well — though perhaps you know that, for he's a Magdalen man too — and Kester's old man was even worse.'

'You remember his father, then?' I said eagerly. Lucius had always airily claimed to come of a long line of debauchers; I had thought it the idle boast of a would-be rake, eager to impress his elders. And yet at eighteen, he had not been half so devilish as he had believed himself: I remembered the trouble he had caused by falling in love with a whore who proceeded to cozen him of fifty pounds and run off with a carter. Small wonder that these

265

days, his chief pleasure lay in causing the wretched creatures pain. But bad friends and a naturally vicious temper had worked their evil influence on his character since then, and now he was as depraved and heartless a young man as one could wish not to meet.

Ginny put the poker back in its stand and sighed. The memory seemed to weary her. 'Yes, I remember him, only too well. His father was a cruel man with a dreadful temper, given to horrible practices, and from what the girls say, his son's even worse. I'm surprised Mrs Pelham tolerates his company, but he's been spending time with her quite regular, from what I hear. Mostly Wednesdays, I believe.'

This was news to me. Bile smarted at the back of my throat. Wednesdays were the days I worked at the Radcliffe on the night shift; there would have been no danger of my interrupting their conference on those evenings. Why had she not told me of their meetings? What was she concealing? What could be darker than her past in Cambridge — so dark that she had felt she must hide it, even from me?

'Dunno why he would've been talking to her on a Saturday night though — Lucky's usually got more pressing appointments of a weekend.' She glanced sidelong at me. 'Or perhaps she was his pressing appointment?'

This was too much.

'What, pray, do you mean to imply? I'll thank you to speak plainly, Mrs Shimmin!' I exclaimed, flushing with indignation. She did not flinch, but regarded me steadily.

'I speaks it as I sees it,' she said quietly. 'Take care, that's all. It's only been that way for a month or two — ever since he come up from the country. He seemed to lose interest for a spell, but now he's back, so something must've changed while he was away. Stands to reason.'

My frustration made me curt. 'What?'

She shrugged with infuriating insouciance.

'Search me. All I'm saying is, there's more to this new habit of his than meets the eye: he ain't the tea-taking type. And why a nice, decent lady like herself should entertain him — well, that's the real mystery, ain't it?'

I grew hot with indignation at her presump-tuousness; yet in my heart I knew she was right to caution me. I was only ashamed that I had not allowed Diana to explain her actions at the time. How I cursed myself again for my impetuosity! The terror that I had somehow damned her on that night by my refusal to for-give, or even to hear her, clawed again at my soul.

'The only mystery,' I said priggishly, 'is where she has got to; and you will oblige me greatly if you tell me all that you know in that regard.'

She shook her head sadly. 'All I know, my dear, is the Kesters are a bad lot; and if Lord Lucky's somehow mixed up in her going astray, you mark me, she's in a deal of trouble.'

I bit my lip.

'So I had feared.'

'You're right to,' said Mrs Shimmin brusquely, 'and I fear it too. I don't mind tell-ing you I've a lot of respect for Our Lady. She had the guts to do something nobody else bothered to; and I don't mean handing out a bob here and a Bible there, I mean really looking after those girls. Looking out for the ones nobody gives a damn about — well, nobody but me.'

For a moment, tenderness stole into her voice; but she recovered herself swiftly.

'But me, I got to make a living, same as anyone. Charity comes easier when you ain't got rent to pay. In any event, the quicker she's found, the better it'll be for my peace of mind. I'll keep me eyes and ears open.'

'Very well; that is all I ask. Thank you for your help. I am most grateful, really.'

She nodded, holding my gaze a little longer than was quite comfortable. 'Just you bring her back safe, young man,' she said, and there was a gleam of steel in her voice, 'and then you can thank me.'

I showed myself out into the cool evening, my soul sinking after the vanished sun. I was out of hope and out of options. And as the trail grew cold, so too did the blood in my veins, chilled by the thought that I had, perhaps, unwittingly — and yet far from blamelessly — sent the woman I loved, the woman I had doubted, and cursed, and spurned in her hour of direst need, to her grave.

It was the Monday after my interview with Mrs Shimmin, when I had near despaired of seeing Diana again, that she quite unexpectedly returned to us — and under the most surprising and terrible circumstances.

The atmosphere in the shelter that evening was subdued and melancholy, as it had been ever since she had disappeared; for the girls had grown to trust Diana, and the protection and care she offered; they had dared, for once, to feel safe in that refuge, and this small solace in their comfortless lives was cruelly stripped from them by her absence.

With the uncanny intuition of creatures used to danger, hardship and death, they sensed Sukey's and my fears without knowing the cause. For my own part, though I count myself no more susceptible to such impressions than any other man, I confess that on that cold, wind-racked night, the fire seemed cheerless, the alleys blacker and the drunkards and ne'er-do-wells loitering upon the Jericho streets more threatening than formerly.

Little did I imagine how very much more sinister they were about to become.

It was around six o'clock, and I was conducting a general examination of one of the birds who had recently come to roost, when I heard a commotion in the hallway, a few doors down from my gloomy little consulting-room. The woman I was assessing, a coarse, hardened creature of about thirty called Louisa, who was well-used to the brawls of public-houses and common lodging-rooms, did not turn a hair; but I, knowing how quiet and orderly a house

Sukey usually kept, immediately ceased what I was doing.

Louisa observed me with a sarcastic squint. Her skin was greyish-red and her eyes blood-shot with drink. Though she did not yet know it, and I did not relish the prospect of telling her, she had scant few months of life remaining to her.

'Summink the matter, dear? Got a rowdy one, 'ave yer?'

I hushed her with an abrupt gesture. My first surmise had indeed been that some inebriate street-walker had stumbled in and caused the fuss — but I soon realized that the cries I heard were not of distress, but of surprise and joy.

I stripped off my apron while the half-naked drab watched me with amused contempt.

'Stay there,' I told her.

'Good job you ain't on my time,' she remarked drily; but did as she was bid.

I hurried down the corridor to the entrance-hall with all haste, quickly buttoning my jacket as I went. As I approached the knot of girls I reminded myself that we could hardly dare hope for anything so miraculous as the restoration of Diana, whole and unharmed. In one aspect of this caveat, at least, I was correct.

For there she stood: defiant and indomitable Diana, Diana of the dark, gentle eyes and low, soft voice, of the impeccable dress, demure manners, mild demeanour and iron determination. She was a dreadful and saddening sight.

Her dress was torn and dirtied, its dove-grey

silk stained dark; in parts by mud, in parts by what could only be blood. The bodice of her gown was awry, the stays bent and snapped, and one sleeve and half her petticoats were torn away; but that was not the worst. Looking aghast upon her poor face, I barely recognized the woman I had known.

The shining dark hair of which she had been quietly proud, brushing and pinning it neatly each morning so that never a wisp drifted out of place, had been hacked off anyhow. Above the left cheekbone, her eye peeped from a tender mound of swollen flesh, discoloured a livid purple. Beneath the bruising, however, she was deadly pale. Scrapes and cuts lacerated her face, neck and fingers, as if she had been defending herself against some frenzied but unarmed attacker. I saw, too, that two finger-nails had been torn off her right hand, though she had curled the bloodied ends into her palm to try to hide them, ashamed of this new disfig-urement.

'Diana!' I exclaimed, and rushed towards her, the girls parting like a flock of chiding birds before me. All my instincts as a doctor implored me to get her into a sickbed as soon as ever was possible; as a lover, to embrace her. But I was horribly aware that despite the ugli-ness of her superficial injuries, the shock and trauma of what she had suffered was a far greater threat to her well-being than a few cuts and bruises or a blacked eye.

She gave me a painful, wary smile, through split and swollen lips — another hurt I grimly laid to Kester's account. Then all at once, her smile vanished and she dropped her eyes, as though she had forgot herself, or done something she had not meant to. I offered her my arm, but she shrank back, as though fearful of my touch.

'Doctor Chapman,' she said, in a clear, casual voice which faltered none the less, like a once-bold horse refusing a fence, 'I did not think to find you here, not after our last interview. Is it your day?'

'My day is every day since you have been gone,' I told her.

She raked her bleeding fingers through the chopped tufts of her hair; trying absently to stroke the ghost of the locks she had lost. It was at once risible and pathetic, like the gesture of one demented. Tears started to my eyes and I turned my head to conceal them.

My averted gaze did not escape Diana's notice.

'I must look a sight,' she muttered, with a trembling half-laugh, and my heart twisted within my bosom.

By this stage the other girls, all except Sukey, who exhibited an exemplary calm, were worse than useless; exclaiming and rushing about to fetch water and smelling-salts and Lord knows what other unhelpful palliatives.

As they pressed around her, Diana's face paled further and, sensing danger, I darted forward. I took her swiftly and securely by the elbow as she started to sway, and Sukey, catching on, moved to her other side. But for our support, she would surely have fallen senseless and struck her poor cropped head on the stone flags. Clearing the tangled fringe from her forehead, I felt Diana's brow and was alarmed to find that despite her mortuary pallor, it was hot as a stove-top.

'The infirmary,' I said to Sukey; and she nodded tightly, as through I merely confirmed a conclusion she had already reached.

'Mary Ann,' she said, in a low, urgent tone, 'go and fetch a clean nightgown; you and I must put her to bed at once. The rest of you,' she added, raising her voice, 'be off! Mrs Pelham needs air; she cannot catch her breath with all you ninnies crowding around like fairground gawpers. Wait in the refectory. Go now!'

The girls scattered, chastened, and Sukey and I half-led and half-carried the swooning Diana to the infirmary, where Mary Ann stood holding a freshly starched nightgown before her like a protective charm.

Leaving the womenfolk to ease Diana out of her ruined garments and into a clean bed, I stepped out into the small kitchen-garden that gave on to the back of the nearby church. The evening was cool and clear, and I gazed up at the steeple which reared like a great obelisk against the infected red of the evening sky. A wandering breeze tousled my hair, and my mind's eye recalled that chopped and matted tangle which had once been Diana's only vanity. I shut my eyes, and there, blazoned on the darkness inside my lids, was Valenti's portrait, her black locks tumbling about her slender shoulders. When I opened them again, they were damp with tears.

I do not know why it seemed to me so much worse that he had cut her lovely hair, than that he had beaten and brutalized her; I only know it sickened me to think what she must have suffered at the whim of Kester and his foul companions — for I was certain, now, that this was his doing.

Collecting myself, I loosened my tie and gathered my thoughts. She would need a thorough examination and something to bring down her fever, as well as a hefty dose of laudanum to drive away, at least temporarily, the demons that beset all those who have undergone horrors of which they cannot speak, yet cannot forget. She had not appeared, at first glance, to have more than superficial injuries, but it did not do to be complacent — especially when I was still mercifully ignorant as to exactly what tortures she had endured.

When I entered the sickroom, however, I was surprised to find Diana alone. Mary Ann would have retired upstairs with the other girls, but Sukey was a more than able assistant in treating seriously ill or injured patients, and I had expected her to stay and help. Yet even *in extremis*, Diana's dark, quick eyes missed nothing; she saw the puzzlement upon my face and coughed out a cracked laugh.

'Don't worry, Stephen,' she said faintly, 'I asked her to leave us for a minute. I wish to speak to you in private.'

'I will hear everything you have to say,' I

vowed, regretting once more that I had not been as patient the last time we spoke. I am not ashamed to admit that there was a certain trepidation in my voice and in my heart; for if what she had to divulge was so shocking that even Sukey could not be privy to it, I was far from sure I wished to hear it myself.

She turned her face towards me as she spoke, her white brow streaming cold with sweat.

'I wish . . . ' she said, and stopped, and began again: 'I wish you to forgive me, Stephen.'

Forgive her! As if I cared now for the minor indiscretions of her past! And yet it was typical of her to attempt to protect me from the consequences of my own folly and turn all blame upon herself. I cradled her limp, bloodied hands in my own.

'Of course, my love, a thousand times, though there is nothing to forgive!'

She smiled faintly. 'You do not yet know what I have done. You were right when you called me a liar.'

I hung my head, too shamed to reply.

She raised a finger to touch my lips.

'I know what you are thinking. But this is not your fault, Stephen.'

I stared at her swollen, ruined face, her half-closed eye. My words choked in my throat.

'Then whose, Diana, if not mine?'

'I brought this upon myself,' she said, and her tone was light and airy, almost cheerful, as she stared calmly up at the ceiling. 'It is entirely my own doing. I made a mistake and lied about it, then lied again, and again, to cover up the old lies. What a terrible tangle of them I made! Like a fly swaddled in a spider's silk . . . I cannot fathom why I did it, now. Those things seem so trivial and strange. I deceived those I loved, and who I thought — I hoped — loved me . . . ' Her eyes burned suddenly with fresh tears.

'O God, Stephen, why did I do those things?' she cried in agony, rearing up in the bed, panting and sobbing. She clung to me with violent desperation; her thin arms circled my chest, her face was pressed against mine, and I felt her wet eyelashes brush my cheek. I stroked the ragged remains of her lovely hair, listening apprehensively to the hard rattle of her breathing.

'Hush, love,' I soothed her. 'You are here now, and I am here, and shall stay. Rest now. You are home.' I laid her back gently on the bed, trying to mask my anxiety. I touched her brow again; the hectic flush had gone, and it was cold and damp as a gravestone after rain.

Her eyes fluttered almost shut.

'I dreaded to find you here,' she whispered, 'and yet I hoped for it too. As long as you were not angry.'

'No, my dear,' I told her steadily, 'I am not angry.'

Her pale lips parted in a vague smile.

'Good,' she said. 'He said I'd never be forgiven, you know. If I came back. If you found out what I had done.'

Her breathing was rapid and uneven, and the chill grip of her fingers faint and fading.

Her smile widened as her eyes closed.

'But he was wrong, Stephen. I can tell you the truth now. I shall tell you everything.'

I left Diana sleeping, and found Sukey in the refectory, the only figure in the long low hall, sunk in an attitude of absolute weariness upon one of the benches, eyes closed and brow pushed against her open palm. Unwilling to intrude upon her in this unguarded state, I paused upon the threshold; but, sensing my presence, she sighed, opened her eyes and smiled at me.

'You caught me napping, Doctor! Sorry, I didn't mean to — I expect you're done in enough for the both of us. Mustn't make it worse, eh? I was just taking a bit of a breather. I'll be right as rain in a minute.'

The disease which still simmered in her blood was clearly taking its toll on her much-tried strength — yet in truth, this was the first sign of weakness she had shown since Diana's disappearance.

'Is she sleeping?' she asked.

'Yes, she dropped off almost at once. I'll examine her properly once she wakes. Though her injuries are unpleasant to behold, fortu-nately they are relatively slight. For the present, I am satisfied that her life is in no danger.'

'Not from her wounds, anyway,' murmured Sukey darkly.

'Are the girls all upstairs?' I asked.

'Some are,' Sukey said. 'Some went out to work, or the pub.' A half-smile.

'I am surprised that any have taken to the streets, considering Diana's state,' I remarked. 'That animal could still be out there — and if not him, another dozen just as bad. Don't they know it isn't safe?'

Sukey shook her head, as though at the backwardness of a normally able pupil.

'You should know what whores are by now, Doctor. If we don't work we don't eat, or, more important for many, drink. All Our Lady can give us is shelter and soup; it ain't enough for most. They get bored and restless and do silly things. God knows I did. Besides, it's all we know; and the risk's part of the game, ain't it? Why stand idle when there's money to be made?'

Sukey was right to chide me for my naïveté; for I confess that I had not wished to acknowledge that sordid truth in my heart. Do not forget, Fraser, that I do not only attend prostitutes in the refuge, but the poor women of Jericho in general, who cannot afford physicians, and so would simply suffer and die in silence were I not there to offer what help I can. Cancer, fever, scurvy, starvation, broken heads and limbs and noses; there are few injuries or indignities the human frame can meet with that my patients are not prey to. The greatest cause of all this suffering is ignorance, followed by neglect; but the next commonest, and the hardest for me to bear, is cruelty: the cruelty of men in particular. A vision of Diana's battered face flashed before my mind's eye, and my hands ached to close about that villain's throat.

'Come,' said Sukey, touching my shoulder companionably, 'let's talk about what's to be done with her.'

We repaired to Diana's bare little parlour at the front of the house. It was a small, neat room with plain whitewashed walls, dark wooden bookshelves on three sides, and two armchairs facing one another before the dead grey ashes in the grate. Sukey had taken lately to sleeping curled up in one of the chairs, so as to be ready at any time for a knock upon the door, or a medical emergency. She pulled her shawl closer about her shoulders and shivered.

'Sorry it's so cold. Seemed wrong to have a fire when she was gone, somehow.'

She flashed another sheepish half-smile; and, drawn and haggard though she was, it was heartening to see that indomitable spirit of hers shine out from her youthful face. I assured her that it was of no consequence to me. Sukey crossed the room, gently closing the heavy oak door to preclude any opportunistic eavesdropping, before seating herself in the chair opposite.

'Well, Sukey,' I said. 'What, then, shall we do with Mrs Pelham? And, more importantly, with her abuser?'

She gave me a narrow, appraising look, then folded her work-roughened hands across her lap and stared into the feathered ash of the cold fireplace, as though flames danced there still.

'What can we do?' she said hollowly.

'Well,' I began, 'we can have the scoundrel up for assault at the very least — not to mention gross indecency, kidnap and perhaps even attempted murder.'

Sukey's blonde head snapped up sharply and she stared at me as I listed Kester's crimes, her eyes widening. Finally, apparently unable to contain her mirth, she let out a single peal of laughter, swiftly bitten back. And yet it was not a laugh of amusement; rather, I heard in it a note of hysteria, even despair.

'What do you find so funny?' I enquired, ice in my voice, my indignation rising.

She composed herself, regarding me sincerely.

'I'm sorry, Doctor. I didn't mean to offend, or make light of things, I'm sure. It's only the idea of us hauling Lord Lucky into court made me laugh.'

'Why, pray?'

She sighed. 'Well — even *you* must see that there's not a cat's chance in hell?'

'What can you mean?' I cried hotly. 'We know beyond a doubt who has done this, and we have two witnesses to the fact — Mary Ann was there too, you know, at Kester's despicable orgy. He left the party and did not return, the very night that Diana disappeared. She has no enemies; not even the Jericho pimps wish her ill! Who else could it be?'

'That's as may be,' said Sukey, a tinge of resignation in her low, sensible voice, 'but we still
can't touch Kester. You're a man of the world,
Doctor, for all that you're so good and kind.
You must know I'm right.'

This was beyond all my reckoning. Undoubtedly, the man was rich and high-born, with
many influential friends, but even he could not
hope to emerge unscathed from such a sordid
scandal. The use and, all too often, abuse of
prostitutes is, alas, tolerated, and dispiritingly
common. The assault and kidnap of decent
women, however, was an entirely different
matter.

'We can and shall touch him,' I averred, 'and
it will be more than a touch, you have my
word!'

Sukey looked at me placidly.

'And how do we identify him?' she asked.
'All the gentlemen wore masks, and they never
took 'em off.'

'If you can call such swine gentlemen!' I
muttered; but she was, of course, quite right. I
began to see that it would not be so easy as I
had thought to drag Kester before the authorities.

'But he was not masked when he solicited
Mary Ann on the street!' I reminded her.

Sukey shook her head. 'All that proves is that
he hosted the night; not that he did this to Mrs
P, or was even present at the party.'

'Mary Ann knew him at once, even in disguise; she could testify to his manner and
voice,' I argued, desperately.

'She might,' conceded Sukey, 'and she might not. You know she's a bit soft in the head. But either way, what beak would take a common whore's word against a Lord's?'

'It will be my word, too,' I protested vehemently. She made a dismissive little gesture with her hand, which angered me more than it ought.

'Very well then, a whore-doctor's word — it ain't much better! And besides,' she added, '*you* wasn't there.'

'I may as well have been. I know what happened and who is responsible!'

'Oh, I'm sure you think you do,' she said with that maddening rationality of hers, 'but you can't *prove* it.'

I was in an agony of restlessness and indignation; I leaped from my chair and paced the room, Sukey's sharp eyes following my agitated perambulations.

'But — curse it, Sukey, it's all wrong!'

'Oh, you won't get no argument from me. It *is* all wrong. Awful wrong. But that's the way it is. One law for the rich, another for the poor. Don't tell me you don't know that. Or d'you think just because she's nice-spoken and nice-looking they'll make an exception? Most folk ain't like you, Doctor. Most folk think like that Sergeant Beaton — if you keep company with whores you ain't much better than one yourself.'

'You have seen her,' I pleaded. 'She is broken — her nerves are shredded, not to mention her gown. Surely we cannot allow such brutality to go unpunished?'

'It ain't a question of allowing it,' she said sadly.

I could not comprehend her attitude of defeat; she who had fought so hard and against such daunting odds to maintain the shelter, to bring light and succour to this dark place, where she knew it was so sorely needed; she who had turned before my eyes from a dissolute, saucy bawd into a disciplined, hard-working nurse. A slow, certain suspicion formed in my mind that there was something else here; something more than a disinclination to engage in a long and difficult battle — a weakness to which she had never before succumbed. But what could it be? She watched my reaction, sitting quietly in her chair: I felt like an insect in a specimen-jar beneath her steady, appraising gaze.

'I confess I am astonished at your change of heart,' I said. 'Have not you yourself suffered at Kester's hands? Can you bear to see yet another woman suffer the same — suffer worse — and allow him to escape punishment?'

'Oh, I hate him all right,' she assured me, 'but one of the things I learned early on — one of the things he taught me, Doctor' — and here her lips twisted in a cynical grimace — 'was to choose my battles; and trust me, this one we've no chance of winning.'

'There is more to this than you are admitting,' I told her. 'You know something about Diana, or about Kester, that you will not speak of. What is it, Sukey? We should have no secrets from one another.'

'It's nothing,' she said, annoyance sharpening her low tone, 'only that Kester's not a man to be trifled with.'

Her words recalled to me Diana's of that night two weeks ago, and her mysterious habit of conducting private meetings with the man — and I thought I understood. What was this extraordinary power he seemed to have over women, that though he abused and insulted them, they would not seek to harm nor even to challenge him?

'I won't have it!' I told her. 'A crime has been committed. If you will not make it known to the proper authorities, then I shall.'

A sharp pang of despair flashed across her face — the first sign of strong emotion she had shown since our conversation began.

'No, Doctor, you mustn't — you don't understand!'

'No, I do not!' I agreed brusquely. 'I certainly cannot understand what motives you or Diana might have for — for protecting him.'

Her head snapped up. 'Protecting him!' she cried, a harsh note of strained laughter edging her voice.

'Yes. In all the time she has known him, Diana has refused to speak a word against that man, though she must have known his reputation. Even when I challenged her, she would only say that they were in private conference, and that it was important. And now look at her! I don't know, nor do I wish to, what has passed between you and Kester. That is your business and his alone — though I confess I am surprised that, even if you are careless of your own safety, you seem to hold Diana's so cheap.'

She did not move or speak, but I knew the barb had wounded her; and I did not care. I surged heedlessly on.

'What does he have over you — what has he *done* to you, damnit?'

At this, her hands flew to her face and I knew I had gone too far, and sought at once to undo my mistake. Overwhelmed by remorse, I knelt impulsively at her feet and tried, gently, to remove her fingers from over her eyes and read what was written in them. She shook me off in a single, fierce spasm and then remained quite still, as if she did not dare to move lest she should lose the remnants of her self-control. Choleric and impassioned though I was, I instantly regretted my harsh words.

'I am sorry,' I told her. 'I have said too much; I have upset you. I will not speak of your past life again, for God knows, you have atoned for it, and these last few weeks I could not have done without you by my side. But whether it is money he is offering you, or protection, or I know not what, you must surely know his promises are meaningless, his money tainted — that he befouls everything he touches, damn it!'

She flinched at the word *tainted*, and her bosom heaved a little. To my astonishment and dismay, I saw a tear slide between her fingers; then another, and another, dropping swiftly and softly as sudden rain.

You know the sensitive ladies of our class, Fraser; you know the sort of green-sick girls and hothouse blooms we are pleased to call the flower of womanhood, who will weep at a sentimental verse and near die of emotion at a fashionable opera. Tears are as common to them, and as freely used, as oaths to undergraduates.

But Sukey is an altogether different creature — coarser, yes, harder; but at bottom, very much stronger. She is a survivor: and until that moment, though I had seen her bruised and abused, threatened and spurned, I had never once seen her weep.

'We are all tainted,' she said in a low, hard voice I had never before heard from her lips. I took her gently by the shoulder; she shuddered violently, as though my touch were repulsive to her — and this, I own, shocked me more deeply than all the rest.

'You want to know what he's done?' She looked up at me, fiercely dashing away the tears coursing down her cheeks with the back of her hand. 'All right, I'll tell you. Listen well and you'll understand why I do as I do and say what I say. You asked for it and you'll have it — I only hope he didn't do the same to her, or there's no God and this is Hell we live in.'

Startled by her ferocity, I moved back to sit in the chair opposite.

'There was a — an encounter — ' she began, and stopped, and breathed deeply, and then continued: 'It wasn't at one of them Wilmot parties — this was a few years back, when he hadn't the powerful friends he's got now — or not all of them. I was a bit fresher then, too; I'd come down from Southwark to visit a friend — sort of a rest-cure, you might say. Sarah Belling was her name — another working girl, but she was kind and generous, though she liked a drink, as we all do. She's dead now,' she added as an afterthought.

'Anyhow, after a few weeks I was back to my usual self and wanted to pay my way with Sarah, who'd given me free bed and board for all that time, on condition that I kept watch for peelers on the street when she was entertaining a client. Sort of a mix of a housemaid and guard-dog, you might say.

'So one fine night, when Sarah was visiting her sister in Ducklington for the weekend, I put on me best togs and went out into Jericho to see what I could see. My idea was to buy her a nice present — a hat I'd seen her admiring in the milliner's on Walton Street — and leave her a bit of rent money into the bargain. I reckoned I could turn five or six tricks if I was brisk, and the same again next night, and surprise her when she got back on Sunday. And God! That part came true enough — though not the way I'd planned. Anyway, it didn't take me long to catch the eye of a posh-looking young gent who was hanging about on a corner by the Duke's Arms, smoking a cigar and clutching a sort of carpet-bag. He approached, nervous-like, and asked if I was doing business, and if I had somewhere to go to, and I answered yes — reckoning him for a shy virgin what wouldn't take more than five minutes to bring off. I'd be back on the street in no time, or so I thought.

'I led him to Sarah's and showed him into the bedroom, told him the price and started stripping off. He sat there staring as I took me stays off, gawping like a fish. I thought maybe he just wanted me to use my mouth, which was why he wasn't getting undressed, so I asked him what he had in mind. He cleared his throat and pulled a pound-note from his waistcoat pocket.

'Well, I don't need to tell you that's an awful lot of money for a street-girl — more, I think, than I'd ever seen together in one place in my life — and I was damned sure he'd be wanting something special for it. And I was right. He asked in his high, husky voice what I might do for such a sum, and foolishly, I replied that I'd do pretty much anything he cared to name. He reached down into his bag — never trust the ones with bags, they've always got something queer in 'em — and drew out the oddest collection of bits and pieces. There was a cup of some sort that looked to be silver, a silver crucifix, four or five inches high, and some candleholders, and I don't know what else. I thought for a moment that he was a phoney-swell, a thief or a confidence man who'd somehow stolen the altar-stuff out of a church, but he promised me it was all his own: 'the family plate', he said. That made what happened next even worse, but it relieved my mind at the time. They was his trinkets and he could do

what he liked with 'em, was how I saw it
— though I promise you, I didn't think that
way for long.'

She broke off and stared blindly, summoning
strength for the rest of her tale. It seemed that
recalling the incident was draining her of blood
before my very eyes, and I urged her to pause
or stop if she needed — but she flapped her
hand impatiently at me and insisted she would
do no such thing.

'You asked to hear it, Doctor, and hear you
will, whether you want to or not,' she said with
a stony glare. 'I'm all right now — I'm here,
ain't I? — but you'll bloody well understand
what that man's like if it's the last thing I do.

'He got — well, first he asked me solemnly if
I was a religious girl. I told him I'd seen the
inside of a church a few times since my chris-
tening, but he might guess I was no nun. He
got out a bottle of red wine and poured a little
into the goblet, drank from it, and offered me
the cup. I sniffed it and it smelt all right, so I
took a little sip.

' 'Drink this,' he muttered as I put my lips to
it, 'this is my blood.' Nonsense, of course, but
it gave me a dreadful feeling of wrong, no
matter that he was no priest and I was no
better than I should be. Now I'm not a Papist
and I don't know their rituals, but that was
when he opened his britches and started saying
something in Latin, something religious-
sounding, and then he got out a little round
biscuit — wafers, they call them, don't they,
and put one on my tongue and told me to keep

my mouth open. He got himself out and said to kneel down — and then I knew where we was going. I did what he wanted, hoping that that was all, and he held on to my hair, talking about the colour of it, like a blonde angel, he said, and telling me all the time not to swallow — which is the opposite of what punters usually want in these situations, but I was in no position to argue.

'After he'd spent himself he collapsed on his knees on the carpet in front of me, so that we was face to face. He yanked open my mouth and saw the wafer still inside.

' 'Good girl,' he gasped. 'You may swallow now, though you'd better hope for your sake God is not watching.'

'I gulped, relieved, and drank a little more wine to wash the bitter taste of him out of my mouth, which seemed to amuse him. He lay back half-naked on the threadbare carpet, and laughed as I emptied the goblet.

' 'Can't get enough of the blood and the body, eh? I'll make a convert of you yet!'

'I smiled obligingly, and made a move towards the dresser, where my precious pound payment lay folded, weighed down with some coin. Quick as an adder, he caught my wrist and twisted it so I cried out softly.

' 'Not so fast, you,' he said. 'We have more business together before you get your reward.'

'He lit a couple of candle stubs he had brought, placing them in the silver candlestick he held, and told me to strip completely and lie down on the bed. I did so, though not without some anxiety as to what he'd do next, and closed my eyes. As he leaned over me with the flame he must have tipped the candle too far, for I suddenly felt a scalding splash on my stomach and nether parts. I yelped and started up, but he pushed me down again with his free arm, his hand over my mouth, and, crawling up on to the bed, shoved himself into me. The flame continued to dance before my eyes and the wax dripped hot on to my naked skin. I tried to yell and bite his fingers, but his grip was too strong and I couldn't move my jaw — indeed, he near stifled me before he was done. As he was reaching the crisis he stopped for a moment, looking hard into my eyes.

' 'I don't know what you're squealing for,' he panted, grinning, 'it's only pain.' He knelt half-up, without disengaging himself, and poured the hot wax on to his palm to show me he could bear it. He flinched at the feeling at first, then his features cleared and he closed his eyes and smiled, and thrust into me so hard I cried out again.

' 'Quiet if you want to earn your money,' he growled, and held the candle so close to my face I feared my hair would catch alight. Then he seemed to relent a little. 'Fight as hard as you will, my dear — scratch and batter me, for as you can see, it will only inflame my passion — just don't screech so, else I'll be forced to silence you, and it won't be with my hand.'

'Well, you may imagine I took full advantage of the permission to hurt him — partly because I wanted to, and partly because I yearned for him to finish quick as possible so I could throw him out and lock the door behind him. Some punters like that sort of thing, God knows why, and I'd run into a few of 'em before, but I put my whole self into hurting Kester. I dug my nails in and smacked and slapped him, bit the fingers he rammed into my mouth and kicked and squirmed — for I thought maybe I could get out from under him before he came again, and that would be one less thing to worry about. But he was too heavy for me, and finally he gave a shudder and a cry and his whole weight fell atop me, and I felt his warm seed seeping between my legs.'

She made a moue of disgust and glanced at me in grim contrition. 'Sorry, Doctor, but that's how it was.'

I shook my head, gesturing her to continue. 'What happened next?'

'Next, he got out the crucifix, and told me what he wanted me to do with it, and it was then that I started thinking it wasn't worth bargaining whatever was left of my soul for the sake of twenty shillings and an easy life for me and Sarah for a few weeks. Wine and wafers don't mean nothing to me, and hot wax ain't so bad, once you get used to it — after all, who hasn't spilled some on themself once in a while? But I don't like messing about with blasphemy and crosses and whatnot, for though I'm no churchgoer and God, far as I know, ain't ever looked out for me, that didn't mean I wasn't going to watch out for Him. There's some things you shouldn't risk, and fooling with damnation is one of 'em. I backed away and told him straight up I wouldn't do it. He smiled nastily.

' 'Then you shan't be paid.'

' 'I shall,' I said, 'and in full, given what you just made me do.'

' 'No,' he said lazily, plucking up the note before I could grab it, 'you shan't.' The look in his eyes was blank and cold, like the eyes of a statue, and suddenly I was very afraid of what he might do if I didn't oblige him — and even more of what would happen if I did. In this business you get an instinct for funny customers, and mine was telling me to get him out of there sharpish; I reckoned that if ever there was a time to cut my losses and chalk it up to experience, it was now. I opened the bedroom door.

' 'You can show yourself out,' I said curtly, 'and then don't ever show yourself here again.'

'I don't think he'd believed that I'd refuse him, having gone so far already, but I didn't reckon he'd turn nasty nor that he'd be too much trouble if he did, though I knew from tussling with him on the bed he was stronger than he looked. But I wasn't prepared for what come next.

'He roared in fury and sprang at me, banging the door shut and crushing me against it, half-stunning me, my face pushed sideways into the panels and my hands pinned above my head. I cried out in pain and fright, but he only grinned like a madman or a savage. I thought he might bite me, or force me, or kill me, even — I don't know what I thought, but perhaps my terror was enough for him, for the fire died slowly from his eyes and he stepped back, letting me tumble to the floor — for the fear and shock had left me weak as water.

' 'Here's what I'll show you, my girl,' he said calmly, as he stood over me, gathering up his things, including his damned pound-note, and buttoning his waistcoat. 'Let this be a lesson. Next time, don't make a bargain you can't keep. It's bad for business.' He grinned. 'And there's always a next time for your sort. I'll see you on the streets, I'm sure.'

'Something cold and hard bounced off my naked breast. I looked down and, through my tears, saw a farthing roll towards the skirting.

' 'For your trouble,' he said, and tipped his hat, and left.'

'My God, Sukey,' I said, grasping her chill hands in mine. 'I had no idea. He is an animal! We must — '

'We mustn't,' she said shortly. 'I tried to. Stupid of me, I know — is it even possible to rape a whore? — but I thought I'd put my faith in justice for a change, for it was assault at least. I found Sergeant Beaton and told him what had passed, gave a description of Kester and offered to speak against him in court. Do you know what he did? He laughed in my face, and took me in for soliciting. They brought in a searcher and she stripped me bare, and a surgeon examined me for disease, then they threw me in the cells and turned me on to the streets the next morning. I don't know if Kester paid

294

them off, or if the police just didn't care, but that was the last time I ever trusted in the law. And let me tell you this: nothing, nothing has changed, and I don't reckon as it ever will.' She forced a sad and terrible smile. 'And my poor friend Sarah never did get her pretty hat.'

Her trembling hands were clenched into fists as she turned away from me, attempting vainly to hide her emotion.

'Go to her, Doctor,' she said. 'If she ever had need of you, it's now. Go to her and pray he never used her as he used me. Some wounds don't heal.'

I rose in silence and closed the door on her hunched, motionless figure, convinced now, and beyond all possibility of doubt, that justice was far more than Kester deserved — and death, infinitely less.

It occurred to me, as I crossed the hallway with slow and dejected steps, that however deep Diana's trauma (and I prayed it did not approach anything that Sukey had just described), her physical injuries were by no means slight and that I must monitor my patient. I resolved to watch over Diana as she slept instead of retiring to my own makeshift bed — for I had passed the last several nights upon the hard couch in my examination-room. I made my way wearily to the infirmary, where Diana lay slumbering; or so I had thought.

Gently, I turned the knob and opened the door a chink; but as I peered through the slender gap into the gloom beyond, the light from the passage glittered upon a pair of eyes, wide open in the darkness.

'Diana,' I called softly, 'are you awake?'

There was a dry little cough from her bed in the corner.

'Yes, Stephen,' she whispered.

I thought of my heated words, my raised voice, which must, perhaps, have carried across the echoing hall, and hung my head.

'Is there anything that you want?' I asked, hoping that I might make amends for waking her by being of some small service.

'Only perhaps a little company,' she said, hesitatingly, as though it were not a request she dared dream I would grant.

'Are you wakeful?' I enquired.

She nodded, her face a pale shadow in the gloom.

'I slept for a spell, but woke when I heard voices; and I was so afraid, alone in the dark, that I could not close my eyes again.'

'Then I shall get a light, and sit with you,' I said, 'for I am wakeful too.' And I suited the action to the words, picking up the candle that burned on the hall table, re-entering the infirmary and closing the door softly behind me.

In the wavering light of the tallow flame, Diana looked small and lost beneath the white sheets of the bed; as though something had sucked the substance from her, and left her a shallow husk. She smiled faintly as I approached and set the light down upon her bedside table. I drew up a wooden chair, and settled myself upon it, preparing to keep vigil until she should sleep again.

'It hardly seems proper,' she said wryly, as I sat beside her, 'you being in here, alone with me. Should I ask Sukey to chaperone us?'

I smiled at her weak jest, and patted her cold, lacerated little hand, which lay outside the bed-clothes like something abandoned or forgotten.

'Don't trouble yourself about it,' I said. 'I am a doctor and you my patient, so it is perfectly proper; besides, everyone is asleep now, you know, excepting you and I.'

'And Sukey?' she asked anxiously.

'She is sleeping in your study,' I said — though I hoped, rather than knew, that my words were truthful. 'We shall not disturb her if we are quiet.'

This seemed to set her mind at ease, and she fell back again on the pillow, her eyes idly following the dance of the candle's shadows upon the low ceiling.

'I'm glad I woke,' she said softly, 'though I was awfully frightened when I came to.'

'Frightened?' I echoed, apprehensively. Visions of what she might have suffered leaped unbidden to my mind.

She twisted her head upon the pillow to look at me, and nodded.

'Oh yes. I had such dreadful dreams, and it was they that roused me. Then I heard you speaking aloud with Sukey, and tried to sleep again, for I did not want to hear something I oughtn't. God knows I've done enough of that, lately.' She shivered. 'But I could not rest, for every time I shut my eyes the dreams rose up again worse than ever.'

'Should you like to tell me about them?' I asked — for I have frequently observed, when treating those who are prey to night-terrors, that the process of describing what is dreadful to them can often banish the phantoms. Sometimes they are even able to laugh at what they had formerly so greatly feared. It seemed, however, that Diana could not speak of her dream-demons to me — or, perhaps, she felt foolish, or ashamed of her fancies, and did not wish to. She shook her head firmly; but then hesitated, as though there were some other matter of which she yearned to unburden herself.

'Is there anything else, then, that you would speak to me about?' I said gently.

Her eyes fluttered closed and she sighed, her breath, light as thistledown, stirring the hairs on my wrist.

'Not tonight, Stephen,' she said, 'for I am so terribly tired. Only stay with me, and keep hold of my hand, won't you?'

I bent to kiss her thin fingers, and they gripped my own tightly, with a strength and vigour I should not have expected of one so exhausted. My mind was still uneasy, however, on one point; and I felt I must ask her the question that burned in my breast.

'Diana,' I said hesitantly, 'I know who has done this to you — I will not speak his name lest it cause you distress — but I swear by almighty God that I shall exact vengeance upon him if it be in my power to do so. But I must

298

know the whole of it, you understand? You must . . . you must tell me if he has done worse to you than outward appearances show. You could be made very ill, you know, if he has touched you, if he has — you catch my meaning, do you not, my dear?'

Her eyes opened and she looked at me steadily.

'I know what you aim at, Stephen. Set your mind at rest. He never got so far — I made sure he did not. Oh! Do not speak of it, please, my love — I have become hateful to myself, but that is not why. I saved myself, Stephen, and damned myself in so doing. That is all I can tell you.'

Her poor cropped head sank back, exhausted beyond her failing strength. It was a queer and uncanny thing to see; for though her gaze as she spoke had been steady, and her voice urgent and clear, now she seemed utterly spent. It was just as if she were a medium through whom some unquiet spirit had been speaking; for her eyes now turned upwards in her head, the lids fluttering like trapped birds. I touched her brow; it was as hot as formerly it had been cold. The fever of her emotional excitement and the strain of her ordeal competed to burn off what little energy remained to her, lending a hectic rosiness to her thin cheeks.

After a while she stirred, as if in a restless dream, and spoke again.

'I am safe here, am I not, Stephen?' she whispered.

'Yes,' I told her. 'All is over now. All is well.'

Her lips moved in a faint smile. 'He told me that if ever I should make my escape, I should find no refuge here. Odd, is it not, that once I took in abused and desperate creatures, and now I come begging succour at my own door?'

'Hush now. Try to rest,' I told her firmly. I pulled the covers up around her and stroked her ragged hair back from her forehead.

'You will stay with me?' she asked again.

Her voice was thin and tremulous, like a lost child's, and my heart swelled with pity, to think that she could imagine my abandoning her to that darkness which had so nearly consumed her. After having witnessed her pathetic entrance, her unsightly injuries, and the nameless terror in her eyes, I could not conceive how anyone with a heart in their bosom might have left the poor girl alone.

'I shall be by your side until morning,' I assured her.

She nodded, settling her cheek upon the pillow, her wan face turned towards mine. After a few minutes her breathing deepened and slowed, though even in her slumber she still clung fast to my hand.

Some time had passed when I looked up to observe Sukey standing in the doorway, staring steadily at Diana in the uncertain flicker of the lone candle. I put a finger to my lips and she nodded once.

'Sleeping the sleep of the just,' she said, in a low, meditative voice. Then she fixed her eyes upon me.

'I expect you're wondering, ain't you, how I

could ever do business with Lord Lucky again after that tale of mine? Maybe asking yourself if you can trust me, seeing as I kept taking his money despite what he done?'

I must admit that the question had crossed my mind; but I did not reply, only held her gaze.

'I'll just say this, Doctor. Needs must when the devil drives, and the devil never drives harder than in Jericho. And no matter how I hate him, living in shame's better than dying in the street any day. I don't ask you to understand, only don't judge me for it.'

'Of course not — ' I protested, but she cut me off curtly.

'Hush, now. She's sleeping.' She glanced back toward Diana's still form, upon the rise and fall of her slender breast, and our two hands intertwined like the hands of spent lovers.

'Life's sweet, Doctor, even for such as me. Even when it's bitter, it's sweet. That's why Our Lady will live, you know,' she said, defiance and longing cracking her soft voice, 'because you give her something to live for.'

And with a swift small smile with something of grief in it, and something of strange, poignant regret, she turned, closing the door gently, and left the two of us alone.

My outward aspect was calm as I watched Diana sleep, but within me my heart pulsed with violent anger: I confess I was as full of rage and murderous thoughts as the vilest blackguard on the streets of Jericho. Kester's absolute villainy could no longer be denied; and whether he had fled beyond immediate punishment or not, I swore silently that Diana would not go unavenged. If not Kester, then the Wilmot Club who had collaborated in his filthy entertainments — the whole damned lot of them should find retribution! Someone must suffer for her suffering; and at that moment, burning with cold fury on Diana's behalf, I did not much care who. Alas! If I had but known how things would fall out, perhaps I might have prayed for mercy as I sat by her side, rather than thirsted for revenge.

I suppose I must have dozed, alone with my patient in the flickering silence of that room; perhaps my eyes closed for a moment; a minute; an hour — I do not know. I could not say what black watch of the night it was when I was awakened by a woman's terrible scream. 'Diana!' I cried, and started violently from my chair. The candle had burned itself out, and I was lost in blackness unrelieved by moonlight, for the shutters were closed tight. The silence following the shriek was thick with the pounding of my own blood in my ears; my brain, still overcast with sleep, was shocked and disordered. Was she gone? Had someone taken her? I bent blindly and felt the bed-clothes; to my enormous relief, Diana's fragile frame still breathed beneath my hands. Her fever had not broken, however, and she panted shallowly, like a dog — perhaps tangled in delirious dreaming. She caught at my fingers as they touched her face.

'What was that?' she croaked, her voice dry as paper.

'Stay here,' I told her in an undertone. 'Do not move.'

'Did I dream it, Stephen? The scream?'

'No. But don't alarm yourself. It may be nothing.'

'Nothing?' she echoed.

'I expect one of the girls has had a nightmare,' I lied, distractedly, though I neither believed my own words nor expected her to. I rose, slowly and cautiously —

'Don't go!' she cried aloud. 'You swore you would not leave me!'

'Hush! For God's sake, hush!' I whispered fiercely. 'For your life, stay quiet! I will return.'

'No . . . ' she moaned hopelessly, tears thickening her voice. Though her distress tore at me, I hardened my heart to her entreaties. I should have been less than a man had I stayed, knowing that another had greater need of me.

When you know a person well, Fraser, you know the rhythm of their step, or the sound of their voice, in an instant — even if they only scream. And when you know someone as I had come to know Sukey over those last few, terrible weeks — when you know *such* a woman, her courage and her strength, the sound of her terror is the most awful in the world, for she does not frighten easily.

Outside in the hall, I crept across the moonlit tiles with infinite stealth, every sense alert and tingling, wondering from whence the danger might come — or already had.

I rounded the corner towards the entrance, and saw that the door to Diana's study swung ajar, and that low firelight flickered upon the opposite wall. I stalked soft as a cat towards the threshold and looked into the room. The dreadful tableau they made there, in the red light of the dying fire, stopped my breath in my throat.

One of the armchairs before the hearth was overturned, as if in the heat of a deadly struggle, and the desk at which Diana habitually worked was strewn with coins, bank-notes and papers in chaotic disarray, as though the contents of a drawer had been upended. Sukey was bent over the desk at an unnatural angle, her face corpse-white. Her mouth and nose were obscured by a heavy, ringed hand clamped tight about them, and she was struggling for air. Behind her, close as a shadow and doubly as dark, his body pressed against hers in a foul parody of intimacy, stood a man I should hardly have recognized as Lucius Kester.

He was a gruesome spectacle. His collar was undone, his shirt filthy with blood, and his cravat torn away. About his naked throat was a livid purple noose of bruises, such as the pathologist finds upon the neck of one hanged. Someone had left their mark upon him, then — but alas! — too lightly, for extraordinarily, despite it all, he yet lived.

They both looked up as I stepped forward. Sukey's eyes widened in fear — I know not whether for her own safety, or for mine — and Kester's narrowed with cruel and cynical amusement. Rather than being amazed to see me, he seemed obscurely satisfied, as if he had been waiting for me to complete this macabre triptych.

His free hand roved swiftly among the disordered coins and notes, stowing them about his person while keeping his victim trapped and dumb. Yet his manner was eerily relaxed, and he showed no hint of desperation. That insouciant coldness of his which Sukey had described was like a deadly tide in which all compassion drowned.

I confess that the sight of him — so cool, so calm — sent a shaft of apprehension into my heart. I had hoped he was either fled for ever, or dead — and indeed, so far as his appearance went, he was not far off it. I would have laid my life that a man of his delicate build and middling strength could not have survived such an attack as he had evidently suffered — and yet, there he stood. He must have had the stamina and resilience of a mongrel dog to have come so close to Death and yet cheated him of his prize! I confess that even in my extremity it amazed me anew, to think of the incredible feats of which the human body is capable in its rapacious struggle for existence.

But his ordeal had taken its toll upon him. His hands were stained with blood and dirt, and his face was ghastly, patterned with a spiderweb of red lines where the capillaries beneath the skin had burst as he fought madly for breath against the strangler's cord. There were black hollows under his bloodshot eyes, which burned fervidly in his dark, congested face. It was an appalling sight — as though a hanged corpse had somehow staggered back up on its feet, to seek vengeance upon its executioner. One would almost have thought that he loved life, so fiercely had he clung to it.

'Doctor Chapman,' said Kester drily, his voice a damaged croak. 'Thank God you're here.'

I ignored his words, turning instead to his captive, who writhed anew in his grasp, perhaps heartened by the sight of me.

'Sukey! Are you hurt? What has he done to you?'

'Nothing,' Kester answered indolently, 'though I daresay the night is yet young.'

I rounded upon him, my eyes flashing.

'Nothing, is it, when you kidnap a woman, half-kill her, and then compound your crimes by taking money from the mouths of women and children!'

I grabbed a bank-note from the cash-strewn desk, brandishing it in his face.

He threw his head back, laughing heartily, and moved his mouth close to Sukey's trembling ear.

'It is not I who steals it from them — is it, Sukey? I've been generous enough with you in the past — but they from me!'

Sukey's frightened eyes widened further, then dropped, and her whole body slumped slackly, as though she had swooned.

'Fear not, Sukey,' I told her, 'I will settle this — ' though in plain truth, I had not the faintest idea how: I was unarmed, and nothing like a weapon lay at hand. Her eyes flickered closed, and a glistening tear escaped from between her lids. That sorry sight cut my soul to its very quick; it was inconceivable that I should stand aside and do nothing; that, weaponless as I was, I should not give my last drop of heart's blood to save this brave, wretched creature.

'Let her go, Kester,' I said in a voice low and stony, 'or by God I'll kill you,' and I was gratified to find that I sounded just as sincere, and as dangerous, as indeed I felt. Kester sensed it too, for his eyebrows raised themselves a fraction, and his sensual lip lifted in a snarl of amusement.

'Will you, Doctor? I say you shan't, you know — for if that hellcat Diana couldn't make an end of me, I fancy I am not for the grave at your healing hands!'

'Release her, damn you!' I shouted, and saw Sukey flinch at the noise, though Kester's icy, sardonic expression did not flicker. He reached out his free hand, and recommenced filling his pockets with the money that lay scattered upon the table.

'Not without what I came for, Doctor. Come now. Where is she hiding? This one won't tell me, but perhaps you value her life more than she does? Perhaps you have as soft a spot for her as she for you, eh?'

I watched him in agonized indecision, afraid that should I rush at him, he would hurt Sukey, perhaps fatally. I turned to look at her, and, seeing the direction of my gaze and the dawning comprehension in my face, she shook her head violently and cringed away — almost into Kester's hateful embrace.

'Don't let him have her, Doctor!' she gasped through his iron fingers. 'Don't you say a word!'

'Quiet, slut!' he spat, and wrenched her head back, forcing from her a cry of pain. Kester smiled to himself momentarily — it was like a flash of lightning across a ravaged plain — then crushed Sukey closer to him, so that she flinched and wilted.

'So she is here, then? And she can, no doubt, hear us,' he speculated. 'Ah, she is a resourceful woman — and she knows who her friends are. But the question is now, which does she prize higher — her lover, or my money?'

Suddenly, he let Sukey go. She tumbled, loosely as a rag-doll, to the floor, and lay breathing harshly and rapidly.

Every fibre of my straining heart yearned to rush to her side: but I was the only thing now blocking Kester's escape — and I swear to you, Fraser, that I knew in that moment that I should never forgive myself, nor be forgiven, if I allowed the monster to go free.

'Diana!' called Kester in that smiling, dead voice of his. 'Come in here, my dear! We have much to discuss, and a friend needs your help. She shan't last long, I'll be bound,' he added, indicating Sukey's sprawled form with a jerk of his chin. 'How is her mistress, by the by? I hope she has recovered from her stay as my guest. We became awfully close, you know, during our time together. She knows almost as much about me, now, as I do of her.'

'Damn you!' I exclaimed, unable to stomach more of his poison.

'Damn *me*!' he grinned, savagely. 'That's good! Damn *her*, rather. Do you know the true purpose of my visits to her, Chapman, and her tolerance of me? You'd rather hear it from her own lips, I'll wager, but I am sure she'll deign to join us eventually. I came to reclaim the inheritance that is rightfully mine — the money she cozened through broken promises made to a dying man and a dead one. At least a whore gives something back — eh, girl?'

He kicked Sukey's unresponsive body, and the blood burned in my veins.

'Lies!' I cried.

'Are they? Lies your sweetheart was willing to pay me not to tell? Lies that can be proven — or could have been, had Hereward not failed me! There exists a painting, Chapman, of your saintly darling, in nothing but her skin, which would show the charitable folk of Oxford and, moreover, *you*, exactly what sort of slut she is. It was given to my friend Henry, her then fiancé, by the artist himself — her lover. I visit Henry in London, often — he is an invalid now, you know, thanks to her! He was most amused to hear that she was in Oxford and up to her old tricks. He told me the whole story — how, even once she had cuckolded him, she would not leave Cambridge until he'd paid her off.'

'I have seen the painting,' I said scornfully. 'It

is nothing. It means nothing to me. She is changed now — washed clean — she is mine!'

Kester's grin widened in vicious delight.

'Yours? You poor dupe! That she can never be! Oh, she told me she feared that she had lost you — and the painting was all you knew about! My God, such innocence! You've no notion of the depths to which that woman will sink, Chapman. You ought to thank me for saving you from a succubus such as she!'

'Stop,' said a voice from the door, softly and yet with such composure that even Kester fell silent.

I turned. Diana was standing, swaying, supporting herself against the door-frame with a trembling hand, like a phantom torn from an unquiet grave.

'At last,' sneered Kester, 'the ghost at the feast. Won't you join us?'

He darted suddenly towards her, as though to drag her into the room, and the dam of my anger broke. I sprang at him, interposing myself between his body and hers, and closed my fingers about his bruised and straining neck, intending to finish what his previous assailant had left undone. We went down together upon the stone floor with a dreadful crash, his bucking body beneath mine. His eyes glazed and glared as we wrestled one another in mutual desperation and hatred. I hardly knew what I was saying as I forced my thumbs against his windpipe, shouting madly into his face.

'Don't touch her! I'll murder you!'

'Will you?' he growled. 'With what? Something like this?'

In a single sudden movement he twisted his body from under mine, pulling from his belt a wicked-looking hunting-knife. He raised it and slashed blindly at my throttling hands, carving a deep wound into my wrist. I cried out, in my agony letting go my hold on his throat. He wriggled away like a snake, backing against the wall, and pointed his blade at Diana, like an accusing finger.

'I'll warrant she's not told you everything, my chivalrous friend. There are secrets she would still not have you know — secrets she paid me to keep. Now, my little huntress, will you tell me where my money is, and let me leave quietly — or shall I tell him what I know?'

'No!' she cried, in an agony of passion — but whether she was refusing to yield to him, or begging his silence, I could not tell.

Kester grinned and advanced on her, the knife held before him, its blade still dripping with my blood.

'No? Very well, then, I shall indulge the doctor's curiosity, for I'm sure he's agog to know. I don't suppose you told him about the child — the child that Henry beat out of you, that you claimed was his?'

I turned to her, and saw the truth in her brimming eyes.

'O Diana!' I said softly. 'O God!'

Kester smiled wider, savouring his awful triumph.

311

'Once she saw I knew everything, you should have seen her pious airs and graces fall away! She was willing to do anything to stop my mouth — anything at all, except pay it me all. She fobbed me off with dribs and drabs at first, hoping, no doubt, to silence me for a time. However, my need grew more pressing, and so I dropped by one night to demand the balance of our account. And then you came, and seemed to know something, and in her despair it seems my hold over her was weakened. Secrets, like nightmares, lose their power once they are exposed to light. But I shall have the money that is mine by right: if my dolt of a father had not tried to unblacken his filthy old soul by leaving it to these whores in the first place, it should have been mine before now. As it is, it was the price of my silence, and for such a secret, I do not think it nearly enough.'

He glanced again, triumphantly, at Diana.

'Wouldn't you agree, my dear?'

But Diana, now, was weeping silently, curled like a beaten spaniel upon the floor. He stared at her as if she were something he had discovered in the gutter which revolted him mildly, but was not otherwise of interest.

'Look at the creature,' he said with disgust. 'Wretched with her own guilt. Ask her!' he spat, suddenly. 'Ask her about the baby! She cannot deny it!'

At this, Diana broke at last. With a cry of fury, she leaped up at him — but he kicked her aside contemptuously, and she fell back upon the stone floor, clutching her arm and whimpering. I tried to go to her, but Kester threatened her again with his boot, and I stopped still, to spare her further violence.

'She said that of all people, she most dreaded your knowing,' he said, conversationally. 'But man to man, I thought I'd better tell you. As a favour. A word to the wise, if you like. Seeing as I'll get what I want out of her anyhow.'

Her sweet mouth twisted with scorn as she struggled up from the ground and stared into his hateful, mocking visage.

'I had rather you killed me, you cur!' she gasped.

He smiled — oh, such a cruel and tender smile!

'I know.'

My heart burgeoned in my breast as I saw the pain seared across her face.

'It does not matter, Diana!' I told her, my whole soul in my voice. 'I forgive you. I love you. Nothing is unforgivable.'

She looked up at me in shock; and seeing I was sincere, her wide eyes filled again with tears. She covered her face with her hands and her whole body shook; a frail sapling in the grip of a hurricane.

'God! God!' she wept. 'What have I done?'

'I'm afraid that your lady is ahead of you, in this as in all things, my poor friend,' said Kester. 'She has already tried to kill me, to protect her shameful secret. Can you conceive of it! So subtle, and so sly, these females — I tell you, Chapman, a fox has nothing on them for cunning or daring, when they set their minds to mischief!'

'What does he mean?' I asked Diana — my voice faltering, but she did not answer me — whether unable, or unwilling to, I could not tell.

'See this?' He gestured at the ring of dark bruises around his throat. 'This is merely unsightly — this did not kill me — but this' — and now he tore open his tattered shirt to expose the heaving breadth of his chest — 'assuredly will.'

With a thrill of horror I saw the familiar, awful pattern of red blisters, the bull's-eyes painted upon his white skin in rings of blood, as though dozens of leeches had crept in the dark to feed upon him and all been torn off at once.

'I'd thought I would die at the hands of my creditors,' said Kester, 'until I crawled back from the edge of death, and staggered into the light, and saw these upon me. You recognize them, don't you, Doctor?'

I nodded. The symptoms were unmistakable. The dreadful mission I had sent Sukey to fulfil a fortnight ago had been unnecessary — Kester had already contracted her sickness from some other source, and he bore the signs of it upon him now, like the mark of Cain.

'Well,' he said, 'so do I. This is the sailors' disease from the Indies. I know the look of it, for my father had a coachman die of it once.

Poor fellow! He was no saint, I suppose, but he did not deserve an end like that. Some it takes quickly and some it eats slow — isn't that right? Him, it took years. First the blisters, then the terrible itching and the scabs, then the flesh turns brown and soft, like a rotten apple, and the bones hollow out like a dying tree. And at last, the madness comes, does it not? The pity and the horror. I was not allowed to see him by that stage, of course, but I heard the servants speak of it.'

He laughed, and it was the rattle of dry bones.

'Swift or slow, I am killed, Chapman, and by one of the girls she harboured; perhaps Sukey herself — it hardly matters. You and she keep breath in them who would otherwise die of it — and they live to walk the street again, infecting honest men! You've as good as murdered me, between you. Only fair, don't you think, that I return the favour?'

Diana must have seen the intent in his eyes then, for 'No!' she shrieked, throwing herself on her knees, her hands reaching to him, beseeching him. 'Leave him be!'

'Back, bitch!' Kester snarled. And swifter than a striking viper, he wrapped his arms about me and clasped me tight before her, a helpless hostage. He jerked my head back, and pushed the point of his blade against the blue vein throbbing in my throat.

'I know this is your area of expertise, my dear, for you've been nursing these girls for a while,' he said conversationally, 'so why don't

you go and get the money, and your best cura-
tives, and perhaps I won't cut his throat? The
disease can be retarded, I know that much, and
once I'm on the Continent I'll consult better
quacks than your sweetheart here. Medicine I'll
need, and cash, in the mean time. And see you
don't try to poison me, for I can read a Latin
label as well as the next man, and I'll bleed
him dry in a heartbeat.'

She staggered back towards the door, weeping and cursing my captor.

'You devil!' she told him. 'You will burn for
this!'

'Yes, yes,' he said, impatiently, his horrible
grinning face, rotten with blood, pressed close
to my own. 'Just be quick about it, there's a
good girl.'

But as she turned hopelessly to do his bid-
ding, a grey-clad figure rose up, swaying, at the
corner of my eye. It held something long and
shining gripped tight as Death in its thin hand,
and its eyes burned black.

In an instant, Sukey was upon him — that
fierce, ravaged girl, dying if she but knew it,
struggling with that fiend — and this time, I
knew, it must be to the death. With her first
wild blow, she struck the upper part of the arm
which held me, and stabbed at it in a terrible
frenzy, finding the brachial artery. His blood
leaped and spurted and he screamed like a
wounded beast and dropped his weapon in
agony. Dizzy with loss of blood, I fell bone-
lessly, slumping on to the floor before the desk
as though already dead. Diana moved to my

aid, but I pushed her away with the little strength that remained to me.

'Back!' I groaned. 'Back, or he'll kill us all!'

But she did not hear me; or if she did, she did not pay heed. She flew at the wounded Kester just as he fell upon Sukey, crushing her with the weight of his body. Diana beat at him with her hands and tried to pull him off the girl, but he lashed out and, with a lucky blow of his fist, laid her senseless upon the cold stones.

With a roar of animal wrath, I sprang at the two figures that writhed together upon the floor, fighting breathlessly for possession of his hunting-blade — for Sukey, I now saw, was armed with nothing but a silver paper-knife. Already the pair of them were slick with blood, hers and his own, like wrestling slaughtermen, and their cries were strangled and wordless. Kester had got Sukey's right hand in his left and was twisting it back and beating it upon the stone floor — but she now had his own knife in her left fist and stabbed at him with the terrible strength of desperation. Yet she was weakening moment by moment, and though she slashed and cut again and again, her blows fell wide or plunged into the soft and meaty parts of his arms.

I did not think. I drove my fist into Kester's snarling face, and felt one or two of his teeth snap from their roots under the force of my blow. Sukey shrieked then, horribly, and I saw he had somehow managed to turn the blade she had wrung from him against her, and that it was sunk inches deep in her chest, which leaked bright blood. I reached for the handle, and with a roar of fury he wrenched it from her body and slashed madly at me, carving crimson ribbons from my shirt-sleeves. I grabbed at the hilt of the weapon, avoiding his wild stabs. Our faces were inches apart, his eyes burning into mine, our hot blood mingling, when I caught his knife by the handle at last and thrust it savagely — once, twice, thrice — into his straining neck.

Kester screamed, a dreadful bubbling howl. It was the sound of Lucifer falling into Hell, and I revelled in it.

I pulled Sukey off him and gathered her to me, dragging her back across the floor, away from Kester's twisting, thrashing body. The knife was gripped in my hand, aimed, trembling, at him, and I never took my eyes from him as he shuddered in his dying agony. His hands, gloved with streaming blood, clutched at his throat to stem the flow; but his wounds were too grievous. I watched unblinking as the life ebbed from his hateful frame. It was over very quickly — a merciful end for one whose life had been without mercy.

When he was quite still, I looked again to Sukey, whose shaking body I still held tightly. As I lifted my hand from the place where he had hurt her, she gasped. I carefully parted the rip in her dress to examine the wound; she had bled but little, and I prayed the injury was superficial. I uncovered it — and my hopes were shattered.

It was a deep clean stab, an inch or two wide, high up on her chest, just to the left of the sternum, where the seat of life lies. The blade had slid between her ribs and found its mark, as unerring and inescapable as an arrow of Cupid — straight into her heart.

'Sukey,' I said, 'can you hear me?'

She nodded, brave girl — O! I never met a braver! — but her face was ashen and her eyes already misting over with the vision of what was to come.

'I'm gone, ain't I?' she said. Blood drooled from her lips as they parted. I nodded, and bowed my head, and wept. She must have felt my hot tears upon her face as I bent over her, cradling her in my arms, for her grey eyes flickered open.

'Never mind, Doctor,' she whispered. 'I won't say goodbye, for I'll see you again, shan't I?'

'There's no Heaven if I do not meet you in it,' I told her; and at this she smiled very faintly, and her eyes closed, and she breathed no more.

There is little left to tell. Once the shock of the night's tragedies had ebbed a little, and Diana had somewhat recovered her strength, for her concussion had been mercifully slight, she went out into the deserted early-morning streets and found a policeman — one with a greater sense of duty, and a keener taste for justice, than the impassive Sergeant Beaton. She told him all — or almost all — that had passed: that Kester had broken in to take the shelter's money, and that I had overcome him. Once the police had done all that was necessary, we bore away poor Sukey, and left Kester to the constables or the crows — I cared not which. Diana, upon whom the ordeal had told sorely, was fainting on her feet by this time, but refused to rest until she had made Sukey decent for the undertaker. She said it was the least and last duty we owed the poor creature, who had, at the expense of her own life, saved both Diana's and mine.

The girls of the shelter gathered silently about her bed, standing solemn vigil over her, their faces white and empty. I had never seen a beautiful corpse before; but in death, her years of hard living and abuse fell away, and she appeared so like the blameless child she must once have been, that I could hardly stand to gaze upon her, and was forced to look away lest my face betrayed my heart.

When Diana slept at last, under the protective watch of a tearful Mary Ann, I walked the half-mile to the Radcliffe, dazed and dazzled by the sunlight I had never thought to see again. I walked like one 'touched' or drunk, Fraser — I stumbled and keeled, exhaustion pulling at me with every step, darkness crawling at the edges of my vision. And yet there was a keen, hectic fever in me too — I had the strange, livid energy that comes when one is beyond fatigue, beyond tears, beyond anything. I felt as if I were living on my nerves alone, and flaring up high and bright, just as a candle flame does, the moment before it gutters and dies.

I had barely strength to see or walk, but

there was one final question I must answer before I could let myself rest.

I felt that I knew already what I would find, even as I pricked my finger and squeezed a single drop of my blood on to the glass slide. That dreadful disease strikes fast and deadly, like a snake: it shows itself swiftly in the body of its host — a few hours, at the outside. And so when I saw the twirling spirochaetes beneath the microscope, I was not amazed, only satisfied — almost relieved, indeed — that at last I knew what I must do.

I did not return to the shelter, to Diana, to say good-bye. It would have been an act of cruelty more than of kindness, and I could not have borne to be cruel — crueller, I should say — to her. But neither could I bear the idea of confiding in her my dreadful situation, and she, perhaps, blaming herself for it. Our bloods had mingled, mine and Kester's, and he had killed me too, though it was he who lay cold in the mortuary. Had he but known it, the awful irony of it, he should have laughed that queer, hoarse laugh of his. Perhaps he mocks me even now, from his station in Hell?

For I was a murderer, and condemned by my own hand. It mattered not that Kester had deserved his death, nor that I had cut his throat in self-defence. His blood was upon my soul; and moreover, Sukey, that poor, brave, loyal creature, had died defending me, and for that, if nothing else — for that, and for everything else — I knew I should never be able to hope for forgiveness. I could not ask Diana to stand by me now that I knew my doom. Still less could I marry her, as had been my heart's desire, for to do so would have been to consign her, and any children she bore, to my own terrible fate. So I took no leave of the woman I loved, for I wanted her to think of me kindly, as of a friend who has gone away.

Set in the balance against all my other crimes, the sin of self-destruction seems to weigh as a mere feather, and so, once I have finished this letter, I will hurry in the direction of the canal, and as I go I shall comfort myself with the thought of how much better the world will be without me in it. I shall consider how fortunate this Earth is, to rid itself of me at last; and how happy and grateful all my friends — including you, old fellow; yes, even you — will be when they understand that I have had the decency to remove myself quietly, without fuss, and plague them no more.

I believe that Diana might miss me, a little, and you, Fraser, as well, but I also know that the misery I have inflicted upon you both far outweighs the scant joy I could ever hope to bring — especially now.

The dawn is just breaking; the day promises to be fine. It is time: I shall write my last words and consign this letter to the porter, along with that damned, and damning, painting. Strange that it should afford me my last glimpse, in this world, of she whom I most treasured in it; but God, as you are wont to observe, Fraser, sometimes moves in mysterious ways.

I shall walk alongside the river, and listen to the twittering of the birds in the rustling leaves, and watch the sunlight glitter upon the tumbling waters. Birdsong has never sounded so sweet in my ears, nor has Nature ever seemed more lovely to me, than at this moment.

And yet I confess that my heart is strangely light — lighter, perhaps, than it has ever been — as I think of how I shall fill my pockets with stones, and walk out into the cold dark water, and so at last bring to an unmourned end the wretched story of your most sincere and sorrowful friend,

Stephen Chapman

BOOK FIVE

The Confession of Anna Sadler

The following document was pressed upon me by its author as one of the last acts of her life, some eighteen years ago. It appears that she had spent the final months of her confinement composing these pages, part confession, part personal memoir, and part letter to her unborn child.

Though I did not peruse them at the time, I broke the seal so that I could include them here now for you, my dear son, to read, in order that you might come to understand her extraordinary history and the truth behind the tragic events of her short life.

It is too late for me to beg your mother's forgiveness for the injustice I once did her — but it is not too late for you to know how great a soul was contained in that fragile vessel, and to honour and remember her, as I do, now that I am setting out upon the bright path to join her.

EF, 1914

My darling child,

The dreariness of the chill spring weather and the tedium of my confinement, coupled with a strange impulse I have been feeling, over these last few months, to unburden my bosom of what has lain weighty upon it for so long, have impelled me at last towards the writing-desk, where now I sit, feeling you shift softly inside me as though demanding my attention. Your father is out upon some errand, and the imploring wind tugs at the ivy that waves before my window, rattling the loose panes.

But my attention is all yours, little one, for this letter, or confession, or whatever I shall call it (and in truth, I know not what it will be until it is finished, for I never tried to set down my life on paper before), is for your eyes alone, as and when I believe you are ready to know all that conspired to make your mother what, and who, she has become.

How strange and dreadful it is to be entirely without desire! I know that some religions believe this to be the apotheosis of holiness, the nearest its disciples can attain to the Godhead, and yet I cannot think it so. To be desireless is to live with one's heart cut out — neither despairing nor rejoicing, never knowing agony or ecstasy, only living as dumbly as a beast between hour and hour, day and day, year upon year. To turn one's face to the wall and have done with life, with care, with all of it. To want nothing. To have nothing. To be as dead within as a stock or a stone.

But I am dead inside no longer, my love. I am more alive than ever I have been! I quicken with two heartbeats. I have you, and you are all I desire. Certainly it is painful, to return to the world after so long out of it — many years for me, as opposed to three days for Christ in the tomb — but the pain is only that of a limb benumbed, shooting darts of sensation, little sparkling agonies, to remind me that at last I live again.

But I digress — this unfamiliar dance of my pen upon the paper has already led me astray, and I must stick to my purpose, little one, if I am to speak of what I know; if I am to lay the facts of my life before you.

Let me begin, then, at the place where every life-story has its start, which is to say, with my birth: I forswore anything but the whole truth a long time ago, and if you will have my tale, it shall be all of it.

I was born Anna Sadler in East Anglia, in the year 1859. My father, Christopher, was of decent enough stock, in a quiet way; his family had lived upon its Norfolk acres and collected rent from its tenant-farmers since time immemorial, after the usual fashion of minor country gentry. Following the age-old convention, my father, the youngest son by some years, who had shown strong artistic promise (and hence, to my grandfather's mind, a disagreeably unconventional streak) in his early youth, was committed to the clergy at the earliest possible opportunity, so as to curb any ambitions he might have in the Bohemian direction.

After he had completed his studies at the University, a living was allotted to him, and he made his way to the vicarage of Hardwick, a little village just over the county border into Cambridgeshire, without much demur — assuming that he would live out his life quietly there, in a modicum of comfort, sketching the natural beauties with which the landscape abounded, and delivering an uncontroversial sermon every Sunday — for at that time he did not feel himself to have a particular vocation.

All this changed, however, when he met my mother at a ball given annually for the local worthies, to which anyone who approached that description was invited, even one so retiring and obscure as he (for merchants' daughters must marry too, you know). But alas for her, my mother was no mere tradesman's girl: she was, indeed, considered the jewel of the Pelham family's three daughters. The Pelhams were an old Catholic clan, extremely well-to-do, and through influence and advantageous alliances had managed to cling on to their fortune and estates even through the turbulence of Tudor times. The family had fully expected to barter off their youngest child to some viscount or baronet at the very least, and were, as you may imagine, extremely put out to discover (when at last she had the courage to make her feelings known) that she had fallen head over heels in love with an undistinguished Anglican vicar.

330

Even his abandonment of the English Church, rescindment of his orders and conversion to Catholicism failed to move them: they would not hear of my mother's marrying him, and so, one day, they made their escape under cover of night in a hired post-chaise, drove up to Gretna Green together, and were secretly wed. No matter that my father, with his living gone and his little inheritance shrunk almost to nothing, had no obvious means of supporting her — nor that she came to his arms unburdened by a dowry, having been disowned by her people: the blissful pair believed that they could live upon love, and according to Papa, managed to do almost that in the first few years of their union, and were very happy.

My memories of my mother are vague and faded now; to me she is a sort of benevolent ghost, a kind warm presence smelling of the freshness of cut flowers, with dark silky curls which I used to wind around my babyish fingers. That is all I have of her, save a little locket-sketch my father drew, in which she looks remarkably like myself at twenty or thereabouts. She died of a weak heart (a condition congenital in her family) a few years after giving birth to me; I had a little brother for a spell of a few months, but when he fell victim to some infant illness, the grief of it carried her away too — or so said my father.

Alone in the world, save for each other, with me but three or four years old, my father decided to turn his hand again to his first love, painting, and make a living somehow as a drawing-master for young ladies and gentlemen. This he managed with some success, though he often fondly attributed the securing of many of his professional engagements to my own constant presence at his side. It seemed that not only did my winning, childish ways charm prospective students and parents alike, but the existence of a little girl, coupled with my father's widowhood, meant that many a mother's mind was set at rest. After all, the chances of the new art-master making love to, or eloping with, her precious daughter were vanishingly small, burdened as he already was with a dead wife and a living child.

And so we went on, my father and I, poor enough for me to have known hunger and privation more than once in my life, but happily secure in one another's company and the strength of our mutual affection. He remained true to his new faith and raised me a Catholic, in my mother's memory, but we had to keep that aspect of our lives secret for much of the time, lest we were regarded with suspicion or horror by his genteel, Anglican would-be employers. As I grew older, and came to know, if not fully understand, such things, I was often struck by the irony of our situation, and amused by the idea of the young ladies and gentlemen whom Papa instructed in the gentle art of drawing discovering that their tutor was not only a Papist, but an apostate from their own church at that; once as accustomed to delivering homilies and singing hymns as the staunchest Protestant alive!

When I was just fifteen, however, my poor father died. He had gone out for several dawns together to sketch herons on the marshes near the little cottage where we then lodged, and at last caught a dreadful chill on his lungs which he could not shake. I nursed him as best I could, but although I looked far older than my tender years (which was subsequently to prove to my advantage) I was still little more than a child, and all my loving care could not, alas, save him. I buried him the week before my six-teenth birthday, and was left bereft, bereaved, and with scarcely a penny to my name. All that my father had been able to bequeath me was a sheaf of his drawings and paintings (which I subsequently sold, all but the locket with the picture of my mother), a little artistic talent, raised to a decent enough pitch by his excellent tuition, and a determination to make my own way in the world, friendless as I was, just as he had.

The question of throwing myself upon the mercy of my mother's family never entered my head; I should rather have eaten stones — but, by a queer coincidence, I was soon to encoun-ter a distant relative of the Pelhams — an individual old lady called Miss Bellingham, who was a lifelong spinster with a modest annuity and an absolute passion for art. As you might imagine, after two or three years of instructing girls hardly younger than myself (for at this time I was giving my age as twenty-one and claiming experience at one of the Paris schools) I was thoroughly sick of the thankless life of a teacher-cum-governess.

Thus, when I made the acquaintance of Miss Bellingham at a watercolour-exhibition, and she mentioned her growing frailty and solitude, and asked whether I knew of anyone who might make her a suitable companion, it seemed as though a gift from Heaven had dropped into my lap. I at once put myself forward, and as she liked what she called my 'grave' looks (she did not disapprove of beauty in young women, but mistrusted 'frivolous, flirtatious prettiness') and had no objection to my artistic leanings — indeed, positively encouraged them — I moved in with the lady two weeks later, and for three happy years we lived very comfortably and amicably together in Fen Ditton.

I had got into the habit, on my half-day off, which fell upon a Wednesday afternoon when Miss Bellingham could best spare me, of going into Cambridge town and entertaining myself by wandering about the streets and seeing what I could see; whether the vivid colours and sounds of the market, or the monochrome phalanxes of students walking purposefully from lecture to library, weighty volumes clutched beneath their arms. My first few forays were, I admit, rather disappointing, for alas, there is little pleasure in window-shopping when one cannot possibly afford the goods on display.

However, after some weeks of exploring the limited opportunities for amusement afforded to a poor girl, barely better than a servant, I was overjoyed to discover the Fitzwilliam's art-gallery, where I stood and gazed for hours at paintings that both entranced and invigorated me. Here, at last, was the genius of which my father had so often spoken; here were the blood-rich Turner sunsets and the smoky, tenebrous hues of the Old Masters, and I felt blessed to be able to sit and drink them in without hindrance — and, moreover, without paying an entrance-fee. Every day that the sun did not shine (and many on which it did) I hastened eagerly towards that haven, and drank my fill of beauty before duty compelled me to return to the *camera obscura* of Miss Bellingham's cottage.

Perhaps unlike most girls of my age, I had never hoped nor sought for romance in those cool, dim galleries — for I occupied that uneasy liminal space between gentility and the common run of honest working people, where those men beneath you in birth think you too fine for them, and those above believe themselves superior to such as you (always excepting, of course, those girls of the middle or trade class who have handsome dowries, invariably the most eloquent way to effect an introduction to a potential husband).

In short, unlike so many of the females dawdling in the Fitzwilliam of an idle afternoon, I was there for the art — and that was where, one fine Wednesday in the spring of 1880, I met Antonio Valenti — or rather, he met me.

Valenti was a remarkably fine-looking young man, with black hair, large dark eyes, and skin kissed by the Mediterranean sun, and I cannot truthfully claim not to have noticed him, artist as he so evidently was, with oil-paint carelessly smeared on his wrists and shirt-tails and sketching-pad prominently to hand, on my previous perambulations around the gallery. However, I was aware that to acknowledge him would be tantamount to encouraging perhaps unwelcome attentions, and so I let my gaze glide over him as though I were a swan and he water, and gave no sign whatever of my curiosity. Naturally enough, indifference on my part piqued interest on his (for wherever he went, I saw that the shop-girls and lady's-maids near fainted at his dashing looks) — in addition to which, he seemed to appreciate my own earnest admiration of the paintings on display, and at last made bold to approach me.

He wasted little time on niceties, but plunged straight in, asking me what I thought of the Gainsborough before which I stood, and, reciprocating his frankness, I told him. Our conversation moved on swiftly; we spoke together of art and artists in some depth, and with such vigour that we were forced eventually by the dryness of our throats to take refreshment at a local tea-room. By the time we parted, I had secured an invitation to see some of the pieces he was working on *in situ*, in his garret-studio; and he had asked me to model for him — a request at which I at first baulked, then laughed — then, when he mentioned the sum he was prepared to pay me (quite half a week's wages by Miss Bellingham's frugal reckoning), began very seriously to consider.

You must remember that I was then barely twenty-one, despite having the bearing and manner of one some years my senior, and extremely ignorant in the ways of the world, and of men in particular. The only man I had known with any intimacy was my father, whom I had admired and adored — and I confess that Valenti's passion for both art and life reminded me with an almost painful tenderness of my dear, dead Papa. I knew how to make my way in the world, I knew how to get by on half-nothing a year; I knew how to conduct myself in front of potential employers, and how to paint a portrait, draw a dahlia and sketch a skull; but I had no idea how to control the wilful wanderings of my heart — for I had never before had occasion to try.

I became Valenti's model; then his friend; then his confidante and pupil; and at last his sweetheart and his Muse. He painted me as Venus rising from the waves, as Sappho composing her love-rhymes, as apple-dropping Atalanta, and as Diana disturbed bathing — but it was this last piece that was his favourite by far, and from which his fond nickname for me, 'Diana', was derived. Of course he knew my true name, but preferred not to use it for reasons of confidentiality (with which precaution I heartily concurred) and so I became 'Diana' to him and his friends: and Diana, for good or ill, I remained.

What Antonio and I felt for one another would now be called, I think, 'puppy-love' — a tender, violent adolescent passion which burned

337

fiercely but chastely like a sacred flame between us. I was never his mistress; he was never my lover, whatever the other models might have thought. He gave me, as a token of the sincerity of his intentions, a little gold-and-garnet ring his mother had owned; I wore it for a while upon my little finger, but soon, in order not to arouse suspicion in Miss Bellingham, strung it on a silken cord about my neck, next to my heart, and touched it often beneath my blouse when I was lonely, and thought of him.

We told each other stories of our families (mine, I admit, somewhat embellished with fancies from my reading of Shakespeare and fondness for opera) and made grand, wonderful plans for our future. We were star-crossed and poverty-stricken, but like all heroes and heroines of stage and literature, we believed that our love would carry us on golden wings far above the petty concerns of the world, and that, somehow, we would contrive to be together, and be happy. Even then, I confess I had some apprehension in my heart as to how we might survive, penniless as we were, for I recalled only too well the heartbreaking struggles of my parents; but I pushed these unwelcome thoughts away, giving myself over entirely to the sweet intoxication of hope.

In short, we adored one another, but being both so poor, could not sanctify our mutual affection with the bond of marriage; nor would either of us have dreamed of consummating it without the blessing of the Church. We were as joyful and innocent as children in our love, but it was, none the less, a childish dalliance; a beautiful dream from which one or other of us was bound, eventually, to wake.

Henry Hereward was the man who broke that dream.

If you, little stranger, should have the dubious pleasure of coming into this world female, I tell you this now: prepare yourself for some very great hardships, for though, God willing, you will be born into a family which shall love you and care for you as much as any child living, the world was not shaped for the happiness of you and I. And if you who stir even now within my womb are a little boy, be thankful that you were born free, white and English — but most of all that you were born male; and have pity and mercy on the members of a sex made weaker less by natural disposition than by the demands, obligations and injustices heaped upon our heads.

Nothing can excuse what now follows, which I undertake to relate with complete honesty in as much detail as I can now recall, except this: I should never have been so severely punished for my actions, had I been a man. None would have been the wiser; my reputation would not have suffered one whit; my life would not have been scattered to the four winds. This does not mean that what I did was not wrong — only that at the time it seemed to me, as one who had suffered poverty, famine and loss, the best thing to do for my own sake and that of my future children.

Nobody, except perhaps Antonio's friend Edward Fraser, knew of our clandestine engagement — our understanding was to remain an absolute secret until Antonio had established himself as an artist or teacher with sufficient income to marry and start a family. This, I confess, I found not only thrillingly romantic on one level (for covert love-affairs were the very stuff of three-volume novels then, as now) but also comfortingly practical — for despite the great esteem in which I still held my beloved father, and the many happy memories I had of my own childhood, I had no wish to raise my children in a situation of uncertainty or want. The height of my ambition, before I met Henry Hereward, was only to marry Antonio, live with him in secure and loving domesticity, and have many healthy and happy offspring.

I have said that Antonio was a handsome man, but Henry Hereward was that infinitely more dangerous thing — a charming one, and rich, and clever, and superior in breeding to boot. No wonder I gave my still-unpierced heart to him! No wonder I became mad for the gleam of his bright eyes, for the sound of his step; for the ring of his voice calling softly to me in the shadows of twilight . . . Lovely women are both celebrated and excoriated by society, but this is quite unfair, for beauty is only a weapon if its owner has the wit to make it one. It is the fascinating, intelligent female against whom you must guard, my little love, whether you grow to be

woman or man; for other women, be they moth-
ers, sisters, sweethearts or rivals, cannot compete
against them; and men's hearts are not proof
against the least of their wiles. This single fact, I
believe, saves those of both sexes from downfall
at the hands of these sirens: that for a woman to
wield such extraordinary influence, to be a
femme fatale, she must, perforce, be beautiful.
Men must only be powerful: that is their beauty,
and women and men alike swoon before it, if it
is compelling and strong enough.

Henry's power was strong enough, and real
too, and he knew and exulted in it. His was a
sharp, agile intellect, which idled for most of
the time, but when forced into action (such as
a philosophical debate with a friend, or an
essay for his exasperated tutors) would produce
such astonishing results with so little apparent
effort that even now it fills me with wonder and
apprehension to think what he might have done
with his brainpower, had he ever had the drive
and inclination to use it fully. But he was an
indolent, sensual fellow, even at twenty, and
though he excelled in every endeavour to which
he turned his casual hand, there was none he
had energy and passion enough to pursue, save
the systematic indulgence of his own appetites
and whims. He was a Catholic, but such a one
as gave my father's adopted faith a bad name;
he would sin on a Saturday night merely to
have something to repent of at Sunday Mass,
and go out again the next week and repeat his
follies, only this time twice as frequently and
twice as badly.

But God! he was charming. When he first caught my eye in Petty Cury, by the market-place, and would not look away nor take my studied indifference for an answer, my heart throbbed a little faster in my breast as I went swiftly on my way, though I knew it ought not to. He followed me all the way to the Hills Road, by the cemetery, where I habitually waited to beg a lift back to Miss Bellingham's from the passing carters — but for shame, I could not bring myself to do so in front of him, and instead pretended that I was waiting for a friend — by which I meant him to understand an older female companion or chaperone, so that, perhaps, he would let me alone and go upon his way.

He affected to misapprehend me, however, and cursed the imaginary 'gentleman' for a cur and a cad, for leaving so lovely a creature alone on the common highway, at the mercy of bold reprobates such as he. I could not forbear to laugh, and chided him that he could not be so dangerous as he claimed, or else I should have seen pictures of his face up in the post-office, where they hang the portraits of wanted criminals, and he smiled very wide and offered to prove it. This was such a quixotic way of effecting an introduction that I was entirely swept away by it, and, dazzled by his peculiar charisma, I allowed him to treat me to tea at a small café nearby.

Though I had got into the habit of concealing nothing from Antonio, and chattering on about the various little events of the past few

days as he painted and sketched me every
Wednesday afternoon, the next week I did not
mention this interlude to my beloved. I was
afraid that he would be jealous, even though as
far as I was concerned it was an isolated incident, not to be repeated, with a man who was
at once well above my own station and quite
self-evidently — self-confessedly, in fact — a
rake. Looking back, I know now that this was
the first evidence of the guilt in my own heart;
for even then I could not help but hope,
secretly, that somehow I might run across this
fascinating stranger again.

Let me put this as bluntly as I may: though I
still loved Antonio sincerely, I fell in love with
Henry, and he — well, he did not, alas, fall in
love with me. He was, however, after a month
or two of accidental-upon-purpose meetings
and intense conversations over tea, then coffee,
then dinner, then wine, very much in thrall to
me. I was, naturally, still a virgin, though he
had frankly made me aware that he was not
lacking in experience in that area, and I believe
he had conceived a mad ambition to deflower
me, which was, I felt, despite my own helpless
desire for him, quite impossible unless and
until we were married. I think he was at first
rather unpleasantly surprised by the strength of
my resistance, surmising no doubt that this was
some wile of mine to render the prize more
attractive, but when he realized the sincerity
and strength of my resolve, he became at once
far more respectful of me than he had hitherto
been — and, of course, more determined to

make me surrender my will and my body to his.

When he began to speak seriously of a secret understanding between us, I knew — and was astonished at the savage joy of my mastery over him — that I had him. Suddenly what had been a flirtatious game, if a dangerous one to my heart and honesty both, was being played in deadly earnest. I slowly came to appreciate that in Henry, I had within my grasp all that my parents had lost for the sake of love, and had been unable to regain. Wealth, position and power, for myself and for the children I would bear, were mine for the asking — and all I had to give in return was that which is cherished most in woman, and which, once lost, cannot be regained.

Though Antonio had seen me nude many times, he had always viewed me as a model though an artist's eyes, and we had never exchanged more than the most innocent caresses, let alone become lovers — for our mutual inclination had been to possess our two souls in patience until the time was right. But now, with Henry's hot eyes upon me, in imagination if not in fact, wherever I went, I began to know the heady, dangerous elation of being savagely desired. I began, myself, to desire; it was a sensation I had never known, as different from the purity of my affection for Antonio as flame from spark, or waterfall from rain. I wanted to be Henry's wife, and have all that came with it, of course — but I also wanted to know and be known; to press my naked body against his — I wanted, in short, *him*.

It seemed, for a brief, wonderful interlude, to be possible. The only real barriers to our marriage (for he knew and approved of my mother's high birth and Catholic antecedents) were firstly, my poverty; secondly, Henry's own disinclination to take on responsibility or obligations of any kind; and, thirdly, his father's approval. As for the first, Henry could supply my lack; the second was overridden by his fomenting lust (and besides, he told me with a comical roll of his eyes, he'd have to marry someone *some* time, and should far rather it was me than anyone else); and the third, he promised me to manage. Perhaps it was foolish of me, but I believed him: Henry was a headstrong and persuasive man, the apple of his doting father's eye, and he assured me that once the old man had met me, our chief trouble would be preventing him from trying to carry me off himself.

And so we struck a deal. You may perhaps think it mercenary or whorish of me, my dear, if and when you come to read this, whichever sex you belong to, but I was determined not to sell myself cheaply — for I knew well enough that with a man like Henry, to make a bargain one way or another was my only option, or else sooner or later he would look in the window of a different shop.

We went to a hotel deep in the country, registering ourselves as a married couple; Mr and Mrs Johnson, I believe. I wore Antonio's ring while we were in public to maintain the fiction of our union; but as soon as the door of the suite closed behind me, Henry tore it from my finger in an access of jealousy.

'Where did you get this?' he demanded, in deadly tones. I stuttered that it had been my mother's, which was almost true — and hated myself for the lie, and the traducement of my secret betrothal, even as the words left my lips. He considered it for a moment, turning it in his thin strong fingers, then smiled and tossed it on the table by the door.

'Cheap little thing,' he said carelessly. 'Still, I suppose it was the best your poor father could afford. I think I can do a little better, however.'

The ring he slipped upon my finger held a diamond larger than I had ever seen, except in a jeweller's window.

'That was *my* mother's,' he said, moving his mouth against my cheek, his breath hot and soft upon my ear. 'Pretty taste, hadn't she?'

I put my forefinger to his lips.

'Not yet,' I said.

He pouted, then grinned wickedly.

'Very well, my dear; you drive a hard bargain, don't you?' He stepped aside and swept his hand towards the writing-desk. The letters I had asked him to compose were laid out on it for my inspection, signed, but not sealed; one to his father, informing him of our engagement, and one to *The Times* of London, announcing it. Both were stamped, and I watched as he sealed them and put them into my portmanteau.

'You may post them in the morning, as soon

346

as you like,' he said. 'When we are at last one.'

I was trembling violently as he took me in his arms; not with terror, but with desire for him. I did not think of Antonio again that night. I was in the feverish embrace of my first and, for a long time, only lover; my deflowerer, my defiler, call him what you will — and though I feared it a little, I ached for it too. I was not a victim, that you must understand, unless it was of my own avarice, ambition and deceitfulness, which were soon — oh, so very soon! — to bring all I had longed for crashing down about my ears. Though Henry made me hate him afterwards, I was the original author of my own downfall, and I accept responsibility for my misery: I am paying for it still. Never be a liar, my little one.

We were lovers, and I was in love with him, and I wanted him too: but I had lied to him and to Antonio, and my sins were soon to find me out.

Somehow, Edward got wind of my engagement to Henry before the party was officially announced (he did not know me then by my true name, so the notice in *The Times* would have meant nothing to him) and told Antonio. Ever since the first moment he had stumbled unawares upon me sitting for Antonio, I had known with a woman's sure instinct that he had no love for me. Years later, Stephen used to tease him, and call him a 'cold fish'; but I had divined his secret, for it was also my own. Stephen was everything to both of us: we would gladly have died for him. Yet that which should have bound us more closely pushed us further from one another, like repelling magnets. I think, perhaps, we understood one another from the very beginning, though Edward might not then have admitted it. But to understand all is to forgive all, and this, at least, we held in common; we loved fiercely, and without compromise.

We who must hold ourselves aloof, who must practise self-control, who must bank the fires of our passion and pretend indifference where we would rage and burn, may sometimes appear heartless, but the truth is quite the reverse. Because we teach ourselves to suffer in silence, the world assumes we do not suffer. Believe me, my little one, it is not so. Perhaps he recognized this quality in me too; I do not know. In any case, I knew at once that through no wish of my own, I had made an enemy, and one all the more formidable for his outward mildness.

Edward evidently feared that the affection of Antonio, his best friend, hitherto centred upon himself, and more than returned (as I could tell), was finite; that Antonio could not give his heart to me without loving him a little less. Certainly, it was obvious that Edward was incapable of loving Antonio without hating me. To his credit, he refrained from abusing or maligning me; but I felt his gaze upon me more than once when he thought himself unobserved, and it was not hot with desire, as is that of most men who bend their eyes upon a pretty woman, but cold with suspicion and dislike. I had no quarrel with Edward, but to his mind, I had stolen his bosom companion, and I knew that sooner or later I should be made to pay.

And that was why he told my secret, and in so doing, shattered his best friend's heart.

What followed at the engagement-party was a dreadful scene — Antonio storming in and throwing down the portrait of me as Diana; Henry white as a ghost, and the terrible hatred in his eyes when he looked at me, believing me to have cuckolded him with Antonio — oh, the awful irony of it! I had privately reasoned to myself that since Antonio's and my betrothal had never been made public, it as good as did not exist, and so I was deceiving nobody — ah, what falsehoods we hoodwink ourselves with, when we are desperate, and desirous, and believe ourselves in love!

I shall not linger upon the awful details of what transpired: it is dreadful to recall, even after so many years, and I have tried many times since, without success, to blot it from my recollection. Suffice it to say that there was a duel; that Antonio was killed, and Henry horribly wounded, and that very same night I discovered myself to be with child, and went to beg Henry to honour our engagement, for the sake of his baby, if not for my own. He called me slut and whore, and insisted that it could not be his — for though he had seen clearly enough the signs of my virginity when we had first made love, he affected to believe that I had taken the opportunity to become Antonio's mistress at the same time.

I wept and pleaded, and swore that I had never known another man; but it did not matter, for nothing could be proved, and Henry now loathed me with all the warped passion of love turned sour. He became furious, and wrenched the diamond from my finger, casting me from him; and then our bodies met again, for one final time, in violence. And when I left him that night, or rather, stumbled away, I had at last lost everything: my hope, my love, my lover — and my child.

It was the war that saved me.

I left Cambridge in poverty and disgrace, and wandered, half-distracted with grief, from town to town, taking odd work where I could get it — sewing, teaching at village schools, housekeeping and even a little modelling for artists, anywhere I was certain I should not be recognized or known. And yet everywhere I fled, still I carried with me my crushing burden of guilt and shame. Both Antonio and my unborn child had died because of my lies; Henry had turned fiend, and been brutally wounded, permanently crippled. Was this what love did? Could I not make amends, somehow? I should have gone anywhere, sacrificed anything — and at last I found what I must do.

From the first moment I volunteered to go out and tend the dying and wounded soldiers who fought so bravely in the Colonies, I knew that this was what I was meant for; and every day of the training confirmed my faith. I felt washed clean, reborn. Each wound I dressed, each man I comforted, healed something in my soul, until at last I felt that, through my usefulness to others, I had become almost bearable once more to myself. I resolved to devote my life to nothing else — and so I have done ever since. Little by little, my repentance was becoming easier; little by little, or so I felt, my sins were receding and fading; were being sluiced away.

There was a girl who trained with me — she was about my age, and had my sort of looks and colouring, and we got on so well together that the other girls joked and called us sisters. She died out there in Afghanistan — of an awful disease that thrives in that foul tropic, caught from the blood of one of the soldiers she tended. It is commonly known as a venereal disease, one I have seen since in many of the street-walkers of Jericho, and so her own colleagues, declining to believe that she had not been whoring, refused to treat her, and when I would not leave her side, cast us both out.

I watched over her as she breathed her last, as she gave me her little gold ring (the only heirloom of value she had taken with her) and told me to go to her cousin in Oxford, her sole living relative, whom she had not seen for some ten years, and tell him she had thought of him at the end.

Her name was Diana Cornell.

The coincidence was too wonderful. My own old appellation; Antonio's secret pet-name for me. I took it as a sign. I believed that God had sent me this opportunity to show me I was forgiven, and could live a new life, free from the miseries and, worse, the terrible guilt, of my old one. I closed her eyes and took her keepsake. And — yes, I confess it — I took her place, too. Her life became mine, her cousin my cousin, and her mission my own — I would save those who had been rejected and cast aside as she had so unjustly been. I would work to cure them, to redeem them, to make them live again, just as she lived again in me.

But I should do this chastely, as a widow. I would keep her name and match it to another, one no-one else would know, but which would remind me daily of both my adored mother, the most generous and loving of women, and her family, whose cruelty condemned her to a life of penury and hardship. I would take my mother's maiden name, and Diana's Christian name, and be born anew, the sins and sadnesses of the past shed at last. And moreover, with Diana's face constantly before my eyes, and my mother's sad fate in my heart, I hoped to ensure that I might never condemn another, as they had once been condemned.

I slipped Diana's ring on to my finger, and became Mrs Pelham.

I returned to London with the rest of that unhappy, decimated army, and immediately wrote to my new cousin Neil Cornell, a doctor in training, to wonder whether he might be able to find me some nursing work near him in Oxford. He gladly obliged, and I was happy for almost three years in that city; first, nursing private patients and advancing my training at the Radcliffe Infirmary (which was in fact where I first saw Stephen, though he never saw me, and it was some months before I could get up the courage to introduce myself to him) and, latterly, at the Victor Street shelter.

I had found my vocation; I had even found love again. At last I dared to hope that I had been forgiven; my sins forgotten, my past misdeeds expunged.

And then came Lucius Kester.

Imagine, if you can, innocent babe that you are, fine boy or girl that you shall, I know, grow to be, the abject horror of something awful, which you had believed dead and buried, rising from the grave to greet you at the very moment of your longed-for salvation. Imagine the guilt and shame of your past mocking you from beneath a mask of mild innocuousness. Imagine the dread of tearing off that mask, and staring your own old sin in the face once more.

Kester was sly and subtle in his blackmail — for that was what it was, plain and simple, and he never bothered to disguise his intention once he knew that his meaningful looks and hints had hit their mark. It seemed that Henry Hereward still lived, as a dissolute shadow of his former self, sponging off naïve expatriates all over Europe and, latterly, in London, where Kester — a boyhood friend of his, apparently — had heard the whole of our doomed and sordid history together from Henry's own lips.

It did not take the astute Lucius long to recognize me in Hereward's description, and he at once determined to extract money from me in exchange for his silence. From the first, he had resented his father's charitable benevolence in willing half his estate to the refuge for fallen women of which I was now the manager — and, as he told me at our third or fourth interview, he intended to claw back all that he felt was rightfully his.

Naturally, I was revolted and distressed in the extreme by this turn of events, and his low and avaricious motives — but none the less, I paid him off, as far as was commensurate with my conscience, by giving to him what would have been my monthly stipend for the position I held, and living as frugally as possible, so that some nights when the girls had all been fed, and there was not even a drop of soup nor a heel of bread left, I myself went hungry.

I should not have done it, I know — I should have abandoned all my lies there and then — but I could not! I could not bear to have my happiness snatched away from me once more. I knew that to be rejected again, and by one who meant more to me than anyone before or since (saving always you, my little one), should break me — should kill me, I believed.

At first my monthly payments seemed to satisfy Kester, and he let me alone for a spell — but then he grew more importunate, more insistent; he would have more, he would have everything! A blackmailer, like a glutton or opium-fiend, is never satisfied, but craves all until all is gone. I delayed, I dissembled; on more than one occasion I point-blank refused — but then Kester would smile, and wonder aloud what my surgeon-sweetheart would think if he were to tell what he knew, and — alas! — at last, I crumbled.

The night that he came to collect what he wanted was the same night that Stephen interrupted our conference. At the time I cursed Fate, and God, and — forgive me — even Stephen's bosom friend Edward, wretched in my misery, for I believed that my secret was out at last, and that all my desperate attempts to keep it had been for naught. Once Stephen had stormed out in fury, I bade Kester leave me at once: I told him that I could not think, that I would see what I could do — I do not know what I said, in truth, for my agony was so extreme and my thoughts so disordered . . . I did not know how much of my history Stephen knew, but from his behaviour, I dreaded the worst. I feared, in short, that despite my craven efforts to escape the long shadow of my past, I had once again lost all that was dear to me.

Kester told me with some asperity that a lovers' quarrel was none of his business, but that he would make it so if I did not have the full amount ready for him by next morning; and that this deadline was not negotiable.

'Think of your fiancé,' he reminded me, in that horrible, light, husky voice of his; 'think of your reputation. Think of everything you have built, everything you have risen above. Do you really want to fall back into the mire like one of your street-girls? For that is what will happen if you cross me, make no mistake. Remember, my dear, for whores, there is no asylum.'

And he bowed in a sardonic travesty of politeness, and left.

When Kester quit the shelter I was, as you may imagine, in appalling distress. Not only had he presented me with a terrible ultimatum, but my own earlier interview with Stephen had shaken me considerably. At that moment I was quite certain all was lost — not only had I already sacrificed Stephen's love and regard for me, but, if I could not buy Kester's silence, my efforts, my position, and all I had worked for over the last few years of ceaseless toil would tumble down in irreparable ruin.

I sat speechless and frozen in my chair in the attitude in which Kester had quit me, beset on all sides by violent and despairing thoughts, and quite unable to move, for I knew not what to do. The hopelessness of my situation paralysed me, and nausea washed over me as my heart quickened and the blood flooded to my head. I laid my face upon the desk, and gave vent to loud, dry sobs which I could not control nor stifle.

The night was inclement, with hard rain beating against the window-panes and restless thunder muttering over the city's distant spires. The very wind seemed to join in my misery, and moaned and howled in the chimney, nearly drowning out my own abandoned cries.

In the midst of my turmoil, however, I was still alive to what passed in the house, and when I heard the sly patter of footsteps in the atrium, followed by the soft creak of the front door, I determined to see who braved the stormy elements at so late an hour. Composing myself, I moved to the window and lifted a corner of the curtain to observe the street outside.

Consider my astonishment when I recognized through the driving rain the unmistakable figure of Mary Ann, who was not only far too fragile to risk exposure to the chill night, but whom I also privately considered one of my successes — a quiet, gentle child with a naturally pious temper, whose only crime was to have become habituated to sin and degradation at an early age, to the extent that she still sometimes puzzled to distinguish between what was right and what wrong.

She was garbed in a light cotton indoor-dress, with nothing but a gaudy shawl and a somewhat battered hat to protect her against the violent downpour. I watched her cross the street, looking anxiously about her, then huddle in a narrow alleyway, almost hidden by its slanting shadows. Wondering what nature of appointment she had gone to keep, and moreover with whom, I stayed at the window, peeping through the curtains. I still do not know why I did not rush out and bring her back to safety at once, notwithstanding the lashing rain, and God knows I have cursed myself many times since that night for failing to do so, given what followed; but so it was, and it cannot be changed now. I can only say that my mind was in a wild storm of confusion and anguish, and that I hardly knew what I did, or how. Rational thought seemed to have forsaken me in that hour, and I had only my woman's instinct to guide me.

After some minutes of watching, I was amazed to see Kester's private carriage, which I had heard rattling off when he had left me earlier, come around the street-corner, and stop directly before the alley where Mary Ann had secreted herself. My hand flew to my mouth. So that was his game! Blackmail, then, was not crime enough for him, but he must add the corruption of children to the catalogue of his sins!

I ran into the hall at once, wrenching the front door open just as a clap of thunder roared overhead. My intention had been to rush over and rescue Mary Ann — tear her from his very clutches, if I had to — but as I cowered in the doorway, half-obscured by shadow, it came to me that a surer way to bring my blackmailer to justice would be to discover whither he was bound and follow him there, perhaps with an officer of the law at my side, the better to catch him in the dreadful act. I cared nothing for my own safety or reputation now; I only wished to revenge myself on my tormentor and save even one desperate soul from sinking back into degradation. To this end, I crept along the street until I was next the carriage — the window-blind was pulled down, so that I could neither discern the occupant of the vehicle, nor he see what lay without — and strained my ears over the pounding of the rain to hear Kester's directions.

It was with a sense of dread, yet little surprise, that I caught the name of the Tolling Bell, a public-house on Pembroke Street notorious for its late hours and loose licence. I was not so innocent nor ignorant as Stephen and the girls thought (as indeed who could have been, who worked daily in the field I had chosen?) and was well aware it was a haunt of the moneyed debauchees of the University. As Kester's carriage rumbled away over the glistening cobbles, I followed at a distance, until it was lost in the darkness.

I hurried to the nearby cab-rank to find someone who would drive me to Kester's destination. Many of the cabmen knew me by sight, and still more by repute, and so I was tolerably certain of their willing cooperation, even if it meant taking me to a place with so evil a name at so unsociable an hour.

My surmise was correct; two hansoms waited at the junction, their horses dejected and dripping under the heavens' assault. I ran up, panting, to the nearest and asked how much it would be to take me to Pembroke Street. He named his price — which was just a little less than I had in my purse — and handed me in, without, to my relief, asking me what business I had there. As we raced along the rain-slick streets, I wrung my cold hands and twisted my numbed fingers together in mounting anxiety.

What if I arrived too late? What if the landlord would not let me pass? What if there was no constable about to whom I could appeal for help? For, although the local police knew well enough the character of that street and the hostelries that thronged it, they were for that very reason quite as likely to shun the place of a night, for fear of trouble, as they should have been to patrol it in order to prevent the same.

My driver, a kindly-looking old fellow with sharp, honest eyes, must have been prey to the same misgivings as I, for as we drew up on the deserted street opposite my destination and I descended to pay him, he loosened his muffler nervously, tipped back his wideawake, and scratched his bald head.

'D'you want me to wait around for a spell, miss, just in case there's any folk might give you trouble?' he asked hesitantly.

I smiled and shook my head with a firm resolve I was far from feeling. I did not wish to involve anyone else in my private and perilous mission, especially not a fellow so elderly and feeble-looking that I fancied a stiff breeze might knock him over.

'Thank you,' I said, 'but I will go in alone. If I require assistance, I shall be sure to summon a constable.'

He looked doubtful, muttering something about not wanting any daughter of his to go about these streets unescorted, but once he understood I was in earnest, he took his fare (and generous tip) without demur. I watched him drive around the corner on to St Aldate's and out of sight before straightening my attire and approaching the door of the public-house. It was firmly closed against the elements and all comers, but faint sounds of revelry drifted down from the third-floor suite, and light spilled from the curtained windows and from under the door before me. I knew I had the right place.

I lifted my hand and rapped thrice upon the black portal. As I stood shaking and drenched in the darkness without the door, I confess I had not the smallest idea what I would say to whoever answered my knock; nor of how I should gain admittance, let alone the private audience with Lord Kester which I imperatively desired. To force my way in would be impossible, for though young, healthy, and, for a woman, strongly made, I should be no match for a hulking doorman, and certainly did not wish to try my strength against Kester's flunkies. Dissimulation, then, was the only option open to me, as so often to females in this world! What we may not achieve by brute force, we must gain by guile. I, whose life has been dogged and near destroyed by lies, my own and those of others, could wish it were not so — but alas! so it is.

The door creaked ajar an inch or two, and a bleared blue eye raked me up and down, partly in suspicion, partly in repulsive appreciation. Draggled and sodden, I must have seemed quite the guttersnipe — for before I could address myself to this ill-favoured Janus, he opened the door further to admit me, jerking a dirty thumb in the direction of a narrow, rickety flight of steps.

'Another one for the Wilmot party, is it?' he said with a leer. 'Upstairs, sweetheart.' His face in the low gaslight had the dull red sheen of an habitual drinker's, and I did not care for the way he regarded nor spoke to me. A rebuke trembled on my lips — how dare he take me for a woman of the night! — but I bit it back, realizing that his mistaken apprehension of my purpose suited my plan better than anything I could have thought of. I ducked my head in acknowledgement, forcing a thin smile, and proceeded up the stairway.

As I ascended, the coarse shouts and laughter from the topmost suite of rooms rang ever louder in my ears; I did not dare think too closely upon what repellent pleasures they might betoken. I hesitated upon the third-floor landing, outside the sturdy oaken door, steeling myself for whatever I might behold within.

I heard a swift, firm step upon the stairs below, and at once confusion and panic overtook me. I was prepared for anything, or so I had thought — except for being trapped here with my only way of escape cut off. To my right stood a small, mean door which I took to be that of a broom-cupboard or storage-room; quick as thought I twisted the handle, slipped through into the dark, close space beyond, and shut it again just as my invisible pursuer gained the landing where I had but moments ago stood. My heart pummelled my ribcage as I leaned against the thin panels and listened, over the insistent pounding of the blood in my head, to the noises from the other side.

There was the slam of a larger, heavier door being kicked open, followed by a ragged cheer from the assembled company.

'More Champagne!' cried a loud, slurring voice, and another, higher and sharper, replied approvingly, 'Good man, Jennings! You're a scholar and a gentleman — whatever the Provost says!'

This witticism was greeted by a roar of inebriated laughter, and the recent arrival (presumably Jennings) stumbled into the room, attended by the heavy clanking of bottles.

Safe from detection for the nonce, I breathed more evenly and felt behind me for the door-handle, lest there was any bolt or lock upon the inside by means of which I could secure myself against intrusion. The cold brass of a hook-and-eye latch presented itself to my questing fingers, and I dropped it home; it was not much protection, but it would have to do. As my eyes adjusted to the gloom of the little closet in which I found myself, however, I became aware that the darkness was not quite so complete as I had at first thought. In fact, the more I searched the blackness, the more I became convinced of the faintest echo of light coming from somewhere within the room, though as my eyes were still mazed and my sight not yet sensitized, I could not say where. I stepped forward tentatively, to try and discover the source of the glow — and brushed against a stiff velvet curtain with my fumbling left hand.

A curtain in a windowless room! Here was a curiosity indeed! Moving with apprehensive care, I felt the piece of cloth with fluttering fingers. It hung at breast-height — rather lower than any window, interior or otherwise, had a right to be — and, to my astonishment, as I edged deeper into the little room, or closet, or whatever it was, I came up against the plush back of a luxuriously upholstered chair set before the curtain, positioned as though for the comfort and ease of whoever might peep through at what lay beyond.

As silently as I could, I settled myself into the chair, holding my breath at each rustle of my skirts, though the uproar from the other room would have drowned out any noise softer than a marching-band. Sitting down, I found the velvet swag was before me, exactly at the level of my head — and saw also that the faint light which bled into the little room emanated from the portion of wall obscured by the cloth. I tried to draw the drape, but it was fixed in position — so, having no other recourse, I ducked my head beneath the curtain just as a photographer might under his black hood — for that seemed to be the principle upon which this spying-booth (and it could be nothing else) had been designed.

Sure enough, directly before me in the thin partition-wall was cut a hole just large enough for a person to press their eye against, and so perceive what was passing in the room beyond. I applied my eye to the aperture; and this was what I saw.

The room was sumptuously furnished in red and gold, the walls hung with a rich scarlet-and-black Oriental paper, and the floor covered by an immense Chinese rug. The main chamber was large, and brilliantly, if sporadically, lit by a blazing array of candles dotted upon every available surface. There were many little occasional-tables crowded with glasses, bottles, hookah-pipes and ash-trays for the cigars fugging the air with their blue smoke, and a number of couches, chaises-longues and sofas against the walls and corners of the room, occupied indiscriminately by the male revellers and their female companions. I also descried a large alcove directly opposite me, hung with curtains which were half-drawn, partly revealing a vast four-poster bed draped with a red silk cover-let already disturbed and rumpled — by what or whom I did not care to imagine.

But the most horrible thing was the aspect of the gentleman-guests. Every man of them was cloaked in black, and masked in the most hideous and fantastical fashion: I saw devils and beasts, dark gods and mythical monsters, but no male human face could I see. Such dastardly cunning! Even the luck-less drabs with whom they had their sport should not have been able to swear who had done what to whom, after the orgy was over. I could not see Mary Ann among the girls, but this was scant comfort, for there were many whose heads were thrown back in atti-tudes of exhaustion and abandon, or whose faces were obscured by their hair, or turned away from me.

The scent of what I assumed to be opium hung heavy upon the air of the room (for my little peep-hole admitted the smells and noises of the party as well as the sights) and most of the girls, some of whom were already in a state of semi-undress, seemed stupefied either by the drug or the alcohol which was still flowing freely. A large, dark-haired man in a scarlet devil's mask, whom I guessed to be the latecomer Jennings (if that was indeed his true name) was going about the room filling up every empty glass with foaming Champagne.

As he approached the couch opposite me, he bent and twitched aside a sheet of some dark satiny material covering a girl who was sprawled, half-conscious, upon the stained plush of the cushions. She moved sleepily, tossing her dark hair aside as the light of the room startled her eyes; and to my horror, I saw that this befuddled creature was none other than Mary Ann, her stays half-undone and her small, wax-white breasts heaving beneath them as though she had been woken from some exhausting dream. She was clearly an object of some interest to many of the party, for she was surrounded by a semi-circle of young bloods, all, as I say, masked, though some threw their cloaks off as I watched, the room being hot and close.

'Give her another taste of the hashish-pipe!' cried one.

'Let her pose for us!' suggested another.

The poor child smiled in a confused fashion,
then, encouraged by the raucous company,
began amusing her audience by striking 'artistic' attitudes, like a model before a drawing-
class, when a slender man of middle height,
wearing the papier-mâché visage of a bear,
shoved into the circle and sat down right on
her naked foot — for she wore but one stock-
ing, the other lying discarded on the floor like
the shed skin of a serpent. Wriggle as she
might, she could not free her foot without him
rising; and so she must have made bold to tell

him to get off her. In the uproar of the room, I did not catch exactly what she said (though the expression upon her face was most importunate) but her words must have angered him, for all that the other men appeared to find them very witty. The whole of the company laughed aloud, in a rather nasty way, and I got the sense that Mary Ann had innocently hit upon a weakness, or a private joke, known to all the gentlemen, regarding her addressee — and one not to his advantage.

It all happened terribly quickly after that. Mary Ann did not seem to realize she had upset her interlocutor until his thick hard hand was about her throat. Forcing her head up, obliging her to meet his eye, he loomed over her, growling into her face.

'*What* did you say, trollop?' he demanded.

O God! I knew that voice! Its harsh, husky music was dreadful to me, and I stifled the cry of disgust which sprang to my lips. It was Kester; no doubt of it. I had heard that voice both wheedling and scorning, in calm and in choler, and there could be no mistaking its peculiar, insinuating rasp. My anxiety for his captive increased a dozenfold.

'Sir, I don't know — ' she choked, terror rising, sudden as tears, into her wide brown eyes.

'Yes you do, damn you! Say it again!' He shook her hard by the neck, like a dog with a half-killed rabbit, and she gasped in pain.

'I'm sorry, sir, I don't, indeed I don't!' Her brimming eyes appealed to him. 'The pipe works strange on me, I think, and I am as apt to forget what I do or say the second after doing it, as the morning after.'

It was plain that he did not believe her; and worse, was further enraged by her refusal to repeat herself. In my time among the unfortunates of Jericho, they have taught me the grim lesson that every girl who has spent any significant period on the street can tell perfectly well when a man is only waiting for an excuse to hurt her. They claim that this sixth sense develops early in their business; for without it, no woman who is exposed to all the dangers and hardships of a prostitute's life can hope to survive long. Mary Ann seemed terribly frightened, and no wonder — I could tell, even at this distance, that she was desperate not to say the wrong thing, lest her tormentor let fly. And yet not to do or say anything could make it worse for her, for he might take her silence for 'dumb insolence' and punish her anyway.

At all events, it was clear that she could hardly speak, thanks to the continued pressure of his fingers around her neck — but she managed to croak out a plea to let her breathe, at which the other men gathered about the pair stirred in sympathetic unease.

'I say, old fellow,' ventured one of them, a slip of a lad wearing the golden, blank-faced visage of a Greek idol, who had an uncommonly deep and rich voice, 'let her go, won't you? She was only teasing, you know.'

This seemed only to stoke Kester's ire, which

rallied like a fire flaming up at the wind down a chimney.

'Teasing? I'll tease *her*, the impudent bitch. I'll tease the damned life out of her!'

Another man chimed in — trying, I suppose, to soothe Kester's indignation.

'Steady on, old man,' the second protested. 'I say, why don't you have some more Champagne?'

I could have told him that this was the last thing Kester needed. Too often I had sat in my study as he talked on in his affected, insouciant fashion, consuming what seemed to me prodigious quantities of brandy from the flask he always carried with him, and wondered to myself why he did not grow muddled or sleepy. It was only after several of these unpleasant sessions that it dawned upon me that his peculiar constitution must, whether by nature or through excessive consumption, be exceptionally resistant to the effects of alcohol — the softening ones, at any rate.

'Get your own damned girl, Carrick!' snarled Kester, never taking his eyes off Mary Ann. 'Or do you prefer damaged goods?'

Through all this, the background chatter and laughter of the other men and girls had slowly faded, until the room was quiet as an empty church; and it was into this tense, tight silence that the next words dropped.

'Don't hurt her, eh, sir?'

It was a new voice, a woman's voice, which addressed him. I thought I knew that soft, wheedling tone; and Mary Ann seemed to also.

Despite Kester's throttling hold, she twisted her head around and up to see who had spoken. Kester seemed quite as surprised as she — and I half-hoped and half-dreaded that he would drop his victim and go after this other girl who had dared to talk back to him in defence of her sister.

'I'll do what I like with her,' he said, tightening his grip still further, as if to demonstrate the truth of his words. The girl stepped towards him and smiled ingratiatingly. She was a tall, well-made creature with milk-white skin and a handsome head of curling auburn hair. I recognized her from her usual pitch at the Plain, where they called her Red Sarah.

'But I like her so, my Lord,' she said, coyly, 'and if you mar her looks, why, it won't be such fun to watch us play together.'

At this, there was an appreciative stir from the other men in the room. I felt the black, dangerous mood that had descended lift and lighten a little — for, as my charges had told me, it is a well-known peculiarity of many men who use prostitutes that there is nothing they like so much as two pretty girls making free with one another, kissing and touching and so forth — just as long as the men may tarry to watch the entertainment, of course.

Kester's eyes glittered behind the mask, and the blood that congested his straining neck began slowly to drain away. He unclenched his fingers from about Mary Ann's throat, and she fell back into the lap of the man behind her, gasping a little. Kester continued to stare at her steadily, and I had an awful suspicion that her distress excited him in some way I did not wish to consider too closely. He did not take his gaze from the gasping girl as Sarah knelt down and began, tentatively, to caress her. His lips only lifted in a ghastly, meaningful little smile, his teeth gleaming horribly beneath the bear-mask's brown snout.

'Well done, my dear,' he told Sarah, as she leaned in to kiss the other, and I saw the mute fear in the redhead's eyes. 'A little *divertissement* is just what we need. But *you*' — and here he pointed a thick finger in Mary Ann's face — 'you had better keep that mouth of yours busy with something other than smart words from now on.'

He knelt up and dusted off his trousers, snapping his fingers at someone beyond the circle for more Champagne, his gaze on the pair the whole time. I think I knew, though, even then, that poor Mary Ann's reprieve was only temporary, and that he should get his revenge on her somehow, before the evening was over. I determined — though I knew not when, and still less how — to stop him before he had a chance to injure her further. The acrid smoke of the opium and hashish, and the sordid sight presented to my eyes, made them sting, and tears sprang to them, as if wrung from them by a harsh cold wind. I withdrew my face from the peep-hole and out from under the velvet curtain, to ponder how I might effect Kester's, or better, Mary Ann's own removal from this perilous orgy.

I could still hear the whoops and claps of the girls' appreciative audience as their invisible performance continued, but I was spared the spectacle of their forced debauchery. I wondered how I might decoy Kester from the room — should I tell the doorkeeper to fetch him down upon some pretext, a matter of my 'payment', perhaps? Or would it be safer for myself and Mary Ann if I waited quietly in my hiding-place (which was, I realized, a secret chamber provided to indulge the proclivities of those who liked to watch the degraded goings-on within) for an opportunity of intervention to present itself?

I do not know what I should have done otherwise, for my mind was overwrought with the strains and reverses of the night, but I must have moved more abruptly than I thought away from the viewing-chink — and in so doing, I shifted the heavy chair against the little room's bare floorboards with a high and piercing squeal.

Most of the company were too busy with their own shrieks and halloas of lubricious enthusiasm to hear the noise above the general hubbub, but to my horror I heard Kester's high, rasping tenor cry, 'Hark! What was that?' in accents of guilty alarm.

'Nothing, Lucky, leave it!' complained the rich-voiced boy in a tone of irritated urgency, and his companions murmured agreement. The artificial panting of the two girls increased in volume — but it seemed that Kester was unenthralled by their antics, for I heard his swift, light step coming towards the door of the banqueting-room, and I surmised that he was going out on to the landing, to see if anyone had come upstairs to disturb the party.

I grasped in those seconds that my only chance of saving myself — and, perchance, Mary Ann — when he inevitably discovered me, was to bluff. He had demanded his money from me by the morrow morn, and if I could convince him I had come to give it him now, under cover of darkness, perhaps I could lure him out of that house of ill-fame and into the path of a constable — or at least, some gentle-man who might take my part and protect me from Kester's ire. The plan was a desperate one, and the hope of finding friendly succour all but forlorn; but it was all I had — and so I stepped out of the closet on to the landing.

His astonishment upon seeing me was my saviour; it allowed me a few precious moments in which to put my finger to my lips, make the most urgent signs of secrecy, and draw him away from the revels within.

'What in Christ's name are you doing here?' he whispered in sharp, shocked tones, scarce able to believe his eyes. Indeed, my sudden appearance upon the threshold of the John Wilmot Club's inner sanctum must have seemed to him almost supernatural — for though he had invited me, jokingly, to their 'little tea-party' ear-lier in the evening, knowing full well that I would decline his repellent offer, he had not made mention of where it was to be held.

'Hush!' I said, and motioned for him to shut the door of the suite behind him, which he did with great alacrity, closing it tight and standing square before it as though to prevent my ingress. He pulled the bear-mask from his face to wipe his brow; beneath it, he was deadly pale, and sweating profusely.

'How did you find me?' he stammered. 'What do you want? This place is not for you!'

'I have my spies,' I told him, disdainfully, 'and they said I should find you here. Your comings and goings are no mystery to me.'

His lip curled in a sneer.

'Nor yours to me, whoremistress,' he said. 'And if you're thinking of blackmailing me about our little Wilmot gatherings, don't forget you have far more to lose in this game than I. Why are you here?'

I took a deep breath and lied.

'I am here to deliver your ransom,' I told him, in a calm voice, 'for you said you would have it as soon as I could lay my hands upon the money, and now is as good a time as any.'

He arched his eyebrows.

'Now? And here? You have a queer notion of the apt time and place for business transactions, my dear.'

'I do not wish to live under the shadow of your despicable threats for a moment longer than is necessary,' I told him, with feeling, 'and I have brought what you wanted, so that I may be rid of you as soon as possible, once and for all.'

His stone-grey eyes lit up with avarice, and he nodded impatiently.

'Very well, then — sooner rather than later, why not? I could do with the cash tonight in any case — these soirées can get expensive. Where is it?'

I snorted, as if at his foolishness.

'I have not been so naïve as to bring it with me into this den of vice, if that's what you suppose! It is downstairs, hidden a little way from here, somewhere we may make our bargain under the cover of darkness — and then see one another never more.'

He favoured me with a narrow, calculating look.

'Very well, I suppose I can leave them to it for a spell. This had better not be a trick, mind — or you know what will happen.'

I bowed my head in acquiescence, and this seemed to satisfy him, for he swiftly opened the door again and shouted through that he was going on a little errand, and should bring back 'a treat'. His words garnered a cheer of drunken approval, and he withdrew, closing the door once more, his mind apparently at ease.

'Don't try anything, now,' he warned me. 'You see that I am expected back, and if I do not return within the half-hour, mark my words, they shall come out looking for me — and their treat.'

I nodded mutely, but my brain was working at a furious pace. My strategy — a risky one — was to decoy him into the street, far enough from the tavern that its denizens would not hear what passed, and, as soon as I saw someone nearby, set up such a hue and cry as to attract notice and excite curiosity for as far around as possible. In this manner, I surmised I might be able to have him arrested, or at least detained, and perhaps even persuade some honest citizens to go in and break up the unholy assembly that caroused behind the third-floor door.

I descended the narrow stairwell in silence, Kester following me, his long opera-cloak dragging softly on the uncarpeted treads. When we passed the giant Janus who lounged at the foot of the stairs, the man sprang upright from his leaning position against the grimy wall, and eyed me with unpleasantly renewed interest.

'Just going outside for a while, Bob,' said Kester casually. 'I have some business to conduct with this young lady.'

'Very good, sir,' said Bob, leering at me and winking heavily at Kester. 'See you in a bit.'

'How far is it?' muttered Kester as we stepped out into the bitter night air. 'This had better not take long.'

'No more than five minutes' walk,' I assured him, setting a quick pace, so as to get him as far from the inn and as near to where there might be witnesses as possible.

We walked in silence for a few minutes, as I navigated the tangle of narrow thoroughfares behind Pembroke which led northwards to Queen Street. He spoke but once; and then, only to threaten me.

'You do know,' he said, 'that if you are leading me upon a wild-goose chase, and there is no money at the end of it, I shall be obliged to take it out of you in kind?' He took my elbow in a hard, painful grasp, and span me about to face him. 'I warn you! I shan't be gentle, and I shall enjoy it.'

In the moonlight, his face had the cruel implacability of a graven image, and I was reminded of those dreadful gods worshipped when the world was young, the granite faces of their idols carved into expressions of savage and sensual joy that have outlasted the millennia.

'I would not dare to cheat you,' I said, my voice trembling with unfeigned fear. 'I have seen what you will do.'

He laughed shortly. 'You haven't seen the half of it, believe me! Walk on. You will understand my anxiety to get this over with before the real fun begins.'

I shuddered, despairing of the still-empty streets, and fearing that I had run my foolish head into a noose after all, when to my overwhelming relief I saw two stout fellows walking along the opposite side of the road, arms slung over one another's shoulders. They were evidently a little the worse for drink, but they looked honest enough, and I hoped their inebriation might embolden them to confront Kester if I began to scream.

Which at once I did.

Kester still had tight hold of my elbow, and the first thing I did on commencing shrieking was wriggle out of his clutches, shaking off his hand and beating at him with my fists, all the time making such a loud carry-on that the men opposite could not fail to stop and stare.

'Help!' I cried. 'Oh sirs, please help me! This man is following me — he means to rob me, or worse! Help, help, I beg you!'

One of the fellows threw off the arm of the other, and wove towards us as I fought with Kester, who had now seized my shoulders and was trying to force a hand across my screaming mouth. Though the stranger's instinct was charitable, alas, I now perceived what I had not before: that he and his companion were not merely merry, but hopelessly, incapably drunk — as I should, I suppose, have guessed they were apt to be in this place, and at this hour. Kester trapped both my flailing hands in one of his own, succeeded in getting the other over my mouth, and turned to face the fellow, who stood swaying in confusion in the middle of the street, with a most charming and apologetic air.

'Don't bother yourself about this one, my friend,' he said, in a confiding tone, 'she's a notorious drunk, I'm afraid, and a little mad with it. I paid up and had my pleasure, and then she tried to charge me again. Naturally I refused, so now she's getting uppity and trying to draw other honest men into the mess.'

I fought him as hard as I might, trying to free my tongue, at least, to denounce his falsehoods — but I could not.

'Seems a bit upset,' said my putative saviour, doubtfully.

Kester chuckled. 'It's just the gin-terrors. She sees things! If we were not here she'd be cursing and yelling at an empty street — and if I didn't hold her back, she'd have my eye out — or yours.'

At this piece of news, the man retreated smartly, glancing nervously over at his friend, who, having lost his only means of physical support, now stared slack-jawed at the scene from a sitting position in the gutter.

'She looks like a mad 'un all right,' observed the first man, watching my vain efforts to free myself with mild interest.

'She's a wild girl, I promise,' Kester agreed, 'a very devil when it comes to rutting, but that always comes at a price. Still' — and here I was horrified to feel his hand move down across my body to hoist up my petticoats, showing off my stockinged legs to the thigh as the amazed drunkards stared and smiled — 'worth a tumble, eh?'

'Oh yes, no doubt,' said the first, ignoring my frantic, sobbing struggles, and chortling in a good-humoured, lascivious sort of way. 'Good luck with 'er, sir! Expect she'll calm down if you give 'er another drink, eh?' And he swayed back across the road to join his comrade. Kester stood, calmly holding me as I twisted in his arms, and watched impassive as my last hopes of rescue stumbled away.

The rest of that night I cannot recollect, though I managed to piece together some of what must have happened later. Still, I am and remain eternally grateful that the memory of what passed after my abandonment by the credulous drunkards has been lost to me, for I do not know whether its awfulness, compounded with the subsequent events that still haunt my dreams, might not have proved too much in the terrible days that were to follow. Our brains are wiser than we give them credit for, and will oftentimes hide from us or draw a veil of forgetfulness over that which it might else kill us to know or recall.

I woke in the dark, and knew at once that I was neither in my own bed back at the shelter, nor anywhere I had been to before. I was lying on my back on a wooden pallet, a cold, moist blackness pressing silence over me like a blanket. I was clothed still, for which I was thankful, and my dress was not greatly torn, nor was I injured, except for a thick, throbbing ache at one side of my head, where I conjectured Kester must have struck me — whether to ensure my silence, or to vent his rage, I could not guess.

The mattress on which I lay was thin and hard and full of lumps, and I smelt corruption and mould on the air, and something else, too — some musky, animal scent, faint but distinct, which I could not put a name to. The darkness was absolute, and the atmosphere very chill and damp. I soon guessed that I must be underground, in some cellar or basement; but in my frightened and bewildered state, for a long moment I believed myself already in the grave.

I tried to rise, but my limbs were weak as water, too feeble to support me, and the pain in my head struck again savagely. Dizzy with the effort, I fell back and crossed my shivering arms over my chest like a corpse, hugging myself for warmth, for my shawl was gone. I suspected that it would do me no good to call out, and so I lay quite still with my eyes wide against the pressing blackness, and waited, as though anticipating my own death.

I do not know how long it was before I heard a door above me creak, and booted feet descending stone steps. I knew then that I was indeed in some chamber beneath the earth; and when a faint light showed at the corner of the room, it shone through a grille of stout metal bars; and I understood that I was prisoner here.

'Diana,' came the soft, hoarse voice of Lord Kester, the voice I had learned long ago to fear and hate. 'Are you awake?'

I lay quite motionless; for though I had but a second before wished for anyone to deliver me from the black dungeon in which I languished, I remembered now that there were many things more dreadful in the world than cold and darkness. My captor would not be put off, though, and the light advanced until his lantern gleamed at the end of the chamber, hard against the iron-barred door of my cell.

Kester's face was in shadow, but his eyes shone in the flame of the bull's-eye as he stared between the bars at me. There was a rusty jangle as he lifted his free hand closer to the lamp to examine something, and I saw a bunch of keys, like a black spider, hanging from his fist. He found the one he wanted; it clattered in the lock, and the gate shrieked metallically as he pushed it open. My eyes, opened the merest slit to watch him, I instantly shut tight, and I breathed a swift prayer, taking care my lips did not move.

I sensed through closed eyelids that the light was getting nearer and brighter, and heard his wet breathing as he knelt down beside me, setting down his lantern with a clank on the cold flags of the floor.

Now, I thought. *Now I might do it.*

I could overturn the lamp, dash it against the wall; I could grab it and swing it at his head, if I were swift enough, and escape that way — for I had not heard him lock the gate again, and in my mind's eye it hung loose and half-open upon its hinges.

And then I felt his hard hand upon my crossed wrists, and heard his dry laugh, and knew I was lost.

'Why, your little heart is beating like a mouse's at the sight of a cat!' he whispered, and there was a delight in his words that was almost innocent — as though he had not expected such a reward, so soon. 'I can see it,' he said, 'here' — and he placed his other hand hot on my throat, where the pulse of life fluttered. 'It is throbbing fit to burst, so you need not pretend to be asleep, or dead, you know.'

There was no further use in shamming, and I reasoned that if I spoke to him, I might persuade him to let me go unharmed. I still had a vestige of faith in his capacity for pity, for it was all the hope I had to cling to. I did not know what else to do. I opened my eyes.

I don't know what I expected to see in his face; a monstrous evil, I suppose, distorting his features; a leer of brutal lust, perhaps. But his expression was thoughtful as he gazed upon me, and his grey eyes soft, almost kind; and that was the worst of all.

'Well, little mouse,' he said mildly, 'what am I to do with you?'

'Let me go,' I said at once. 'Let me go and I will not tell, I swear it, I will not give you up to the police; I shall go away, leave Oxford, and we need never see one another more — '

He lifted his hand from my neck, halting my desperate babblings with a single finger laid across my lips.

'It's no good, you know,' he said conversationally. 'I shan't let you go until I have done with you, and I fancy that won't be for a while yet.'

I shuddered at the sinister import of his words.

'What do you mean?' I asked, dreading the answer.

'I mean that you are to be my guest for a little, Diana — or do you prefer Anna, now we are alone? I'll not call you Mrs Pelham — we both know it is a false name and title, and besides, I think we may dispense with the formalities now.'

His guest? His captive, he meant; his helpless victim. I quailed to imagine even an hour more of this torment.

'How long?' I whispered.

'Long enough,' he said. 'As long as it takes you to tell me where that payment of mine is stowed — for my need of it is becoming rather pressing, you know, and I mean to have it even if I must beat it out of you.'

I struggled up and spat in his face: he recoiled, but did not leave go of me.

'You shall not have it even if you kill me! I have already lost that for which I cared most — my reputation is nothing to me now, for Stephen knows my secret, and has spurned me. My work is all that remains to me: it is the only good thing I have left in this world, and neither you nor anyone will rob me of it!'

He took his hands from me and squatted back on his haunches with a faint smile upon his face, taking care not to soil his clothes with the damp and dirt of the floor.

'Such fierce defiance! But you'll sing a different tune before long, I warrant.' He cocked his head and lifted over it the leather strap of a canteen slung around his shoulder, which in the darkness I had not previously noticed, setting it beside me.

'In the mean time, I've brought you water,' he said, 'and Towers will bring your supper later, when he returns. I've promised him the keeping of you for his pains, by the way, so be good to him, though he's an ugly brute, won't you? He doesn't get much in the way of female company, and you'll soon enough see why.'

'Good to him?' I whispered. 'And shall you be good to me?'

He shrugged as though the question were facetious.

'I'll feed and keep you,' he said, 'that's good enough.'

'As a prisoner!'

His eyes slitted and hardened and he looked at me as if I were a rat that had bitten him.

'You've seen the inside of worse places than this before, my dear, I have no doubt. So don't pretend you cannot bear it, else I'll make it so you can't.'

I believed him. I had noticed in our previous dealings that he had a curious way of treating people — not just myself, or the girls at the shelter, but his friends and fellows too — as though they were actors, or animals, perhaps, disporting themselves for his amusement, but incapable of real volition or genuine feeling. Sukey had said that she had once seen him strike a girl for some piece of impudence, and then seem puzzled and impatient when she was hurt after, as though she were shamming to annoy him. He reminded me of those cruel boys who throw stones at cats, or burn ants beneath a glass, only for their own entertainment.

And yet the gentleness that had shone in his eyes only a moment before was as inherent in his character as coldness or choler. Sukey had told me that fits of generosity, even remorse, came upon him sometimes after he had ill-used her, and he would grow sentimental and affectionate as any girl, treating her with a tender care almost more frightening than his cruelty

— for she knew it could vanish in an instant, leaving him harder than ever. It was this quality in him to which I sought to appeal, when it showed itself; and I dared hope that if I could move him, he might relent somewhat in his softer mood — even, perhaps, let me go.

I closed my eyes and turned my head away.

'My head hurts dreadfully,' I said in a weak voice.

'A blow to the skull will do that,' he said shortly. 'You are a strong girl, Diana,' he added, 'more resilient than you look. It took Towers and I quite some effort to get you to stay quiet, for even after I knocked you once, you would not quite go out — you continued to struggle and rave. Things have not all proceeded quite as I had planned them, I own, but it could have been worse. So congratulations, my dear, on your new position as my companion.'

'Companion?' I said warily; I was all alertness now, the pain in my head quite forgotten.

He nodded, reaching out his hand; I flinched, but he only moved my hair away from my face, stroking it a little. Though his touch was warm, I could not forbear from shivering at it.

'Yes. I must lie low for a bit, Diana — though not, admittedly, as low as you.'

He smiled at this weak sally, and I stared at him in blank, speechless horror.

'I owe some money, you see — a trifling amount really, but more than I can put my hands on at present — and since you did not have the grace to bring my payment as you promised, I must keep you here until you tell me where it is. Don't worry about imposing on me, or outstaying your welcome, though, for I'm quite willing to take my time. Besides, I am looked for, and don't wish to be found at present.' He studied me knowingly. 'I warrant you understand my predicament.'

I did, naturally, for God knows I had fled my sins in the past; but his words none the less surprised me. He was free enough with money, of course, but knowing his inheritance to have been handsome, despite his father's dying gift to the shelter, I had thought him rather a wealthy spendthrift than a profligate. I had assumed his penchant for blackmailing and extortion was merely a means to extend his future pleasures, rather than pay for those of the past.

I should have guessed, I suppose, given how far gone he was in other ways, that he was sure to number gambling among his vices. The bookmakers of Oxford, I knew, made a hand-some profit out of young gentlemen with expectations, and were prepared to play a very hard game to collect what was due them. A gentleman might owe his tailor or his servant a score of guineas for a score of years; but if he were not prompt in paying his bookmaker he risked both life and limb.

'To whom do you owe this money?' I asked him.

He waved a hand impatiently. 'It doesn't matter. There is nothing I can give him as col-lateral — even you, my dear! The unreasonable fellow demands cash on the nail. So here I am, gone to ground like an animal, and none to share my solitude but you. Perhaps we will become friends, by and by, though you hate me now?'

He smiled a little sadly at me; and I sensed that the melancholy, feeling mood was upon him.

'Perhaps we will,' I said carefully, 'if you'll only treat me kindly.'

'Treat you kindly!' he scoffed, laughing as at some joke private to him. 'What! As kindly as you treat your whores, teaching them to make their beds and say their prayers, as children do? Do you know what they call you behind your back? 'Our Lady'! Do you think I don't see how you sneer at them beneath your mask of virtue?'

This was insupportable, and warm blood sprang to my cheeks.

'I protect them and care for them,' I said vehemently, 'which is a great deal more than most do. You ought not to mock virtue, you who know nothing of it.'

He leaned in close, shaking his head a little in disappointment.

'And *you*,' he said, 'ought not to ape it, being what you are.'

He grasped a thick fistful of my hair, and wound it around his fingers, pulling it tight so that I gasped and my face came near his; and still his eyes were calm and mild, his voice soft.

'You think yourself quite the living saint, Diana, do you not? Like Miss Nightingale and

389

Mr Gladstone combined, with your saving and your sanctimony. But I could tell such tales of you as would make your doctor's golden hair curl, couldn't I?'

I snorted. 'You cannot hurt me more than you already have,' I told him — at which, strangely, he looked amused.

'Is that so?' he said. 'Well, we shall have to see about that, shan't we?'

I did not know what he meant by that, nor did I want to. I twisted my head against his grasp; but he held my hair tight and would not let me go.

'No use wriggling,' he said. 'You are caught just like Absalom tangled in the tree.' A thought seemed to strike him. 'Do you know, Diana, what Porphyria's lover did to her with her hair — her long lovely hair, just like yours?'

I shook my head, as far as I could. He gazed down at me as if calculating something.

'You'll be better educated before our time together is over,' he mused, 'but for the moment, it may be better you don't know. In the mean time, I'm finding you rather impertinent, so perhaps I shall teach you your first lesson in privation.'

He let go my hair suddenly, like a trinket he had grown tired of, and his gaze, hard and cold now, moved down my body. Instinctively, I shrank from his glance; but he did not move to touch me, only laughed and stood, turning towards the door.

'Don't worry, little mouse,' he said, 'this cat will toy with you a while longer before it comes to that. And believe me, you'll be grateful enough for my company by then.'

He made to leave, at which a sickening horror of being left alone again in that profound darkness assailed me; to my shame, I proved his words true, and struggled from my poor pallet-bed, weak as I was, following him to the door. Though I begged and pleaded for my freedom, or at least a light to chase away the shadows, he pushed me roughly back and told me to be quiet. Clinging to the iron gate, however, I glimpsed more of what was beyond it, discerning a short passage and a set of worn stone steps, leading up into blackness.

As he turned his back upon me and ascended, I put my head against the bars, and by the dancing lantern-light could just make out a sturdy oak door at the top of the steps, weathered and ancient. I noted that when he opened the door to leave, no illumination spilled through it from beyond; neither daylight, gas- nor candle-light; and this was how I knew that in the world without my prison it was also night-time. And as the door closed again, cutting off the light from his lamp, I was left all alone in the black and utter dark.

I had made up my mind that Kester should not break me, however, and so I occupied my time not in weeping and bootless self-pity, like some girl in a Gothic story, but by thinking as hard as I could of a way to get out of there. In this I was hindered by my ignorance of the events on the night of my abduction, such as how I had been transported, and, crucially, whither. The thick stone walls of my cell meant that no noise reached me from outside — and, I felt sure, no sound made inside the room, however loud or distressed, would penetrate them. I had been right not to cry out when I first awoke; for I might have torn my throat out with screaming and still no-one should have come.

First, I established that the grille to my cell was quite firm in the wall, tugging it hard several times to make sure; and further, that the bars were at once too thick to dream of breaking, and too closely spaced for me to squeeze through. There was no light in the place at all, save that which Kester had brought down with him. From the little I had seen, I guessed this was an old place, and one some miles out of Oxford, perhaps up on Headington Hill, or north beyond Summertown. I supposed it must be a large house, built for a wealthy family; for how many places that are not also ancient and grand have so great a cellar, whether it is used to keep women or wine?

But my clever deductions did not comfort me, for as I sat and worried at the few clues I had, I grew more and more despairing. Every fresh piece of the puzzle seemed to make my prison darker and surer around me. I felt as though the walls of my cell drew closer, creeping up on me in the blackness, as I realized that even if I could somehow escape, I would have no idea where I was, nor which direction to run in, when I got out; and no-one to whom I could appeal for help. It was not a consoling thought, and I hugged myself harder in the chill dark.

My unhappy and fruitless musings were interrupted after some time (I know not how long, but it seemed to me hours) by a key grating in the lock of the stair-head door. I uncurled myself from my damp pallet and staggered up, the blood rushing through my cramped limbs, feeling along the wall in the blackness until I reached the gate. I had hoped to renew my attack on Kester's better nature; but it was only a servant who came clumsily down the steps, a wooden trencher in one hand and a candle in the other.

On the rough platter lay a crust of bread and a piece of cheese, which set my mouth watering, for I calculated that I had not then eaten for at least a day and a half. The man did not open my gate, but set the trencher down before it, where I could reach the food through the bars. I looked in his face and smiled my thanks as he did so; but he would not look at me.

I did not know whether it was shame at his office that made him coy, or disgust at my filthy and raddled appearance — but as he withdrew from the bars I put out my hand to catch his arm. This startled him into gazing directly at me, and then I knew him for Towers, my Lord's personal manservant and driver, whose impassive visage I had glimpsed once or twice when Kester's carriage had waited outside the shelter for him to emerge.

Close up, he was, as Kester had promised, an ugly enough creature. His face was white as a

393

slab of lard, with small dull eyes, rough skin pitted by pustules or pox, and a nose made crooked by somebody's fist. His hair was black and thick, standing up at all angles like a bear's fur, and indeed, apart from that white face of his, he seemed bearlike altogether, with his shambling movements and great heavy body that held the promise of a terrible strength.

He had seemed part chauffeur, part bodyguard when I had remarked him before; but now I saw he was Kester's accomplice too. Indeed, I guessed with a shiver that he must be quite as vicious as the one he served — for what honest servant would have conspired in such a villainous scheme!

None the less, I touched his arm, and looked deep into his little pale eyes, which seemed almost as frightened as my own. I wondered whether he had seen prisoners down here before; and what he might tell of their fate.

'Towers, is it not?' I said softly, remembering Kester's promise that he should bring me my supper.

He nodded very slightly, as if afraid someone might see him do it.

'My name is Diana,' I said.

'I know,' he muttered. 'I have seen you.'

The queer way he said it — as though simply knowing me by sight was a source at once of shame and excitement — called to mind Kester's words about promising Towers 'the keeping of me', and I shuddered at the memory of the servant's avid, watchful glare. Towers

394

must have spied me more than once through my study window, or coming and going at the refuge when Kester paid his visits — and I guessed, from the hungry way he stared at me through the grille, that he had too much liked what he saw.

I withdrew my hand quickly.

'I am sorry to meet you again, under such circumstances,' I said. 'It cannot be . . . pleasant, what he has made you do.'

At these words, his face set against me, like stone.

'I oughtn't to talk to you,' he said.

'Very well,' I said quickly, 'I shall not bother you; only, if you have a pitcher of water, just to wash my face in — or if you could fill up the leather bottle, I would be most obliged. I fear I am hardly fit to be seen — I must look like a blackamoor!'

He considered me slowly; there was evidently some truth in my words, for he nodded once and put out his hand to the bars.

'Bring me the canteen and I'll fill it.'

I fetched the empty bottle, passing the strap through the bars for him to pull it through; and as I did so an idea came to me, which I thought I might make use of later. By the time Towers returned with water sloshing in the canteen, I had made short work of the bread and cheese, and was dabbing up the crumbs from the rough wooden plate. He shoved the bottle back at me through the bars, and I thanked him profusely. I decided to test my luck further.

'Might you leave me the candle, too, at least?'

He frowned, the shifting shadows of the lamp making his face still uglier against the dark, like a jack o'lantern at Hallowe'en.

'What for?' he asked shortly.

'Only to see to wash myself,' I told him. 'I don't want to knock over the canteen in the dark — and after all, I must know where the dirt is to get it off again.'

He considered my request slowly. I realized that he was now beyond the remit of Kester's instructions, and was having to think for himself what he should do. I held my breath and hoped.

'What if you set the cell or yourself on fire?'

I admit I had considered attempting to torch the damp straw strewing my prison, but had dismissed the idea as being impractical — for even if they heard me calling, and came in time, I could scarcely hope to melt the bars out of the walls before I burned to death.

'Why should I do that?' I asked, innocently.

'To get yourself taken up to the house; or only for spite, perhaps.'

I laughed, lifting the damp rags of my petticoats and thrusting them through the bars for him to feel.

'How should I burn these? It is so moist down here that even the bricks sweat. I could not put anything to flame, least of all myself.'

As he bent to touch my wet skirts, his wide nostrils flared, and it occurred to me that from that position, he could not only glimpse my naked ankles and calves, but could smell the sweat and salt of my body. I smiled down on his whorled crown as he bunched my dress in his great fist, examining it closely for an unnecessary length of time. The fabric was as wet as washing, and he appeared satisfied, for he straightened and stepped back. He took a candle from his pocket, opened the door of the lantern, and lit the new one from the flaming stub.

I dropped my skirts and held my hand through the gate: as he passed the burning candle to me, our fingers brushed; mine cold, his warm.

'Thank you,' I said. He nodded.

I held the candle fast and cherished the little flame in my cupped hand, delighting in it as a mother delights in her baby. Quickly, I backed away from the bars so he could not suddenly change his mind and snatch it from me again. He watched me retreat, my face lit up, for I was really overjoyed at even such a tiny piece of kindness. I suppose he must have felt some stirring of pity, for his mouth twitched, once, as at a spasm of pain, and he passed his hand across it. I did not notice him turn and climb the stairs — for a big man, he could creep very quietly — but when I looked up again, he was gone.

I did not see another soul until what I suppose must have been the next day, but I took care not to waste the time and light at my disposal. As soon as Towers slammed the stair-top door,

I began a minute examination of every corner of my cell. It was a mean, low little room, and my inspection did not take long; but in the course of it I discovered some things that were, if not exactly useful, most curious and interesting — and, I am afraid to say, very alarming.

The dimensions of the cellar itself were not large; the ceiling above my head rose to a height of perhaps seven feet — just enough for a person of middle size to stand without hindrance. The floor was of thick stone flags crusted with immemorial dirt; some light-starved plant matter grew in the dank corners, and moulds of various kinds and dull colours spread between the crumbling bricks. Had the cellar been of stone entirely, I think I should have been more comfortable there, but the porous mortar had allowed decay and damp to take an advanced hold on the place — though not so advanced as to allow me to loosen the stones from the walls, though I broke my finger-nails in trying.

However, as I scraped hopelessly at the seeping bricks, I discovered to my alarm that I was not the first prisoner of this dungeon to try and claw my way out. I had set my candle down upon the floor, securing it with a drop of its own wax, the better to work at what I thought might be a loose brick. The strange shadows cast upwards by the flame upon the rough stones revealed something I had not hitherto noticed: several parallel scratches scored deep in the wall, as though made by the nails of a desperate hand. I spread my fingers and fitted them into the grooves. My hands are not small, but the width between the lines showed me they had been made by someone with fists far larger than mine.

Having remarked one set of scratches upon the bricks, I slowly became aware of many more; most were at the height of a man — that is to say, a little above my own reach — but some I found low down, almost at the level of the floor, as though my predecessor had lain upon the stones in agony and scraped at whatever he or she could touch. Still more reached almost to the ceiling, implying either unusual height in the one who had made them, or a desperate stretch. You may imagine how these discoveries worked upon my susceptible mind; and I wondered if I ought to snuff the candle, so as to preserve not only my sole source of light, but my dwindling store of courage.

I could not do it, though; for after so long in the blackness, that brave little flame seemed to me the most precious thing in the world; nay, the only thing that could keep at bay the nightmares in the wavering shadows. I wished later that I had put out the light when I had thought to — oh! how I wished it! — and spared myself the horror of what I found next — but I suppose I should have come across it sooner or later, and perhaps to have stumbled upon the thing in the dark would have terrified me even more.

I had determined to acquaint myself with every cranny of my cheerless abode, and it was in the furthest corner of the room, remotest from the door and my poor pallet-bed, and thus most obscured by shadow, that I made my last, most chilling discovery.

I had believed the strange black shapes on this far wall to be tricks of the guttering candle-light, or perhaps an illusion caused by my dazzled eyes throwing ghostly images on to the darkness. But as I approached and the shadows fled, I saw that the objects were real enough. What loomed into the light was a stout iron bolt, hammered hard into the wall, from which dangled a thick, rusted chain, with a cuff or manacle at the end. No sooner had I started back in fear from this thing, than I perceived another upon the adjacent wall; two bolts, two chains and two manacles, for the arms of she or he who had come before me.

The foetid, musky smell I had noted on first awakening was stronger in this gloomy nook; and the scratches yet more numerous, cross-hatched against the ancient brick so it showed orange and clean where the surface had been scored away. I recoiled again; and stumbled upon some object that lay on the flagstones, and clanked. Down where a man's feet might be, were he to lie in chains, was another set of shackles fixed just above the floor. I shrieked, kicking at the chains as though they were alive and meant to catch me — and in my fright, the candle dropped from my hand and rolled on to the floor, my single small flame extinguished, plunging me into blackness.

Until that moment, I had thought my spirit strong, and I confess I had taken a foolish pride in my own feeble bravery; but this discovery, and the loss of my light, undid me entirely. I think, indeed, it would have shattered the nerves of anyone: such horrors, such darkness, and all through the rest of the night, such awful, echoless silence, broken only by the pitiful sound of my own weeping.

I woke with Kester standing above me, his lantern in one hand and the half-burned stub of my candle in the other. He was smiling with his teeth only; and I did not like to see them gleam so, in the low light, like the bared fangs of a wolf.

'So,' he said, 'Towers has taken a fancy to you?'

I sat up, shrinking back against the dank wall, pulling my wretched gown closer about me. There was a dangerous edge to his voice, as though he suspected me of deceiving or tricking him in some fashion.

'Why do you say that?'

He thrust the candle-end at me as if it were the damning evidence in a capital trial.

'Why else would he give you *this*?'

I looked past the light he held at the spots of brightness that were his eyes, and lowered my voice to a modest murmur.

'It was only so that I could see to wash myself. I think he did it more for your sake, than mine.'

His eyebrows rose as he considered my filthy state.

'Indeed?' he said archly. 'Well, you have not

done a very good job of it.'

I bowed my head. 'I became frightened and dropped the candle.'

At this, he laughed with a queer note of glee.

'Frightened, she says! But what could have frightened you, little mouse? There is nothing else living down here, you know — not any more.'

I must have paled at that; for his grin widened, and he squatted before me, bringing the lantern near my face, the better to enjoy my discomfort.

'The only thing in this place of which you ought to be frightened,' he said softly, 'is me — especially if you prove an ungracious guest. You must understand, my dear, that you are a prisoner here, and learn to comport yourself accordingly. How shall I teach you to respect your state, I wonder? What will show you, little mouse, that this cat is not to be tricked nor trifled with? What is it they do to women convicts, to make them know their place? Ah!'

An idea had evidently struck him, for he looked horribly pleased with himself as he set down the lantern and reached into a deep pocket inside his jacket, drawing out a hunting-knife, perhaps six inches long. My eyes widened in dread, and this set him laughing with malicious delight. Oh! The uncanny dead sound of it in that black and noisome place — I shall not forget it as long as I live!

Suddenly his other hand shot out and grasped my hair, which tumbled in disarray down my back, and gathered it into his hard fist. He tugged it sharply so that tears sprang to my eyes and my head was forced back, exposing my throat. I felt my pulse flutter wildly in my neck as he poised the knife over it — then, at last, moved the flashing blade beyond and behind. A foolish, secretive smile crept across his lips.

'It is not what you think,' he said — and I felt a rough sawing sensation and heard a thick ripping sound, as of torn cloth, and my head fell forward, released. He showed his hands to me: in one he still grasped his wicked-looking blade — and in the other, the thick, black rope of my own hair, which looked, clutched in his pallid fingers, like a garland of dark seaweed, or a bunch of withered stalks with all the blooms cut off.

'There!' he said. 'Chopped and chastened. I flatter myself a Millbank wardress could not have done it better! And if you displease me again,' he added grimly, 'I'll shear the rest too.'

He stuffed my lopped-off locks carelessly into his pocket and sat back on his heels, stowing his knife back inside his coat and surveying my shocked and miserable state with satisfaction.

'I suppose it wouldn't cheer you to know that your new hair-style makes you look quite fetching? Rather like a Christ Church chorister, if hardly as innocent.'

I said nothing, but gazed upon the floor, willing myself not to weep, as the terror which had flooded me slowly receded.

'You should not have begun sniffing around, little mouse,' he scolded, 'for it will do you no good. I declare, you look quite a-quiver! Have you smelled a cat down here — or perhaps a ghost?'

I kept my head bowed and made no reply.

'What has it found, to scare it so?' he crooned, as though addressing a child. It was so unnatural a thing to hear, there in that sickening dungeon, that his quiet voice tore at my nerves more than all his violence had.

'Chains!' I burst out in his face, and he jerked back, surprised at my sudden audacity — and at the vehemence still in me. It gave me a surging thrill of joy to see that I had unsettled him, and I pressed home my accusation, my voice low with fury. 'Chains, and shackles, and scratches on the walls, made by human hands, human nails. That is what I have found!'

He folded his arms across his chest with an air of smug satisfaction.

'Oh, have you now?'

I stared at him. 'Monster! Do you deny it?'

He cocked his head, considering.

'Chains I grant you; but as for the other — you will be pleased to know that you, my dear, are the first person to have the honour of staying in my subterranean hotel. There was no man or woman here before you.'

I knew he aimed at something beyond my grasping — but my head was muddled with privation and fear, and I could not think what it might be.

'What do you mean?'

'Exactly what I say.' He examined me as

404

coolly as if I were a student and he my schoolmaster, waiting for me to find out the answer to his riddle.

'I have seen the gouges in the bricks,' I told him. 'Someone was here, I know it. Someone died here. I *feel* it!'

At this, he shook his head and his boyish lip curled in a sneer. He reached forward his hand; I flinched, but he only chucked my chin and tutted.

'You are not as quick as I had hoped, Diana, for all your pert ways. It was no human that made those marks.'

This was worse than I had thought; my mind reeled with all the horrible beasts I had heard of or seen, and the notion of whatever it was having been chained up mere feet from where I slept, be it ever so long ago, gave me a chill that shuddered through my entire body.

Kester stood abruptly, stretching his limbs, and wandered to the far corner where the heavy iron manacles weighed on their chains, as still and ghastly as men long hanged. He thrust the lantern out at them, and they seemed to quiver.

'Allow me to tell you the history of your former cell-mate,' he said. 'After all, this is quite the aptest place for a ghost story — and I doubt your dreams should be any pleasanter were I to leave you in ignorance. Will you hear it?'

I regarded him with resigned calm, for we both knew that if he wished to speak, I must listen.

'It cannot be worse than anything I have already imagined.'

'Can't it now? We'll see. The first time I entered this place,' he said, 'I was thirteen years old. I was visiting the estate to see my cousin, who was back from University for the Long Vac. I was a sickly and ill-grown boy — difficult to conceive, I know — ' and here his mouth bent in a thin, self-mocking smile.

'In any case, my mother got it into her head that it would do me good to spend some time with my cousins, especially Charlie, the elder, who was quite the darling of the family — handsome, a fine sportsman and awfully clever, of course. He had passed the first months of his holiday in travelling about Europe — not the Grand Tour, exactly, but an exotic enough jaunt, nevertheless. When I arrived I found there was a small party of his college friends visiting for a few days. Charlie was in a high state of glee, and promised us that he had brought back something from the Rhineland which we should be very interested in seeing.

'It was the Saturday night, and my uncle and aunt were away, calling upon some local gentry or other. In their unmourned absence, we had feasted royally, with the gluttony of schoolboys, and after dinner we all trooped downstairs to this cellar in a thrill of tipsy anticipation to view our promised entertainment.

'I had drunk far more than I ought, and being unused to wine, felt rather ill and dizzy. I wondered whether I might not be sick when we

406

reached the gate and the stench of the cell rolled over us. It was a thick, sour animal smell, of something kept too long in its own filth, and it made me gag; but I did not turn back: I did not care to seem afraid or unmanly in front of the older fellows. Moreover, I was afire with curiosity to see what manner of thing Charlie kept so close and secret down here.

'We all crowded around the bars, trying to spy what lurked within, for we could hear something pacing and growling low; roused, no doubt, by the noise we made and the scents of food and wine upon us. Charlie pushed through the throng, armed with a lamp and a stout wooden stick. He banged on the bars with the latter, to make the beast come into the light, and we heard it roar, but still did not see it.

'Harry — your own dear Henry Hereward, in fact, who was the younger brother of one of Charlie's intimates — was the only one of us not pressing eagerly at the gate, and from the pallor of his face I deduced that either he had seen what lay inside, and did not want to again; or that he was afraid of it, and wished to be as far from its lair as possible.

' 'Quiet!' shouted Charlie. 'Move back there! He won't come if you crowd him — or if he does, you'll regret it!'

'Charlie passed the lantern to Harry, and pulled a handkerchief from his pocket, in which was wrapped a strip of venison filched from the dinner-table. He draped the meat over one of the cross-bars of the grille and kept us back from it with his stick, as a great black shape in the darkest corner raised its head, sniffing, and shambled towards us. We gasped softly as its questing snout came into the circle of light; then its bared yellow teeth; then, at last, its little sharp eyes, black as buttons and glimmering with a savage intelligence.

'We stared at the bear, and the bear at us, and I do not know who had the best of the contest; for suddenly it was over. The bear darted out a paw to snatch at the meat, hooking it with one curved claw, then dragged it into his mouth and began tearing at it with those dreadful fangs.

'Somebody laughed. It was not a true laugh — more of a high-pitched giggle, half fright, and half desperate, drunken gaiety. I was stood near the back of the crowd, next to Harry, and our view of the animal was partly obscured by the men in front, so that we could only see the bear's head and paws. The others began to laugh too, but strangely, with the hysterical mirth that bespeaks the relief of some great tension. Strain as I might, I could not see what in the animal's terrible and savage aspect could have caused such amusement.

' 'Why do they laugh?' I muttered to Harry, who shook his head mutely, not looking at me. But Charlie heard my words, and seizing me by the shoulder, pulled me to the forefront of the huddle, so that I, too, could share in the joke. I saw then what had so amused my fellows, but I could not join in the merriment. I was still very young, and quite sentimental, you see, and my natural tenderness towards my fellow creatures had not yet been entirely knocked out of me — in fact, you will be pleased to hear, I retain a trace of it still.'

And again he smiled that joyless, secret smile.

'The bear was dressed in what must once have been a somewhat garish waistcoat, an odd patchwork thing stitched together out of colourful silks and velvets — rather fine, in its way, and dotted with sequins and glittering beads, where they had not been lost or torn away by the creature's clumsy claws. This garment, which was very worn and soiled, was fastened about the animal's body by buttons of horn; but it hung loosely, as though it had at one time been tailored to fit, before its wearer had lost flesh through starvation or disease. It was a spectacle at once risible, and insupportably piteous: this fierce creature caged, though not tamed, fed with table-scraps, provoked with sticks, and dressed in a harlequin's rags for the cruel entertainment of a gaggle of boys.

'Confused and enraged by the laughter of my fellows, the beast snarled again, batting hard at the iron bars; but this show of temper served only to increase their amusement, and the others — all but Harry and myself — roared and leaned on one another helplessly, their paroxysms sounding in my ears like the shrieks of the mad or the damned.

' 'Is he not handsome?' cried Charlie, grinning with delight and banging his stick against the bars to knock back the beast's scrabbling claws. 'I call him Dandy, because of his fine dress, you know! I got him from a travelling circus. The Prussian who kept him said he had grown too sullen, and would not dance any more. But I can make him dance!'

'He turned to his sniggering audience.

' 'Shall I make him dance, boys?'

'They bellowed their assent.

'Charlie worked his stick through the bars and poked the bear hard in its soft belly, slackened and mangy with famine. It roared, showing its teeth at him, and shrank away, but then Charlie rattled his lantern at it threateningly, as if he meant to bring the flame closer to burn it; and waved the stick again. I saw what I had not noticed before, that the end of the stick was blackened as though it had at one time been set alight, as a brand — and that the bear's flesh was pitted and scarred with burns, some old and some still raw-pink against its dark, patchy fur.

'Slowly it rose up on its back legs; it shuffled hesitantly, and began to caper for us, a sickly, dragging shamble. It was an ungainly thing, clumsy and unbalanced, and further weakened by its years of captivity and abuse. Its powerful arms, their thick talons blunted by fruitless clawing at the walls, hung limp at its sides as it stumbled through its miserable jig. The sparse beading upon its jacket jerked and swayed as the creature moved, clattering against the buttons; and I thought it the saddest, most hopeless sound I had ever heard. Though I had watched unblinking until that moment, when I heard that lonely rattle of glass on bone, I turned my head away and closed my eyes.

'Charlie noticed my distress, and put his mouth to my ear.

' 'Don't you care for his dancing, Lucius?' he whispered softly, so that only I might catch his words. 'Could you do better? Shall I make you?'

'I turned and stared into his eyes; my own brimmed with unlooked-for tears. He saw these tokens of my boyish tenderness and sneered.

' 'Where's your sense of humour, Lucky?' he asked loudly, and suddenly pulled his stick from between the bars and dug it sharply into my ribs. I gasped in shock and pain, and the others turned to stare at me.

'It was like the moment when a pack of hounds at last corners the fox, just before they leap upon it to tear it to pieces. Every man's breath caught in his throat; ready to mock and torment not the bear — but me. I was their victim now, and I quailed at the apprehension of what they might not make me do.

'I did not dance. I seized the end of the stick resting against my chest, and pulled it out of Charlie's hands, and thrust it though the bars again. I jabbed at the bear, viciously, repeatedly, as hard as I could; I stabbed the creature until it bled as it danced. And then — then, I threw my head back and laughed.'

Kester's face was turned towards the far wall, lost in shadow, as he fell silent. His eyes sparkled fiercely in the candle-light as he gazed at the chains before him.

'Why do you tell me this?' I said, my voice hoarse. Kester's tale of the bear, pathetic and horrible as it was, had wrenched tears to the back of my throat; I choked on, but could not swallow, them. He blinked and glanced across at me, as though wakened from a dream, his brows creased in a peculiar, confused expression, something between defiance and defeat.

'Oh,' he said, 'did I not say? Charlie used the chains on Dandy, when he wanted to restrain him. He would give him brandy to drink, wait until he fell insensible, and then shackle him up. Sometimes he would set one of the dogs on him, for sport, but only when Dandy was cuffed — otherwise, he said, it was not a fair fight.'

'Poor creature!' I exclaimed softly. Kester picked up one of the manacles, weighing it in his hand like some drawing-room curio.

'Poor dogs, too, my dear. Dandy must have killed half-a-dozen of them before Charlie tired of the spectacle. That bear was a vicious animal at the end, for all that it was weak, and sick, and sorely injured by its battles. Finally, even the fiercest dog would whine and cower when set in the cell with it; for the creature had come to be nothing but misery and madness. Even Charlie could not make Dandy dance, by then; for with the slow wisdom of beasts, he had learned at last that the cruelty did not end, even when he danced.'

He looked over at me, and the force of his shining grey eyes upon mine was such that I felt as if he had struck me. In the glimmer of the lantern-light they seemed hollow, like blown eggs. His gaze did not rest upon me, but ran through me, as though there were nothing between himself and the walls of the cell but black air.

'Am I to be your bear, then? Shackled and tortured for your amusement?' I demanded at last. 'You should kill me now, if so — or I shall find a way to do it myself.'

He did not answer for a long moment; then he let go the manacle he held, wiping his soiled fingers upon his shirt. His voice when he spoke again was soft and thoughtful; against my will, I found I almost pitied him — or rather, the boy he had once been, made brutal by brutality.

'After that night, when I descended again into the cellar with the others (for we never went alone; I do not think we should have dared) I sometimes felt as though *I* were that bear. I dreamed of it at night; I trembled at its anger, yet I also wept at its pain, at the cruelty we showed it. And then the very next day I would compose myself and chase my pity away, as one might shake off a nightmare. On those days I would laugh at its maddened antics, and be the cruellest of anyone.'

'And now?'

'That's the queer thing.' He shook his head, wonderingly. 'I recall it clear as anything; I tell you the story of the boy who wept for the suffering of a beast. Is it a sad tale? I suppose so; I hardly know. All I know is that once, when I thought of it, it made me wretched; so furious and disgusted I felt like gnawing my own flesh off my bones. And now' — and here he spread his fingers wide, like a magician showing his palms clean and empty — 'now, I feel nothing at all. Not triumph, not despair; neither hope nor fear. It is how I imagine the dead must feel, if they know anything at all. I have tried to make myself sensate again: I have beat at the doors of my soul, indulged my lusts, courted pain and pleasure both — but I have come at last to believe that I am not made like other men. I have a fancy that there is stone or bone where my heart should be — or perhaps only emptiness.'

He looked steadily at me then; at my torn and bedraggled dress; at my face, smeared with dirt and streaked with tears born of pity and terror. His eyes in the darkness were as hollow as his hands.

'Do you know, all of a sudden I am awfully tired?' he said. 'I don't think I shall bother you any more tonight.'

He took up the lantern and made for the door, fumbling blindly beneath his shirt for the key. I watched him close and lock the gate behind him, and then turn back, holding up the lamp to stare at me.

'Good-night, my dear,' he said. 'You are not the bear — ' and his voice was filled with a dreadful sort of kindness. 'At least,' he added, 'not yet.'

I shall pass over the particulars of the next few days I spent in that place, for relentless suffering grows as tedious to recount as its opposite, limitless pleasure. Instead I shall write generally of what I endured and what I learned, though the remembrance of it is almost as painful as its re-enactment. Enough to say that I was used very roughly, and my growing conviction that my captor was, if not evil entirely, more than a little mad, was horribly confirmed at every fresh turn.

How shall I describe the strange, contradictory behaviour shown me by Kester? How can I expect you to believe what I tell you? It is so outlandish, so beyond all reckoning, that had I not seen and suffered it myself, I should dismiss it as the ravings of a lunatic. Yet I emerged, despite all, quite sane, and have grown to value the balance of my mind yet more highly, having been thrown into awful intimacy with one so deranged.

Madness is not something to be laughed at or dismissed. I had always understood that in a vague, impersonal way, never affording its victims much thoughtful consideration. But my awareness of its horrors and dangers was reinforced during my incarceration with one who walked the lip of its abyss. Madness, I know now, is a dreadful thing, at once pitiful and frightening. It consumes like fire, or disease; and like them, destroys everything it touches. I blush now when I remember how the women at the shelter used to giggle about poor Long Polly, the idiot girl on Ship Street who was too simple to get money from the men who shared her favours, and I am ashamed of not upbraiding them for their cruelty. At the time I dismissed it as harmless; the petty foolishness of ignorant girls, but now I knew better. And John Small, the unlettered poet of Magpie Lane who stood shaking like an aspen as he declaimed his apocalyptic verse beside the Martyrs' Memorial, the children mocking and teasing him: his antics used to frighten me, but I had only pity for him now. I prayed for them both in that dark time, whenever I had strength to pray.

And yet I did not at first suspect that Kester was mad. Peculiar, yes — as are so many young men of his class, who have been indulged beyond desiring, and to whom the world is a plaything of which they soon tire — but hardly mad. His eccentricities had not alarmed me when I had first encountered them: to drink heavily and with a steady, fierce determination to drive one out of oneself is alas all too common, and I had remarked it before in some of the doctors and even the nurses I had known in my time overseas. The horrors which those whose business it is to heal encounter during war are no less dreadful than those witnessed by the soldiers, and will not admit of obliteration. Small wonder so many seek oblivion at the bottom of a bottle, and find it there!

But Kester appeared so deceptively mild; he was not especially tall nor strong, and his countenance was somewhat plain — neither very handsome nor very hideous. His sole claim to beauty was a soft and sensual mouth, rosy as a girl's, which contrasted eerily with his grey, fishlike eyes. He did not wear his vices in his face, as some men do, though perhaps he was yet too young for that. His aspect, when he was not drunken nor angry, was unassuming. It would not be easy work to pick him out of a crowd. In short, in looks and bearing he was altogether quite ordinary. I wonder sometimes, when I think back on it, if that was not the very thing that haunted and enraged him. I wonder whether if he had been handsome, like Henry, or even very ugly, like poor Towers, he should have been a different man. I cannot say.

What I can attest to is that whatever the cause of this frightening upset of his reason, his madness hid itself behind his inoffensive demeanour, just as an awful and stealthy disease sleeps in the blood until the moment when it bursts forth in all its horror. That moment was the penultimate night of my incarceration — a night when my hopes of rescue or clemency were shattered beyond repair, and I realized with dreadful certainty that I must escape my prison, or else surely die there.

Our relationship became, over these days and weeks, a strange one indeed — one which I have not power to explain, for the uneasy intimacy of the bond between a prisoner and her

417

gaoler, especially when the latter's rationality is not to be relied upon, is quite as indescribable as it is bizarre. Kester regarded me with a queer mixture of awe and contempt; indeed, he seemed quite as fatally fascinated by me as a moth by a flame, visiting at odd hours merely to stare at me as I slept. I would wake sometimes to find him gazing through the bars of my cage with a puzzled, yearning expression, as though at some wonder from another world; and yet at other times he bore a look of hatred and repulsion, so that I cowered and turned away.

He had moods when he harped upon my 'unnatural' character constantly; when he admired aloud my fortitude and staunch resolve not to give up my secret, even in the face of bullying and violence. Yet in the next breath he would jeer at my 'wrong-headed idealism', and lament that such an 'extraordinary creature' should waste her time and talents on helping the hopeless. His words and actions were at war — for he had taken to reading to me to pass the time, and so was not he, himself, devoting his energies to improving me (though he professed to think me so little worthy of his attention), just as though I were a recalcitrant child and he my tutor? I did not know from one moment to the next what I really was to him, for in the same half-hour he might abuse me for a slut, flatter me like a suitor, and lecture me as a pupil. I do not think he knew himself what he truly felt.

Once, though, feeling braver than usual, I

decided to prick his pomposity when he went
on in this fashion, remarking that I had never
heard a man rail so passionately against a
woman unless he was in love with her. At that,
his soft lips spread in a bitter grin, and he
denied the charge absolutely, saying I was
worse than Lilith, Adam's faithless first wife,
and that he should as soon kiss the mouth of a
cobra. At this I thanked God silently — for if
he found me so repulsive, I reasoned, he would
not stoop to visiting upon me the worst punishment any woman can endure.

Often during our 'lessons', when my
responses displeased him, he would glare at me
and mutter under his breath that if only I had
more sense, or less, I should make a better
companion, and a black mood would fall on
him. He once said that a woman should be all
brain, like the lady-students of the University
halls, or all body, like a whore, but that this
in-between state of mine was dangerous, and
would not do.

In these fits of temper he talked to himself
often, quite as though I were not present. (He
had a wonderful gift of ignoring other people
entirely, as if they simply did not exist, that
reminded me somewhat of my first lover,
Henry; I suppose the gentry learn that trick in
their cradles, so that they may more easily close
their eyes to what it does not suit them to see.)
Then he would shake his head, and settle his
nerves, with an effort of will. 'She must break
sooner or later,' he would remind himself. 'She
cannot stand it long — then I shall have what I

419

need.' Though he muttered low, I caught his words, my hearing sharpened by the long, slow hours of darkness; and his self-reassurance strengthened my grim resolve to die before I let him have what was not his.

His favourite authors, and those whose works he most frequently read to me, were an obscure essayist called George Delon, and a Frenchman called de Sade, who had consorted with whores and all manner of humble and criminal persons, and had preached equality for every man under the sun — his logic being that all humanity was equally sordid and low. This gentleman had done a deal of horrible things for the most philosophical reasons, Kester claimed, and had been an atheist and a blasphemer too, and this seemed to enchant him. He declared frequently that de Sade had lived at the extreme edge of sensation and morality; that he was a pioneer, penetrating the uncharted reaches of the soul, just as our modern explorers pierce the savage heart of the dark places of the Earth.

He said that de Sade, like no other man, had seen the beauty of decay and the fascination of sordor and despair — had sought to embrace and understand them, and thereby to conquer them — or some such decadent, undergraduate nonsense. Though I could well understand the fascination an adept of pain might hold for one who, like Kester, professed himself spiritually numb, I confess I hardly listened to his ramblings, so faint was I with hunger and dejection. Perhaps the oppressiveness of my cell

420

worked upon his imagination somewhat, and he felt some foul frisson in night by night descending the creaking stair to call upon his caged woman — but how different would it suddenly appear to him, I thought, if he were in my place and I in his! He would not find himself so indifferent, so affectless and full of *ennui* then!

I have often considered that the attraction of any prison for idle visitors must be one with that of the bedlam and the graveyard; the fortunate fact that, while they thrill to its horrors, they are not compelled to remain there — for the moment, at least. And so Kester's fine words about holy terror and the sublime heated my blood, for I knew that only one who had never experienced poverty, hunger, or true and terrible fear could find them exciting; and, moreover, that he enjoyed my captivity as a sideshow to titillate his corrupted appetite for degradation.

I set a guard upon my tongue, however, and refrained from expressing my private thoughts upon the matter, for fear that his amused condescension would change to baleful ire. One time only, my self-control slipped, and I remarked tartly that if de Sade had ever been upon the edge of morality, I was sure by now that he had tumbled off. At this, Kester's eyes flashed and I thought for a moment he might strike me for making light of his idol; but then he laughed out loud, as gay a sound as I had heard in that place, and said he was glad I had learned something under his tutelage after all;

and that de Sade himself should have liked me, for I was both cynical and witty.

Extraordinary to relate, I felt a queer surge of gratitude and pleasure at this compliment, quite against my will; perhaps because it was so unlooked-for. I have heard it said that it is easier to endure the most extreme privation, cruelty, and pain, as long as it is consistent — for then it is all you know. Let only one crumb of bread break the fast of famine, however — let but the pain ease for a moment, or the torturer speak a tender word, and all is ten times worse than it was, for then you are reminded agonizingly of what you have lost; and remember that things were not always so.

His quick eye saw the flush of gratification sweep across my cheek, and he smiled. I realized my face had betrayed me, and blushed deeper with shame; for I knew I ought to hate my gaoler, not seek his praise. But you must understand that by this stage, my little world had shrunk to a point; my earth was the chill stone floor, my sun his candle, my day and night his coming and going. For in such darkness, and cold, and awful loneliness, whom else was I to turn to? Towers had stayed dumb as a stone since that first night, perhaps fearing that any new kindness shown me would court a further reprimand. So I ask you, though Kester was my abductor, and my gaoler, and frequently my tormentor too, yet in the absence of any other comfort, whose step should I listen for, and whose face should I long to see, but his?

Some nights, when he was especially restless, he read verse or pamphlets to me for hours — declaiming and commenting and prodding at every phrase or idea, for it was not his style to let the words speak for themselves. Then, part-way through, he would fling down the book in an agony of anxiousness, and turn his face to the wall, or pace about my cell like a caged animal, with an expression as black as thunder, and as forbidding. He would turn abruptly and stare at me, his grey eyes dark with something like despair, and seemed to be upon the point of confiding something — but he did not. And I came to suspect that his debts could not be so light as he had pretended; that he had been uncomfortably deep in them for a long time since, and the situation in which he found himself was far more perilous than he would admit. I believe, indeed, that for every day that passed with my secret intact, he grew more and more to fear for his very life.

It made me wonder, and tremble as I wondered, just how much money Kester must owe, and to whom, to make him so mortally afraid.

What vice could possibly have told thus heavily, even on so deep a purse as his? And what creditor could have kept him in terrified hiding; silent, hunted, spending half his days underground, in an animal's cell, with only his intransigent prisoner for company? I did not know, nor wish to imagine. I knew he was afraid; and I feared his fear, for at its worst pitch, it turns men into cornered beasts, and drives even the mildest to dreadful acts. And, despite his deceptive slightness and harmless bearing, Kester was far from the mildest of men.

Do not imagine, however, that my compliance with his odd whims was due to a docile acceptance of my fate. Faint and enfeebled though I was, I still lay awake each night, staring into the dark, trying to think of any way I could escape my prison. I had given up on the taciturn Towers early on, for it soon became clear that he was of that breed of servant who is more like a dog than a man, and beg though I might, he would rather hang himself than betray his master.

I would not have baulked at attacking Kester himself, except that I had no weapon, and nothing that could be fashioned into one. I considered wresting the key of my cell from him; but he always locked the oaken door above and the iron gate behind him, and wore the keys on a silk cord around his neck, slipped inside his shirt where I could not get at them; and so my position seemed hopeless. My only chance was to snatch the keys when he was locking or unlocking the gate — but how to overpower him was more than I could fathom. For though not large he was yet a man, with a man's force and vigour, and I merely a woman, ill-used and underfed; in addition to which, he had an unexpected, wiry strength that belied his delicate looks, which I had encountered on the dreadful night he abducted me.

I concluded reluctantly that my only remaining ally, if I was to leave that place alive, was

Hope itself. I hoped I was mistaken about my captor's increasing desperation. I hoped that Kester's determination to outwait my silence would soon crumble. I hoped that the tenderness he sometimes showed was his true nature, and that the other aspects of his character — the fury, and petulance, and worst of all, the fits of numb, deadly calm, clear and cold as well-water — were but passing phases. I hoped fervently that his moods and vices were not the substance of his soul, but only hid the good part of it, just as clouds hide the sun, and yet by its warmth are finally burned away.

My hopes were disappointed.

The next night, he came to me for the last time. The first I knew of consciousness was the slam of the door at the stair-head, and the thud of feet stumbling down them. I started up at once from my pallet, for in the cold discomfort of that dungeon I slept lightly as a cat. I felt swiftly along the wall and grasped at the bars of my gate, coming face-to-face with a wild-eyed Kester. We stared at one another through the grille; and for a moment, I felt that I had stepped unawares into a mirror-world, where he was the prisoner and I the gaoler, so miserable and racked did he look as he hung on to the bars for all the world as though he might fall. Even in the golden glow of the candle, he was deathly pale, and the lamp shook in his hand.

His breath stank of brandy, and his clothes and hair were foul with the musky reek of cigar smoke. I concluded with dread that, bored alike of his own company and mine, he had been getting drunk upstairs, alone or with Towers, and had descended to taunt me, just as if I were that poor bear which had been my cell's first prisoner.

'What is it?' I cried — for my frayed stamina could brook no more strange torments. 'What do you want of me?'

He shook his head in an ecstasy of despair, his eyes glistening — I knew not whether with fury, or terror, or pity. His mouth worked, but he did not speak: the expression on his slack face spoke of fear rather than spite, and at once, my heart shrank, and my fevered imagination conjured some grotesque accident or crisis.

'What?' I asked again, more urgently.

'They are coming for me,' he slurred, with the fatal air of one in whom hope is stillborn. 'I am betrayed.' And now I saw that his brow was damp with perspiration, and that he gasped and breathed hard, as if he had been running or brawling. He fumbled in his jacket with a vague hand, removing a letter, stained and crumpled as though grasped in a sweating fist for some time. He unfolded it clumsily, staring at it with reddened, unfocused eyes, as though it might, on second reading, prove innocuous.

'Today I received this letter from my friend Carrick, telling me I am discovered, and my hopes of evading my creditors, or even surviving to pay them off, are utterly dashed. Somehow my pursuers have tracked me down. He urges me to fly for my life!'

He laughed emptily, screwed the paper into a ball and flung it on the floor in disgust, leaning his head wearily against the bars. I should have reached through and scratched or strangled him then, in his moment of weakness and despair, as he cooled his fervid brow upon the iron of my gate — and yet, I could not.

'But surely — ' I began, breathlessly — for my heart leaped in my breast at the thought that if I could somehow aid him in his distress, he might grant me my freedom.

'Surely nothing!' he spat, his misery changing to fury. 'Don't you understand, cretin? I am looked for and I shall be found! They will kill me! Thanks to your infernal stubbornness, I have no funds to pay them back; nor even to flee the country. Why would you not yield? Will you hold out, even now? Only lead me to the money and you may yet be saved!'

'If I lead you to that money, which I swore to devote to the destitute and desperate, I am damned,' I told him coldly. 'Though you have done all you could to break me, you have failed. I have not surrendered, and I never shall.'

He pressed his wild face against the bars.

'*I* am destitute, damn it! *I* am desperate!'

'Through your own wicked fault!' I rejoined. I admit that, although I have never been the gloating, envious sort who takes pleasure in another's despair, at that moment I thrilled to the tables turning, and exulted in his misery. What joy it was to see him beg! What terrible triumph! The flame of hope flared in my soul

427

— he was grasping at any straw, and in this state I felt sure I could bend him to my will somehow, and persuade him to release me.

'Imbecile!' he raged. 'If I die here, you surely shall too!' His grey, hard eyes searched mine for any indication of weakness or of pity, and I laughed — laughed in his face!

'Do you still believe that life can be sweet to me?' I said scornfully. 'Beaten and starved; cursed, lost; loveless and friendless? Death would be better far than this! Oh! If you knew how I have prayed for it! You have taken everything from me — and I had rather die than give you what is not yours.'

He stared at me, and read the truth of my words in my eyes. He staggered away from the bars and slumped against the back wall in an attitude of utter defeat.

'Then I am a dead man,' he muttered. 'O God, God! What am I to do?'

At last, I thought, *you shall know what it is to be powerless, and terrified. Though no cage encloses you, you are trapped now, like a beast in its lair.*

'There is nothing to be done,' I told him, and I could not keep the note of triumph from my voice. He lifted his head and stared at me through the bars; his face was bleak and bloodless, all hope drained from it. Slowly, with a deliberation that frightened me more than any violence, he set the lantern on the stones beyond my gate, never taking his gaze from my own.

'Perhaps you are right,' he said, leadenly. He

reached inside his shirt, tugging on the silken cord that swung about his neck, from which depended the key to my cell. 'Though I had hoped it would not be like this.'

'What?' I asked, panic mounting in my breast, thrusting itself against my ribs. My head throbbed and span, and the darkness loomed ever blacker before me, until the only points of light in the world seemed to be those which danced in my gaoler's eyes.

He ignored my question, fumbling the key into the rusting lock.

'I made a friend of her, did I not?' he muttered to himself. 'I read to her, and conversed with her, and treated her pretty kindly, really, when one considers what I might have done. I believe she had even begun to hope I could be redeemed, like one of her street-walkers.'

He made one last turn, and the lock squealed open — but instead of entering, he held the door of my prison shut with his own strength alone, leaning on it hard. He pushed his burning white face up against the bars, and I saw that film of madness descend, like a cat's third lid, over his blank grey eyes. His mouth was only inches from my own, his breath warm and bitter, like ashes.

'I kept you and fed you, I barely hurt you — and still you would not give me what I wanted. Ah! Women! Well, I suppose it is for the best; the time is come.' He cocked his head and grinned. 'Even the divine Marquis never did what I shall do to you, you know, my dear. The last transgression. The worst. Oh, do not blanch and look coy! It is not what the priggish call 'the fate worse than death'; it is merely what you have courted all along. Have you guessed?'

I had: and the knowledge dried my voice in my throat. I could not answer, but only stared. He drew the keys up again to his breast, tucking them fussily back into his shirt, as though preening himself before a mirror.

'I had hoped it would be magnificent, my first time — and yours, of course, for there never comes another for one partner in this dance. I had planned to do it at my leisure — after you had told me where to find my money, of course — but you were too bull-headed for that.' Regret flickered across his face. 'I should have lingered over you, Diana, for hours. But be comforted — at least now it will be quick.'

It is possible that I would not have done what I then did, had I not realized in that moment that he had been scheming at my death for some time. For who should ever have heard my screams, or found my corpse? Had our strange closeness, our discussions and our lessons, been merely the sauce to his violent desires, whetting his appetite for my blood? And if it is terrible to kill a stranger, how much more must it stir the evil passions of such a man to slay a creature he has known and spoken with, one so abjectly at his mercy, and entirely in his power?

I looked into his eyes, and knew it was true. I saw at last that all the poetry and philosophy, all his compliments and confessions, had been nothing but play-acting, a pleasant fiction to lend poignancy to my murder, or to soften my heart before tearing it out. This explained his uncharacteristic restraint in leaving my virtue untouched, which I had wondered at before. Now I understood his diabolical subtlety in not visiting that worst violation upon me; he had been saving it for the ripe moment, the better to savour my humiliation before ending it with my death. Just as a farmer fattens and pampers the calf before the slaughter so that its meat may taste the sweeter, so had he fed and watered my soul to reap a fuller harvest.

My breath left my body in a terrible scream. I lifted my hand and pointed past him, my finger trembling, up towards the stony dark of the staircase. He whipped around in terror and staggered against my cage, his back to me, staring into the blackness.

Quick as thought, I snatched my leathern water-bottle off the floor and flung its tough strap through the gap in the bars and over his head. Before he could gasp for breath, I jerked the rough noose back, crashing his skull against the iron gate, and pulled the leather tight about his throat, leaning into it with all my bodily might. His fingers scrabbled at the strap, but it was as sturdy and thick as a belt, and he could find no purchase. The more he struggled and choked, the harder I pulled, twisting to tighten it, strangling him slowly — God, how slow it was! — but surely.

Though I know it was only to save myself,

and that had I done otherwise I should not
have lived another minute in that prison, still I
cursed him aloud for making me a killer. I spat
words of hatred at him as he thrashed, spas-
ming against the ringing iron of my cell-door.
He bucked and twisted violently at first, his
flailing fist catching me a blow on the eye, but
finally his twitching slowed, his tongue flopped
flaccidly from between his lips, and his bulging
eyes fluttered shut. But still I hung on tight as
Death to that band of leather as I wept, whis-
pering in his deaf ears, damning him over and
over for blackening my soul with the stain of
murder.

When at last I released the strap and let it fall, the fingers of my right hand were quite numb from where it had been wrapped about them as I hauled. Wiping my mouth, I found that my lips and tongue were streaming with blood, for I had bitten them hard in my efforts to hold him, and had not felt the pain.

Slowly, clumsily, I pushed wide the gate, pitting my weight against that of Kester's motionless body. For a moment I stood quite still, amazed that my blood-chilling scream had not summoned Towers; but then by the feeble light of the lantern I saw that the sturdy door at the stair-head remained closed, cutting off all noise from below. I picked up the lamp, crossed myself and walked up into the unknown.

It was dark inside the house, and silent as the grave, for which I gave thanks — for I think that had I emerged into daylight, my dark-adapted eyes would have dazzled, and I should have been as blind and helpless as a mole. As it was, I found my way easily by the light of the guttering lantern. I moved through cold chambers and dust and empty shadows; here was a back-stairs passage for the servants, a mean kitchen-corridor, and then at last the huge, abandoned kitchen, and a back-door opening on to the wide vastness of my freedom.

I stood there for a long, ecstatic moment, snuffing the lamp and closing my eyes, the better to savour the chill freshness of the sweet open air. And then, like a fox pursued by the hounds of Hell itself, I fled. Like Lot abandoning the cities of the plain, I did not hesitate, and I did not look back; I ran and ran, just as fast as I could, until I came back home.

The events that followed my return to the shelter I shall not speak of: it is all known, that which is important, and I hardly remember what I myself witnessed — only patches, like spots of sunlight on a forest floor, stand out clear to me; and these I do not wish to recall. I dream of them still, sometimes — they burn my mind's eye with their horrible brightness, so that even years after, there are nights when I wake in breathless terror, and must blink them away.

All I will say is that there were four people in my study that awful night, and by the dawn's breaking, there remained but two — and now one alone lives. The rest is a matter of private grief, and public record. Ask me if you must, when the time comes; but I hope that when you are grown you shall understand (by natural instinct, rather than — God forbid! — personal experience) that there exist things too terrible to be relived, and know that this is one of those.

I have always found it ironic that in the time that followed this penultimate tragedy of my life, I gained a reputation among those I encountered as a woman of almost inhuman calm and patience, one whom neither the ravings of drunken whores nor the sneers of narrow-minded enemies could move. Some nicknamed me the Stone Angel, in honour of my imperviousness to criticism (and sometimes violent opposition). I thought of the statues that are said to weep blood, and smiled privately at the aptness of my appellation — but only a little.

For, little one, though I never showed it by word or deed, I carried myself through those years as a cup full to brimming; I was a vessel of tears, and could not afford to upset myself. After that final, awful night, Stephen vanished from Oxford without warning and without good-bye; and the wound he made then in my heart could not be healed by the vague, cryptic letter that eventually reached me, protesting much, yet explaining nothing. He did not trust me; therefore, I reasoned, he could no longer love me. The life of my soul was at an end — but the life of my body persisted obstinately. For the sake of those who depended upon me, if for no other reason (and I could think of none), though my heart bled daily, I had to continue; I had to endure. This was the true reason for my supreme, supernatural calm: had I permitted a single drop of my fathomless sadness to spill over, I should have emptied myself entirely; I should have drowned in my own intolerable grief.

The greatest agony of loss consists in not knowing why, or how, that which is gone has been taken from you. The secret viper in the bosom of one who mourns as I mourned is the same as that which torments the mother whose child is snatched away: year after year, the tiny spark of hope burns undimmed, that what was lost may perhaps be found again — or that he who is gone might yet return.

I shall write no more. Already my tears, so long denied, so fiercely and carefully contained, are falling upon these pages, just as the rain dashes its cold drops against the window. The words of Tennyson return to haunt me: 'Death has made his darkness beautiful with thee' — and Stephen seems to stand before me now, a lost ghost in the blackening night beyond my window . . . but I will not think on him any longer — I cannot —

No more. No more.

I am mistress of myself again. It is the strange effect of my interesting condition, no doubt, to make me suddenly so weak, where I was ever strong: I shall not let it conquer me again.

I promised to tell you the truth, my little one, in these pages, and so I have, except where the truth is unspeakable. Let it lie; let it die: and I hope that you may, one day, forgive this last of many failings in your otherwise most loving and devoted mother,

Diana Fraser

EPHEMERA

Letter from Edward Fraser to Stephen Chapman

Saclose Hall, Gloucestershire
31 MARCH 1888

My dear Chapman,

I am gladder than I can say — and yet, in some measure, sorry — that my duties at my father's bedside have taken me away from town, and from you, for such a long spell. The doctors all agreed that he would not outlast the month, but their predictions have proven pessimistic, and my father's strength far greater than they had imagined, thank the Lord. He always was a tenacious fellow, and it seems he is quite resolved not to go to his reward until all the morbid paperwork — as to Wills, dispositions, the correct provisions for my brother George, myself, and various distant relatives, &c. — is complete. He is absolutely an inspiration; I wish you could see him, you who love life and toil endlessly and all but thanklessly to preserve it. I am humbled with admiration for him.

However, it pained me greatly to read your last letter, in which you spoke of your determination to preserve the silence betwixt Diana and yourself, so as to leave her free to marry elsewhere should she choose, rather than tell her the true nature of your situation. I understand, of course, that you are working day and night on finding a remedy for this terrible illness you have contracted, and that you hope to be able to claim her again once you are cured — but although I have the utmost faith in your talent and dedication as a researcher, these dreadful maladies are not so easily conquered.

To put it frankly, I do not think, Chapman, that you have seriously considered what might happen if you never succeed, and can never confess to her the secret you still hide. You will alienate her, and deprive yourself of the invaluable support and companionship that she might give. I say again that if you deal honestly with her, Diana will understand, and will wait for you, until the ends of the Earth, if need be — and that moreover, she would rather be told the truth, however dreadful, than any number of lies, be they never so kindly meant.

You say that you cannot be a husband to her, in your present condition — and yet, what is marriage? I shall refrain from quoting chapter and verse at you, for I know you don't like to be subjected to what you call my religious cant, but I contend that marriage is a condition as much of the spirit as of the body — perhaps even more so. It is more than simply the physical love of one for another; it is a union of souls before God, purer and deeper than mere love of the flesh, and will outlast even the stars in the Heavens, if it is only true.

You say that if you were to marry her, you should thereby deprive her of that crowning joy of womanhood, which is to be a mother — and yet, is she not already, in some wise, a mother? Does she not care for, and nurture, and shelter those girls of hers, who are as helpless and vulnerable, and in their souls (I now truly believe) as innocent, many of them, as any newborn babe? You say that once you have found the treatment for your disease, you will go to her, and tell her plain that you were infected, and that was why you did not dare ask for her hand — but who knows how long that will take, and how many bitter years of misunderstanding and sorrow will have passed between you, before you can enlighten her to your real motive for abandoning her?

For that is what you are proposing, Chapman — to abandon the woman who loves you more than does anyone upon this Earth — excepting, perhaps, one other. And she *will* think it is because of her past life; that you have not and cannot truly forgive her — and she *will* blame herself. For, when a love-match falters, that is what women, be they never so strong-minded, invariably do.

I will put it as plain as I dare to you, Chapman, in the hope that you will break the habit of many years and heed my advice, if only this once: Mrs Pelham does not need another man. She does not need children.

She does not deserve to be 'released' from her engagement to you under false and feeble pretences, however nobly meant, and she does not need to be 'spared', as you term it.

You have often told me that she is a woman as remarkable for her intelligence and strength of character as for her beauty and virtue — and yet you refuse to do her the courtesy of telling her the truth, and allowing her to forgive you, as you once forgave her. I tell you as a friend — as an old, and true, and, I hope, a trusted friend — that this is sheer folly and hypocrisy, and no good will come of it. My opinion of her has changed greatly over these last weeks, as you know, and I cannot believe that you will demand any stronger proof of my sincerity than that I, once her severest detractor, am become her champion! The irony is not lost upon me; but believe me, in the end it is for your own happiness that I am fighting.

Tell her. Go to her. Beg her on your knees, if you must — though I hardly think it will come to that, given how completely she loves you. What she needs is the truth, my dearest Chapman; what she needs, is *you*.

With my sincerest warm wishes, I remain, as ever, truly,

Your most devoted friend,

Edward

Letter from Stephen Chapman to Diana Pelham

Jericho, Oxford
6 APRIL 1888

My dearest love,

If I were to make this letter as brief as it is
painful to me, I should never set pen to paper
at all — only, perhaps, write it invisibly, in my
own tears.

You of all people must know how deeply I
admire and esteem you; how closely knit are
our souls and minds, and how loath I should
be to injure you, were it in my power to spare
you any hurt, however slight.

And yet it is to save you from still more pain
and sorrow than I have already caused you,
that I write to let you know that I am releasing
you from our engagement, and earnestly entreat
you to consider yourself a free woman from
this day forth. This I do from no other motive
than my profound and sincere love for you, and
my desire that you should have the chance at
happiness which I have now forfeited for ever.

Poor Sukey said to me once that we are all
tainted. O! how I wish it were not true, but it is
— of me, perhaps, more than anyone. And so, I
beg you, do not ask me why I do this; only
know that for your own sweet sake, it must be
done. Please do not reply at all, my dearest,
except to say that you have received this of
mine, and that you accept we must part. I
don't believe I could bear to read anything

more than that, for I am hardly proof against the entreaties of my own heart; I should weaken at any of yours — and that I cannot do.

Keep steady, though, won't you, my angel? — and think of me kindly sometimes, when you are happily married, and dandle your baby upon your knee. Or hate me, if you must — but whatever you do, know that as sure as the sun rises, I have done this out of love for you. I could not bear for you to lose faith in me, for I never did in you, and never shall, till my dying day.

One day — God grant that it is soon! — I shall be able to explain my reasons to you. I hope, on that day, that to understand all will be to forgive all, and that you will be able at last to take pity on the poor, unhappy, unworthy creature who shall none the less remain, until the very breath leaves my body,

Your ever-loving
Stephen

Letter from Edward Fraser to Diana Pelham

Wiesbaden, Prussia
12 JANUARY 1895

My dear Mrs Pelham,

It distresses me almost beyond the power of expression to write and tell you of how these last few weeks upon the Continent have been.

444

You know, of course, that Stephen's condition deteriorated very severely over the last winter we had, which was so bad, and his physician advised me emphatically that a spell in sunnier climes was the only way he could hope to out-live another year, if the disease continued to progress at this rate.

It is a strange and terrible thing to watch a man so comparatively young — a friend, more-over, with all the blessings of intellect, body and spirit that God could possibly bestow — decline and wither so fast, like fruit rotting upon the vine. I regret to say that his condition (some tropical ailment he contracted from the corpses at the Radcliffe, he maintains) is still without cure.

And although he himself has for these past seven years bent the enormous power of his will and intelligence upon solving this terrible riddle, it remains uncracked — and if he cannot do it, I know not who shall. He has made great strides, to be sure, in retarding the development of the latter stages of the illness, fighting it each step of the way — but though the odd battle here and there may be won, I fear, as I know must he, that the war is all but lost.

His limbs have grown so weak and wasted that he is now unable to walk, and he is so thin and fleshless that he shivers like an aspen at the least breeze. When we go out with the other invalids, here in the mountains, I must keep the blankets of his bath-chair tucked up around his neck as though he were a babe with a chill. Though it shatters my heart to see him so reduced, I try to put a brave face upon it, and buck him up, and rally his spirits with cheerful talk as far as I can.

More and more, he loves to speak of the past, now, rather than of the future; I think perhaps he knows that there is little enough of that left to him, to be able to discuss it with any hope or certainty. Also, his memory has begun to fade; his once quick and brilliant apprehension is misted, and his recall, formerly so acute, has become patchy and jumbled. And yet at some times he is as astute as ever he was, and jests and disputes with me (and even teases me rather mercilessly) just as in the old days.

The last doctor I consulted (a specialist in diseases of the blood, or nerves, I forget which), who had been a contemporary of Stephen's at Magdalen, told me to think of his brain as being like a sheet of blotting-paper, or a palimpsest, where, though some words stand out clear and sharp, they are often only fragments, and the rest of the sentence is lost. Equally, there are words overlaid on one another, so that although clearly printed, they cannot be read. I never had much of a head for science, so I believe this notion makes it easier for me to understand Stephen's struggles, and to be patient with him when he grasps for a memory or idea and cannot reach it, even when he has no patience with himself. I think you ought to know that he speaks often of you, and that when he does so, it is always in tones of the deepest and sincerest affection.

The thing that upsets me the most about

this vile illness of his is how cruel and slow it is — how it robs its victim of his health, youth, comprehension and, at last (so they tell me), volition. When we roomed together at Worcester, people would often mistake me for his elder brother, or even his father, as we walked along close at one another's side, deep in conversation — for though he was barely twelve months my junior, I have always looked far older than my years. But this is now reversed; and I am obliged constantly to explain that it is not my aged and invalid parent I care for, but my contemporary and friend.

And yet there is a strange mercy in the creeping decay of his poor brain; for the memories the sickness consumes are, more often than not, the most recent — which is to say, the recollection of struggle, and hardship, and disappointment. It is as though where once we walked side-by-side along the same road, now, though I continue on, he is retreating, going away from me again, backwards whence he came, stopping occasionally to wave from an ever-widening distance. My greatest fear is that one day soon I shall grow so small and far-away that he will not know me any more. I hope not. I pray not.

At twilight yesterday, he asked me to wheel him out on to the hotel terrace, to watch the sun set on the little lake below. I lit his cigar for him (for his hands are weak and clumsy now, and he can barely hold them still for trembling) and stood beside him in companionable silence, smoking and gazing out upon the waters brushed with red fire. When it was dark at last, and the stars that are so huge and bright up here in the mountains had come out, he turned to me and remarked casually that he had never seen Worcester lake look so well. The darkness hid my tears, thank God — for I could never have made him understand why I was weeping.

I am sorry. I do not wish to burden you with this sad news. Such piteous scenes as I daily witness, I should learn to keep close to my bosom, and not distress my only remaining correspondent with them. I had sat down meaning to write to you that all is as well as could be expected, that we think of you often, that the mountain air is doing him a power of good, &c. — but I am afraid my resolution has failed. You are the only one to whom I can speak of him, as he has become and as he formerly was; the last person who will know, and remember, and truly understand.

It makes me laugh, almost, to think of the lengths to which I once went to try and conceal our correspondence — for now, when he asks me what I am writing, I say that I am composing a letter to you, and he smiles and remarks that he must drop by the shelter, as soon as he has caught up with his lecture-notes, and discharged his duties at the laboratory. Perhaps, he said tonight as I retired to my room with paper and ink, he would pay a call upon you tomorrow.

We went to Lourdes last month, at my insistence. I reasoned (though he would not have called it 'reasoning') that where science has failed, faith might find a remedy. It saddened me strangely to see that where he would once have scoffed at me for my credulity, now he meekly obliged. I suspect that perhaps he did not any longer understand the significance of the place. The springs did him no good, in any event. Maybe my faith was not strong enough; maybe it is simply that there are no miracles any more. His vigour is entirely spent; his mind wanders where it will. It is ridiculous, and pathetic, like the dance of a dying bear — and yet I should rather weep at this sorry spectacle, than laugh.

It will not be long, now, I am afraid. Prepare yourself for the worst news: but know that you are in his heart at the last; and let him be in yours. Pray for him — and, if you have any pity or love left over — perhaps, also, for me.

I remain, madam, your loyal and most respectful friend,

Edward Fraser

Letter from Edward Fraser to Diana Pelham

Wiesbaden, Prussia
17 JANUARY 1895

My dear Diana,

You must know what this letter, coming so hard upon the heels of my last, cannot but mean, and you will, I am convinced, forgive me for not setting it down in so many plain words. This must seem mere superstition or cowardice in me, I know, to be unable to state the stark truth of what has passed; but it is yet so raw in my heart that I can hardly bear to write even this. I should splash the paper so that it was unreadable, if I thought too long on his end.

I know that the pain of his loss will burn as strong in you as in me, for what I feel now is a grief so like madness that I almost hope it shall prove to be such; that I merely dream, and will wake again soon to a world of joy and mercy. I tell you this because I do not wish you to dismiss what I am about to say without giving it your most serious consideration.

He asked me with his last breath to take care of you, and a promise made to a dying man is the most serious sort of undertaking possible. I shall take care of you for him, Diana — I hope you will pardon my temerity in using your familiar name, but it seems to me that we have been so long friends, now, that you might overlook and forgive my presumption — I shall look after you for the rest of my life, or your own, if you will only let me.

It seems, as I sit here, staring out at the black mountain air in which the stars shiver, so agonizingly bright, as though they too feel the pain of his leaving — it occurs to me that you and I are like the twinned halves of a broken mould, two leaves of wax; and that what unites us is the shape of his absence between us. The best of him, I think, was in loving you; and the best of me, I know, in loving him. I should be so sorry to lose any part of him more than has already slipped away; and I trust that if I were ever by your side, helping you, comforting you, caring for you, that aspect of Stephen which burns in us both should never be truly extinguished. The saddest thing of all, my dear Diana, is not that he dies; but that we live on. We must learn to do it the best way we can.

I do not propose that we live together fully as man and wife, if you do not wish it; I would respect and understand completely your desire for celibacy. In order to extend the legal protection of what wealth and position I have to you, however, it will be necessary, should you agree to it, that we marry, though we may live as chastely as sister and brother. I know that you will shake your head — perhaps in horror, perhaps in disgust — but I pray you, do not tear this letter up or throw it away; for I have thought all of this through prior to laying it before you, and I assure you before God of my total sincerity. So I beg you, Diana, read on, for his sake, if not for mine.

Let me attest that no-one knows better than I how you (with Mrs Shimmin's invaluable help, of course) have done prodigious wonders at the shelter; no-one is more sensible of how many unfortunate souls you have saved, and how many have been brought around to a useful and honest existence by your tender ministrations, coupled with your dauntless zeal and the wonderfully inspiring example you set. But it is terrible, miserable, tiring work, and you are no longer in the first bloom of youth,

Diana, no more than I.

Hertford College, despite my long absence caring for Stephen, has agreed to take me back as a Fellow — I have a very nice set of rooms in college, and though it is so masculine an institution they will not, I am assured, baulk at my marrying — in fact, there is a pretty little cottage out by the Marston Ferry Road which they keep for just such an eventuality. When my father died, my brother George gained the estate, of course, but my father left me a capital sum, far more than I had any right to expect, and I have not touched the principal ever since, but lived off the interest these several years past.

I do not say that I could make you happy, Diana; only Stephen could do that for either of us, I suspect — but I can make you secure, and I can ensure that you want for nothing — neither the physical comforts so crucial to a decent life, nor the tender support of one who still has, I hope, the honour to call himself,

Your most devoted friend,

Edward Fraser

Notice in the Oxford Times, *6 April 1895:*
'Births, Marriages and Deaths'

MARRIED: Dr Edward Robert John Fraser, bachelor of the parish of Jericho, to Mrs Diana Pelham, *née* Cornell, widow of the same parish. At three o'clock, in the church of St Mary, by the Rev. Jonathan Forrest. Witnesses: Mr George Fraser, brother of the groom, and Dr Neil Cornell.

Notice in the Oxford Times, *20 July 1896:*
'Births, Marriages and Deaths'

BIRTH: To Dr & Mrs Edward Fraser, a son: Stephen Jonathan Neil Fraser, at eleven o'clock in the evening of 18 July; 6lb, 3oz.

Notice in the Oxford Times, *20 July 1896:*
'Births, Marriages and Deaths'

DEATH: Mrs Diana Fraser, *née* Cornell, wife to Dr Edward Fraser, mother to Stephen Jonathan Neil Fraser, in childbed on the evening of 18 July. Funeral 21 July at the church of St Mary in the parish of Jericho. Survived by husband and infant son. No flowers.

21 December 1896

Today is the shortest day; but she died at the height of summer, and the men and women of Jericho turned out and silently lined the streets to pay their last respects to her as the funeral cortège rolled slowly by. Even the carters and cabmen stopped their work and held their caps against their chests, with their heads bowed to show solemn reverence. I rode behind the hearse, looking neither to right nor left, not even when I saw Mary Ann, of whom Chapman had spoken so long ago, weeping on her husband's shoulder as though all the rain in the heavens would fall from her poor red eyes. I envied her her grief: for my own eyes were as dry and clear as a snowless sky; and my heart felt like a cracked stone. They laid her to rest in the little churchyard of St Mary, where we were married, in the grave next-door to Chapman's still-untarnished tomb. Even then, I could not weep.

I think that perhaps I shed all the tears I had in me when Stephen died. He was the keystone that bridged the gap between us, and when he was gone, we had nothing left but the emptiness of his loss. I had hoped that our child might have brought her happiness at last; but it was not to be. She looked upon his face, smiled once, faintly, as I brought his brow to her lips to kiss; then her eyes closed, and she was gone. But when her last breath escaped her body, she was still smiling, as though she knew she was going to join her baby's namesake, the husband of her soul, and was glad to have brought our boy into the world, though it cost her her own life.

The closing years of this century have brought me such great grief in so short a time that I could have wished it, or indeed my own unhappy existence, already over, were it not for the sweet sake of my son. But he lives on, a lively, lusty boy of five months now, and so I must do the same. I confess that in all my strangest fancies I had never imagined myself both widower and nursemaid; but so it is, and so it shall be, however much the good folk of Jericho laugh about it behind the curtains of their parlours, and my bachelor colleagues at the University arch their eyebrows at it in the Senior Common Rooms. I have discerned something of his namesake in my son already, you see; he delights in making me ridiculous, and forces me to laugh at my own pomposity and folly.

The fateful portrait I had thought to bury with Diana; but I could not do it in the end, for it reminded me so happily of her, and of my dead friend Valenti, and it comforted me to gaze upon it, and see Chapman's beloved in the flush of her youth and hope once more. I think, also, that little Stephen may one day like to look at it, for it is the only remnant of his mother left to him; that, and one other thing — a letter that she wrote in the final months of her confinement, which she pressed upon me, abjuring me not to touch or open it until I judged that he was old enough, and could read it himself. It lies, sealed and virgin, in the little jewellery-chest she put aside with a pair of pearl earrings and a necklace in case the baby should be a girl.

The painting hangs before me as I write these words; I believe I shall entrust it to my brother George, who has excellent taste in art, as a Christmas present, when Stephen and I go to visit him at Saclose Hall. Perhaps if, one day, George reads this collection of old papers, he shall find that that picture has a history more dramatic and intriguing than any number of Canalettos and Turners.

As for the remains of Chapman's estate, once his inheritance and annuity were eaten up, it was pitifully little in the end. I have entrusted his scientific papers to his former mentor and benefactor, Professor Marstone, in the hope that that eminent gentleman might be able to make some use of what I fear towards the end were little more than meaningless scribbles. I have made the Professor understand that there can be no question of publishing Chapman's earlier researches into the disease under his own name, brilliant though they are, for they would bring shame upon his memory. Thanks to his practice of testing his riskier remedies upon himself and recording the results as a sort of running narrative, it would become unmistakably clear to even the dullest reader that he was in fact suffering from the terrible malady he so vainly and bravely attempted to cure. And I will not allow him to be scorned and calumniated, even in death.

Any advances in that field shall be made under Marstone's aegis, and his alone; but I know that Chapman would not mind — his monument, like Diana's, is all around, in the lives which he saved and reclaimed. He never craved glory, nor even thanks: his only desire was ever to help and to heal. If my son lives to be half the fellow my friend was, he shall be a man indeed.

However, I am aware now that I must begin to take better care of myself if I hope to live to see my boy grow to manhood; I have never been what anyone might call a hearty fellow, but the years of caring for Chapman, then, latterly, for Diana in her troubled pregnancy, have taken a heavy toll upon my own health. It is time I began to live again as other men do, with regular habits and little excitement, for the storm of my life is over, and if, by chance more than design, this bark floats still on the waters, I ought not to tempt Fate any more — I must steer for a calmer harbour.

George spends most of his time in London these days; he has assured me that he shall be more than happy to let Stephen and I reside at Saclose Hall, where we may live a quiet life together. I have made up my mind to leave Oxford: thanks to my father's generosity, I have no real need of my Fellow's pitiful stipend, and besides, this place holds nothing for me now but the ghost of happiness long past, and the spectre of pain all too recent. Besides, I am determined to be a true father to my son: I will not be the 'cold fish' Chapman once thought me. I will not have Stephen say that I was one of those morose, remote *paterfamilias* whose own loneliness and misery was inflicted on everyone around them. What love is left in me will be all my boy's — and we shall be happy.

For I have carried these twin burdens of mine too long; well beyond what I had thought must be the end of my endurance, and thank God, at last I may set them down. My love for my friend was ever the greater of the two. It has stunted me, crippled me; made me as mad and as blind as he himself became in the very last ravages of his illness. He was right when he spoke of love as a disease; perhaps, one way or another, love is what will kill us all in the end. But we gladly shoulder this load, heavier than Atlas's — because we cannot do otherwise.

My second burden has been the truth of what really happened to Stephen Chapman; why he became what he did, to the grief and distress of his friends; why he could not wed the one woman in all the world whom he loved beyond life itself. Why this brilliant boy plunged himself into obscurity and poverty, living a hermit-like existence (except, of course, for me) in the pursuit of a goal of which he could speak to no-one.

He once mused bitterly that his former colleagues must have thought he had turned alchemist and was pursuing the philosopher's stone, so long did he work and so little did he speak of his endeavours. Perhaps the cure he dreamed of was a philosopher's stone, of sorts. Perhaps, and especially now that he has failed, and lies cold beneath the earth, it will never be found. I confess that now he is gone from me, I cannot really bring myself to care one way or another.

And so I lay down my second, my last load:

this, the truth; every word of it. It had to be told, and I had to tell it. I am sure I shall be long dead by the time it is read, if ever it is — if this manuscript is not forgotten entirely in some obscure corner of Saclose Hall's library, or destroyed by fire, flood or accident, as is so often the case with the papers of obscure and friendless men.

Or perhaps, one day, I will show it to Stephen, along with his mother's letter, when he is old enough — when the wounds that now pierce my heart are healed, and can be displayed and spoken about, like battle-scars old soldiers show.

And to be entirely honest, it does not matter to what future reader this saddest of stories is finally revealed; whether he cares or is indifferent, whether he weeps, or laughs, or is incredulous. I have told it: that is enough. It is done.

Epilogue

Saclose Hall, Gloucestershire
10 DECEMBER 1914

Stephen,

I wrote these words nigh-on twenty years ago, in the depths of my despair, in the cell of my own loneliness and self-loathing. The world to me, then, seemed entirely lightless, and bereft of even the possibility of joy.

Since that time, I have not despaired. I have never again felt the touch of the abyss, for I have had you, my boy; and in you is all my love and hope. It is through you that my life has gained purpose and sweetness. These are words fathers do not say to their sons, nor husbands to their wives, yet they should be said, and often; for love is the pearl beyond price, the divine gift, which raises us above our weak and imperfect selves and burns with a hard, astonishing flame against death's darkness. The grave is cold and silent enough, and soon enough in coming. We ought not to be cold and silent too.

But let the truth be told: if I must go, I go willingly, joyfully; my only regret shall be leaving you alone in the world, for since your uncle George died we two have been the lonely last of the Fraser clan. Not that this is such a weighty matter; I know you will have made

460

great friends by the time this war is over, and when you go on to Oxford afterwards, I trust you will make even greater ones, just as I did — though they are almost all dead now. In fact, saving you alone, dear boy, and some acquaintances with whom I now correspond less and less frequently, I do believe that there is no living soul who owes me the courtesy of a mourning tear. Yet that is not a source of regret to me, for I have done what I set out to.

It is the strangest thing, but now that I know what has been troubling me these past few months, and am quite assured that I am soon to die, it is as if a great weight has been lifted from my shoulders. I feel almost insubstantial, as though my bones are suffused with light. It is as if I am becoming air, sunbeam, shadow; I feel that, if I cared to, I could pass through solid objects and tread the air along the street, floating a few inches above the ground. All nonsense, of course; I have eaten little today, or indeed in the last few weeks, and in truth I am frailer and thinner than I was, but that means nothing; my physical health was broken long ago.

It is my head that is lightest. Sometimes, though I know it to be impossible, I believe that I see your figure, my dear boy, or that of my dead friend Stephen, whom you resemble in some ways that crack my heart, just as you do your mother . . . I see your shape in the shadow behind a door; recognize your gait in a stranger's on the street. Sometimes I fancy I hear your voice against the harmonics of a high

461

wind, or in the murmur and babble of a crowd in church. I start, and turn — always, the hope leaps in my breast like sudden tears; but of course, you are not there.

I am reminded of a desperate fortnight, long years ago, when I wandered Oxford, lost as an unshriven soul, searching, though I knew it not, for my other self, my friend Chapman; restless, relentless, crazed alternately with hope and fear. I envy my younger self. At least, back then, I knew somehow that he was there to be found; just as I know now that you are not lost to me, only gone away for a little while, for which I thank God daily.

I think of the dead often, now. Dr Dunseath brings me morphia for the pain, and it fires my memory, my imagination, in ways I had not dreamed. I might at last have found my only vice, were it not that I shall surely die before it has the opportunity of killing me! I must and do believe that my friend Stephen, and your mother too, are somewhere — not physically, mark you, but in spirit — souls surviving just as that wonderful picture of Diana which hangs in the Great Hall at Saclose has survived — a depthless, changeless thing of beauty, untainted by time or mortality.

Chapman confessed to me once that he believed in neither salvation nor damnation, unless it was upon this Earth, in our hearts; in this life. Once, I thought this meant he could not be saved. I am no longer that blind and unyielding man — but even when I was, I should gladly have swapped places with him. I imagined that my spotless soul would descend and his rise, and perhaps, when we passed, there would be a moment of recognition; no more. And now I wonder whether he was not right, after all; for I can imagine no damnation more absolute and no Hell bleaker than a world without love in it.

And so, my boy, I dare to hope; I hope that I will live to see you marching through the snow towards home; I hope that my life has not been lived entirely in vain, even if the one truly good thing I did in it was to bring such a fine young man into the world; and I hope, above all, that when you have read these words, you will forgive your father his many failures, faults and weaknesses. Those who strive to be good are doomed to fail; but they are happy in this world who have loved, for that greatest of gifts rebounds upon the giver. Whether they have been loved in return is immaterial: the heart cannot remain inviolate — it must be pierced. The joyful sacrifice, the willing submission, is all.

All that consumes me now, Stephen, is a desire to see you one last time; to be beside you, to be able once more to touch your hand, to hear your voice, to see your spirit shine out through the fathomless laughing brightness of your eyes. Wherever you are now, that is where I direct all my thoughts and energies, and shall until you return to join me.

Come back safely to me, dear boy; do not let these be the last words I write to you. I have a little bet with my medical man that I'll outlast the New Year, and I know that I shall, if you'll only come home soon. Don't let me down! — or else it will be you that owes the good Doctor that five pounds, and not I, you know.

Your loving father,
Edward Fraser

THE END

Author's Note

This book is a work of fiction, not of history. While I have tried, as far as I was able, to be historically accurate, where the story demands it certain events and places have been fudged or invented, and where I have been unable through research to discover answers to my questions, I have used my imagination.

The Ox's Head and the Tolling Bell pubs, for example, are made up; though the latter is located, in my mind, not too far from where the Old Tom now stands. I have tried to stay faithful to the spirit and style of the period, and hope that if any minor inaccuracies have slipped through, they will not spoil your enjoyment of what is, after all, only a story.

Katy Darby

Acknowledgements

I owe a huge debt of gratitude to everyone without whom this book couldn't have been written (and, more importantly, re-written); most of all my first readers, Jim Chamberlain, Quintin Forrest, Veronique Baxter and Martin Pengelly; the Oxford writing group of John Marzillier, Jenny Stanton, Lucie Whitehouse and Anne Church Bigelow; my tutors and fellow students at UEA, especially Paul Comrie and Murray Garrard; Arthur Conan Doyle, Wilkie Collins and those Victorian authors whose work is a constant source of inspiration and pleasure; and (last but not least) Alex, Bex, my parents and my lovely friends, for their constant encouragement and amazing tolerance . . .

Final thanks go to those without whom *The Whores' Asylum* would never have been published and read: my agents Vicky Bijur and Arabella Stein; my editor Juliet Annan and the team at Penguin; and everyone who reads and enjoys it.